KILLER CONVERGENCE

A Matthew Paine Mystery

KILLER CONVERGENCE

A Matthew Paine Mystery

LEE CLARK

Cypress River
Media, LLC

Burlington

Cypress River Media, LLC
Burlington, NC 27215
CypressRiverMedia.com

First Edition: April 2025

The publisher is not responsible for websites (or their content) that are not owned by the publisher.

Clark, Lee.
    Killer Convergence / Lee Clark. – First edition.
        Pages ; cm. – (A Matthew Paine mystery)
    ISBN 979-8-9905936-1-9 (hardcover) – ISBN 979-8-9905936-2-6 (paperback) – ISBN 979-8-9905936-0-2 (e-book) 1. Paine, Matthew (Fictitious character) 1. Paine, Matthew (Fictitious character)

Matthew Paine Mystery Series

Pre Kill (prequel short story)

Dead Spots

Prefer Death

MIA

Christmas Punch

Iced

Forbidden Relics

Killer Convergence

Dedication

First, to my father, Ray Clark, a truly generous and loving father, and then to my husband, Bill, another of the best fathers I've ever known, I dedicate this book. To dads everywhere, know that there are few people who are, or ever will be, more important to your children than you.

As always, I am beyond grateful to my amazingly loving and wonderful heavenly father who has given me the words again for Matthew's journey. Many earthly fathers try their best, but ultimately, there's only one who loves us perfectly and unconditionally. I am most thankful to God, my heavenly father!

Contents

PROLOGUE ~ SUMMER 1998

The tall, lanky youth had no idea this was the day his world would turn upside-down as he sauntered down the steps of the activity bus. A basketball under one arm and a gym bag dangling down his back, he laughed at a joke about one bodily function or another his friends had just made.

"Good one!" he said, in a voice that had already dropped to a far lower register than those of any of his friends. He rubbed the coarsening blond peach fuzz on his chin with his thumb as his well-worn high-top basketball sneakers landed on the shoulder of the rural road beneath the bus steps. "Are we playing this afternoon?" he asked, over his shoulder.

"We just played all day at basketball camp," a red-faced youth objected, sweating profusely in the July heat on the unairconditioned activity bus. "Anyway, I can't. The chain on my bike broke."

"Yeah, I can come over after I finish my chores," responded a second youth from aboard the bus. "My mom won't let me go until she checks behind me."

"On a Tuesday?" asked the disembarking youth, turning back to the bus door. "I do my chores on Saturday."

"Yeah, she's such a dragon!" the boy answered as the bus doors whooshed closed between them.

Secretly, the youth wished his mother were home. She wouldn't be, though. He'd be coming home alone to an empty house today as he had for the past two years. She regretted it, he knew, but she seemed resigned to her fate. Working was apparently a necessity when you were married to a police detective whose salary wasn't quite sufficient to make all of the ends meet. She worked tirelessly to make life homey for her only son. He'd find snacks she'd left for him with silly notes attached in the refrigerator when he got home.

Still, coming home to the empty house was better than some of the lame after-school and summer programs he'd been enrolled in when he was younger. Given his considerable size, he'd never been bullied by the other kids, but neither had he ever felt like he belonged among them. Being home alone in the afternoons wasn't so bad, he told himself as he dribbled the basketball down the shoulder of the road before turning the corner onto his short neighborhood street. It made him sound grown-up and important to his friends. That was OK, he guessed.

His house, the last on the left of the dead-end street, was a neat split level built in the latter 1960s. Well maintained with a lawn that was always neatly trimmed, it was one of a few houses on a street that should have been fully developed. Instead, there were multiple wooded lots, overgrown with saplings and weeds, interspersed with a few houses along each side. Focused firmly on the ball, the boy made his way down the street.

At the end of the street in front of his house stood a basketball goal, the hoop of which was long since devoid of netting. Rusting and leaning slightly, the goal post stood like a tired sentinel keeping a watchful guard over the small neighborhood. That was fine with him. He didn't need netting or a fancy backboard to dominate in a basketball game because he could out-shoot and out-maneuver all of his friends. With his long limbs and height, already six feet tall, he was much more agile than a guy like him had a right to be. Unlike most of the boys his age, he wasn't tripping over himself in an awkward attempt to dribble the ball around their makeshift court— though he was a head taller than all but one of them.

Looking up as he approached his house, a wide smile spread across his face. "Amma!" he exclaimed, snatching up the basketball and breaking into a run.

He'd spotted his grandmother leaning against her aging sedan, and he saw nothing else. This was an exciting development, he thought. It would mean chocolate chip cookies and the Norse mythology and folklore tales of his ancestors at bedtime—all of which he'd never admit to anyone that he still enjoyed immensely. He was twelve, after all, not five, and bedtime stories weren't cool.

As the boy closed the distance between him and his grandmother, something seemed off. Why was she outside by her car in front of his house? Had she just arrived? Why wasn't she inside waiting for him with those cookies that made the house smell heavenly and his mouth water in anticipation? Her arms had been crossed, and she looked odd, as if he'd done something wrong and a reprimand was imminent. But he was sure he hadn't. He could think of nothing.

Drawing nearer, he glanced over at his house, which was set back from the road on nearly an acre of a heavily wooded lot, and slowed to a walk.

Several cars were parked in the driveway and yellow tape was strung between the clump of trees in the front yard, blocking entry to the house. His house. People came and went from it, and his grandmother wasn't stopping them. Why was she just standing there? He ran to her. The tall, solid woman wordlessly enveloped him in a bear hug as he wrapped one skinny arm around her and clung to the basketball with the other.

"Your things are packed in the trunk," she said, calmly but firmly pulling away from him. "You're coming home with me."

"What? Why? For how long? Did I do something wrong?"

"No, Kærasti. You didn't. Somebody did. But it wasn't you," she thickly replied. As she explained what had transpired in his own home that morning after he'd left, the basketball dropped from under his arm, unnoticed. It slowly rolled toward the goal at the end of the street, as sullenly as the boy felt. Bumping the bottom of the post, it stopped in the grass at the base, and there it remained.

A plethora of protests and questions poured from his lips. His mind raced, refusing to believe what he'd just heard. Understanding the words as his mind began to sense the truth in them, his heart ached and convulsed in ways he couldn't begin to express.

"Words, Kærasti. So many words," his grandmother dismally replied. "Words change nothing. Action is what's needed. Get in the car. We have to leave before it starts."

"Before what starts?" he asked, confused to the core of his being.

"The questions. There'll be time to answer those later. But not now. Let's go before they see you. They'll know who you are," she added in her commanding Norwegian dialect the boy knew was more pronounced when she was mad or upset.

Even as she said it, a man coming out of the house turned his head in their direction and strode purposefully toward them. Suddenly, a deafening roar stopped the man in his tracks. He ducked, all but dropping to the ground as a large shadow accompanying the noise raced down the street and disappeared.

The thunderous jet engine provided a momentary pause for everyone but the boy and his grandmother. Obediently, he climbed into the car. Choking on his tears—trying to emulate the brave and stoic ancestors his grandmother had told him about—he refused to allow them to fall.

1 ~ WHY DEATH?

Matthew Paine hated funerals, particularly those of young people whose lives were cut short. Funerals for older people, presumed to have lived full lives, were still depressing. The young family physician from Peak, North Carolina, tirelessly worked to improve the quality of his patients' lives. When someone died it felt like a personal affront—like he'd somehow lost the war—even when the deceased wasn't his patient. Death was an extension of life, he knew, and there was a hundred percent mortality rate—sooner or later. That logic, however sound, felt hollow on this chilly, blustery spring morning.

There was something unsettling about death. He'd seen far too much of it lately.

It had been a rough year working alongside Homicide Detective Warren Danbury, on and off, as a medical consultant with the Raleigh Police Department. After befriending Danbury the year before, Matthew had done far more than consult medically. He'd been drawn into a world of violence, evil, and needless death—one he'd never intended to encounter quite so closely.

A peace had filled him when he resigned, yet again, from his consulting role. He planned to stay that way—both peaceful and unencumbered with police work.

In the case of Danbury's grandmother, Matthew hadn't known she existed before three days ago when she had died. In the cemetery behind the redbrick church on the outskirts of Peak, a few mourners paid their respects. They were spread out in sparse groups—tucked into protective gear against the wind and misty rain—separated against a virus claiming lives at a rapid pace.

It was an isolated way to leave this world, Matthew thought, on a damp, dreary Thursday morning in early April. Nobody yet knew enough about the COVID virus to stop it. Extreme caution was more than advised. It had been mandated.

The virus had very recently appeared in North Carolina in small pockets. One of those had run rampant through the facility where Danbury's grandmother had lived—if you could really call it living—and she had succumbed. From what he learned of her from the graveside service, which was far more than he'd ever gotten out of his stoic friend Danbury, she had been a wonderfully vibrant woman.

A stroke had taken much of her mobility nearly ten years previously. On the heels of that, dementia had begun to claim her mind. Beneath her tough exterior was a warmth and a heart of gold. The past ten years of her story, he learned, had been sad ones. It was probably sweet relief she'd left this earth at long last, but that was a horrid thought, and he shivered in his suit at it.

The daughter of immigrant parents from Norway, Freya Danbury had married and been widowed young. Those experiences produced a woman as tough as nails but who loved her only son fiercely until mourning his loss, too, at a young age. She had raised her only grandson well, extolled the pastor. It was what family did, she'd insisted, and she never regretted a moment of the hardship she'd endured to do so. Danbury—as he was called by nearly everyone—was the only son of an only son. That must have been a lonely childhood, thought Matthew as he pondered all of this new information.

Glancing at the tall, broad-shouldered detective—who he had always thought looked like a misplaced Viking—Matthew wondered what had happened to his parents. Danbury, he knew, was a very private person. He was learning more about the guy in this one day than he'd known since they'd met. You don't, thought Matthew, have to know a person's past to know who they are at the core of their being. At least that was true in Danbury's case.

Matthew had seen him repeatedly drop everything to help people. The guy was stoic. He spoke as few words as humanly possible in a staccato speech pattern that was at first annoying, but then became endearing somehow. With Danbury, if two words would suffice, four would never be uttered. He had a dry sense of humor and a completely unreadable face and demeanor. That was particularly true when he was in what Matthew had termed "cop mode."

Penn Lingle—who had recently become Danbury's fiancée and was the only person who called him Warren—could read the big detective better than anyone else, except perhaps the grandmother he was saying a final goodbye to today.

Matthew cast a surreptitious glance around at the few tiny groupings of people dispersing as the service ended. Afterward, making his way to the historic Lingle Plantation—the home of Penn and her younger brother Leo—Matthew was in awe of the pervasive quiet enveloping the little town of Peak. He lived on the outskirts of town, though his office was near the Lingles' house.

The main streets of downtown Peak were deserted. Most businesses were closed. Matthew chided himself for expecting to see tumbleweeds rolling down the empty streets at any moment. There was something eerie about it he hadn't gotten used to.

Arriving at their house, Matthew changed into jeans and a soft Henley T-shirt and joined Penn and her brother Leo with Danbury as they gathered around the kitchen table. The old historic family home shuddered and moaned in the stiff wind on this bleak spring day. Most of the town thought the house was haunted. On days like today, Matthew fully understood why.

"Warren was my mother's surname. Before she married my father," Danbury morosely answered a question Penn had asked over a steaming cup of coffee as if he were a million miles away in another era or dimension. "My grandmother disliked it. She never said so. Not directly. She preferred a strong Norse name. Like Odin or Thor. Maybe Gunnar or Leif."

"I get it," answered Penn. "I've never understood why my otherwise sensible parents named me something entirely frivolous like Penelope. Or Leonard." She gestured to her younger brother. "Those aren't family names. At least your parents had a reason."

The room was silent for a few moments, the only sound a rhythmic one from a grandfather clock that stood in the hallway off the kitchen and the creaking of the old house in the wind.

Quietly, Penn asked, "Do you want to talk about her? I'm a great listener, and I'd love to know more."

Matthew nodded his agreement. Leo made excuses about going to check the security cameras on his joint business with Penn, a currently closed gym and spa, and slipped out of the kitchen.

"Yes and no," said Danbury, staring into space. Anguish was etched on his face as he rubbed his thumb across his square jawline and over his clean-shaven chin.

Matthew wondered if he should slip out as Leo had, but some indescribable force held him in his seat. There was a tangible urgency in the room. Penn had every right to probe and draw her fiancé out, but Matthew didn't want to intrude. He wanted to honor Danbury's privacy while showing support, though the line between the two wasn't clear in that moment.

"It isn't your grandmother that's bothering you, is it?" asked Penn.

"No," said Danbury, meeting her eyes. "It isn't."

"What's on your mind?" she asked.

"An old cold case," Danbury said tersely. "A personal one."

Penn asked gently, "Can I help?"

"You can," said Danbury. "Your perspective could help. It's completely different from mine. It might produce new leads. Things I wouldn't think of. You can help too, Doc," he added, including Matthew in a sweeping glance.

Surprised, Matthew leaned forward, elbows on the table. "I'll help if I can," he answered sincerely. To that statement, he wanted to add the disclaimer "in anything but police work." He refrained.

"What can we do?" asked Penn, reaching for Danbury's hand.

"My parents. I need to know," Danbury slowly answered, as if he'd had to consider each word carefully. He added, so softly Matthew wasn't sure he'd heard him correctly, "What really happened."

"Oh," said Penn, nodding like she knew exactly what Danbury was talking about as Matthew, who had no idea, asked, "Oh?"

"I didn't pursue it when Amma was alive," said Danbury. "Even after she wouldn't have known. It felt dishonoring. But now I need to know."

Matthew waited patiently for Danbury to explain. Penn stared ahead in silence, twisting the new diamond engagement ring Danbury had just given her, obviously concerned.

"I thought I knew him. My father was my hero. But I was a kid. What could I know?"

Matthew nodded encouragingly, though he didn't understand. A quick glance at Penn told him she understood completely. Concern clouded her bright-blue eyes.

"A lot of it is blank," continued Danbury. "I don't remember the weeks before. Or the day it happened. It's hazy in my mind. My grandmother refused to talk about it. She pursed her lips tightly whenever I asked. Eventually, I stopped asking.

"I never thought it was true. But I need to know. Definitively. I've left it alone for nearly twenty-two years. Out of respect for the woman who raised me. She selflessly took me in. And worked hard to support us," he said, looking meaningfully at Penn. "If it is true, I can live with it. But I have to know to move forward."

"I've told him it doesn't matter to me," Penn said to Matthew. "We're getting married, regardless of what his father did or didn't do all of those years ago. But it matters deeply to Warren. Will you help him, Matthew? I know you wanted to get as far away from police work as you could, but the case is over twenty years old."

She was pleading with Matthew, and his friend was obviously still hurting from something in his long ago past. How could he tell them no, even if it meant getting involved in police work again?

"You know I'll help," Matthew heard himself agree. "What are you trying to find out?"

His eyes full of pain, Danbury softly replied, "If my father shot my mother. And then himself."

2 ~ PRESUMED INNOCENT

"Oh," said Matthew as the information about Danbury's parents' death sunk in. He couldn't imagine how soul crushing that would be. Danbury had not merely lost his parents at a young and vulnerable age. He had lost them in such a way that challenged his father's hero status, forcing him to question it throughout his life.

"When and where do we start?" Matthew asked through the steam of his coffee.

"Thanks, Doc," said Danbury, his voice tinged with sincere warmth. "Right now. I got copies of the files from the initial investigation. A lot is missing. Things that should be there. I'm asking questions. Discretely. A couple of officers are still at the precinct. Two who were around then. Neither were involved in the investigation. Though they remember it. I'm tracking down two others. They were involved. Both retired. I'm locating people who were interviewed. That's harder than you'd think. After almost twenty-two years."

"What do you need me to do?" Matthew asked.

"I created an online document. Listing what I know. Mostly, it's questions," said Danbury, pulling his phone from his pocket and tapping it. "I shared it with you. There isn't much. I copied the files. From the initial investigation. A set for you. Then you'll know what I know."

"You can share those files?"

"What files?"

"Oh. You know I'll do what I can as discretely as possible."

That was all Danbury needed to pull his hand gently away from Penn and mutter, "I know," as he left the room. Matthew shared a wry grimace with Penn before Danbury returned with a large, thick manila envelope.

"Guess I've got a little light reading to do," said Matthew, thinking he had time to help because the COVID pandemic had turned his usually hectic schedule up-side-down. As he and the senior partners tried to protect themselves—and their patients—from the deadly virus, E-visits made up the bulk of his patient interaction.

"Did any of what's in here jog your memory?" he asked, as Danbury slid the envelope across the table to him.

"Not much," said Danbury. "I wasn't home that day. The files detail time frames. Ballistic reports. Finger prints. Or lack of them. And the time of death. That was around noon, based on a 911 call. It's mysterious. Nobody admitted to making the call. Jaber lived across the street. There's an unsigned statement that I think is his. Says he was home. He saw nothing and nobody. Heard nothing. Denied calling 911. There's a transcript of the call. You'll see it in there. Pretty generic. Reported hearing gunshots fired. Gave the address. The caller hung up. When asked his name. If the caller was male. There's a question about that too."

"That sounds suspicious," agreed Matthew, nodding, "There was no phone number for the incoming call?"

"Dispatch didn't record it. If they were able to see one. Or it was removed if they did."

"It was a traumatic experience that you likely blocked from your memory. You were a child, so that's reasonable. Do you remember anything at all of that day?"

Deep in thought, Danbury stared as if he were looking beyond Matthew and Penn, like they weren't in the room or in the same time and space. Finally, he replied in a stream of consciousness, "It's scattered. That morning. Pop-Tarts, not eggs. Mom usually cooked eggs. Brain food. Protein. But she didn't. Pop-Tarts were great. For a kid. Basketball clothes. A glass of milk. My gym bag. A basketball," he said and shivered slightly. "She must have told me she loved me. She always did. I don't remember seeing my dad."

Pausing, Danbury sipped his coffee. "A normal day, I guess. Summer basketball camp. Probably a bus ride home. I don't remember it. Or walking up the street. I must have. Nobody picked me up. The house. Cars. People. I couldn't make out what was happening. What they were doing. My grandmother. Amma telling me to be brave. But maybe that was later. It all jumbles in my mind. That's it. I get shadowy glimpses. And then it's gone."

"It's OK," said Penn, getting up and standing behind Danbury, massaging his broad shoulders and neck.

"Can you remember anything unusual about the days before? Did your parents seem stressed? Were they having serious discussions or arguing?" asked Matthew.

"Not that I can remember," answered Danbury. "I never heard them argue. But I was a kid. Would I have noticed tension? Paid attention to know?"

"What about other people?" asked Matthew. He—who had mostly watched and listened when Danbury conducted interviews and chimed in to help when a more empathetic touch was needed—had taken the lead in questioning the interrogation expert. It was an odd juxtaposition, but the role felt strangely right. "Was there anybody else around the week before? Family? Or friends? Your grandmother? Or anybody unusual?"

Thumbing his chin, Danbury said, "My dad's best friend. They worked together. And had served together. In the Marines. He was around a lot. And his wife. Heather. I hadn't thought about her in years. Her name just came back to me. She was around a lot. Maybe not that last week. But often."

Danbury added, "Sitting at the kitchen table. Drinking something. Talking to Mom. Whatever they were discussing was serious. They paused when I came in. Then started up again. After I went upstairs. Their voices were hushed murmurs. A distant undertone of voices. It blends into the background. You tune it out. Maybe I heard words. If I did, I don't remember them."

After a sip of coffee, Danbury said, "And lunch at my grandmother's house. The weekend before. Sunday, maybe. She had no use for church. But she cherished family traditions. Like lunches together."

Matthew could relate to enjoying family traditions. He sorely missed his family since the pandemic began. "You were at your grandmother's house here in Peak the weekend before your parents died?" he clarified.

"I'm pretty sure."

"Did they talk about anything serious or that sounded important?"

"If they did, it was after I left. My dad gave me cash. To get a root beer float. At Peak Eats. Sometime after lunch. That was odd. Now that I think about it. But I was a kid. A root beer float was a treat. I didn't question it."

Matthew missed Peak Eats. The downtown café or diner, depending on who you asked in town, was temporarily closed due to the pandemic.

"We need to check a storage unit," said Danbury. "My grandmother's. I didn't know she had one. Until yesterday afternoon. Her lawyer gave me the key. And told me where it is."

"Huh," said Matthew. "Did she open it when you cleaned out her house and moved her into the care facility?"

"Couldn't have," said Danbury. "She wasn't capable. Not by that point. Had to have been earlier."

"You don't know what's in it?" asked Matthew.

"No idea. Ready to roll?"

Penn made sandwiches for them, Matthew hung his suit bag in his Honda Element, and they piled into Danbury's big, black SUV. As he rode nibbling his lunch, Matthew flipped through the files in the folder.

Diagrams of the crime scene appeared to have been sketched by hand. Two bodies were depicted, one on a sofa and another looked to be draped over something—a stool, maybe. A gun was sketched on the floor. Matthew wondered if the drawing were anywhere near to scale.

The gun seemed to be some distance from both bodies. Wouldn't that have been improbable if the shooter had been one of them? he wondered.

The body across the stool was labeled "Erik Danbury." Danbury's father had been given one of the strong Nordic names that hadn't been bestowed on his son, Matthew mused. The other figure, sketched on the sofa, was labeled "Gayle Danbury."

A small rectangular object was depicted on the floor closer to the man's body than the weapon, and it was labeled "pager."

"Is this your dad's pager?" he asked Danbury.

"Likely so. It's not listed."

Shuffling through the files, Matthew looked for an itemized list of the objects in the room. He found none and asked Danbury about that. Objects like the contents of pockets might provide important information.

"There's no itemized list. It's missing from the file."

Returning to the files, Matthew found several statements taken from neighbors. An unsigned one claiming the person being interviewed was home all day but had heard and seen nothing had a note jotted on the corner. It indicated the interviewee lived across the street.

"This is the one you think was Jaber?" Matthew asked, holding it out for Danbury to quickly glance at.

"It is."

"That's odd. If the houses are in close proximity, he should have heard the gunshots. Unless he had a TV or music cranked up. He claims not to have been the 911 caller."

Wondering about the distance between the houses and who else would have been around to hear gunshots, Matthew pulled his phone from his pocket and searched for the address on the report. The map image showed a short street that dead-ended into airport runways. There was a small buffer of trees between. One house was directly across the street and another on the right just as you'd turn onto the street.

"There are three houses on this street?" Matthew asked.

"There used to be others. A few more. I'm surprised those are still there."

"Were the other houses close enough for one of those neighbors to have heard the gunshots and called 911?"

"It's possible," answered Danbury. "The other neighbors were interviewed. Most weren't home. Nobody admitted to calling 911."

According to the report, the call had come in at 12:12 p.m. on Tuesday, July 7, 1998. Flipping through the pages, Matthew found a coroner's report. It put the estimated time of death for both victims between 8 a.m. and 12 p.m. that day. The incoming call was just outside that window of time but still close enough to be accurate.

Matthew flipped through the rest of the pages. Conrad Manchester had been interrogated several times. The transcripts showed the questions circling and returning to four central issues. The primary one was whether Conrad had been at the Danburys' home the morning of the incident. Another was Conrad's feelings for Danbury's mother. The interrogator all but accused him of killing Erik and Gayle Danbury because he was in love with Gayle. Ownership of a gun and sunglasses were also discussed.

That made little sense, though, as the other person interrogated more than once was Heather Manchester. That must be Conrad's wife who Danbury remembered seeing in the kitchen talking with his mother. That also made her Gayle's friend—and potential confidant—and Conrad Erik Danbury's best friend. Stranger things had happened than a love triangle gone wrong, Matthew thought. Somehow, that didn't feel right in this case, though he had no idea why he thought so.

Nothing about this felt right, Matthew realized as he nibbled his sandwich. Returning his attention to the files, he pulled a smaller envelope from the large one. It contained photographs of the crime scene. Faded with age, they showed a lot of blood surrounding both bodies, which meant they likely hadn't been moved.

Were there defensive wounds anywhere on them? He'd seen no mention of it in the files, and he flipped back to the coroner's report. It was, from what he'd learned of police work over the past year, a sparse report. The time of death was noted, and the cause of death was listed as fatal gunshot wounds for both victims. Neither had any life-threatening illnesses or other injuries found. Little else was included.

Why, Matthew wondered, would the death of a police officer receive less than a thorough investigation and detailed reporting? Was it because he'd been presumed to have killed himself? Or was it because his best friend was accused of killing both him and his wife? He asked Danbury none of those questions.

"Conrad Manchester," Matthew muttered aloud. "Here's the record of his interrogation. He was your dad's best friend, right?"

"Questioning. They didn't call it an interrogation. But yeah, that's him."

"It's just a word. They all but accused him of having an affair with your mother and killing your parents as a result." Noticing something short of a flinch from Danbury, Matthew added, "Sorry, Man. I guess this is still raw for you."

"It is hard," Danbury agreed, his voice husky with suppressed emotion. "I knew it would be. But I need the truth. Whatever that is."

"Do you think it's possible? That this Conrad was in love with your mother and killed your parents?"

"Almost anything is possible. My dad trusted him. As far as I knew. Unless that suddenly changed. My grandmother would have known. But she shut me down when I asked about it. I wish I'd tried harder. She was a steel trap. She never shared secrets. Or gossip. Unless it was necessary somehow."

Matthew tapped his phone to search for information on Conrad Manchester. Multiple searches came up empty. The only information he could find on the name was nearly as old as the murder. Newspaper records quoted Manchester as saying he wasn't guilty of the murders, hadn't been near the Danbury home that morning, and had no idea why they'd have been targeted. He was also quoted as saying he didn't believe Erik Danbury had killed either his wife or himself, though other unnamed sources within the police department disagreed with his assessment.

"Interesting," Matthew muttered.

"What is, Doc?"

"There's no address and nothing after 1998 on Conrad Manchester."

"Yeah, I know. I've looked."

"Heather Manchester," he muttered. Another search turned up an obituary for someone with that name in early 1999. "On February 3, 1999, a woman with that name died in a single car accident in Raleigh. Born in 1963, she'd have been thirty-six at the time of her death. That would have put her somewhere in the vicinity of your parents' ages."

"Right. I found that too."

Scrolling through the obituary, Matthew saw that her husband, Conrad Manchester, survived her. One brother and her parents had preceded her in death. No children were listed, nor were any other relatives, an address, or career. It was surprisingly sparse, but Matthew was getting used to that. Lack of information seemed to be the theme for investigating the death of Danbury's parents.

"You were right about these files," said Matthew, sliding it all back into the folder. "Most interesting is what I don't see. Even the coroner's report is short on details. That's surprising because your father was an officer. You'd think his own precinct would work more diligently to figure out what had happened to him."

"Unless they thought they knew."

"You think they were covering for him? Not putting details in the file that could have incriminated him further? Or investigating thoroughly and proving his guilt?"

"Maybe. It's one possibility. Too soon to tell," he said, turning into a storage facility and tapping in a code to raise an electronic arm admitting them. "There, on the left."

Danbury pointed to one of the biggest units, parked, and they slid out. After examining the lock, Danbury pulled a key from his pocket and clicked it open. As the door rose, Matthew saw it was full, stacked floor to ceiling with furniture and boxes.

"It's from my parents' house," said Danbury, flipping a light switch and looking around. "It's like it was put here yesterday. And never looked at again. My grandmother had her reasons. I wish I knew what they were."

"Do you think it's all in here? The furnishings from the house you grew up in?"

"Looks like it. It'll take time to go through it. I can't get through it all today. There are other things we need to do. We'll have to come back. There," he said pointing, and making his way through a U-shaped aisle that had been thoughtfully left to access the contents. "That's my father's filing cabinet."

Sliding it out slightly to open the drawers, Danbury flipped through folders. "There's not much here," he said.

"Maybe his files will show us what he was working on at least," said Matthew. "Are they dated?"

"They are. My father was meticulous. These outline private security work," he said, pointing. "He worked a second job. For a security company. Iron Clad Security. I don't remember the company. If I ever knew it."

Pulling a folder out to scrutinize the contents more closely, he added, "It's out of Washington."

Matthew tapped his phone to enter the company and location. "It was in DC," he said. "Iron Clad Security at that address went out of business back in January of 1999. That's shortly after your parents were killed. You think that's a coincidence?"

"Neither of us believe in those," answered Danbury darkly.

That was an early point of connection when he and Danbury had first met. It was one of the few things they had initially agreed on.

Scanning through the folders, Danbury said, "Information is redacted. In all of these files."

"Any idea what that could have been?" asked Matthew, looking over his shoulder.

"None," said Danbury, picking up a nearly empty box and tossing the folders in. "I'll take these with me."

"Now what?" asked Matthew.

Danbury made a complete loop through the unit, flipped off the light, and locked up.

"Going back in time," he replied cryptically, putting the box of files in the back of the SUV.

The misty rain had stopped and the sun was trying to peak through the cloud cover this afternoon. Despite it, Matthew felt a darkness and an overwhelming sense of urgency. A surge of energy ran through his body that he couldn't explain. What could possibly be pressing about a twenty-two-year-old cold case?

3 ~ RETURN OF THE SON

They turned onto a road that looked to have once been paved but now had more cracks than asphalt. A profusion of young spring weeds had sprouted in the cracks. Danbury's SUV handled the eroding street expertly as he maneuvered it to the end. Pausing, he stared before turning into an equally fractured driveway in front of the house on the left. It had once been painted white, Matthew thought, but the paint was grayed and peeling.

Emerging quietly from his side of the vehicle, Matthew watched as Danbury stood surveying the house and yard. Suddenly, an earsplitting roar filled the atmosphere. Startled, Matthew covered his ears and half ducked at the thunderous rumble. That was accompanied by the shadow of a massive object passing overhead and shooting quickly down the street.

"Whoa!" yelled Matthew. Danbury, who hadn't reacted at all, looked quizzically over at him as if Matthew's response were familiar.

"That," said Danbury calmly, "is why this street was never fully developed. And why my parents liked it. This lot isn't huge. Not quite an acre. The two lots beside it weren't developed. All the trees meant privacy. And tree forts. With a huge yard to play in."

Tall oaks surrounded the house—with a clump of trees in front—and across the lots beside it that Danbury had indicated.

"The property was buffered from development. At least of houses. The strip of trees at the end of the street. And along the far side of the house. Those were thicker. Back in the day."

Clumps of brown weeds were reviving with new growth all around them, particularly between the driveway and the tree line. Briers and brambles intertwined, climbing up each other like ladder rungs. Some sort of creeping vines that Matthew couldn't identify rambled high into the trees.

"The airport owns all that," continued Danbury, pointing beyond the end of the road to the tree line. "Their property wraps the end of this street. The state park is on the other side. It was peaceful, secluded. When my parents bought the house. Before that new runway was added. On the other side of that tree line. Planes used it sporadically, at first. When I was little. You get used to it after a while. Believe it or not."

Matthew glanced dubiously at him as Danbury explained, "The second terminal was added. Around 2008, I think. After I'd moved to Peak with my grandmother. That noise became constant."

"If there were other houses on this street, what happened to them?"

After a second plane lifted just above their heads in a tornadic roar, Danbury said, "My guess? That forced most of them out. The houses must have been razed. These properties belong to the airport now. Mostly. They were bought up."

Danbury's childhood home and the house across the street, in far worse shape, stood as stubborn monuments to the past between the airport property and the rest of the street.

The driveway wasn't extensive, but it was at least double the length of many new houses, assessed Matthew. At the end of the street where Danbury had pointed, stood a bent and twisted basketball pole. It leaned at an odd angle, as if stubbornly refusing to fall. Its broken backboard, attached at a single point, dangled from the rusted post.

It could have been an exhibit in a modern art museum, Matthew mused as he considered a title for the piece. The whole thing looked as if it would fall over in the next gust of wind. As he fought the urge to go finish it off and kick it over, he was disturbed by the oddly destructive impulse. Something about this place affected him in an unsettling way.

"Was that yours?" asked Matthew, pointing to the mangled basketball post.

"Sort of. My dad put it up. Somebody he knew got rid of it. It belonged to all of us."

"I didn't know you played basketball," said Matthew, remembering Danbury had been a football star in high school.

"I don't. Not since July 7, 1998. Exactly three months after my twelfth birthday."

"Oh," said Matthew, understanding the implication and the significance of the new information. "Who owns this property now?"

"Apparently, I do. I learned that this week. I assumed my grandmother had sold it. Years ago. I don't understand why she didn't. She wanted nothing to do with it. She never came back. And wouldn't let me. She could have used the money. The airport must have offered plenty. They badgered my dad about it. He swore he'd never sell. A local politician tried to force him out. It was a whole ordeal. I vaguely remember it all."

"Could that have had anything to do with what happened to your parents?" Matthew asked, trying to ask the question as gently as he could manage.

"It's one possibility."

"Why is the house still here, if the property was the objective?"

"Exactly. We need more information."

"I assume Amma had it emptied," said Danbury, approaching the house under an attached carport. "Given the furniture in the storage unit. Looks like it's been boarded up for a while. I doubt there's anything here to find. Not checking isn't an option. Particularly not now."

Making fast work of prying up and pulling off the boards blocking the side entrance, Danbury produced a key to open a creaking and sagging door. He stepped through.

Matthew looked over his shoulder. He couldn't shake the feeling they were being watched, though he saw nobody. The sensation caused a slight tremor down his spine. He told himself the only eyes that could be watching likely belonged to wildlife which had made their home here. Still, the chill was bone-deep and the sense of being watched no less real.

Catching his breath, he stepped into the house. The smell of earthy dampness and something overpoweringly feral, that distinct odor of wild animal, assailed his nostrils. The split-level house obviously hadn't been home to people in years.

A kitchen opened off to the right with what appeared to have been a breakfast nook beyond. Shafts of light slanted through cracks between the boards on the windows. That and the slender mag light, which Danbury pulled from the side pocket of his black cargo pants, provided enough light for Matthew to see an archway into a front room on the left. It was, as Danbury had supposed, devoid of furnishings.

Danbury led the way upstairs where there were doorways into three empty bedrooms. The windows on this upper floor were also boarded from the outside; muted light filtered between the cracks here too. A hall bath and a closet provided two more doorways on the short hallway.

Matthew following Danbury through the upstairs. A master bedroom was on the front of the house, a door inside led to a bath with a small closet beyond.

The bedroom on the back corner of the house Matthew guessed to have been Danbury's by the way the big detective paused and looked around the empty room, as if remembering how it had been set up in his youth. He went to the corner closet and opened the door, running his fingers down the inside trim. Faintly visible were markings, Danbury's growth progress as a child. The lines stopped just above his shoulder. The guy had been tall even as a twelve-year-old. Danbury's face, as usual, was unreadable.

After checking a second back bedroom and the accompanying closet, the linen closet, and the hall bath, Danbury reached up and pulled an overhead cord to draw down folding stairs to attic space. The ancient cord snapped in his hand, forcing him to wiggle his fingers in behind the bowed door to pry it open, pulling it down. The springs and scissor mechanism screeched in protest at the disruption; dust and dirt rained down.

Matthew watched dubiously as Danbury climbed the first four steps to get his head above the ceiling and shine the mag light around. The steps held his weight. Apparently satisfied there was nothing to be learned above, Danbury stepped down, folded the stairs, and pushed the door into place.

Downstairs, a front door was on the level with the kitchen with a coat closet behind it. After examining that middle floor, closets, and kitchen cabinets, Danbury squared his shoulders. He descended slowly down five steps into the lower level of the house.

"This is it," said Danbury softly. "Where they were found."

Matthew waited without comment while Danbury paced the room, as if in a trance and seeing it all again in his mind. "A sofa was there. A loveseat here. There was a rug. In the middle of the floor. A footstool was usually here. Beside the loveseat. It was moved. In the crime scene photos, it was beside the recliner. My mother was on the loveseat. My father was slumped over that footstool."

Danbury moved to where the footstool would have been in the pictures he described and knelt to examine the floor. Matthew couldn't see his face, but his shoulders visibly stiffened. "There's a dark spot here. Blood stains that weren't removed," he said simply.

That it remained was a wonder, thought Matthew. But then, he assumed the house had been undisturbed, except by rodents, after the contents had been removed. He couldn't imagine how it must feel—seeing it all again for first time in nearly twenty-two years.

At the front of the house, Danbury examined a laundry room with connections but lacking appliances, a half bathroom, and a tiny room where he paused and stared. It was slightly larger than a storage closet.

"This was my dad's home office. There wasn't much in it. Just a desk and chair there." He pointed to the side wall. "The filing cabinet was over there. The one in the storage unit."

After they'd examined every crevice of the house but found nothing, Danbury locked the door behind them. "For whatever that's worth," he muttered.

"Now what?" asked Matthew.

"I want to talk to Ms. Rosa. I've been trying to find Jaber. From across the street. I don't have a last name for him. Online, I can see the year the house was built. And that it was sold in 1998. Right after my parents died. I can't see the ownership transfer. There's no information on the earlier owner. The tax records don't go back far enough. It's currently owned by a foundation. An elusive one. There's no information about it."

The house across the street looked like something out of a horror film, Matthew thought, shading his eyes against the bright, early spring sun. Nobody had bothered to board it up. It might have once been painted blue, but it was hard to tell. More of the gray boards showed than the peeling paint that had presumably covered them. Most of the windows were broken, and the roof was sagging in several spots. The carport roof was barely there; the post on the front corner was missing.

"Do you want to look at that house?"

"Eventually. I was in it once or twice. As a kid. I want to talk to Ms. Rosa first. She can enlighten us. If anybody can."

"Ms. Rosa?"

"The house on the right. Where we first turned in. Sweet lady. She baked the best peanut butter cookies. We'll have to go slow. She'll ask where the fire is. If you talk too fast. I thought she was ancient back then. Everybody looks old to kids. I think she really was though."

"She still lives there?"

"I hope so. The house is in her name. She knew everything about everybody. She wasn't a gossip. Or a nosy neighbor. She took care of people. When they were struggling. Neighbors talked to her. There were five other houses. Two across from her. One between those and mine. And two between her and Jaber."

"Do you know what happened to the people?"

"No. I've searched records. Trying to find them. I hope Ms. Rosa can tell us. They disappeared. Like the houses."

4 ~ REVISITING

They slid from the SUV in front of the one house at the entrance of the street. Silently, they traversed a short cement walkway—recently cleaned—to a low front stoop. The brick house was a single story with two windows on either side of the centered front door. White flower boxes beneath all four windows contained profusions of blooming spring flowers in a myriad of colors.

Danbury pushed the doorbell, which Matthew noticed included a security camera, and they waited. Eventually, scuffling noises from within grew louder until the solid door was opened and the storm door cracked by an elderly woman stooped over a walker. She wore a faded flowered house dress with a matching kerchief around her head. Her dark skin had so many wrinkles her face resembled a topological map. Leaning out to study Danbury, she opened the door wider.

"As I live and breathe! Warren Danbury, is that you?" she asked, peering intently at him through a pair of thick glasses. The exclamation startled Matthew because they hadn't had a chance to introduce themselves. Another pair of glasses, he noticed, hung from a chain around her wrinkled neck.

Matthew wondered how, after twenty-two years, she could recognize the big detective so quickly and easily if Danbury hadn't been back to the old neighborhood.

"Yes, Ma'am," he replied, ducking his head in deference. Indicating Matthew, he quickly added, "This is Doctor Matthew Paine."

"You brought me a doctor?" she asked in mock concern.

"I'm not here in that capacity, Ma'am," said Matthew. "It's nice to meet you."

"Well, come on in!" she exclaimed, pulling the door open wider.

"No disrespect, Ms. Rosa," said Danbury, "but we can't stay."

"Oh," she said, obviously disappointed.

"How are you?" Danbury asked politely. "Do you need to sit?"

"As long as I'm on this side of the grass, I guess I'm OK. I don't have nary an ache nor pain. I'm just slow moving. And I'm fine with my walker. I need to be up and around a bit."

"How's Jimmy? I lost track of him," said Danbury, then added, "after I moved."

Taking her cue from him to skirt the issue, she responded, "I was hoping you'd come back to visit sooner. We missed you when you left. Jimmy, especially. He has a good job, works for himself. He's married with two little girls, cute as they can be."

"Jimmy is Ms. Rosa's great-grandson," Danbury explained to Matthew. "We played together. When we were kids. Whenever he was here. He didn't live here. But he was here a lot."

"Ain't that the truth?" said Ms. Rosa with a partially toothless grin. "He might as well have lived here. His momma worked two or three jobs, and it won't never enough. He was here with me a lot. You were always such a help to him, with his math, particularly. I'm not sure if I ever told you how much I appreciated that. He struggled in school so much. Jimmy worked hard, but it wasn't easy for him."

As she complimented Danbury, the big detective hung his head and shifted from one foot to the other. Matthew did his best to hide the amused smirk he felt creeping up to his face, though one eyebrow raised involuntarily. Danbury could have withstood severe interrogation, faced ruthless killers, or stood in front of a firing squad without flinching. But this sweet elderly lady's praise made him fidget.

"Jimmy's been real helpful around here. He installed a security system on the house. I have a little camera that's on the table by my chair in the sittin' room. It shows me who's here when somebody's at the front door."

When Danbury hadn't responded, Ms. Rosa said, "Cat got your tongue, Boy? You used to talk a blue streak. You chattered like a magpie about everything under the sun."

That, thought Matthew, his eyebrow raised, was the most surprising thing he could have heard. The big detective had been a man of few words since he'd known him. The fewer the better.

"You grew up into the strong silent type, huh?" she asked, chuckling. "And handsome too. You always were a head taller than all the boys your own age. What are you doing with yourself these days?" she asked, giving him the perfect segue to what he'd come to discuss with her.

"I'm a homicide detective. With the Raleigh Police Department," he answered.

Somehow, she managed to whistle between her missing teeth and he dove in to the discussion he'd wanted to have with her.

"I'm working on a cold case. I hope you can help me. If you will, Ms. Rosa?"

"I'll help you if I can," she responded, nodding her head. Her face showed both kindness and wisdom.

"Do you know how to find Jaber? And the other people from the street? I don't remember many of the others. Only one other house had children. And they were older than Jimmy and me. What's Jaber's last name? I searched for him. But it's harder without the surname."

Confusion clouded Danbury's face as the old woman threw back her head and a belly laugh burbled up and out of her open mouth.

"Jaber won't his first name," she said. "Nor his last name neither. His name was Jason Byrd. People called him Jay Bird. Jimmy couldn't say that when he was little, so he called him Jaber, and it stuck."

"Oh!" said Danbury, adding a chuckle to her laughter. "I never knew that."

"I hadn't thought about old Jay Bird in years," she said. "He moved out right after you did."

"Did anyone else move in? After he was gone?"

"No, siree. That house has stood empty and rotting for years. Jimmy went in it once and said it was like Jaber walked out and took nothing with him. The furniture was all still there, and Jimmy said there was clothes in the closets."

"Did Jaber live there alone?"

"As best I could tell, he did. There were people in and out, his cousins he called them, but there ain't no telling what he was really up to. I'm sure your daddy knew, being a police officer and all. But he didn't never tell me, and I didn't ask. Your daddy was a gentleman."

"What about the others? The neighbors on the street?"

Danbury had pulled an electronic notebook from a side pocket in his cargo pants. He tapped to add the information as Ms. Rosa told him about the neighbors who had lived in each of the houses.

"It was all real secretive-like. I don't know where any of 'em went nor why. They were just there one day and moved out the next. I never did understand it. Then a couple 'a months or so later, the crews and machines came in and the houses and trees disappeared. In just a couple of days, all of it was gone. Burned up or hauled off in dump trucks, like it hadn't ever been there."

Danbury clarified the timeline of each family moving out and asked Ms. Rosa for names and approximate ages of each the former neighbors. Logging the information, Danbury asked question after question, attempting to get as many details as she could remember about each one.

"How odd that they all moved out abruptly," Matthew chimed in. "Did anybody approach you about selling your house or moving?"

"They did. Regular as clockwork for a while. Until I'd had enough of it. It was back before the other neighbors moved out, back when they were bothering your parents. I reckon they were badgering us all. Somebody called every week, and they came by about once a month trying to buy my property. Then, I told them the same thing your father said he did. And they stopped bothering me."

"What was that?"

The old woman's face drooped and she stammered, trying to recover, "Well, it won't nothing much."

"Ms. Rosa," said Danbury earnestly. "It's why I'm here. I'm investigating their deaths. I need to know what really happened. Anything you can remember might help. Whatever you can tell me."

"Your father was an honorable man, Warren. He didn't kill himself, and he'd have never have harmed a hair on your pretty mama's head. He loved that woman with everything he had. I knew it then, and I know it now."

"Then help me prove it. Tell me what he said."

"Because of what happened," she said, tentatively, alluding to the death of Danbury's parents without stating it outright, "I remembered exactly what he said. And I always did wonder if that wasn't why it happened."

"What was it, Ms. Rosa?" asked Danbury. "What did my father say?"

"Well, he told me that he told them he'd sell that house over his dead body! Those were his exact words too."

"Oh," said Danbury and Matthew in unison.

"All of those politicians wanting to take this street out and put in another runway. Like anybody wanted another one of those. And there's land 'a plenty on the other side of the airport. But that didn't slow them down one bit. Somebody had their sight set on this street and this property. They badgered us all, I can tell you that! And then they just stopped."

"I wonder what changed," said Matthew as Danbury thumbed his chin.

"I've wondered that same thing," she answered.

"Was Jimmy here?" asked Danbury. "The day it happened?"

"He won't. He was in summer school. He went home to his mama's house that afternoon. You got off the activity bus by yourself that day. You don't remember that?"

"No, ma'am. Not much about any of it," said Danbury, his brow furrowed in concentration.

"It'll come back, if you want it to," she said soothingly, reaching over to pat his hand. Danbury nodded as Ms. Rosa continued, "Jimmy found your basketball at the end of the street, and he kept it for years. He was hopin' you'd come back for it and visit. He moved right in here after all of that happened. I guess he was afraid for me too. But they left me alone after that, those people trying to buy my property."

"You were tuned in. To what went on here," said Danbury. "Did anybody see anything? The day my parents were killed. Or hear anything? Anything unusual?"

"I tried real hard to think about that then. Won't nobody much ever here during the daytime, except Jaber sometimes. I think he worked at night, if he worked at all. Jaber told the police he didn't see nobody down there all that day or hear anything. He told 'em he was in the front of the house where he could have. No cars or people came down there after you left for school that morning."

Ms. Rosa screwed up her face and then added, "But that was after he'd already told me that he had. He said he saw a car leaving right after he got up about lunch time. He was a little fuzzy on the details about what it looked like when I asked him."

"What did he tell you?"

"He said was a sedan that might have been gray or tan. I reckon he forgot all about that when the police asked him. Maybe he didn't want to get involved. But he told me he saw that car. I didn't see nothing, but I did hear a car leaving the neighborhood that day."

"You did? What time was that?"

"I didn't know exactly when the police asked, but sometime before I had lunch. I remembered it because it was speeding out 'a here like a bat out 'a someplace hot. I thought they should have known better, to slow down in a residential area. But I didn't never see it. I just heard it."

"You told the police about it?"

"I did. I thought maybe it was one of Jaber's 'cousins' driving out too fast. Then Jaber said there won't nobody at his house but him that day, so I figured maybe it was somebody looking for a shortcut to the airport. That happened sometimes back before then. People thought this street went through. It didn't happen so much by then because we'd gotten that 'Dead End' sign put up there at the entrance."

Further questions of Ms. Rosa yielded nothing new. Danbury eventually said his goodbyes with a promise for future visits.

"Did I miss something?" asked Matthew as Danbury stared at the dash without starting the car.

"Ms. Rosa's statement. About the car speeding away. It wasn't in the police report," said Danbury.

"Oh," said Matthew. "Now what?"

"Now we're going to Jaber's," said Danbury, starting the SUV and backing down the driveway. "It probably won't help. After all of this time. But best to be thorough. If it's safe to go in it."

They made their way down the street and up what was left of the crumbling driveway. Water had washed one section of it completely out and chunks of cement stood up at odd angles on either side of a trench with small drying puddles. Danbury stopped the SUV before that section.

Picking their way over the driveway debris, across what had probably once been a sidewalk, and to the front stoop, Matthew stopped. "You first," he said, grinning.

"Yeah, thanks, Doc," answered Danbury, stepping up two steps to the door. The front stoop, at least, was concrete and still solid. Danbury pushed the door open with an effort. It dragged across the floor inside and rusted hinges protested.

The inside of the house was worse than the outside, Matthew thought as they stepped tentatively in. He caught a whiff of a vaguely familiar rank smell. Grunting, Danbury pulled out the mag light and began shining it around the dark corners and closets downstairs.

Furniture had not been removed, as Ms. Rosa had said, which made it all the more a disgusting jumble.

Bits of papers and fabric remnants—that could have once been most anything—dirt, grime, dead leaves, and debris that had blown in cluttered the floors. Detritus, that Matthew was neither sure what it was or that he wanted to know, was too thick to determine what the floor had looked like. It was blown in heaps against the lumps that had once been furniture in the front room.

Broken shards of glass peeked between the piles of trash and sparkled in the beam of Danbury's mag light. Examining the rest of the downstairs, they found it to be in similar condition. As Ms. Rosa had said, it looked like the occupant had walked out and never looked back.

The smell Matthew had noticed earlier had become horrific as they peered up the stairs to the top floor. "Something died in here," he stated the obvious.

"Recently," added Danbury.

Climbing the stairs slowly, Matthew was reluctant to find the source of the odor.

"Maybe it's just a possum or raccoon or something," said Matthew, hopefully, though he didn't have much expectation of that being the case.

"Maybe so, Doc," responded Danbury, though his voice held a decisive lack of conviction.

The house was similar to the one Danbury had lived in across the street, Matthew noted as they crossed the narrow upstairs hallway. Danbury went first to the back of the house into what appeared to be the master bedroom.

Following, Matthew froze in the doorway. In the cool damp eeriness of the house, amidst a premonition of warning—then decisive knowing—an overwhelming chill crept up Matthew's spine.

Had there been glass in any of the windows that they'd seen so far, Matthew would have recommended opening one. The potency of the smell caused his stomach to roil.

Making his way around the heap that had once been a bed, Danbury held his light firmly on a figure slumped against the far wall. His posture stiffened. As if he had snapped to attention, only Danbury's extended arm holding the light and his face tilted downward broke the posture. His sharp intake of breath invaded the silence of the room.

"Hey, Doc," he said, blowing out the breath at last and motioning for Matthew to join him. Between the lower portion of the body against the wall and the collapsed and sunken bed, the space was tight. Matthew managed to wedge between them, without touching anything, to stand beside Danbury.

Twisted at an angle, a man's body was slumped against the wall. His right wrist hung on the edge of an upholstered footstool as if he'd been hugging it. Flitting quickly in and then back out of Matthew's mind was the thought that this was an unusual place for a footstool.

Studying the oddly positioned figure, Matthew felt a sadness wash over him at the wasted life. It wasn't an unusual feeling—given the last year he'd been working alongside Danbury—but it was an unwelcome one. He had studied and worked to improve and save lives. Stumbling upon one ended abruptly and purposefully felt like an assault on his profession.

The man was neither young nor old. Older than both men who had found him, Matthew assessed, maybe by a decade. Given the state of the pale upturned face, it was difficult to know definitively.

He was clad in military garb—dress blues, Matthew guessed. The blue of the uniform was a washed-out gray, the brass buttons tarnished. Stripes of piping, once red but now faded, trimmed the edges. An array of pins and ribbons, barely visible from the position of the body, adored the left side of the chest as it met the floor. The man's hands were covered with white gloves. An autopsy would determine if there were defensive wounds beneath the gloves. Matthew had no desire to look.

More interesting to note, though, was the gaping hole in the side of the man's head at his right temple. The cause of death should be easy enough to determine. He knew, though, that these situations weren't always what they seemed. They couldn't assume the gunshot wound was the cause of death and overlook something else.

Dancing momentarily around the room, the beam from Danbury's mag light came back to rest on the figure and the area immediately surrounding him.

"No blood spatters or pooling. No obvious murder weapon. Unless that's under him," said Danbury more slowly and softly than usual.

"Or under this heap that was once a bed," added Matthew. "But I don't see how. It's collapsed on the floor."

"Could be," agreed Danbury as Matthew contradicted his own assertion. The beam of light returned to the deceased man, running down every inch of the uniform, illuminating all of the details. With the beam focused on the face of the deceased, Danbury was studying it intently.

"Do you know him?" asked Matthew.

"I don't think so. He looks familiar. Like he resembles somebody. Not the person himself. If that makes any sense."

"It does," said Matthew. He'd met people who closely resembled someone else he knew, but they weren't related at all.

Glancing around the room, Matthew again felt the eerie sensation they were being watched. The eyes of the corpse were closed, the colorless face relaxed in death. He certainly wasn't watching them. It had been several days, at least, since he'd watched anything or anybody, Matthew surmised sadly.

Danbury knelt beside the figure and began checking the pockets of the uniform. "Not expecting to find anything," he said, over his shoulder, but then he pulled something from the man's pocket.

Shining his mag light on the object, Danbury reacted in the last possible way Matthew could have anticipated. Jumping up, Danbury ran to the hole in the wall that had once been a window, leaned through, and retched violently.

5 ~ RIGOR NO MORE

Confusion circled Matthew's brain like water down a sink drain. Concern for Danbury was foremost in his mind. Over the past year, he'd watched the big detective's face remain expressionless, an unreadable mask, as he'd dealt with worse things. He must have encountered many more across the course of his career. Normally, the guy barely flinched. Surely, the smell of a putrefied corpse hadn't garnered that response. What had?

"Danbury," said Matthew, softly. "What is it?"

"My father's ID," answered Danbury, turning from the window, his face white. He braced himself against the wall and grimaced. "His military ID."

"Your dad was a Marine, right?" asked Matthew, raising an eyebrow. "And then a detective?"

"He was."

"Is the ID actually his? Or a forgery made to look like it?"

"Looks like the real deal. That's who he looks like," Danbury added, thumbing at the corpse while trying to regain his composure. "He has a look of my dad. The shape of his face. The set of the chin. The square jaw. That's who he reminded me of. I didn't figure it out at first."

Matthew could see the likeness as he pointed it out, to Danbury himself. "Where could somebody have gotten your father's military ID?"

"Maybe from the storage unit. We have to go back anyway. Harder to check for what isn't there. Because I never saw what was there. Before my grandmother died." Danbury hesitated, the color returning to his face, and added, "And you never saw that reaction just now. That never happened."

"What reaction?" asked Matthew tactfully. "I see nothing but a corpse in an old abandoned house, as grotesque as that is."

"It is," agreed Danbury.

"Who is he really, do you think? That's a Marine uniform, right?"

As Danbury nodded confirmation, he said, "The uniform might be my father's. It would have been inspection ready. Back in the day. I noticed it immediately. Somebody went to a lot of trouble to get everything right. It wouldn't have been stored that way. If it is his. With the decorations attached. Not likely. Somebody put it together. They knew what they were doing."

"What do you mean?"

"Every detail means something," said Danbury, and Matthew waited for further explanation.

"That's an alpha dress blue. Worn for formal occasions. Like weddings or funerals. The red stripe. That's the blood stripe. Officers would have that. Corporals and higher ranks. My dad was an NCO. That's noncommissioned officer. He enlisted without a college degree. Then climbed the ranks to become an officer. The eagle on the belt buckle. It indicates that status."

"Climbed ranks as a noncommissioned officer?" Matthew repeated, trying to comprehend the significance of what Danbury was saying. Having no close family in the military, he lacked the background for understanding.

"Right. Dad enlisted right after he graduated high school. Never went to college. He became an officer, but began as an enlisted Marine. From Private to Private First Class. Then Lance Corporal to Corporal. That's where the NCO comes in. A noncommissioned officer. Then Sargent and Staff Sargent. See the arm? It shows the rank. Gunnery Sargent. That was my dad's rank."

"OK," said Matthew, nodding his understanding.

"The metals on the left breast pocket," Danbury pointed. "Those look like his. And the ribbons on the right. Some accomplishments don't have metals. They have ribbons. Those look like his too. It's been years since I've seen them. But it all looks right. All positioned correctly. An eighth of an inch down on the pocket."

Matthew asked, "Can we get an ID on this guy through the Marine Corps? From fingerprints maybe?"

"Maybe. If the guy was a Marine. Or maybe his death was punishment. If he dressed as a Marine but wasn't. Stolen valor. But a true Marine wouldn't kill him. Not for that. Semper Fidelis."

"Always faithful?" asked Matthew.

"Exactly. Always faithful in everything. All of life. Not just to the Corp. It's drilled into every Marine. My father lived that. I know he didn't kill my mother. It's one of many reasons I know that. He'd have died protecting her. And then there was this. In the pocket with the ID," Danbury held out something near the window for Matthew to inspect. The scrap of yellowed paper with blockish letters read:

I KNEW YOU'D FIND HIM EVENTUALLY.
KEEP LOOKING OR ANOTHER ONE DROPS IN 24 HOURS.

The chill down Matthew's spine felt as if it had grandchildren. He shivered forcefully in the damp, dank bedroom before stiffening, trying not to give in to it.

"Twenty-four hours to find the killer and prevent another murder?" asked Matthew.

"Sound like it," said Danbury. "This was stupid."

"How so?"

"If I had any doubt at all," began Danbury, "that my father was innocent. That it wasn't a homicide and suicide." He hesitated. "I have none now. My parents were killed. Somebody just told me that. Loudly. How long, Doc? When was he killed? Can you tell?"

"With that smell, rigor has come and gone."

Squatting and forcing his mind into the professional mode he used to detach himself from patients' discomfort in order to help them, he looked over the corpse. Danbury handed him a pair of gloves.

Snapping the gloves into place, Matthew lifted the man's right arm at the wrist. "Rigor mortis has come and gone. That's usually about twenty-four hours after death. It's been more than twenty-four hours since he was killed. If that's what the note means, another victim might already be dead by now."

Suddenly, the continual sense of urgency Matthew had felt since the day before made sense. He looked up to see Danbury nodding.

"Putrification, as I'm sure you also know, can set in about four days after death. Autolysis has started with the odor and some discoloration. The skin isn't turning dark yet, what I can see of it. There appears to be slight distension and bloating, so less than ten days in," he added, looking up at the big detective. "Three to ten days is my best guess, give or take. That's a generalization. An autopsy will help with the cause but might not get you much closer on the time of death. There are bugs on the body, so a forensic entomologist might help."

Before either of them had a chance to say anything further, Matthew jumped backward in alarm as the arm of the corpse he'd just laid back on the footstool moved. His foot caught, wedged between the footstool and the edge of the collapsed bed as he tried to stand. Tumbling backward, he landed sprawled on the bedding remains as a rat ran out of the sleeve of the dress blues. It darted across the room and disappeared behind a bedraggled dresser.

Cringing at the thought of what he'd just landed in, whatever had been breeding and dying in that bed for the past twenty plus years, Matthew scrambled trying to get to his feet and then froze on his knees looking up.

"Danbury," he hissed, nodding at the corner of the ceiling.

"Let's go," said Danbury, turning to leave the house abruptly after his gaze followed Matthew's.

Outside, Matthew pulled his gloves off and bent over, hands on his knees, deeply breathing in the spring air. He wondered if he'd ever get the stench out of his nostrils. Danbury peeled off the gloves he'd donned, pulling the ID and note he'd found backward into one of them. Retrieving an evidence bag, he dropped it in and put both bags in the back of the SUV.

Danbury called his precinct in downtown Raleigh. Matthew heard him report the body, provide their current location, and request a tech team as well as the medical examiner. He asked for a missing person report and gave a description of the body.

"And one more thing. Any new missing person reports. Take them seriously," said Danbury into his phone. Then he added, "No, no other descriptions. It could be anybody."

"I had the creepy feeling that we were being watched the whole time we were in that house," said Matthew after Danbury ended his call.

Continuing to brush himself off, Matthew still felt like things were crawling on him. He resisted the urge to sprint down the road in an attempt to outrun any tiny hitchhikers. He couldn't get a hot shower and his clothes in a soapy wash fast enough.

Motioning to the house across the street, Matthew said, "I had the same feeling outside of your house over there, but not inside."

"The tech team is coming. To sweep for more cameras. And bugs. The electronic sort," Danbury added, his mouth twitching in amusement as Matthew continued to brush himself off. "Both houses."

Matthew nodded and Danbury continued, "They're gone now. Whoever was watching. They've dropped the connection. As soon as they saw you seeing it. They're in the wind. That device was tiny. Nice job spotting it."

"Happy to help," said Matthew sardonically, scratching and twitching. "Maybe the twenty-four hours before another victim dies starts now. If the killer was watching us, then he knows exactly when we found this guy. How long until your team gets here?"

"Maybe a half hour. The ME will be longer. Ours is detained. A case across town. They're contacting somebody else."

Matthew felt the urgency to do something, but there seemed to be nothing to do now but wait, impatiently and uncomfortably, for the professionals Danbury had summoned. In the interim, he had new questions. Deciding the direct approach was best, he asked, "Your father was military for how long before becoming a detective?"

"He was in longer than I was. He took orders better. And went farther. I took some courses to get to Chief Warrant Officer. I wasn't going much higher. I went to college. Got a degree instead."

"In criminal justice at East Carolina University."

"That's right," said Danbury, looking impressed that Matthew had remembered. "My dad got out and moved back here. To get close to my grandmother. I was young. About six, I think. Dad joined the police force. He finally made detective. A year or two before he was killed. He identified more with the military. 'Once a Marine, always a Marine' was his motto."

"And the uniform? You called it alpha dress blues?"

"Right," said Danbury. "An old one. No active Marine would look salty like that. Never faded or tarnished. Their uniform would be crisp. Polished."

"You think that sickening display and the note was meant for you?" asked Matthew softly.

"Had to have been," said Danbury as Matthew nodded agreement. "Ironically, it gives me what I need. I can reopen the case. Somebody tried to send a message. Stupidly. It points to a killer. One who is still around. With an agenda." After a pause, Danbury added, "That display was off, though."

"How so?"

"The way the body was positioned. It wasn't like my dad's. He was found downstairs. Not in the bedroom. Draped over a footstool. A hassock, he'd have called it. Gunshot wound to the head. To the left side, not the right. My dad was right-handed. That never made sense as suicide. The weapon was on the floor. Like it had dropped from his hand. His fingerprints were on it. That's not hard to do. Post mortem. There was a blood stain. You saw it. There was no weapon here. Or blood spatter. Or pooling."

"Meaning that the body was moved?"

"And staged. Elaborately."

"I know not pursuing this isn't an option," said Matthew. "Now what?"

"We find Jaber. Jason Byrd," Danbury amended. "And we go through the storage unit. Its existence was the other surprise. Besides the house here."

"Because this uniform came from the storage unit?"

"Had to have. It wasn't in my grandmother's house in Peak. I went through everything. When she moved to the memory care facility. Nothing of my parents' was there. That didn't shock me. My grandmother wasn't sentimental. She was tough. Like forged steel. She'd been through a lot. The surprise is that she saved it all."

Freya Danbury had mostly raised the stalwart detective. Stoic in anybody's estimation, Danbury had likely gotten that from her, Matthew realized.

Distant sirens faded into flashing lights as a brigade of police vehicles approached. Danbury conferred with two uniformed officers who alighted from a police cruiser while Matthew tried to stand still, not to scratch itches, imagined or actual. Between thoughts of things crawling on his skin and the imminent threat of another murder, he caught mere snippets of the conversation. Danbury outlined their movements, then the details of the body as they had observed them.

"Grab a mask," Danbury told the man he was mostly talking with. "You'll need one. It's rough."

"Do you want one of mine?" the man asked. "It has peppermint oil in it to mask the odor, or at least knock it down a notch."

"Sounds good," said Danbury, taking the proffered mask. "I'll be right back, Doc. Then home to Peak. I know you want a shower."

"More than anything I've wanted in a while," replied Matthew, one eyebrow raised as he tried to scratch his sides and as much of his back as he could reach.

Danbury's abrupt return from the house interrupted Matthew's contemplation of potential murder victims, perceived parasites, and the smell that hadn't receded in the fresh air.

"Bad news," began Danbury, climbing in the SUV. "His fingerprints aren't in the system. Not with a quick scan. Meaning he has no criminal record. We'll run them through multiple databases. Knowing who he is would help."

As Matthew climbed in beside him, he continued, "Good news. There's a forensic conference in Raleigh this week. Our ME can't get here. But her backup is at the conference. He'll be here shortly. Bringing a forensic entomologist. Like you mentioned. She was there giving a presentation. A woman by the name of Tegan McFarland. They'll be here later this afternoon."

"That is good news," agreed Matthew. "She should be able to give you a more accurate time of death based on the bugs' life cycle."

"A TOD would help. To run against missing person reports. We'll start there anyway. From your estimate."

"Good idea. Somebody must know this guy isn't where he's supposed to be. Even if you can't ID him from fingerprints immediately. What's next? After my hot shower," Matthew clarified. "We were going to the storage unit and then to find this Jaber person. Did the corpse change that order of operations?"

"Marginally. Stopping to see Ms. Rosa first. Just for a minute. I want to reassure her. She can't have missed this. She knows something is going on."

"OK," Matthew agreed.

"Then your shower. Back here to meet the ME. Then the storage unit. It's just outside Peak. Then to find Jason Byrd. I have an address for him now," Danbury added.

"Good idea," said Matthew, thinking that was a packed agenda for the remainder of a Friday. "Ms. Rosa will want to know what's going on with all of the police vehicles. Maybe she saw or heard something earlier this week. We didn't know to ask her that. She has the security system she said Jimmy installed with at least one camera facing the street on her doorbell. Maybe there are more. One of them could have captured the killer going by."

"What I was thinking. Worth an ask. Jimmy will have to help. I doubt she can check the camera feeds."

"Mind if I hang out right here and wait for you?" asked Matthew.

"Sit and scratch, Doc," said Danbury, smirking at Matthew as he slid out.

Matthew sat in the running vehicle and did exactly that—scratching first around the back of his neck, then his back and shoulders—while Danbury tromped up onto Ms. Rosa's porch. This time, she met him at the door. After a few moments of gesturing and nodding on both their parts, she disappeared and returned a few minutes later, handing Danbury a scrap of paper. She waved from the door as Danbury climbed in the SUV.

"Doc, you reek," Danbury said as he and Matthew returned the wave and he backed out of the driveway.

"I thought it was just in my nose," said Matthew, squirming and scratching more.

"If it is, it's in mine too. And in here," he added, motioning to the inside of the SUV. "Confined space."

"Is Ms. Rosa OK?"

"I explained what's happening. At a high level. I figured she'd look to see what was going on. She did. When she heard sirens coming. She's fine. Tough lady. Heart of gold with nerves of steel. And stubborn. Like my grandmother. She said Jimmy tried to get her to move. She refused. Dug her heels in. Says she's staying put. Nobody's running her out of her home."

"I can see why he'd want her to. She has no neighbors. You'd think it would be lonely out here. I guess she's been safe enough, so far. Did she see anyone or anything this week?"

"Nothing unusual. The postwoman. And a delivery guy. Jimmy sent her groceries. A service guy from a company she trusts. Somebody Jimmy knows. He checked her air conditioning. None of them went down the street. They turned around here. And went back out."

"Can she access the video?"

"No. But you were right. There are multiple cameras. She says Jimmy can see them. I got his number, though she was reluctant. She's afraid he'll force her to move. I'll call him on the way."

"That might not be such a bad thing. She's a nice lady," said Matthew. "I wouldn't want anything to happen to her out here by herself. Being the only occupant on the street, she's also the only one who could have seen anything happening down there. The killer must know that. I hope it doesn't make her a target."

He felt more than a twinge of unease over her lonely living situation and the threat of another murder hanging over them. It wasn't, he knew, an idle one.

6 ~ DEBUGGED

As he stepped from the most wonderful long, hot shower he could remember ever taking, Matthew pulled a towel around his waist. Max, the large, gray tabby cat, regarded him with huge, serious eyes from his perch on the sill of the bathtub where he habitually hovered while Matthew showered.

Feeling truly clean again after incessant scrubbing, Matthew wiped the steam from the mirror. He'd been told he looked like Liam Hemsworth with brown eyes, but he didn't see it in the reflection staring back at him.

Thankful to be rid of anything that might have been crawling there, he ran a towel through his short, wavy, brown hair. He'd tossed his clothes into the washer as soon as he entered the house and set it to a long wash cycle with extra detergent, an extra rinse cycle, and hot water. Though those things weren't likely to help as much as the dryer cycle, it made him feel better.

Consulting his phone, he still saw no message notification from his girlfriend, Cecelia Patterson – Cici to her friends. She was finishing a year-long assignment with a high-profile client in London for her Raleigh law firm. Normally, they video chatted every morning. When she hadn't answered the video chat request this morning, he texted her. He found it disturbing that she still hadn't answered.

What motivated her was an enigma. It was, she asserted, the work she longed to complete before returning home. He had no choice but to believe her, and yet, something seemed off about it. He couldn't put his finger on exactly what that was, he thought, as he dressed.

Recently, they had come to a standoff about her plan to return home. He found her stubbornness about staying in London confusing. She had been adamant he not get involved in any more police work. That, she insisted, was because she wanted him safely awaiting her return to finally build the life together they both wanted. Why, then, hadn't she gotten on the first flight home when the onset of what was now being labeled a pandemic started shutting things down? He had warned her it was likely to do just that.

Procuring an engagement ring for Cici had been on the top of his list of things to do before she came home. Obtaining rings for Cici and Penn in a pandemic had been no small feat. It was possible only because a college fraternity brother and friend of Matthew's father, Joc, owned a jewelry store. Though a nonessential business, he opened it secretly for an hour to Danbury and Matthew. While Danbury purchased Penn's ring, Matthew selected an emerald-cut diamond—with the triangular side diamonds he knew Cici wanted—in a platinum setting.

To divert his thoughts from Cici, Matthew returned his mind to Danbury's conundrum. Strapping his watch on, he saw the time. He needed to hurry to meet Danbury back at the murder scene. Matthew insisted on driving himself to leave when he chose and not be on Danbury's shifting schedule.

Danbury had called Jimmy—putting the call on speaker and introducing Matthew—on the way to Matthew's office to retrieve his Element. The guy sounded genuinely happy to hear from Danbury— right up until he'd explained the reason for his call. Jimmy agreed to meet them back at his great-grandmother's house after he'd finished up the job he was supervising.

"OK, Big Guy," said Matthew to Max. "I'll feed you a little early because I have no idea when I'll be back tonight. I'm sure you won't object." He scratched the big tabby cat under his upturned chin.

After feeding Max, Matthew slipped out, locking up behind himself. He chose his Honda Element, over the C7 Corvette that shared his garage, and backed out onto Chester Road. A mere mile-long rural street that dead-ended into his condominium complex, the location was perfect. Beyond the condos ran a right-of-way for utilities, which prevented anything from being built beyond his unit, the last one on the right. The units on his side of the street met with the back nine of the King's Country Club golf course. It provided peace and quiet—a respite from the world—at least most of the time.

He spotted his neighbor, Mrs. Drewer, out for an afternoon stroll with her little Pomeranian, Oscar. Matthew pulled alongside and dropped the window to greet her. She scooped Oscar up and stood well back from his window as she returned the greeting.

"What's that smell?" she asked, crinkling her nose.

"Bug spray," answered Matthew. "Long story, but I didn't want a bug infestation in my car. How're you?"

"I'm well, thanks. You're a doctor. How much longer will this awful virus run amok, do you think?"

"I'd love to tell you that it will be over soon. But honestly, Mrs. Drewer, I'd be lying if I did. I think we'll be stuck with it for a while until it mutates into something less deadly and stops killing its hosts. That has to happen, but there's no way to know how long it'll take."

"I appreciate your honesty. I was afraid you were going to say that."

"I'm not an infectious disease specialist, but the experts seem to think that we're in for the long haul."

"I don't suppose you have any special sources to get toilet paper?" she asked hopefully. "The grocery shelves are bare of it, and paper towels. Oh, and those antibacterial wipes too. I can't find any anywhere."

"I'm sorry, but I don't. My office just got paper supplies in a couple of weeks. I have no idea when we'll be able to get more, but I could slip you a roll or two if that would help."

"That's so kind, but I'm not completely out yet. I'll let you get on your way," she said, sighing deeply. "You take care now."

"Stay well, Mrs. Drewer. And have a good afternoon."

"You too." She waved as he raised the window most of the way and made his way out.

During what should have been a busy travel time, the I-40 interstate was unbelievably sparsely traveled. Traveling anywhere at any time was much faster and easier. People were either working from home, if they could, or sadly not working at all. Still, he'd far prefer congested, slow-moving traffic to a pandemic.

As he made his way back across town, he pondered the body they'd found, what it signified, and Danbury's unexpected response to it. Somebody was sending a message, but what was it? And why? Why threaten to kill again as a taunt? If it was the same killer, he'd literally gotten away with murder over twenty years ago. Why resurface now in such an obvious way? If it was a copycat, what was the point?

Was the assassin trying to prove something? That he could murder repeatedly, and Danbury couldn't catch him? Maybe. If that was the case, the killer didn't know much about the big detective. Taunting him was an ignorant move on somebody's part. Danbury was tenacious when he wasn't personally involved in an investigation. Matthew couldn't imagine how much more so he'd be now that he was.

The crime scenes, new and old, ran and reran through his mind as he compared them. They put him no closer to answers. Scanning for Danbury's black SUV, he turned onto the street. It wasn't at Ms. Rosa's house, so Matthew made his way down to where the SUV and a myriad of other vehicles crowded the narrow dead end.

Danbury stepped out of the house, as Matthew pulled up to the only spare spot nearby, accompanied by an unfamiliar police officer in uniform. With them was a man in a dark suit, and a woman clad in scrubs, a white coat, and some sort of chunky shoes. Matthew alighted and approached the huddled group. The freckled face of the young woman looked up at him through huge glasses.

She had a mask pushed up on her head and her brown hair was pulled back tightly into a knot at the nape of her neck. The effect was like some sort of exotic female bird. Everything about her was brown. Her intense hazel eyes locked on Matthew as he approached, as if she were looking deeply into his soul and immediately knowing all about him. It was unsettling.

In her hands, she cradled plastic containers as she returned to the conversation with Danbury and the uniformed officer.

"I'm certain," she said softly but insistently.

The uniformed officer nodded, slid into the nearest police cruiser, and picked up the radio. The man in the dark suit Matthew recognized as an assistant ME he'd worked with before but whose name eluded him. Nodding in acknowledgment of Matthew's presence, the guy slid into the medical examiner's van backed up to the upended slab of pavement in the driveway.

"Hey, Doc," said Danbury and introduced him. "Matthew Paine. Tegan McFarland. Doctors all. General practitioner. Forensic entomologist, and nematologist," Danbury added.

"Nice to meet you," said the woman softly without reaching for his hand. Matthew was relieved. Handshaking seemed to be a thing of the past with the pandemic, though some people still seemed to insist on the formality. The containers she held almost reverently. They looked to contain bug larvae.

"You too," said Matthew, with a nod of acknowledgment to the woman he'd already dubbed "the bug lady" in his mind.

He imagined some sort of super hero with special bug powers. Drawing himself back to reality before his mind ran too far with that thought, he wondered how long the string of letters following her name would be. His was merely DO, Doctor of Osteopathic Medicine. Hers must be far lengthier.

"Dr. McFarland was explaining," said Danbury.

"Skip the formalities," she interjected. "Call me Tegan."

"Tegan," Danbury began again, "was explaining the time of death. It's more recent than we thought."

"Oh?" asked Matthew.

The woman said firmly, "Definitely. I don't believe these are common blowfly larvae. They appear to be from black soldier flies."

"Black soldier flies?" repeated Matthew, not understanding why the distinction mattered.

"Right. Adult black soldier flies look a bit like wasps, but they have only two wings instead of four, and they don't have stingers. They're common to this region, but not on a corpse. They were planted there, probably to throw us off track on the TOD."

"They were placed on the corpse purposefully?" Matthew clarified.

"That's the best explanation for their being there," she responded simply. "Normally, black soldier flies lay their eggs in porous substances like rotting wood in a forest, not human remains. They lay eggs in conditions that are acidic, usually warm and wet, with abundant rotting material for the larvae to feed on. They feed on waste products."

Before Matthew could ask further questions, she went on to explain, as if lecturing a class on the subject, "If they're in urbanized areas where rotting plant life and naturally occurring organic matter is less prevalent, the black soldier fly will lay eggs in waste areas like compost bins or dumpsters. Those have similar odors and provide for the larvae nutritionally. They can also feed on animal waste. Commercially, they're useful to reduce animal manure, like in poultry and swine facilities."

"They won't feed on human remains?" asked Matthew.

"Possibly. But likely only in areas with poor hygiene. Not likely on a human face unless it's severely decomposing. Your victim in there isn't to that point; not even close. These little guys have ravenous appetites," she said sweetly, indicating the larvae in the plastic containers. "They're much older than the death of the victim, though. They're at least two weeks old. The eggs would have hatched after about four days. These guys have been around maybe ten days beyond that. But they're struggling, lacking proper nutrition."

"Meaning," summarized Matthew, "that we can't tell anything about the time of death from these particular bugs."

"Exactly right. But other larvae, the type I'd expect to find, was also present. I should be able to tell you more from that."

"Rigor mortis has come and gone in the corpse," Matthew said pensively.

"That cycle has completed, but recently," she confirmed. "Your corpse has been dead less than two days. Thirty-six hours or so, I'd guess."

"But the odor," objected Matthew. "That indicates the beginning of the purification process."

"Ordinarily, yes," she answered. "If the corpse were emitting the odor."

"It isn't?" asked Matthew, confused.

"Sorry, Doc," said Danbury, looking intently at him. "But no."

When further explanation about what had caused the horrid smell wasn't forthcoming, Matthew thought he might not want the answer to his next question. Steeling himself, he asked quietly, "Then what was?"

"Dead rats," said Danbury. "Lots of them."

"They were under the bedding beside the corpse," offered the bug lady.

"Oh!" said Matthew. "You mean the one I . . ."

"Yeah, that one," answered Danbury softly. "Placed there, purposefully."

Matthew's skin felt like it was crawling again. A shiver ran down his spine.

7 ~ The Creeps

Drawing a deep, calming breath, Matthew asked, "Any ID on the corpse?"

"Not yet," said Tegan. "He's been photographed, and everything is logged. We're running prints through multiple systems now. They'll bring him out and load him up momentarily." She motioned to the white medical examiner's van where the assistant ME still sat.

"There was no blood pooling beneath the body. I checked." Then, she added, "We'll know more when they get him into autopsy."

"His body was moved," said Matthew. "Postmortem."

"Exactly right," she said. "Likely dressed and moved either quickly before rigor set in or immediately afterward. That's hard to say. The body position would indicate that somebody had attempted to drape him over the stool. It didn't fully conform, so it might have been in partial rigor at the time. That's conjecture on my part."

They all stepped aside as a stretcher with a black body bag was wheeled out of the house and down the sidewalk where they'd been standing.

"Well," said Matthew, when both the body and Tegan the bug lady had departed, "one thing we can conclude. The murder must have happened after the death of your grandmother, not before. The killer isn't clairvoyant."

"True," said Danbury, rubbing his thumb across his chin.

After giving the tech team working the scene a few final instructions, Danbury said, "Back to Ms. Rosa's. Jimmy is waiting for us there."

"Gladly," answered Matthew. He'd had more than enough of this end of the street.

It felt ridiculous to drive two vehicles up the short street to the only occupied house on it, but Matthew followed Danbury, and both parked out front. The driveway was occupied by a truck. A dually, it was a heavy-duty pickup truck sporting two rear wheels on each side. The bed was loaded with equipment. A rack above the bed contained ladders and tight coils of some sort of flexible piping. The logo on the side showed two sections of cable with a spark in the middle and read "Jackson's Electric."

As eager as he was to meet Danbury's childhood friend, Matthew wished he were meeting Jimmy Jackson under different circumstances. Before they'd managed to get to the door, it was opened by a man who looked to be in his mid-thirties. Clad in a T-shirt, jeans, and loafers, his wide smile appeared genuine as he held the door for them.

"Warren Danbury!" he said. "Where have you been keeping yourself all these years?"

Danbury stepped forward, and the two men hugged, clapping each other on the back.

"Hey, Jimmy. Good to see you."

"You too, Man. Real good to see you. Come on in."

As they stepped into the hallway, Matthew pulled his mask up onto his face, as did Danbury, while the introductions took place.

"Good to meet you," Jimmy said to Matthew. "Grandma said you'd been by earlier. She's back here dozing in her chair. C'mon in and let's have a look at this video. Then you can tell me what's going on."

"There's not much to tell," said Danbury. "I came to ask some questions, and try to find the old neighbors. Ms. Rosa told me what she knew. Then I went to Jaber's house. I didn't expect to find much."

"And you found a dead guy," said Jimmy over his shoulder.

"Yeah, we did."

"Do you know who? Is it Jaber?"

"No. This guy was younger. Early to mid-forties. Jaber would be what? Maybe sixty by now? No ID yet. We're working on it."

"Have a seat, and let's see what we've got," said Jimmy, motioning to the two seats at a round kitchen table.

Matthew's foot tapped, both in anticipation and in impatience. The clock was ticking on the next murder, and he felt like they were moving through mire, not making much progress at anything he'd equate with speed.

As Jimmy retrieved a laptop computer and sat down, Matthew heard a snort from the room beyond. Ms. Rosa wasn't exactly snoring in her chair, but nearly so.

"She's had a busy and stressful day," explained Jimmy. "The body down the street upset her. Maybe this will make her decide it's time to move from here. We offered to add a bedroom and bath onto our house, a suite just for her. She thinks she's putting me out to move in with my family. She's the whole reason I have a house and a family. Without her, that never would have happened. She kept me on track and focused to get through high school, then encouraged me to get a technical degree. I owe her so much more than an addition on my house."

"She's an independent woman. Always has been," said Danbury. "She has a mind of her own."

"That she does!" agreed Jimmy, his dark brow furrowed as he tapped at the keypad. "I hope this will make her decide that it's time to move somewhere safer with people around her. There's nobody here to protect her."

"It would be easier for you if she did, wouldn't it?" asked Matthew, after pondering for a moment. "That might be the key to talking her into moving. If she's concerned that she'd be a burden to you, maybe convincing her that it's a bigger burden having to come by here and keep up with the extra house would make the difference. That and the worry she causes you because she's here alone. You have to go out of your way to get here and check on her. It would be much easier on you if she lived with you."

"You might be onto something," said Jimmy, grinning admiringly as he turned the computer so that Matthew and Danbury could see the screen. "I had the plans drawn up for the addition, probably five years ago, and put the foundation in. I could get the rest of the materials and get back to work on it. Good idea. Thanks for that."

"Sure," said Matthew, leaning forward to study the screen. The images were slightly grainy but discernible.

"How far back do you want to see?" asked Jimmy.

"Thirty-six hours," answered Danbury promptly. "To start with."

"Here's Thursday morning. Yesterday, about two in the morning," Jimmy clarified. "This camera is the clearest with the widest angle. It's under the eaves on the left side of the house. You can see the street and the driveway up to the front stoop."

Running through the dark video quickly at first, a few moths flitting around the light were all there was to see. Gradually, as the morning lightened, Jimmy backed up and slowed the feed. A panel van pulled into the driveway. The logo on the side was difficult to decipher. A man, clad in a blue work jumpsuit, slid out and approached the door.

"That's the HVAC guy coming to check her air conditioning unit and clean the ductwork under the house," said Jimmy.

They watched as he stood in the doorway, presumably talking to Ms. Rosa. He motioned to the side of the house, then stepped off the porch, walked toward the camera, and disappeared under it. A few minutes later, he returned to the truck. Pulling various unidentifiable items off of it, the guy disappeared behind the house again. After two more trips, the front of the house was quiet. Jimmy ran the video feed forward faster.

"Whoa!" he said as both Danbury and Matthew leaned forward. Something had gone quickly down the road in front of the house. Jimmy slowed the video and backed it up, though the vehicle was still speeding past. He froze the image on the screen.

"It's silver," said Matthew. "Or gray, maybe."

"A minivan," added Danbury. "Not a new one. It's boxy."

"It's an old Ford Aerostar!" said Matthew as recognition of the shape solidified in his mind.

"You're sure?" asked Danbury.

"I am. My parents had the last year model when my sister and I were kids. They drove us all over the place in that thing. Family vacations to the beach, mountains, and historic places in North Carolina and Virginia. Can you see the driver?" asked Matthew, craning forward.

"No. There's a passenger. Large and dark. Black clothing and hat. Or hoodie, maybe. What's that timestamp?" asked Danbury, leaning forward as Jimmy froze the video.

Jimmy read it off to him, and Danbury tapped his phone to make a note of it.

"Why would the killer wait for daylight?" asked Matthew.

"Good question," said Danbury. "Maybe an important one. The time of death was more recent than we thought. The killer tried to obscure it. But it took time. Preparing and dressing the body."

"Ah, the killer didn't have as much time to do all of that as he wanted us to believe. He ran out of time to stage the body overnight," Matthew concluded.

"What I was thinking," said Danbury, returning his gaze to the frozen image of the van on the screen and staring at it as if it held the answer. "No business logo. Nothing identifying. Can't see the plate. Not from this angle. Can you find it coming back?"

"It won't have a license plate because it doesn't have a back bumper," said Matthew. "That's why it took me a minute to realize what it was. It's missing some pieces. The right front fender is damaged or missing altogether. It's hard to tell, but that's darker than the rest of it," Matthew added as Jimmy allowed the video to move forward again.

"Can't be too many of those still on the road," said Danbury pensively.

"If you can find it, it should be easily identifiable by the shape it's in," said Matthew. "It looks like it belongs in a junkyard, not on the road. Maybe we can see more of it when it comes back out."

Jimmy ran the video at double speed until the van reappeared nearly an hour later.

"The HVAC guy is still behind her house somewhere," said Matthew. "He won't likely have seen anything."

Jimmy backed up and froze the feed, zooming in to see the driver's side of the van. The image pixelated when it was blown up.

"The driver's side is in worse shape than the passenger side," noted Matthew. There were dents down the length of the van. "The driver is large and dressed darkly too, unless they switched places on the way out."

"Can you send that to me?" asked Danbury. "The video feed. To a digital drop box?"

"Sure."

"Thanks, Jimmy," said Danbury, picking up a pen from the table and jotting information on his business card before handing it over. "I appreciate your help."

"And you're a cop now," said Jimmy, shaking his head in mock surprise. "I should have seen that coming. Like father like son. But I didn't think you'd go that route."

"What did you think I'd do?" asked Danbury.

"I figured you'd have gotten a full-ride scholarship to some fancy college to play basketball and then gone pro."

"Oh," said Danbury. "I haven't played in years. Not since I left here."

"Seriously?" asked Jimmy, the surprise showing clearly on his face as he looked up from the computer screen. "You had a gift. Nobody our age, or even older, could touch you on the basketball court. You dominated it."

"Things change," said Danbury simply.

"There you go," said Jimmy, closing the computer. "It's on the way. I put my number on there too so you can stay in touch."

"Thanks, Jimmy," said Danbury, rising from his seat. "I will. And you too. Call or text any time."

"Sure, Man," agreed Jimmy as both he and Matthew rose to their feet.

As they were making their way out to the front door, Ms. Rosa snorted more loudly this time, then called out, "Jimmy?"

"Go ahead," said Danbury, clapping Jimmy on the back. "Let me know if I can help. Persuade her, or move her. Whatever you need."

"Thanks," said Jimmy, turning back down the hallway to check on his grandmother. "I will."

The sun was lowering toward the tree line as they left the house. Dusk was approaching, but Matthew knew their day would extend for hours beyond it.

8 ~ BYRD'S THE WORD

"We're going to find Jaber?" Matthew asked.

"Yep," said Danbury as they stepped from Ms. Rosa's doorstep to the waiting cars. "You sure you need to drive? I can bring you back."

"Back here?" asked Matthew. "No thanks. No offense to Ms. Rosa and Jimmy. They're nice people, but I've had more than my share of this street." He fought the shiver down his spine accompanying his words as he remembered the feeling of things crawling all over him earlier in the day. That was a sensation he wouldn't soon forget, and it was tied, at least in his mind, to this street.

"OK, Doc. Have it your way. I'll text the address," said Danbury as he slid behind the wheel of the SUV.

Matthew plugged his phone in to charge in his Element and tapped the address Danbury texted. It wasn't very far away, just up in the edge of Durham. Another message had been delivered while he was in Ms. Rosa's house. Relief swept through him to see a response from Cici.

Her building had been without power since the day before, her phone battery drained. Apologizing profusely for not being able to talk to him, she said she was heading to bed and she'd catch him in the morning. Before leaving Jimmy's driveway, he answered saying he was sorry she'd been without power and hoped she had everything she needed.

Where the sun danced on the tall trees, a blaze of color lit the tops of them. In London, it was late evening.

"Let's catch up by video chat tomorrow, my morning, your afternoon," he added in a text message before turning on the stereo to his eclectic playlist. Cranking it up, he tapped his left foot on the floorboard and fingers on the steering wheel as he sang along to the music. It was his attempt to keep his mind off of the ticking clock he could see in his mind. Like a fuse burning to a bomb in a cartoon, he felt the weight of time slipping away.

Trying to redirect his thoughts from the doom and gloom of another impending murder to positive ones like chatting with Cici in the morning, he followed Danbury up Highway 70. They turned into a residential section where the houses along the streets were in neat rows. Deeper than they were wide at the street frontage, they looked to have been renovated from a bygone era.

Pulling in front the address in his navigation app, Matthew noted it was a step up from the house he refused to think about across from where Danbury had grown up. This one was larger, but marginally well kept. Weeds sprouted in profuse clumps in front. Shutters on the windows flanking the front door were askew. Above a covered porch spanning the narrow front of the house was a second story with three windows. From the center one, a light shone brightly into the gathering dusk.

Matthew donned his mask and followed Danbury—wordlessly—up five steps onto the narrow porch. Knocking loudly, Danbury pulled his badge from his pocket. Apparently, Matthew thought, this call would be handled as official police business and not a friendly visit from a long-lost neighbor. Shuffling feet descended the steps hurriedly, and the front door was flung wide.

The man who stood there jumped back in surprise, and the smile quickly faded from his face.

"Oh," he said. "Who are you, and what do you want?"

"Detective Warren Danbury, Raleigh Homicide Division," answered Danbury, flashing his badge for inspection.

"Police? I don't need no trouble, Detective. Did you say Danbury?"

"I did."

"Lemme see that thing," said the man, reaching for the badge and pulling it, Danbury's hand and all, closer into the light spilling out from the hallway behind him.

"Are you Jason Byrd?" asked Danbury, pocketing his badge.

The man arched a brow as he took his time responding, which made him appear to be leering at them. His face was a mass of wrinkled, sagging skin, as if he'd lost weight and the skin hadn't retreated with it.

"I guess it ain't no good telling you I'm not. Danbury, huh? That rings a bell. Like the family that used to live across the street in Raleigh?"

"That's right," said Danbury calmly.

"That'd make you that tall skinny kid, all growed up," he said and leaned out, sending a stream of brown liquid from his mouth past Danbury and off the edge of the porch.

That's the fastest way to mouth cancer, thought Matthew. He said nothing aloud but watched the guy intently as the scenario unfolded.

"Right. The son of Erik and Gayle Danbury. That's what I want to talk to you about."

"Your parents?"

"Partially," said Danbury. Introducing Matthew, he asked, "Can we come in?"

"A doctor?" asked the guy, evaluating Matthew dubiously from head to toe. Obviously accepting that, he stepped aside and said, "All righty then, but make it fast. I have a cousin comin' over any minute now. C'mon back," he said as the storm door closed behind them and he didn't bother to close the solid one.

"Nice place here," said Danbury. Matthew followed, surveying his surroundings. He peered up a narrow staircase and into the doorways on either side of the front door. The smell of stale smoke was pervasive.

"Yeah, it ain't too bad," said Byrd, leading the way down a long, narrow hallway to a kitchen and eating area spanning the back of the house.

"Looks like a step up. From the one across the street."

"Yeah, I guess so," he said. "Swappin' that house was the best thing I ever did. I got a deal; I can tell you. I won't too excited to move at first. Then they made it to where I couldn't say no. They swapped that house for this one without a sale. I didn't have to report it, and I could keep my disability too."

Matthew had no legal background in real estate, but he wondered how that was possible.

"Disability?" asked Danbury, who Matthew knew would have researched this guy thoroughly and already known that. Clearly, he wanted to hear the story from Byrd himself.

"Yeah, from that war over there," Jason Byrd said vaguely. "Since I got this here disability, I can't work a heavy job. I need that check every month."

Matthew saw no obvious disability, but he said nothing as Danbury asked, "When did you swap houses?"

"Maybe about a month after you all moved out from over across the street. If that," he said.

Pulling a bar stool to a high counter on the back side of his kitchen counter, he motioned for Matthew and Danbury to take the remaining stools. Despite a cigarette already burning in an ashtray on the counter, he picked up a pack, tapped it on his hand, removed the wrap, and pulled another one out. Lighting it, he stuck it between stained teeth where it hung for a moment before he closed his lips and took a long drag from it.

It was a wonder, Matthew thought, that this guy was still walking the planet. If he'd been smoking and chewing tobacco simultaneously any length of time, he shouldn't be.

Blowing smoke toward the ceiling, Jason Byrd asked, "I reckon they tore that ole house down. Is it a runway now?"

"You haven't been back?" asked Danbury.

"Just once. 'Bout a month after I left. I came back to look around."

"Why?"

"To see what was going on down there. When I saw the house still there, I figured I'd check if I'd forgotten anything."

"Forgotten?" asked Matthew. "Did you take anything with you?"

This honest response the guy apparently found amusing, and he howled with laughter.

"Why should I have? This one was furnished. Nicer than anything there." Then, he narrowed his eyes through the smoke and asked, "How'd you know that?"

"The house is still there," answered Danbury.

"It is?" the guy asked, appearing genuinely surprised.

"Like the day you left," said Danbury. "Who bought it?"

"I don't know. It was all kind of quiet-like. Hush, hush, you know."

"Why did you think that was?" asked Danbury.

"I didn't think," he said, cagily. "They gave me a good deal. I took it. Figured I'd be stupid not to."

"It was just a house swap?" asked Danbury pointedly.

"That's right."

"Nothing more?"

"Well, there might 'a been a little bit of cash for my trouble. But we ain't talkin' about it because I need my disability benefits, see?"

Undaunted, Danbury changed the subject abruptly. "Twenty-two years ago. What do you remember? About the day my parents died?"

"I told 'em everything I knew, but it won't much."

"What did you tell them?"

"Just that somebody had been over there that morning."

"You told the police that?" asked Danbury calmly.

"Yeah, I reckon I did," said Byrd fidgeting. "Now look, that was a long time ago. I don't remember it like it was yesterday or nothing. I won't there first thing that morning. I was out from the night before at a poker game. When I got home, everything looked normal. Until I went out to check the mail. Then, that car left your parents' house. But I didn't see nobody get in it or who was drivin' it, and I didn't get a license plate, like I told the police. I saw it like I'd seen it before, and that was all."

"You saw that same car before?"

"Yeah. Lots of times."

"When?"

"I don't know exactly. It came and went. Or one that looked just like it."

"What did it look like? Can you describe it?"

"It was brown. Or silver. Or tan. It was a sedan. Nothing flashy. I don't know what make or model. Maybe Ford or Chevy. I told that all to the police when they asked me."

"Did you hear anything? Before or after the car left?"

"Naw, I didn't hear nothin'."

"You didn't hear gunshots?"

"That'd be somethin', wouldn't it? I just told you I didn't hear nothin'." Stubbing out his cigarette and lighting a new one, he added, "If you're a cop now, you can go look at that report, right? And see exactly what I told 'em back then."

"I have," said Danbury. "None of that was in it."

"I told 'em everything I knew. That was it," the guy answered, his face draining of color.

"You told them you were home. All morning. You saw nothing, and nobody. No cars. Nobody on foot. Nothing unusual. And that you heard nothing."

"I didn't hear nothing!" the guy said defensively.

"You didn't hear gunshots?"

"Naw!"

"And you didn't call 911?"

"I didn't call nobody."

"I see," said Danbury. Changing direction, he asked, "When you swapped houses, was there other criteria? Anything else they asked of you?"

The guy squirmed more on his stool and his face flushed. "Naw, just to move out quick. That was all."

"Who asked you?"

"What do ya mean, who asked me? Who asked me what?"

"Who made the offer to swap houses? A person? A group? A corporation?"

"Ain't never heard of a corporation offerin' nothin' but trouble," the guy answered, puffing out a billow of smoke. "What do you think? Sure, it was a person! A guy wearin' a nice suit. I figured he was either a pimp, a gigolo, or some important person in that suit. I wasn't sure which at first and I didn't trust him. I told him I wasn't goin' nowhere and to get off of my property."

"Did he?"

"He did, but then he came back the very next day in a fancy big car, flashin' cash and with some woman in a suit too. She didn't look like no whore, so I figured he won't a pimp."

"What did they look like?"

"Are you kiddin'? That was over twenty years ago! I don't remember what they looked like. They were just people. Brown. All I remember is lots of brown. They won't ugly, but there wasn't anything exciting about 'em. I mean, she was OK, but nothin' I'd want to get cozy with, if you know what I mean. Pretty boring looking, except for that cash they were flashing around. And that car. I think it was a Rolls Royce. It was nice."

"Neither of them had scars? Tattoos? Piercings? Anything identifying?"

"Man, I don't remember! What have I got to do to get that through your thick skull? It was a long time ago. Hell, I don't remember what I ate for breakfast this morning!"

"Then what happened? The day they came back?" asked Danbury.

"Then they said they'd give me the cash. On the spot. If I rode with them to see this here house. It was a wad of cash," the guy added.

"And you took the deal?"

"They had paperwork all ready for me to sign. I wouldn't do that on the spot. I ain't stupid. There was this other guy here at the house. A lawyer. He gave me his card and told me to let him know when I was ready to sign on the dotted line."

"Do you remember the lawyer's name?"

"I got no idea. I keep telling you, that was over twenty years ago!"

"But you trusted him?" asked Danbury persistently.

"Naw, I don't trust nobody. I got a cousin 'a mine to look over the paperwork before I agreed to anything. He called that lawyer back. Told me it was OK. Then I signed the papers."

"Would your cousin remember?"

"He ain't remembered nothing in almost eight years. He's dead."

"Tell me this," said Danbury, going back on the offensive. "Who asked you to lie? Nearly twenty-two years ago?"

"I didn't lie! I don't remember how it all happened. That was a long time ago!" he exclaimed.

"Either you did then, or you are now," said Danbury calmly.

The guy must be a chronic liar, thought Matthew, because he'd told Ms. Rosa he saw a car after he got up at nearly lunchtime. In the version he'd told her, he was home the night before and slept in that morning.

Standing so abruptly the stool nearly toppled over behind him, the guy said, "I ain't lying! You need to get out of my house. My cousin will be here any minute."

"OK. We're going," said Danbury, holding his hand up. "Just one more thing, Jaber."

They guy tried to look menacing, but then he rolled his eyes and burst out laughing. "Ain't nobody called me that in a coon's age," he said.

"Mr. Byrd," Danbury amended, standing to his full six-foot-four-inch height and rolling his shoulders back. "You said you were out. The night before. What time did you say you got home? That morning."

"I don't know why I should tell you nothing else, but I don't guess it matters so much now. It won't too early," Jason Byrd answered through the haze of smoke. "I fell asleep on a sofa when I got out of a hand of poker and woke up hot that next morning. There won't no air conditioning on, and I couldn't wait to get home. It was probably almost lunchtime before I got back."

"You checked your mailbox? As soon as you got home?"

"Pretty nearly as soon as. I was lookin' for a check that hadn't come yet."

"Thank you, Mr. Byrd. I appreciate your time," said Danbury formally as Matthew followed him back down the hallway to the front door. "If you think of anything else," added Danbury, retrieving a business card and holding it out to the guy.

When he didn't take it, Danbury laid the card on a little table by the front door.

"I won't. And if you got any more of those questions that you think you need to come ask me," said the guy as they stepped out onto the porch, "don't," he added, heaving the door closed heavily behind them.

"Nice neighbor," said Matthew sarcastically as he pulled his mask off at the curb. "Oh man, I'll never get the smoke smell out of these clothes," he added, thinking this would be the second set today to go directly into the washer as soon as he arrived home.

"Yeah, but helpful," said Danbury. "He didn't remember what he told the police. I've seen that happen before. Time passes and witnesses forget. Both what they said and why they said it."

"Which story do you think is the truth?" asked Matthew. "That's the third version of it we've heard. He told Ms. Rosa another one entirely."

"I'm betting on this one. It was unrehearsed. And uncoerced. Did you see his face? When I called him on it?"

"I did. The proverbial deer in headlights. He suddenly remembered all the things he wasn't supposed to say, but it was too late because he'd already said them. That made him scared and then angry."

"You saw all of that? You're a psychiatrist now?"

Matthew chuckled. "I've learned to pay attention to patients, watching their reactions for what they don't say. I saw the range of emotions cross his face and in his body language. Anger won out, but that's not where he started. Surprise, then fear, then anger."

"Nice, Doc."

"It's why you keep me around, right?" Matthew joked. "What's next?"

Danbury checked his watch. "Are you hungry? Penn cooked. We can stop by. Then go back to the storage unit. See if my dad's dress blues are there."

"Right behind you," said Matthew.

A home-cooked meal he didn't have to cook sounded wonderful. He hoped the storage unit would provide something useful. Glancing at his watch, he realized he was still calculating the hours since they'd found the body and been given twenty-four. It wasn't enough time. There was never enough time to get ahead of maniacal killers, he thought in frustration.

9 ~ REDACTION REVEALED

During a rushed but scrumptious pot roast dinner with all the trimmings, Danbury and Matthew updated Penn and Leo on the strange happenings of the day. They omitted most of what happened in the bedroom with the corpse.

"I would ask you to promise me that you'll be careful," Penn said. "But I suppose that's like asking birds not to migrate south for the winter or fish not to swim upstream."

"I'm always careful," he reassured her, leaning over and kissing her on the forehead. "More so now that I have something to lose."

Matthew thanked Penn for dinner and walked out to the front porch ahead of Danbury to give them a moment alone. Danbury followed, closing the front door softly behind him.

"You riding with me, Doc?"

"No more abandoned houses, dead rats? Or live ones?" Matthew added.

"No promises," said Danbury, smirking.

They climbed in Danbury's SUV and went back to the storage unit.

Flipping on bright rows of overhead lighting, Matthew was unsure if the contents of the storage unit reminded him more of a time capsule or a rummage sale. He watched silently as Danbury squeezed through to the back of the unit. Reaching out, he touched a dresser, a small desk in the far corner, and then a disassembled bed.

"This was mine," said Danbury, touching the long posts of the bed.

"I had just gotten it. Extra-long, twin bunk beds. I wanted to bring it with me. My grandmother said no. I needed a fresh start. Maybe she was right. But something familiar, something of my parents. That would have been nice."

Was Danbury talking to him, Matthew wondered, or reminiscing aloud? He didn't think it required an answer as he watched in silence. Danbury made his way around the unit, touching various objects. Pausing again, he reached out to touch a wooden box. He opened it. Inside, it was lined with velvet and there were chess pieces tucked into slotted sections formed for them.

"It was my dad's," said Danbury quietly. Turning abruptly, he added, "Let's start searching."

"What are we looking for?"

"We'll know it when we see it. Might be what isn't there."

"Like your dad's dress blues?"

"Exactly. My dad's office furniture first. It's along that far wall," said Danbury pointing. "The filing cabinet I cleaned out. I want a better look at it."

Making his way around the end of the U-shaped configuration, Danbury pulled the metal filing cabinet out and looked behind it. He began pulling drawers from it and flipped them over, one by one. Systematically, he did the same thing with the desk, looking under and behind each drawer, shining his mag light into the recesses from which they'd come.

"Nothing. Whatever I'm looking for won't be in an obvious place. If Dad was up against something," Danbury began, and then hesitated, "he'd have put it somewhere nobody would look."

Silently circling the space, Danbury landed on the other side of the unit and dropped to his knees in front of a trunk. It looked like an old steamer truck from at least the century before.

"I remember this," said Danbury, suddenly enthusiastic. "It was in the attic. I played up there sometimes as a kid."

When jiggling and wiggling the latch yielded nothing, Danbury studied the lock more closely with the mag light. "This has been jimmied open. Then locked back. There are scratch marks. Fresh ones."

Danbury pulled a penknife from his pocket and worked at the lock gently until he could flip it up. Lifting the lid carefully, he peered inside.

"My baby blanket," said Danbury, pulling it out and laying it aside. Next out was a long white dress with a pleated front. The arms and area across the chest were too small for the length of it. Danbury held it aloft, turning it this way and that.

"A christening gown?" asked Matthew.

"Maybe so," said Danbury, laying it aside.

"My mom's wedding dress," he said, gingerly pulling a thick, sealed bag from the trunk. He pulled out shoes, a hat with a veil, two old family bibles, a neatly folded American flag, and then an old metal lockbox. "This has been opened too. Forcibly," Danbury added, pointing to gouges on the outer edge where the lid met the base. A smaller blade on his pen knife had that, too, open in short order.

"My dad's military records," said Danbury, sifting through. "Transfer to special training. His officer training. Honorable release forms."

Danbury peered back in the trunk. "That's it," he said. "It's what isn't here. My dad's dress blues were in here. His ribbons and decorations were in that metal box. I remember seeing it. That was all in here. When I was a kid."

"Huh," said Matthew, eyebrow raised and foot tapping in concentration. "There are security cameras here, right?" he asked, dreading the chore of sitting through hours of video and maybe finding nothing useful. "I saw a sign to smile because you're on camera as we pulled in."

"There are. Mounted at the front gate. And at either end of each row. But they're useless. I contacted management. Asked for a list of numbers used to access the facility. For the past month. They stalled. Said they'd have to check legal procedures. I haven't heard back on that yet. The security system was repaired yesterday. The cameras have been offline for a week. Nothing was recorded."

"That's convenient," Matthew said, then paused as Danbury replaced the items in the trunk and flipped the lock closed. "What are you thinking? That your dad was into something or knew about something he wasn't meant to, and he hid the evidence of it here somewhere?"

"Had to be something like that. It's less likely to have been about the house. And the airport expansion. If it was, why are the houses still there? They got my parents out of the way. And Jaber. Why walk away then?"

"That's a good point," Matthew said, looking around. "What could be worth killing for, potentially three times?"

"You tell me, Doc. Then we'll both know," said Danbury, rubbing the stubble on his chin in obvious frustration. "You up for looking?"

"Oh yeah," said Matthew. "Where do we start?"

"At the front," answered Danbury, and they began examining a kitchen set near the opening of the storage unit, pulling it outside the unit and moving it aside.

Nearly four hours later, they had pulled out most of the furniture, piece by piece, and gone over it carefully from every angle. They had unpacked, sorted through, and repacked box after box. Finally in the back corner of the unit, Danbury paused in front of the small desk that was part of his childhood bedroom furniture.

There was nothing remarkable about it. It had matching rows of three drawers on either side of a cutout in the center into which a chair had been shoved. On the seat of the chair sat a dusty box, another one was wedged underneath. Working to free the chair, they rummaged briefly through the boxes of childhood memorabilia, records, and awards before setting them aside.

Mechanically, he pulled the desk out from the back wall far enough to look behind and under it, shining his mag light all around it. Danbury pulled each drawer on the left side out and looked under and behind them before moving to the drawers on the right. They were all empty; the contents appeared to have been moved to the boxes in and under the chair. Suddenly, he stopped. Pulling out a long narrow top drawer on the left he had just put back, he held it up to the one mirroring it from the right side.

"Hey, Doc," he said, turning to show Matthew the discrepancy.

"One is deeper than the other," said Matthew, leaving the box he'd been going through and joining Danbury in front of the desk. "About six inches longer."

Without further conversation, they each grabbed an end of the desk and slid it out into the U-shaped walkway. At the right back side, Danbury knelt with the mag light and slid his hand over every inch of the surface.

"Nothing," he said. "Let's flip it. Pull the drawers out. And turn it over."

Matthew helped to accomplish this task, and Danbury wiped away cobwebs and grime from the bottom corner of the desk.

"Hold the light," said Danbury.

There, behind a decorative cutout groove, was a wooden knob in the right back corner of the desk. Twisting and pushing the knob yielded nothing, but when Danbury pulled it, they heard a click. A crack emerged in the back corner of the desk, revealing an opening behind the desk the height and width of the right set of drawers.

Matthew adjusted the light so that Danbury could see to reach in and pull out an expandable portfolio folder. It was some sort of brown paper composite, about three inches wide, with a fanned bottom. A flap over the top with a hook-and-loop closure obscured and protected its contents.

"Bingo," said Danbury. "I didn't put this there."

"You didn't know there was a compartment back there?" asked Matthew.

"Nope. Never noticed the difference in the drawers. I was a kid," Danbury answered and shrugged.

Matthew nodded without comment, shining the mag light in the compartment and revealing it to be otherwise empty. They flipped the desk upright, reloaded the drawers, and slid it into place against the wall. Putting the boxes back, Matthew managed to wedge the chair back in place in the kneehole.

Pulling the kitchen table and chairs back into the unit, they slid it awkwardly beside the wall and dragged two chairs up to it. Danbury retrieved the box of folders he'd pulled from his father's file cabinet, a box of clippings and notes he'd removed from his mother's desk, and added the folio they'd just retrieved.

They donned their jackets, and Danbury pulled the door to the storage unit closed. The April night was chilly. Matthew surreptitiously checked his watch. It was already after ten. It'd be a long night, he thought, squelching a yawn. But they had a ticking clock, and if there was anything in these files that would help prevent another murder, he'd give it his best shot, however long that took.

Stacks of folders emerged from the folio—none of them labeled that Matthew could see—as Danbury slid the contents out onto the table. Some of the pages looked similar to the heavily redacted ones from the file cabinet. These files, though, were intact.

On the bottom of the stack from Danbury's childhood desk was a legal pad. More than half of the pages had been ripped from it. The top page was blank. Danbury laid that aside, then sifted and reorganized the remaining printed pages in silence, while Matthew rearranged the resulting stacks, spreading them over the table.

"What are we looking for?" Matthew asked.

"I'm not sure yet. These files are contracts. They're mostly local customers. Some were simple security system installations. A couple were surveillance. Here's one for hours billed. His travel expenses to Texas. And a bonus for finding a missing woman. I remember that. A college student out jogging. Early morning. She was abducted. A mile or so from home. It was in the newspapers."

"I saw an article about that," said Matthew, who had begun to sift the letters and news clippings from Gayle Danbury's desk. "Here it is. Your mom must have saved it."

"That sounds right," said Danbury, placing the article in the file folder with the billing information. "He wouldn't have kept articles or accolades. Only what was important to him. That she was found safely. And business information, of necessity for taxes. But Mom would."

Danbury returned to matching the files with redacted content from the file cabinet to the versions from his childhood desk. Matthew reached for the legal pad from the bottom of the stack of folders and papers. He held it up to the light to see if there were any impressions in the top sheet of paper. The pages were blank, but as he flipped through them, a folded page fluttered to the table.

Retrieving and unfolding it, Matthew asked, "What's this?"

"That's my dad's handwriting," answered Danbury. "It's pretty distinctive."

It was, Matthew agreed. The script was tall and narrow, with a heavy right slant and sharp points on the tops and bottoms of the letters.

"What does this mean?" asked Matthew.

"Basic Kiswahili," read Danbury. "Vowels each make one sound. Per IPA."

Beneath that sentence was a list of Roman vowels written out in the NATO codes. Alpha, Echo, India, Oscar, and Uniform each occupied a line with odd letters and symbols beside them.

"Kiswahili," muttered Danbury. "A language. Swahili? IPA isn't likely a beer," he added, smirking.

Matthew began tapping on his phone to search.

"It is. Kiswahili, or Swahili, is the language spoken mainly in eastern Africa." After more searching, he added, "IPA is the International Phonetic Alphabet. It's used mostly by linguists, singers, actors, and people learning a foreign language to verify pronunciations."

"Eastern Africa? My dad was stationed all over. Back in the military. But not in Africa. As far as I know. Why learn Swahili?"

Danbury asked rhetorically.

"Is there anybody around from back then who might know if he'd been there? Or was going?"

"Nobody around now," said Danbury, thumbing the stubble on his chin. "I talked to two officers. Both were on the force with Dad. They're still active officers. Neither had much to say. They weren't involved in the investigation of his death. And neither worked directly with him. Conrad Manchester, my dad's best friend. The guy in the files you read. He was always at the house. He would know. If I could find him."

"You don't know where to look?"

"I haven't seen him in years. Not since I moved in with my grandmother. I was twelve. My memory of him then is clear. What he's like now is anybody's guess. I did try to look him up. A few years back. There's no trace of him. I need to try harder. That was already in my plan. I asked the officers about him. Neither knew where he was. He resigned abruptly. Neither knew why."

"If he'd been to Africa, you wouldn't think that'd be a secret. Except that this legal pad was in with the things your dad hid, if he was the one who hid them."

"Likely so. Dad had a purpose for hiding it. I need to find Conrad Manchester. I don't know who else to ask. I wish my grandmother had talked about it."

"There's more here," said Matthew, returning to the legal pad page he'd unfolded and reading from it. "'The next to last syllable is ALWAYS stressed. Examples: Kiswahili, *Asante sana*, Nairobi, Samburu.' Nairobi. That's the capital of Kenya, right? That's on the eastern coast of Africa, so that fits."

"*Asante sana*," said Matthew, tapping his phone, "is thank you very much. Samburu is a place. It's in Kenya, north of Nairobi. It's a whole territory. More like a county. Oh, and it's also the name of a people group. The native people who live there are called Samburu. There's one more thing here jotted under the rest," said Matthew returning to the page. "'Most brutal Maasai.' Does that mean anything to you?"

"It doesn't," said Danbury, shaking his head.

"It sounds familiar. They're another Kenyan people group or tribe," said Matthew, tapping his phone. "They're fierce warriors, related to the Samburu somehow. I thought I'd heard of them."

His hobby as a history buff shining through, Matthew added, "Kenya was a British colony, but not for as long as you'd think. It was sometime in the 1920s until the 1960s, I think. There was an area in the northern territory, maybe it was Samburu, that the British sent troops to conquer. More than once, the British were annihilated. They stopped sending troops and declared that region off limits. It remained more Kenyan than most of the rest of the country. But what does any of this mean to your investigation?"

Danbury sighed in frustration. "I wish I knew. I don't remember Dad talking about Kenya. Or African tribes. Or Swahili. But this was hidden away," he said, thumping the page from the legal pad. "It must be important. Maybe it's somehow related to his death and Mom's. It's worth looking into. As soon as I figure out how."

Returning to the files he'd been sifting through, Danbury pointed. "The redacted information on these contracts. That's not amateur. Not likely side jobs. It's something official. Maybe governmental."

"Governmental?" asked Matthew. "You mean other than your dad's military service or local police work?"

"It might be military," said Danbury. "As a consultant. Third party. That's a possibility."

"Huh," said Matthew, looking over Danbury's shoulder as he flipped through the pages of one folder. "The top pages look like contracts, or multiple pages of a single contract. The latter ones look like lists of some sort."

"Yeah, they're contracts. There's no who or what on this version," Danbury held up the set of files from the filing cabinet. "And the dates. Those are redacted too. Why keep these with so much missing? Some of them match these. The ones from my desk with the information intact. These aren't government contracts. They're with contract companies. Looks like contractors that work with government agencies. The terms are nebulous. What was redacted seems inconsequential. All we have are names. We need to search. Find information on these companies. If they're still in business."

Danbury's phone sounded with a sappy country song. Matthew raised an eyebrow at him when he reached for it.

"Hey, Penn. Yeah, we could use your help," said Danbury. "OK if I put you on speaker?"

"Sure, what do you need?" Matthew heard Penn say as Danbury put the phone on the table.

"To search for a list of companies," said Danbury. "Security companies, I think. See if they're still in business. And whatever else you can learn about them."

"OK, shoot," said Penn as Danbury picked up the files he'd matched to the redacted set.

That made sense to Matthew. If the information on that set of files was important enough to redact the information, then that was a logical place to start.

"OneStar," said Danbury. "HighestTech. Pinnacle. Capital Tech. Windsong."

One by one, Danbury went through the companies and carefully spelled the names, providing suffixes like Inc. and LLC.

"OK, got 'em," said Penn. "Are there locations? Street addresses or at least cities?"

"On some of them," said Danbury reading the street address and states listed. "No locations on the others. That field is blank. That's odd. Why redact blank fields? On the other two that don't have addresses. There's one more. The contract lists a missing person. From a tech security company. Satellife."

"That is odd," she agreed. "OK, I'll search for these and check that one first. I can add what I find into your shared document, if that's the best way to do it. I'll let you know if I find anything interesting."

Danbury agreed, and they ended the call. He'd barely put the phone back in his pocket when it sounded again with the same country song. Pulling it out, he answered. Matthew could hear Penn yelling from where he sat beside Danbury.

"Slow down. I can't understand," said Danbury, standing, alarmed. "Did you turn it off? OK, go unplug your router. The box on the shelf. Right, the one in the library. I'm on my way."

"What's wrong?" asked Matthew.

"Penn found a link. With downloadable information. About Satellife," said Danbury as he rolled up the door and began shoving boxes and furniture back in the storage unit. "She clicked it. Her computer went haywire. She couldn't turn it off. Or control it."

"Anything I can do?" Matthew asked as he hauled furniture and boxes back inside.

"You can head home. I'm going to check Penn's computer," said Danbury. "I'll probably need to take it to my office tonight. Got a buddy there who can work on it. Tech genius."

Matthew marveled at the sleep Danbury didn't seem to need. The guy could run on a few hours a night and seemed none the worse for it.

Finally able to close the door, they were turning off the lights and locking up as Matthew asked, "What's next for the investigation?"

"A road trip. Paying a couple of visits. You free tomorrow?"

"Yeah, tomorrow's Saturday. Where are we going?"

"To see a couple of former officers. They were on the force with my dad. These two might be more willing to talk to me. Or feel less pressure not to. The two I already talked to had little to say. They both could have. There was something they weren't telling me. I got that distinct impression. Maybe because they're still active officers."

"When and where?"

"Meet me at Penn's? How's six?"

"See you then," said Matthew, climbing into his Element. He was thoroughly exhausted and more than a little worried about what would happen in the next ten hours or so.

10 ~ CONTEMPORARIES

The sun began to create a warm glow on the eastern horizon behind him Saturday morning as Matthew drove into Peak. Both his heightened awareness of the clock ticking down to another murder and his inability to connect with Cici that morning left him feeling heavy. She was having connection issues. He wished he'd gotten to see her face or at least hear her voice. She'd gotten a terse text message through telling him she was safe.

"Tell me what do you need me to do today," said Penn, handing each of them a bagged lunch for the road as Matthew joined them on the front porch of the Lingle Plantation.

"Would you make some phone calls?" asked Danbury.

"Sure. Who am I calling, and what am I asking?"

"Something Doc said. It's a long shot. But worth a try."

"What's that?" asked both Matthew and Penn in unison and then looked at each other and laughed. Laughter felt good, Matthew thought. It eased the tension he felt. Danbury must be feeling it too, that sense of urgent strain.

"Junkyards. Any you can find in Raleigh, Durham—the surrounding areas. Call them and ask about an old Ford Aerostar. Silver or gray. Ask if anybody is looking for parts to repair one. Or if they know anyone who owns one. Parts have to come from somewhere. For an older vehicle."

"Good idea," said Matthew. "Those things haven't been manufactured since 1997."

"OK, got it," said Penn cheerfully. "What time would you like dinner?"

Matthew looked at Danbury, who promptly answered, "How's seven?"

"It'll be ready. We're having chicken and dumplings tonight," announced Penn. "I know it's one of your favorites."

"It is," agreed Danbury.

Matthew thought the guy was salivating as he leaned over and kissed his fiancée goodbye. Nodding, Matthew thanked Penn for the bag lunch and the invitation to dinner.

"I helped talk you into this," said Penn. "The least I can do is feed you."

Fair enough, thought Matthew as he followed Danbury out. Climbing in the SUV, he assumed his job would be navigating. "Where are we going?"

"Partstowne."

"Northeast of Raleigh?"

"Right. Up 401. Above 540."

"Got it," said Matthew as Danbury provided an address, pulled out onto the quiet streets of Peak, and headed toward Raleigh. A jazz playlist, one of a few genres they could agree on, provided background music. The SUV was otherwise quiet, leaving Matthew to his own thoughts.

What does Africa have to do with a new runway at the airport? Are the two things related? Probably not, Matthew concluded. An open mind, he knew, was often the key to understanding much of anything when it came to murders, miscreants, and motives.

"Tell me about who we're going to see and what you need me to do," said Matthew.

"Chad Dwyer. He was on the force. With my dad and Conrad Manchester. Word was he was Manchester's protégé. He left Raleigh to be near family. When he started his family. Or so he said. The timing is suspicious. It's the same time Manchester left."

"Anything else you know about this guy?"

"Not much. Clean record. Solid officer, from what I could find. I want to talk to his partner too. Brian Ogilvy. Left about the same time. Retired. He was older than my dad and Manchester. I hope he's still around. He was nearly sixty when he left."

"Which would make him nearly eighty-two now."

"Right. Living on a lake. Farther north of Raleigh. With his daughter. We'll check that next. His last known address."

As they lapsed into silence, Matthew's mind began to create a timeline of events. The only event preceding Danbury's parents' death on July seventh of 1998 that they knew of involved airport expansion. The RDU airport had gone international in 1987. He'd looked that up, for whatever it was worth. Somebody, in early 1998, had badly wanted the street where Danbury had lived to build more runways.

After that, a plethora of events had occurred in such rapid succession that it couldn't be a coincidence. It must all be related somehow, but the connections weren't clear. Tapping his phone, Matthew added a dated timeline in the bottom of the file they were constructing. It was his attempt to get it all straight in his own mind.

Matthew added the early 1998 harassment to sell the properties. Danbury's parents were murdered on July 7, 1998, three months after his twelfth birthday. After a calendar search, Matthew added that it was a Tuesday. Maybe it mattered. Roughly a month later, Jaber moved from across the street.

In January of 1999, the security company Danbury's father had worked for on the side, Iron Clad, went out of business. Manchester's wife, Heather, died in a single car crash in February. Somewhere in that same time frame, not one but at least three police officers left the Raleigh police force: Conrad Manchester, Chad Dwyer, and Brian Ogilvy. Dwyer was Manchester's protégé and Ogilvy retired, Matthew added, eyebrow raised and foot tapping as he studied the timeframe.

What were the exact dates? Tapping his phone to search, he saw Iron Clad went out of business on January thirtieth of 1999. Heather

Manchester died on February third of that same year, mere days later. He wondered if Conrad Manchester had worked for Iron Clad at the time and when he'd left the police force and disappeared. As he made a note to ask, the navigation app telling them to exit Highway 401 onto 401 Business shook Matthew from his own thoughts.

A few turns later landed them in a respectable-looking neighborhood with rows of houses appearing to be far less than twenty-two years old. They couldn't have been built more than ten years ago, Matthew assessed. The houses were close to the road and to each other, deeper than they were wide, with sidewalks on both sides of the street. The house they approached had a driveway extending down the left side that looked to be newly paved. On it, a dark-blue SUV was backed in with the hood up.

As they parked, a man looked up from under the hood. His gaze appeared neither welcoming nor menacing, merely curious.

"Did he know we were coming?" asked Matthew, thinking he knew the answer to his question.

"Nope. Wanted to catch him by surprise. No time to create a story. Or corroborate one."

"With who?"

"I wish I knew. Maybe nobody. I could be off there."

"I'd put my money on your intuition," said Matthew, meaning it sincerely. Danbury was rarely wrong in his assessments, particularly of people, and most notably of other cops.

"Hey," said Danbury, approaching the guy, with Matthew beside him. "Are you Chad Dwyer?"

"Who wants to know?" the guy asked quizzically, squinting up at him. It almost passed as recognition, but not quite, Matthew thought.

"Warren Danbury, Homicide," he answered, pulling and displaying his badge for verification.

"Oh! I thought you looked familiar," said the guy as confusion turned to something else on his face. Was it fear? Was it merely recognition? It was definitely guarded. The guy had morphed into, "cop mode," that state of giving nothing away, a face that became a mask without emotion that Danbury had perfected.

"You're Erik Danbury's son, aren't you?" asked the guy. "You look just like him."

"I've been told that before. This is Matthew Paine. A physician and friend of mine." As Matthew and the guy exchanged nods of acknowledgment, Danbury added, "That makes you Chad Dwyer. If you knew my dad."

"Oh, yeah. I didn't answer you, did I? I'm Chad. How's it going?" he offered his hand to shake, then quickly withdrew it, wiped it off with a cloth, and offered it again. "Sorry, I'm checking the fluid levels in my car. It's making a knocking noise, and I'm not sure why."

"No problem," said Danbury, shaking the proffered hand amicably. "I won't take much of your time."

"Sure. Today's my day off."

Danbury nodded. Matthew figured he probably already knew that.

"What do you need?" Dwyer asked, leaning back against the front of the car as if he was shooting the breeze with a friend and should have a beer in one hand.

"Information about my dad," said Danbury.

"Oh," said Dwyer. "I didn't know him well, mostly through Conrad Manchester. I didn't work with your dad much. I was a rookie cop back then. Conrad was training me when Erik signed on. I knew Conrad better. He'd been trying to talk Erik into moving to the Raleigh area."

"What did Manchester tell you about him?"

"Only good things. I mean, they were best friends, weren't they? Conrad trusted him completely. Said Erik was a straight shooter who always had your back, no matter what. That's why Conrad wanted him to move and join the department. That, and something about Erik's mother living in the area finally convinced your dad to take the job. You were a little guy."

"I was six," confirmed Danbury.

"That was the other thing Conrad mentioned. You were just starting school. Your dad wanted you settled in a place where your family could stay so that you could put down roots, not be moving around with his military assignments."

"Do you know anything about that? My dad's military career? Ever hear him and Conrad talking?"

"A little bit. They talked some over a beer or two at the pub. A couple of times."

"Did they mention any specific places? Anywhere they were assigned. Particularly overseas."

"Somewhere in Europe. Germany, maybe? And they were in Japan together. I do remember that."

"Ever hear mention of Africa?"

"Africa?" the guy looked surprised. "Not that I recall, no." Regaining control over his neutral cop face, Dwyer added, "Your dad never stayed long when we went for drinks after our shifts. He'd stop in, have a beer, and then head home to you and your mom. Or to a second job."

"A second job?"

"I think he worked for a security company part time, after hours."

"That's right. Did you know my mom?"

"Only from a distance. I saw her a few times, but that was about it. I didn't understand why your dad had a second job back then, but boy I do now," he added jovially, motioning to the house behind him. "I was young and single when I was working with Conrad. When I got married and started a family, I understood."

"How many kids do you have?" asked Matthew, joining the conversation.

"Just two. And that's plenty. They're into everything. All sorts of activities after school. At least they were until this pandemic hit. Now they're trying to figure out school assignments online. The virtual classroom set up is a mess, so far. This half of the school year is going to be a total loss from what I can tell. My wife and I are trying to tutor them, work through their school books and assignments with them."

While the guy was excitedly chatting about his family, Matthew asked, "How old are they? What grades are you dealing with?"

"Ten and seven," he said. "They're in grade school still, fourth and second. Some of that new math—I have no idea what to do with it. I'm glad I married an accountant. My wife is working from home, and she helps them with that."

Matthew looked meaningfully at Danbury before asking, "When did you move away from Raleigh? Did you move here then?"

11 ~ INCONSISTENCIES

Chad Dwyer paused. Matthew wondered if it was because he realized what he'd just admitted. His move from Raleigh couldn't have been when his wife was pregnant, as the rumor mill had suggested. His oldest child wasn't old enough.

"We moved to Partstowne when we left Raleigh. But not into this house until almost eight years ago. When my daughter was on the way. We'd outgrown our little two-bedroom condo."

"I bet so," said Matthew, commiserating with the guy, trying to put him at ease. "I have a condo, and it's not where I'd want to raise a family either. I love it for now, but it's too small and there's no yard for kids to play in. This is a really nice neighborhood. It looks like there are lots of kids around. I saw bikes out all over as we came in."

"Oh yeah. The kids ride bikes together outside on nice days."

"What made you leave Raleigh?" asked Matthew, returning to what they truly wanted to know. "It's a nice place to raise a family too."

"My wife's family is all here. I don't have much of one. My parents divorced when I was little, and mine is scattered. When we started our family, we wanted to be here."

"You came here for the support of family when your wife was pregnant," said Matthew, smiling at Dwyer. "I get that. I'm close to my family too, and I'll welcome their help when I have kids."

"Yeah, something like that," he answered vaguely.

Danbury redirected with a couple of earlier questions and then said, bluntly, "I'm investigating my parents' death. Is there anything you can tell me? Whatever you can remember from back then. Something you heard or thought? Anything might help."

"I heard rumors, but that's all they were," Dwyer said, wiping his hands on the towel again. "I doubt we'll ever know for sure."

"Not for lack of trying," said Danbury. "Tell me what you remember."

The guy shifted from one foot to the other before answering. "There was a theory that a third person was at their house. One witness who lived nearby said he was home all morning and nobody came or went from the house across the street. I never believed that."

"Jason Byrd?"

"Yeah, that sounds right. At the time, I thought he was a real bird. He was a shifty one."

"You met him?"

"Not at the site of the murder. He came into the station once to give his statement. Flitty was the word that came to mind after watching him being interviewed. Like his name fit. You know the type."

"I do," said Danbury. "Tell me about the third person."

"It was speculation. 'Scuttlebutt,' as your dad and Conrad called stuff like that. But it's right, more often than not. A third person was probably there."

"Why do you say that?" asked Danbury.

"I've always thought it's why Conrad left. Cops tend to protect cops, but there was suspicion cast on him. It was like a shadow that followed him around. I got the impression he felt like he couldn't shake it and finally decided to move on."

"Not because his wife was killed?" asked Danbury softly.

"I don't know. Maybe that had something to do with it too."

Matthew's eyebrows rose. Danbury had framed the question as if Heather Manchester was murdered. All they really knew, up to this point, was that she'd died.

"She was murdered?" asked Danbury more pointedly.

"Ah," the guy took a deep breath and leaned back against the car as if the energy had just been sucked out of him. "It was rumored that she was, yeah. Right on the heels of your parents' death. Conrad was crushed by all of that and under suspicion again."

"He was?" asked Danbury. "Why was he suspected?"

"Of your parents murder?" Dwyer hesitated. "I guess you have the right to know. Rumor was that Conrad had a thing for your mom. But he had a solid alibi at the time of their murder. He was off duty and at home with his wife, Heather, that morning. She provided the alibi, but she couldn't be forced to testify against him anyway, so I'm not sure how helpful it was or how well believed."

Pausing, he added, "Of his wife's murder, well, nobody really knew what that was about. Speculation was all over the place. It made no sense if he had murdered your parents. I mean, Heather had provided his alibi. And it's not like he would have been getting her out of the way to be with your mother. She was already gone. I never believed he had anything to do with either one."

"Why not?" asked Danbury.

"He wasn't wired like that and he hadn't snapped. I knew him well enough to know that. Heather was a nice person and a pretty woman. I can't say if he was in love with her or if he had a thing for your mother. I never saw it, if he did. Anyway, he wouldn't have let that get in the way of the friendship with your dad. That went deep. They were like brothers."

"Do you know how to find Manchester? I looked. Turned up nothing."

"Wish I did. I've got a lot to thank him for. He was a great mentor. The best."

"He just disappeared? And you don't know where he went?"

"Pretty much. He cleaned out his house when his wife died. I have a few pieces from it here," Dwyer motioned behind him at his house. "He abruptly tendered his resignation and disappeared. I thought he'd at least tell me where he was going, leave a forwarding address. I kept hoping he'd turn up. But he hasn't. He could easily find me. Obviously, it wasn't hard," he added meaningfully.

"Did Conrad Manchester have a second job too?" asked Matthew. "Outside the police force?"

Dwyer stared hard at Matthew before saying, "Why do you ask?"

"Specifically," said Matthew, "did he work for Iron Clad with Erik Danbury? Or after Erik Danbury's death?"

"I'm not sure," said Dwyer evasively. "He stayed busy. With what, I don't know. He kept it to himself, whatever it was."

"Is there anybody else who might know more?" Danbury asked.

"Not that I can think of," said Dwyer. "We all scattered. There are a couple of guys still around the Raleigh area, I think."

"Yeah, I found two of them. They weren't helpful, told me nothing. Like why the case wasn't closed. That's a basic question."

"Probably two reasons for the case being left open, though I'm speculating again," said Dwyer. "I'm sure you've already considered them."

"Not casting blame on a fellow officer. Or on my dad because I'd have lost his benefits. If it was ruled a suicide," said Danbury.

"That's my best guess. Another thing we'll probably never know."

"Thank you, Dwyer. I appreciate your honesty," said Danbury. "Here," he added, pulling a card from his pocket and handing it over. "Let me know if you think of anything else. You know the drill. However insignificant it seems."

"Sure, Warren. It's good to see you."

"Good to meet you too," said Danbury. As he and Matthew climbed back in the car, Dwyer ducked his head back under the hood.

"Ten to one," said Danbury, heading out of the neighborhood, "that he's on the phone. Within the next minute."

"Calling who?" asked Matthew.

"We'd be headed there. If I knew that. Maybe we are."

"You said you have an address for Dwyer's old partner, farther north."

"That's right. Brian Ogilvy. I didn't ask Dwyer about him. Because I didn't want Ogilvy forewarned. If he's still alive. Dwyer might have called him anyway. We'll take our chances in driving up there."

Checking the time on the phone and cringing that it was passing quickly without gaining information nearly as fast, Matthew entered the address Danbury called out into the navigation app. It was over an hours' drive. From there, it would take nearly two to get back to Peak. Matthew figured they'd make it back in time for Penn's dinner.

Settling in, Matthew opened the shared document and saw Penn had listed twelve junkyards, with their phone numbers and addresses. She'd begun to make notes on each entry. Five listings had notes. None of them reported knowing about a silver or gray Ford Aerostar.

As Matthew began adding notes about their interview with Dwyer, Danbury's phone sounded with the sappy country song ringtone. Clicking to accept the incoming call on the car's speaker system, the big detective didn't answer in his usual, brusque manner with "Danbury here." Instead, he said, "Hey, Penn. How's it going?"

"I found it!" she announced triumphantly. "The last junkyard I called has a Ford Aerostar parked by their gate that they swear was moved. It isn't exactly gray or silver, but it's in primer. One of the guys who worked there, before COVID shut down most of the business, is restoring it for his sister. She's a single mom with three children. He's been working on it on the side, coming in evenings, to try to get it reliably back on the road."

"When did they think it was moved?"

"The business owner said the guy working on it parked it outside the gate Wednesday night. It's where he always puts it when he's finished each evening. When he came back Thursday evening about six, he insisted that it had been moved. And that there was more than a quarter tank of gas missing, nearly half a tank. The wires under the steering column were hanging down. The junkyard owner said he hadn't moved it and told the guy he was imagining things."

"That's great work, Penn," said Danbury appreciatively.

"Thanks. There's more."

"Let's hear it," said Danbury.

"The junkyard owner gave me the guy's contact information, and I called him. He repeated that it had been moved, and he said he knew that because there was a gash all the way down the driver's side of the van. It was the side he'd just finished restoring, and he was hopping mad about that."

"I guess so," said Danbury.

"He suspected that the son of the junkyard owner had been joyriding, but he said he couldn't prove it. That van gets about fifteen miles to a gallon of gas, he told me, and it's a twenty-one-gallon tank. His best guess was that the van had been driven about a hundred and twenty to a hundred and fifty miles before it was returned."

"Wow, that's a trip," said Matthew under his breath. "A lot of driving for one night, anyway."

"What's the address?" asked Danbury. "I'll call the office. Have somebody go check it."

"It's in the shared document," she said, and Matthew refreshed it to see that the sixth entry had a plethora of new information beneath the name and address.

"I see the contact information for the Aerostar owner," said Matthew. "The junkyard is located out 401, ironically, but in the other direction. South of Peak."

"It is," said Penn. "I'm nothing if not thorough."

"Thanks, Penn," said Danbury. "That's a huge help. I really appreciate it."

"You're welcome. Anything else I can do?"

"Not without your computer. I'll check on it when I call in about the Ford Aerostar."

"If you think of anything else, let me know. Where are you now?"

"Headed north, up to Lake Morris. To talk to a guy who was on the force with my dad."

"Be careful, Warren. I mean it. Let me know if there's anything else I can do from here. And if you're going to be late for dinner, let me know that too. I'll keep it warm for you."

"Should be there in time," said Danbury, who never willingly missed a meal.

Matthew had heard Danbury advise, on multiple occasions, to eat and sleep when you could because you never knew when you'd get to do either one again. Matthew had no idea how prophetic Danbury's credo would prove to be.

12 ~ CRUSTY AND DUSTY

The multistory house they pulled up to looked like it belonged on the water. From the street, a long gravel driveway led in, turning to pavement where it looped before the house. The drive continued, disappearing beside the house down a slope to the right.

The lot was heavily wooded with bird and squirrel feeders dotted among the trees. The squirrel feeders looked as if they were more to entertain the viewers than to feed the squirrels. Windmill contraptions were attached to the trees; the end of each blade donned half-eaten corn cobs. The squirrels must, Matthew concluded, have coped.

A covered porch graced the left side of the house and a swing hung there. Between it and the door on the right of the porch was a wicker settee with overstuffed cushions.

As Danbury pushed it, the doorbell sounded hollowly from within the house. Masks in hand, they waited. Finally, a woman came squeaking down the hallway—that they could somewhat see through a stained-glass panel to the left of the door—in rubber soled shoes. When the door opened, she appeared younger than Matthew had anticipated. He guessed her to be in her late thirties or early forties, trim and fit.

Startlingly green eyes peered up at them above a black mask she was pulling into place. Dressed in a snug black warm-up suit and black jogging shoes, but for her dirty blonde hair, she'd have looked like a sleek Halloween cat ready to pounce.

"Hi, I'm Detective Danbury," he said, flipping his badge open for inspection. "And this is Doctor Matthew Paine." As he was flipping it closed, the cat woman reached for it.

"May I?" she asked. Danbury shrugged. Without releasing his hold on it, he allowed her to turn his badge this way and that, inspecting it. She alternately studied the badge and his face for a moment longer before agreeing, "So you are." Releasing her hold, she allowed him to take the badge back. "What can I do for you, Detective?"

"I'm looking for Brian Ogilvy."

"So is everyone else. At least your identity is plausible."

"Somebody else has been here looking for him?"

"You'd better come in," she said, waving them through the house and out onto a covered screened porch on the water side. "Please, have a seat. Would you like something to drink? Some hot tea, perhaps?"

"I don't want to take up your time," said Danbury, but he sat as instructed, and Matthew followed suit.

"What you really want is to take up my father's time. Wait here, I'll get the drinks."

"She's a bit crusty," whispered Matthew, pulling his mask off in the fresh air. "Jaded, I mean."

"Daughter of a career cop. She knows a thing or two about how the world works," replied Danbury softly, removing his as well. "She doesn't waste time with nonsense. You have to respect that."

"I guess," said Matthew, leaning back and taking in the scenery. The view, from the second story of the house that had been the first story from the street side, was spectacular. Perched on a hill above the lake with a gently sloping pathway to the water's edge, the house overlooked a wide cove beneath.

A few trees were grouped to the left and more to the right, but none obstructed the path or the view of the lake. A dock with a boathouse extended off to the right, having been thoughtfully placed so as not to obscure the lake scene. Water lapped gently at the pylons on the dock in a softly flowing breeze.

As they sat quietly taking it all in, a door somewhere beneath them opened. The stopping and starting of a quiet motor and the sound of voices, one male, the other female, muted the sounds of the lapping water beyond. After a few moments, a motorized wheelchair emerged from beneath the porch where they sat and wended its way toward the water.

Its diminutive occupant was barely visible above the wheelchair. Spiky gray hair stuck out at odd angles beneath a Greek fisherman's hat, giving the figure the appearance of being male. Walking along beside was a young woman, lithe, in purple scrubs, and carrying a large bag over one shoulder. Neither of them looked up or back.

The pair maneuvered onto a tiled seating area with a fire pit under the edge of the tree cover off to the left. Beyond the seating area and the tree cover was a grill enclosed in a rock chimney with picnic table seating.

When the wheelchair was situated, the young woman perched in an Adirondack chair beside it and pulled a book from the bag she had placed on a low table between them. Flipping pages until she was satisfied, she settled back into the chair leaning toward the man in the wheelchair. The sound of her soft voice wafted upward. Blending with the lazily lapping water, her words were lost on the wind.

"You think that's Ogilvy?" Matthew all but whispered.

"I hope so," Danbury answered.

Before they could speculate further, their hostess returned and set a tray neatly on a low wicker table in front of them. She poured hot water into mugs, adding tea bags and asking about sugar and cream. Sliding napkins underneath, she handed them out.

"Now," she said, perching on a wicker chair across from them. "I'm Sheila, the dragon lady you have to go through to get to my dad."

For once, Matthew saw something register on Danbury's face. Some thought of recognition flitted across it and was just as quickly gone. What sparked it from what she'd just said wasn't obvious. Perhaps it was neither what she said or how she said it; maybe it was something else entirely.

"I won't have you upsetting him, so state your business, here and now," she added.

After a perfunctory sip of tea, Danbury quickly explained that their fathers had worked together. He told her how his parents had died when he was a child. What he wanted most to know, he explained, was if her father remembered anything, particularly anything unusual, that happened around that time. Any information leading to the who or the why behind their murders would be helpful, Danbury clarified. He hadn't, Matthew noticed, mentioned the most recent murder.

Then, in an uncharacteristic display of transparency, Danbury added, "I've always wondered what really happened. I'm an only child. My grandmother raised me after they died. But she wouldn't talk about any of it. Ever. She died this week, and now I need to know. Whatever happened, I need closure."

"You don't believe it was a murder-suicide?" she asked, scrutinizing him carefully with her squinted cat-like eyes.

"No. I don't. Neither do people I've talked to so far. They're pretty tight-lipped about it. Particularly the two still on the police force. Your dad's former partner was slightly more helpful. He knows more than he's saying. Or suspects more. Either way, I was hoping your dad would enlighten me. There are lots of pieces. But they don't fit. No picture is forming. Not a glimpse."

She took a sip of tea before she said, "OK, I trust that you are who you say you are. You can talk to him. But," she held up a hand before continuing, "if he starts to get agitated, you walk away immediately. Swiftly and silently, you walk away. Capiche?"

"Yeah, I got it," said Danbury.

"Good. His health hasn't been great for the past nine years. He can hear reasonably well, though you might have to raise your voice a little. His eyesight is still strong. He won't miss anything about your mannerisms or body language. So don't try to BS him." Standing and leading the way through a screen door and out onto the edge of a high deck with railings, she added, "Come on down this way."

"One more thing," said Danbury.

She stopped at the top of a stairway, turned, and rolled brilliant green eyes up at him. "What's that?"

"You said other people were here. Asking for your dad."

"That's right."

"When?"

"On Friday."

"Yesterday?"

She nodded.

"Who?"

"A man and a woman."

"Can you describe them?"

"OK, so we're doing this," she said. Crossing her arms over her chest, she launched into a detailed description. "They were suspiciously nondescript, dressed neatly in brown suits. Medium heights and weights, probably in their mid to late thirties. No distinguishing birthmarks, scars, piercings, tattoos, or anything else, before you ask. Nothing stood out at all. Both had medium brown hair. His eyes were brown, his skin olive. Hers were hazel, her skin pale. They said they were with an insurance company and handed me their business cards. That proves nothing. Anybody could print those in a flash. Besides, I know our insurance providers. These weren't them. They had John Smith and Jane Doe sorts of names."

"Do you still have the cards?"

"No."

"Would you recognize them again if you saw them?"

She screwed her face up before replying, "Maybe. They were wearing masks, so I didn't see their lower faces. I swear we all look like bank robbers and marauders running around in those things."

"What did they want?"

"They said they wanted to talk to my dad about his life insurance."

"And did they?"

"Absolutely not! I sent them packing," she said before turning and descending the steps. "I told them not to come back," she added over her shoulder. "There's a shotgun behind every door in this house. I pulled it out just enough for them to see. They got in their car and left."

"What sort of car?" Danbury asked as they made their way down the path toward the water.

"It was as generic as they were. A Toyota sedan, a newer Camry. It was a dark color, either navy blue or charcoal, but not black. And no, I didn't get the plate number. They parked it, nose in, a little way down the driveway under the shade of the trees and then backed it out. It isn't registered in Virginia. It had no plates on the front."

She was definitely the daughter of a cop, Matthew thought. She gave all the right answers to all of the questions an officer would ask—without being prompted—and she'd thought to notice it all.

As they followed her down to the seating area, halfway between the house and the water's edge, the breeze kicked up and caught Matthew's windbreaker. April, this year, had been cooler than normal. The breeze off the water was chilly and the day hazy, one where it was difficult to determine whether you needed sunglasses. The water, dotted with puffs of wind, sparkled in some places and was a dull gray in others.

"Dad?" said Sheila loudly. "You have visitors."

Matthew followed her and Danbury to stand in front of the elderly man, who was shrunken into the motorized chair and covered with a lap blanket. Like his partner, the old man gave Danbury a hard stare of scrutiny. On the lake, a small fishing boat puttered into the cove. A flash of sunlight glinting off of a fishing rod in Matthew's peripheral vision caught his attention momentarily.

"Do I know you, Son?" asked Brian Ogilvy, squinting up.

"You knew my father, Erik Danbury. I'm Warren."

"Well, now," the older man said, smiling widely. "Come and have a seat. I don't get many visitors. My daughter wouldn't allow them anyway." He winked at her fondly as he said it. "You must have answered all of her questions right.”

“I told her the truth,” said Danbury.

“OK, Dad, I’ll leave you to talk for a bit. Do you need anything? A warm drink?”

“No, no, I’m fine, thanks.”

With that, Sheila turned and made her way back to the house, and through the downstairs door Ogilvy and his aid must have exited.

After a moment of small talk while the young woman fluffed pillows and repositioned blankest for him, Ogilvy said, “Why don’t you boys pull up some chairs and let’s talk. I’m just a pile of dust these days, physically, but my mind is sharp as it’s ever been. Britton,” he added, turning to the young woman who had been fussing over him, “why don’t you go back up to the house? We can read some more after my visit with young Warren here.”

“Yes, Sir,” she said. “I’ll hang out downstairs by the door so that I can see you. If you need anything, just wave, and I’ll be right back.”

“Thank you, Dear,” he said as she turned and headed for the house.

Danbury was moving to the seat on the far side of the motorized chair, and Matthew was just about to perch in the Adirondack chair Britton had vacated when everything around him erupted into noise, color, movement, and confusion.

“Doc! Get down!” Danbury yelled as he dove for the old man in the wheel chair, knocking him to the ground behind the chair and landing on top of him. In his peripheral vision, Matthew saw a flash of light from the water and heard a loud popping noise as he dove into the sandpit under the grill beside him.

Before he could move, he heard a scream. Immediately afterward, a door slammed, and a female voice yelled threats and curses that would embarrass a sailor. A loud booming burst was followed quickly by two more.

Matthew turned his head, spitting out sand, to see Sheila returning from the water’s edge with a shotgun. The little boat that had so peacefully puttered into the cove was tearing off out of it, powered by a motor nobody would expect to find on a fishing boat.

"Dad? Are you OK? Were you hit?"

He shook his head no after the latter question, but didn't answer verbally.

When the scream came again, Matthew brushed the sand from his face and his mind, looking around to find the source. Britton lay, writhing, on the ground partway between the house and sitting area, holding her bloodied calf and crying out for help.

"Are you OK?" Matthew asked Danbury as he scrambled to his feet.

"We're good. Go," sand Danbury, rolling Brian Ogilvy over gently and beginning to check him, head to toe, asking if he could wiggle his extremities. The old man looked to be in shock and was shaking violently, but there was no visible blood.

"Sheila! Call 911 and get blankets!" Matthew yelled, sliding to his knees beside Britton. "I'm a doctor, and I've got you," he said, checking her over as quickly as he could manage. Finding no other injuries beyond a profusely bleeding calf with a bone that had at least been broken and perhaps shattered by a bullet, he pulled off his jacket and then the cotton Henley shirt beneath it. He wadded the shirt into the wound, tying it around and holding pressure on it with his knee while tying the jacket above her knee to staunch the bleeding.

"Yeah, police and a bus. Right, gunshots fired!" he heard Sheila shouting into the phone. She repeated the address twice. If she could climb through the phone and make the process any faster, she would have, Matthew thought as she darted past him into the house.

Britton shook all over and moaned softly as Sheila dropped the blankets beside Matthew and ran back to her father.

"I've got him. He's OK," Danbury said as he helped Brian Ogilvy into a sitting position. "I'll get him into his chair. And back in the house. As soon as he's ready."

"Sheila, roll up a blanket and put it under her leg here," Matthew instructed, raising Britton's leg slightly, holding it steady in both hands. "And one over her."

Praying the blood loss would slow, he was debating how much he could pull the leg taut, holding it in traction to keep the muscles elongated with the broken bones.

"Do you have another blanket?" he asked Sheila. When she held it out, he asked, "Britton, can you lift your head a little?" On a sobbing breath, the young woman lifted her head. That was a good sign, he thought. Her breathing was panicked but strong.

"Fold that one under her head there. But not too high. Talk to her about anything she likes or likes to do. Happy things," he instructed Sheila. Grasping Britton's wrist to check her pulse with one hand, he held her leg with the other. Wishing he had three or four hands to monitor it, he was satisfied he'd slowed the bleeding and returned his focus to the leg wound.

Sheila dropped to the ground behind Britton's head and brushed her hair from her face. Caressing the young woman's face gently between her hands, Sheila began to sing, quietly at first, and then more confidently as Britton's body noticeably relaxed. His arm and back muscles beginning to ache, Matthew continued to hold both pressure and traction as they awaited the ambulance.

It seemed like an eternity before they heard the sirens and then saw the lights. Identifying first himself and then the wound as a gunshot to the emergency workers, he helped move Britton onto a backboard, to a stretcher, and then into the back of a waiting ambulance. His thoughts muddled, Matthew stepped back as they closed the doors of the ambulance.

"Is there anybody we should call?" he asked Sheila as the ambulance pulled carefully down the long driveway. "Does she have family?"

"She has a brother just up I-85 in Virginia. He's her emergency contact and next of kin. I'll call him," she answered, tapping her phone. Turning her back to the departing ambulance, she identified herself. Matthew couldn't hear what else she said as she walked toward the house. Distant sirens indicated the ambulance's tires had connected with asphalt and was on the way to the hospital.

Before entering the house, Sheila glanced back. Her expression was an odd one. Her cat eyes stared at Matthew as he rolled his shoulders and stretched sore arm and back muscles. Standing in the middle of her driveway, shirtless, muscles flexing, he had no idea why she gaped at him.

Taking a moment to steady his nerves, Matthew stood thanking God nobody had been killed and praying for Britton's well-being. He asked for the best of surgeons to be either already at the hospital or on call and able to get there quickly. His blood-soaked shirt he spotted on the ground behind where the ambulance had been parked. That, he thought, was useless to him now. His jacket had remained with Britton as she was transported. Picking up the shirt, he put it beside Danbury's SUV.

Two police cruisers were parked at odd angles in the paved circular drive, an officer still occupying one of them. Matthew could hear a radio squawking and static between the voices. Now what? he thought, ambling toward the house and letting himself in.

13 ~ By all Accounts

The door swooshed closed behind him as Matthew entered the lake house and called out, "Hello?"

At the other end of the hallway, wood and glass-paneled doors opened, and Danbury emerged with the motorized wheelchair. Of course, they have an elevator, Matthew thought. The multistory house has to be traversable to Ogilvy.

"Is Britton going to be OK?" the old man immediately asked.

"I hope so," said Matthew. "I was able to slow the loss of blood significantly, but that leg is in rough shape. There are compound fractures. One of the bones might be shattered. She'll be rushed into surgery, and they'll determine what those repairs will look like. There's a long road of recovery ahead."

Sheila stood on the deck beyond where they were gathered in the kitchen, looking haggard. Up the steps behind her tromped two uniformed police officers. An older male officer was followed by a younger female officer. Motioning them to follow, Sheila entered the house, and her focus immediately shifted to her father.

"Dad, why don't you go get some rest? I'll answer their questions to file a report," she said. "Come on in, Officers," she added as they hesitated.

"We're fine out here for now," the older one, a heavyset man Matthew guessed to be in his early forties, answered. The name tag on his uniform said "Beck." Matthew couldn't see the nameplate of the officer behind him.

"I'll answer their questions, Sheila. But without this ridiculous mask," he said, ripping it off of his face.

"But Dad, that protects you from the virus that's killing people."

"Look at me, Sweetheart," he said. "If that doesn't get me, something else will."

"I'm trying to keep you safe and well," said Sheila. "Put your mask back on, and I'll talk to the police."

"Not this time," he said. "There are things they need to know. As does young Warren here. Things he deserves to know. What happened in the past seems to have a bearing on the present and potentially his future."

"But, Dad," she protested. "You need your rest."

"Nonsense, My Dear," Ogilvy said calmly.

"But this will put you in danger."

"It is what's most needed right now to keep us out of danger," said Ogilvy patiently.

"Dredging anything up now from all those years ago can't possibly help."

"You need to trust me that it will," he answered, his patience noticeably waning.

"But, Dad," she began to protest again.

"Sheila!" he boomed. "Enough!"

That such a powerful voice could come from a diminished body was remarkable. Sheila cowered as if she'd heard it before and knew repercussions were imminent. It was, Matthew thought, like the elephant tied as a baby that continued to think a simple stake and rope held it in place as an adult. She'd been conditioned to respond to that voice, though it's owner could hardly punish her now.

"I'm sorry, Sweetheart," Ogilvy said to her. "But this is what's best. Normally, I allow you to fuss over me as much as you like, and I do what you ask. This time, though, you're wrong. The only thing that will remove us from danger—both of us, you and I—is to share what I know. Then I'm not the only one who knows it. That removes the target from my back. Do you understand what I'm telling you?"

"I do, Dad. I just want you to be safe. And as healthy as you can be for as long as possible."

"I know, and I appreciate everything you do for me. Now I'm going to do something for both of us. I'm going to set a few records straight, at least as much as I'm able. Then I'll be safer, and so will you. Because more people will know the truth."

"If that's all it took, why didn't you do it before now?" asked Sheila, looking genuinely puzzled.

"Because I didn't know who I could trust with this information until now. And it wasn't relevant to anything anymore. Now, it seems it is."

"OK, Dad. What do you need me to do?"

"We're going to my old office upstairs. There are documents in my safe I'll need to you retrieve. They might shed some light on some of this. I'll hand those off to the right people. Warren Danbury is the right person, and I want them on file with the local police in possible connection with the shooting today."

"All right," she said, turning with him as he punched the button on the elevator to go up. "The stairs are over there," she pointed to everyone else. "And for Pete's sake, put a shirt on!" she fussed at Matthew.

"I would if I had one," he responded, annoyed at her being annoyed as he stood there feeling exposed. "Do you have a grocery bag or something I can toss my bloody one in? I'm not sure it's salvageable, but I can try to wash it out later. And I need to wash up."

"The washer's in there," Sheila said, pointing to a door off the kitchen. "There's a scrub sink. Trash bags are under it. Detergent is in the cabinet above the washer. Help yourself."

"I've got spare shirts in my go bag," said Danbury, tossing Matthew the key fob to the SUV. "Check the black bag. In the back."

"Thanks."

As he removed his watch to wash his arms and upper body, Matthew checked the time. If Ogilvy had been the intended target twenty-four hours after they'd found the first corpse, then maybe they'd prevented him from being the second victim. The timing was almost right. A momentary hope flitted through his mind. Had they prevented the second murder? He thought of Britton and that hope faded. Had one victim been exchanged for another?

Why, then, didn't the feeling of urgency abate?

Donning Danbury's spare shirt, Matthew retrieved his blood-soaked one. The stains might never come out of the shirt that was once dark green, but he thought he'd try. He took Sheila at her word to help himself.

Back upstairs, documents of some sort were spread across a large wooden desk. Ogilvy was in his chair behind it, organizing them. Looking over one shoulder was Danbury. Sheila stood protectively on the other side. The two masked officers watched and waited impatiently as Matthew hovered in the doorway.

"What I'm piecing together is an integral part of what happened here today," answered Ogilvy. "I'm certain of it."

"Sir, would you like a police detail assigned? For a few days or until we apprehend the shooter?" asked the female officer.

"Yes," said Sheila as her father said, "No," in unison.

Looking up at her earnest worried face, Brian Ogilvy acquiesced. "OK, yes," he answered before returning to the papers in front of him. "Now, let's try to make some sense out of all of this."

The female officer slipped by Matthew out into the hallway to call in the request. The older officer seemed to notice Matthew only when he walked into the room.

"We need to hear what happened today from each of you," said Officer Beck. "While it's still fresh in your minds. Let's start with you," he said to Matthew. "This way, Sir," he added, leading the way back down the stairs.

Curious to know what he was missing upstairs, Matthew

reluctantly followed.

"Start with the incident today," instructed the officer. "Tell me the chain of events as they happened, all details you can recall."

Matthew began with their arrival and being scrutinized closely by Sheila before she allowed them to talk to Brian Ogilvy. He mentioned she had other visitors the day before also asking to speak with her father. "Those, she said she'd turned away," explained Matthew. "Sheila can provide details. She paid close attention."

After Matthew had finished his account, Beck summarized, "What you're telling me is that you had just met retired Officer Ogilvy. You hadn't had a chance to talk to him when the shots were fired. And you didn't see the shooter. Is that correct?"

"That's what I'm telling you," said Matthew. "It's why Ogilvy agreed to share whatever he's sorting upstairs now and why he said it pertains to the shooting today. As for the shooter, I saw what I thought was a fishing boat puttering into the cove. It had a single occupant, as far as I could see, but I didn't turn all the way around to look. I caught the flash of something on the boat in my peripheral vision and assumed it was a fishing rod. Retrospectively, it could have been a weapon."

"How soon after you saw the flash did the shooting begin?"

Searching his memory, Matthew said, "Probably just a couple of minutes."

"How far out was the boat from the edge of the shore down there?"

"I'm not sure," answered Matthew, trying to remember and then put the perceived distance into words.

"A football field? Two? More?" asked the officer.

"I'm not much on football," answered Matthew honestly. "But I'd say about two football fields, maybe slightly less."

"About two hundred to two hundred and forty yards," summarized the officer.

"Something like that. Likely Danbury can give a more accurate estimate. He actually played football," Matthew said with a grin.

"You're trying to determine the skill of the shooter?"

"And the type of weapon. Ballistics should help with that. If the bullet is still with the victim. We'll check the area down there more closely in case it isn't."

"It had to have been a rifle or something like that," said Matthew. "If what I saw wasn't a fishing rod, my perception was a long object that caught the sunlight."

"The guy didn't have time to switch between the two? A fishing rod and then a weapon?"

Matthew's eyebrow rose and his foot tapped in contemplation. "He might have," he answered. "That could explain why the trajectory was off, if he swapped too quickly."

"The trajectory?"

"The bullet went high above Danbury, Ogilvy, and me. It hit Britton as she was walking up the pathway to the house. The weather conditions might account for that."

"How so?"

"It was hazy out. The water was murky gray and choppy. An intermittent breeze kept the water churned up in spots. You could see puffs of wind out there. Waves were lapping against the pylons of the dock before the boat came into the cove. I noticed the sound from up here on the porch. Conditions weren't ideal for visibility or steady aim."

"Anything else you can recall?"

"Not right off. If I think of anything, I'll let you know."

"OK, here," said the officer, handing Matthew a business card. "Would you send Ms. Ogilvy down next?"

"Sure," said Matthew as he shoved the card into his pocket and bounded up the steps two at a time.

Sheila's last name is Ogilvy? He pondered, thinking nobody had said otherwise. Somebody, somewhere in their family, had money beyond what a retired police officer's pension would draw. The multistory house on the lake had an elevator. Maybe he was wrong to suspect Sheila or the retired Officer Ogilvy of anything nefarious. Maybe she had a cushy job with an amazing income. Or maybe there was family money somewhere.

He hoped they were innocent near victims and not deserving deviants of the shooting that had seriously injured Britton. Or was Britton as innocent as Sheila had insisted? As suspicious thoughts clouded Matthew's brain, he wondered when he'd become so jaded.

Prying Sheila away from her father to send her downstairs took the intervention of both the young female officer, who was listening intently to Danbury asking questions when Matthew entered, and Brian Ogilvy. When her father insisted, Sheila went. Her reluctance to leave his side was palpable.

Slipping into her place behind Ogilvy, Matthew studied the array of folders and papers now neatly organized on the desk. Danbury held a stack in his hands.

"What you're telling me," Danbury was apparently summarizing Ogilvy, "is that they knew."

"Right. I don't know why the rest of the initial report that you have disappeared or who was responsible for that, but this is the original version. I made copies to cover myself when I left. They were looking for scapegoats. The evidence didn't support a homicide and suicide, but it did raise other questions that somebody didn't want to answer."

"Meaning what?" asked Danbury.

"Look at this one," said Ogilvy, handing Danbury a folder. "What do you see?"

The pages shuffled in the otherwise silent room. Sheila's raised voice faded into the background as she was protesting from downstairs that she'd already answered a question. Danbury stopped flipping and stared at one specific page as if his eyes would burn holes through it.

"I see," he said. "Why hide it?"

Matthew was dying to ask what he saw and was relieved when the young female officer asked instead.

"There was evidence," began Danbury, "of a third person. Hard evidence. Somebody was in the house that morning."

"That corroborates the car that Jason Byrd now says he saw leaving," said Matthew.

"It does," agreed Danbury. "Sounds like an issued vehicle. Police or governmental."

"Jason Byrd," repeated Ogilvy thoughtfully. "Was he the neighbor across the street from your parents?"

"Yeah, he forgot his original story," answered Danbury. "The one he told at the time. Now, he says he came home shortly before noon. From an all-night poker game. He saw a nondescript sedan leaving. He'd seen it there before."

"Or one like it," offered Matthew.

"Right," said Danbury. "When I called him on it, he became hostile. Said he couldn't remember that long ago. I think he remembered perfectly well. But too late. He'd already told me the truth. Not the lie he'd been paid to tell over twenty years ago."

"That makes sense," said Ogilvy. "Could he remember anything else helpful?"

"If he could, he didn't," answered Danbury. "He had to have been paid off. With a nicer house and money. He knows more than he's saying. He thought it was about airport expansion. We wouldn't rule that out, except that it never happened. Not in that direction. His old house is still there. As is my parents.' Why kill over it and then not do it?"

"Unless it got too heated and whoever had killed for it was about to be exposed," said Ogilvy.

"That's possible. I need another go at him. See if he recovers the rest of his memory."

"It would likely take a payoff again to get him to talk now," said Matthew. "He'd want something in return for telling you anything."

"Or a threat," answered Danbury.

"He might have already gotten one of those," said Matthew meaningfully, without mentioning the body found in Jason Byrd's old house aloud.

Nodding, Danbury returned to the stacks of papers. "What else is here?"

"There was an investigation opened on Conrad Manchester," answered Ogilvy. "He checked all the right boxes for a suspect, except one. He had an alibi. His wife said it was his day off, and he was home with her from about six the night before and all morning until he got the call about Erik. He left for the crime scene when that call came, but he was with her until that point."

Ogilvy handed Danbury another set of pages in a folder.

"He admitted that he'd had a thing for your mother when they were younger," continued Ogilvy. "It's all there in the transcript. But he said he realized, pretty quickly, that your parents belonged together, and he backed off. Then he met Heather, who became his wife, and that was that."

"They grilled her too," said Danbury, flipping through the folder Ogilvy had just handed him. "Harshly."

"They did. It was way over the top," agreed Ogilvy. "To her credit, she didn't budge. She said she knew about his past feelings for your mother, and it didn't matter because he chose her. They made some nasty insinuations about her being second choice, but she stood by Conrad. She insisted that he loved her, chose her, married her, and was with her all night until about one thirty that afternoon when the call came in about your parents."

"She was supposed to have been at work?" asked Danbury, pointing to the file.

"Right. They all but accused her of lying that she was home not feeling well."

"Somebody expected her to be away. To have been at work all day," said Danbury.

"I thought the same thing when I read that transcript," agreed Ogilvy. "Like somebody was framing Conrad, but it backfired because Heather had a migraine and stayed home. And he was there caring for her. Statements from two people she worked with in that file confirm that she called in sick and that she wasn't at work at any time that day."

"I see. This looks more like what I'd expected," said Danbury. "From a murder investigation. The files in police storage were sparse. I knew there had to be more. How did you know? Why did you copy these? And save them all this time?"

"This," said Brian Ogilvy, handing Danbury another file folder.

"You were questioned too?" asked Danbury as he scanned, flipping through the pages in the file.

"I was. I got the feeling it was a witch hunt. It was a balancing act between sullying the name of your father and the department and finding another scapegoat to take the fall. In the end, they quietly stopped looking without officially closing the case. Check that last page. That'll tell you why I made a set of these files, as did Conrad Manchester."

"Oh, I see!" said Danbury, flipping pages.

"What is it?" asked Matthew, unable to stand the suspense any longer.

"The third person who was there. The top suspect was Conrad Manchester, initially. His weapon killed my parents," said Danbury slowly. "Looks like he was being set up, but then he had a solid alibi."

"Right," said Ogilvy. "The gun was supposed to have been locked in Conrad's police locker. It was his personal weapon, but it was the one he used on the job. It stayed at the precinct when he was off duty."

"Then it became about finding another scapegoat," said Danbury. "Pinning it on somebody with access to the police locker. It says your fingerprints were on the bullets."

"Exactly," answered Ogilvy. "Though I had no motive, what you're reading there is the transcript of them all but accusing me. Maybe they were my bullets taken from my locker and loaded into the murder weapon. I have no idea how they got there."

"Looks like they were accusing you," said Danbury.

"It's why I kept the files and why I never showed them to anyone else. I had no clear picture of who I could trust. I didn't make these files disappear from the official police records. Neither did Conrad Manchester, though we seemed to be the two with the most motive to do so. And the most to lose if they resurfaced. If the investigative efforts renewed, what's in those files would supply a reason to suspect us first."

"What about Conrad's wife? Was she killed to silence the alibi?" asked Danbury.

"It's what we both suspected, but we couldn't prove it," said Ogilvy, handing Danbury another file. "Or it was to send a message. The investigation of her death was negligible. Nobody wanted to hear from Conrad that she'd been killed and that it wasn't an accident. Here, you can take all of these files with you. I have no further use for them now that they're in the right hands."

"Hold on a minute," the female officer, who'd been standing quietly by, objected. "We'll need copies of those too. You said you wanted them on file with our office. That's smart, if you think that's what was behind the shooting today. Nobody was killed, I hope," she added, looking over at Matthew.

"I hope not," said Matthew simply.

"But an attempt was made on one of your lives. Sounds like it was yours, Sir," she addressed Ogilvy.

"Could Britton have been the intended target?" asked Matthew. "Maybe there's something in her past."

"No," Sheila insisted. "I had the deepest level of background checks run on her and vetted that information myself. She and her family are squeaky clean. I wouldn't have let her anywhere near Dad otherwise."

Not yet willing to let it go entirely, Matthew turned to Danbury. "Does Britton look anything like your mom?"

"Nothing at all," answered Danbury, shaking his head.

"If this is what it's about," interrupted the female officer, indicating the folders of files, "then the shooter didn't want you handing off any of this information. How did he know you had this?"

"I don't know that he did. It might have been as much about not wanting me to share what I know with anybody else who would care. Warren fits that category. Would you run the copies, please?" asked Ogilvy of the young officer. "The printer makes copies, and it's over there in the corner."

"I suppose since you didn't call me 'Sweetheart' or 'Honey' or ask me to fix coffee for you, I will," she muttered under her breath, scooping up one of the file folders from the desk and setting to work.

"She makes a good point. Who knew you had these?" asked Danbury, indicating the folders.

"Just Conrad Manchester, as far as I knew," replied Ogilvy. "But maybe I was wrong about that."

"If nobody knew you had copies," began Danbury, "and neither of you removed files, the official police versions. Somebody else had a reason for wanting them gone. And to silence you."

"Well, don't take my word for it," said Ogilvy. "Go ask Manchester."

"I would if I could!" said Danbury. "Nobody seems to know where he is. Or how to find him."

"I might be able to help with that," said Ogilvy, leaning back into the cushions of his motorized chair, looking drained but satisfied.

14 ~ AGED REVELATIONS

"Tell me," said Danbury.

"Conrad Manchester went off the grid purposefully. I left the police department the end of July of 1998 after the scrutiny I'd come under for something I knew nothing about. I decided I could do without that added stress. The job was hard enough without dirty politics. Our police chief at the time seemed as baffled by all of it as we were. I don't know where his orders came from or why. I knew I'd never get to the bottom of it, and I wasn't sure I wanted to. I didn't know who I could trust anymore, so I retired."

"Then what?"

"I went to work for a security company that your father had worked for. Conrad was working there too. He switched from consulting with them part time to full-time employment after your parents' death and the subsequent investigation."

"Iron Clad Security?"

"That's the one," said Ogilvy, perking up slightly with the reminiscence. "A fresh start was what I needed. I had suspicion hanging over me within the department. It seemed that somebody wanted it to be continually stirred up, like they were looking for a new angle. Transferring precincts was one option, but Sheila was in high school, nearly finished, and I didn't want to move her. The money was better in the private sector too. Her college fund needed a boost."

"Conrad Manchester worked for Iron Clad," muttered Danbury.

"He did. Part time, as needed at first, doing consulting work."

"Then he went full time when he left the precinct?"

"Right."

"Before that, though. He worked both places? At the same time? Like my dad?" asked Danbury for clarification.

"For several years, he did. And then, everything happened at once. The end of January of 1999, Iron Clad suddenly went out of business. They abruptly closed up and shut down. We never understood why. I was notified by a phone call, and they sent me one last check. That was it. The next week, Heather Manchester died suddenly and suspiciously in a single car crash."

"Tell me about Iron Clad," said Danbury.

"There's not much to tell," said Ogilvy, sinking back into his chair, wiggling to get the pillows adjusted. "I worked for them for about six months, August of 1998 through January of 1999. I had a home office in my house in Raleigh with what you see around you here." Matthew took in filing cabinets, a credenza, a small side table and chair, and cabinets beside the copier in the corner.

"It was a small company, with a single owner," Ogilvy continued. "I reported to one of the directors. Both he and his peer were out of Alexandria, Virginia—near DC. They came down here to North Carolina a couple of times, the owner and directors, once when they hired me and again right before Christmas of 1998."

"December of 1998? Before they closed a month later?"

"Right. They took some of us out for a Christmas dinner at that nice restaurant near the airport."

"They gave no indication that anything was wrong? That they might be closing?"

"None. It was the opposite, in fact. It sounded like they were expanding and growing, looking to hire more people. They asked if I had any recommendations."

"Did you ever go to their offices? In Alexandria or DC?" asked Danbury.

"I didn't. Conrad did a few times that I knew about. I'm pretty sure

Erik had been there too. I scrambled to find another company doing the same sort of work when Iron Clad closed. I landed with a nice one out of Nashville. I worked for that company until my health declined. Then I moved in here with Sheila after she divorced. About eight years or so ago."

"What were you doing for Iron Clad?" asked Danbury. "What sort of work?"

"Some of it was routine surveillance. I was on protection details in those early days. A few of them were celebrities—athletes and performers. One was a high-profile politician, I think. I did sweeps ahead of their arrival in hotel suites and conference rooms. I guarded back doors, that sort of thing. I never met any of them, which was fine with me. Their paparazzi was enough to deal with when they weren't there in person."

"Who were they?"

Danbury nodded at the first two names, which Matthew assumed to be the athletes because he'd never heard of them. The name of a singer Matthew recognized and two well-known comedians followed. Then Ogilvy stopped and scratched his nose. "I can't remember the politician's name," he said. "It seems like he was a foreign diplomat of some description."

"Not American?"

"At the time, I didn't think so. I never talked to him directly. Americans have surnames from all over the world, so it's possible. I don't recall now why I didn't think so."

"Would you recognize it? If you heard the name now?"

"I wouldn't guarantee it," said Ogilvy sadly. "I never met the man. If I had, I'd have remembered better, I think. You know, the name and face association."

Danbury nodded. "My dad and Conrad. Did they do the same sort of work?"

"I think so. Some of it was less exciting, like installing cameras and security systems. I never did any of that, but I think both Erik and

Conrad did. They were both tech savvy. In what places and for what purposes, I don't know."

Accessing the online document they'd compiled on his phone, Danbury slowly read the names of all but one of the other security companies they'd compiled from his father's records, pausing after each one. "Do these names mean anything to you? Ever heard of them?"

"No," said Ogilvy, shaking his head slowly. "Those don't sound familiar."

"What about Satellife?"

The older man paused; his head turned quizzically to one side. "That rings a bell," he said. "Though I can't remember the context, it has a negative connotation in my mind. That much I can tell you. It seems like Conrad was involved, or maybe he's the one who mentioned it," he added, his face contorted as if he were struggling to scrape together details from the far recesses of his mind.

"I'm sorry," Ogilvy finally said. "But that's all I've got. I can't remember exactly why it's familiar or any details about where I heard it or what I heard about it."

"That's OK," said Danbury. "It's a start."

"Did you ever hear them talk about Africa? Southeast Africa or Kenya? Or about learning Swahili?" asked Matthew, joining the conversation.

"Kenya," Ogilvy repeated, turning to stare hard at Matthew. "Yes."

"Did my father go?" asked Danbury. "To Kenya? Or southeast Africa?"

"I think he and Conrad were planning to go," said Ogilvy. "They were secretive about it, though, so I doubt anyone knew."

"But you knew?" asked Danbury.

"Only after the fact. Conrad still wanted to go, right after your father was killed. He thought it might clear his name and reputation, but I have no idea why or how that connected to anything. And then something changed. I asked him about it once, probably late in 1998, and his reaction was pretty extreme."

"How so?"

"He hissed at me, so quietly that only I could hear him, never to mention it again. I had no idea why that struck a nerve with him, but it obviously did. I didn't mention it again. Not long after that, Iron Clad went out of business and Conrad's wife died. He disappeared, and I never had a chance to ask him about it again, even if I'd wanted to. I'd forgotten about it until you asked just now, in fact."

"You can find him, can't you?" asked Danbury. "Conrad Manchester."

"I wouldn't go that far," said Ogilvy.

"What are you saying?" Danbury persisted.

"That he left me strings of numbers, lightly disguised. Two strings. Separately. That's it. He said I'd know what to do with them if I ever needed to find him. At the time, I thought they were coordinates. A location. I looked them up that way on a map once to see the general location. If I'm right about that, they're in the middle of nowhere. Which stands to reason if you're going off grid."

"How far in the middle of nowhere?"

"In the Virginia mountains, the far western part of the state. It's nearly West Virginia, but not quite. I'll see if I can find them for you."

Before he could say more, Sheila returned to the room and glared at Danbury and Matthew. "He's tired," she said. "You've worn him out."

"I think being shot at would do that, My Dear," said Ogilvy. "But I'm fine."

"Good to hear," said Officer Beck from the doorway behind Sheila. "Because I need your statement. Yours too, Detective. Would you come with me now?"

"Fine," said Danbury turning to go downstairs with the uniformed officer. "I'll be right back."

"I'm nearly done here," said the younger female officer from the corner of the room. "I just need more paper."

"It's under the cabinet there that the printer is sitting on," said Ogilvy. Then began to mutter, "Now what did I do with those strings of numbers? Did I put them together? I wouldn't have. I stored them someplace safe."

Matthew assisted with the printer. When the paper was reloaded, he turned to see that Ogilvy had drifted off to sleep in his chair, his chin dropping to his chest. Sliding into the chair opposite to wait, Matthew checked his watch. Were they still on a countdown? He wondered, his foot tapping with nervous energy.

"Whattlesby!" exclaimed Ogilvy suddenly, bolting upright and making Matthew jump.

"Sir?" Matthew asked. "Waddle what? Were you dreaming?"

"Yes and no," Ogilvy. "I had an epiphany. You know, that eureka effect when you stop trying to think of something and let your mind relax and wander to other things. Whattlesby!"

"What's Whattlesby?" asked Matthew. "Is that a place? Or a person? A place named after a person?"

"I think it's the surname of the political figure, the diplomat. The guy we were providing security for. That was the last job I had at Iron Clad just before they went out of business."

"Oh," said Matthew. "That's not a name I've ever heard. Maybe it's common in other parts of the world. Let's look," he said, pulling his phone from his pocket and tapping it. "Any idea how to spell that? *W A D L*," he began.

"No, I think it's *W H A T T* and then maybe *L E S B Y*."

"I'm not finding anything," said Matthew.

"Maybe that's not right," muttered Ogilvy. "But I believe it is."

"Do you remember his first name?"

In deep concentration, softly muttering combinations of names, was how Danbury and Officer Beck found the older gentleman when they returned.

"Officer Ogilvy, I need your statement now," said Beck. Matthew vacated the seat in front of the desk for the officer to slide into it, tablet in hand, and begin questioning. Ogilvy's account added that the fishing boat was slightly more than a football field away when the shot was fired. He had seen it too and validated Matthew's assertion that the guy was holding a fishing rod.

"OK," said the female officer from the corner. "I've reloaded your paper again, Sir. And I have everything duplicated twice so that you can keep a copy."

"I don't want one here!" exclaimed Sheila. "If it causes all of this."

"It won't now, My Dear," said Ogilvy to his daughter. "But she's right. We don't need any of that here."

"Mind if I take the original?" asked Danbury.

"It's rightfully yours," said Ogilvy.

"We've got the other two then?" asked the female officer. When nobody disagreed, she picked up both stacks and asked, "We done here, Boss?"

"For now," said Beck. "We'll leave the second car here. And swap out the next shift in a couple of hours. They'll be doing some foot patrol throughout the night, given the water frontage and that the shots were fired from there. They'll keep you informed when the new guys arrive," he added to the father and hovering daughter behind the big desk.

"Thank you," said Sheila, sounding genuinely grateful.

Sheila's phone dinged. Pulling it from her pocket, she announced, "It's Britton's brother. She's still in surgery, but he's gotten a report that it's going well. They're pinning bones and putting plates in place. It'll be a while before she's out."

"That's great news!" exclaimed Ogilvy. They all agreed.

After she'd shown the two uniformed officers out, Sheila returned to stand guard over her father, obviously wanting the plain-clothed officer out as well.

Ogilvy sat in his chair muttering in streams of consciousness with

Matthew and Danbury looking on. He said, so softly that they barely heard him, "The numbers as letters. I mean, the letters were numbers! I've seen that recently. The strings Conrad left, I'm sure they were coordinates, but the numbers were simply letters. Oh, I know!" he exclaimed with gusto. "I used the strings as passwords so that I wouldn't forget them. Sheila, get my notebook, please."

"Yes, Dad," she said obediently and wearily. From a wall safe behind a panel, she pulled a small leather-bound notebook and handed it to her father.

"It has all of my passwords in it, you see," Ogilvy explained to Matthew and Danbury. "Years ago, I could remember them all. But, years ago, I didn't have so many to remember!"

Flipping it open as Matthew pulled paper from the printer and a pen from the desk, Ogilvy called out: "CF.IVMI," Flipping pages, he then said jubilantly, "and -HB.CIHBJ!"

"OK," said Matthew, jotting the alphabet in block letters with a number assigned to each. "That's 36.922139 on the first string, and the second is -82.398210."

"Looks like coordinates. As you said," confirmed Danbury. "Thank you," he said, in a soothing voice that Matthew had only ever heard him use with Penn. "That's extremely helpful. If I caused this today, Sir," he added, and then paused, "I apologize."

"It's not your fault. I'm not sure if they were watching you or me. Either way, we know somebody is watching us both now. You more so now because I've shared everything I know."

"Everything you know that you know," said Matthew meaningfully. "I'm glad the police will be here for a few days. Hopefully, we can get to the bottom of this and find the 'them,' and then you can have peace again."

"Sometimes, Son, it's a little too peaceful around here." He smiled up at his daughter. "Do come back and see me, whether you figure this out or not. I'd like to have a real visit and shoot the breeze about old times. You do look so much like your dad, it's unbelievable," he added, shaking his head.

"Thank you, Sir," said Danbury, shoulders back, standing tall.

"Watch your six out there, Son. Somebody else is watching it."

"Yes, Sir," Danbury said, and they turned to leave.

"Don't forget your shirt," said Sheila. "The washer should be finished by now. Toss it in a bag," she added.

Sheila didn't bother to show them out. Instead, she wheeled her father to the elevator and tapped the button. "Are you ready for dinner, Dad? We have some leftover stuffed pork chops, new potatoes, and asparagus from last night," Matthew heard her offer as he and Danbury made their way down the stairs.

Pulling his sodden shirt from the wash, he stuffed it into a bag without looking to see if the stains were still there and followed Danbury out the front door. As promised, a police car remained in the circular drive. An officer inside was lit by the display of a computer screen on the dash in front of him.

"I need to call Penn," said Danbury as Matthew tossed the bag into the back of the SUV and climbed in. "We won't be back by seven."

"Hardly," said Matthew. To the left of house over the lake, the sun sinking.

"We'll be later. We have another stop to make. You need food now?"

"Where are we going?"

"To talk to Byrd. There's a signed statement from him. In Ogilvy's files. He said he was home. He saw a sedan leave, somewhere before noon. Like one he'd seen before. It's what he told us. He made that initial statement," said Danbury, "which was later replaced with one he didn't sign. I need to talk to him, pronto. He's withholding something else. I'm certain of it. And I think it's important. He can point us to whoever paid him off. Could be the killer."

"You think he saw the person who left your parents' house that morning?"

"It's possible. And we need the number strings. To see if they're coordinates."

"I can search for those," said Matthew, pulling his phone out. "Penn said chicken and dumplings tonight, right?"

"She did." Danbury nodded, grinning.

"I'll try to wait," said Matthew, buckling up as Danbury set their destination on the navigation app.

"Yeah, me too. She'll be fine that we're late if I call. She'd be madder if I wasn't hungry when I got there."

That, Matthew thought, was illogical because he'd never seen Danbury refuse food, ever. When Danbury ate, it was in mass quantities.

"Jason Byrd won't be happy to see us," Matthew said, tapping his phone to find the coordinates while Danbury tapped his to call Penn. "Maybe we should just tell him we discovered that we're his long-lost cousins."

Chuckling when she answered, Danbury agreed. "Hey, Penn."

Hearing one side of the conversation felt like eavesdropping, but it wasn't as if he could help it.

"I'm sorry," said Danbury. "We'll be later than seven. We got held up. We're just now leaving. And we have one more stop. It should be quick. No, you go ahead. Don't wait for us. Well, OK then. I'll see you in a couple of hours. Love you too."

It was strange hearing Danbury express feelings of any kind. Of course, he loves Penn, thought Matthew. They're planning a life together. It was the first time he'd heard Danbury say it aloud. He ached to talk to Cici, hear her voice, see her smiling at him with what he'd termed her bedroom eyes, the expression she wore only for him as she gazed lovingly at him.

Pushing those thoughts from his mind, he confirmed, "If these strings are coordinates, they are in the middle of nowhere in western Virginia."

After a moment of tapping and expanding the map on his phone, he added, "There's nothing but mountains that I can see from the satellite view. There's a narrow road near there. The nearest town looks to be to the west. Coalglow, Virginia. I've never heard of it. Have you?"

"I haven't," answered Danbury pensively, shaking his head.

"We're going tomorrow, aren't we?"

"If you're up for it, Doc. I'm going tomorrow."

15 ~ STUNG AGAIN

Danbury pulled along the curb in front of the house Jason Byrd had moved to all those years ago. The light in the center window above the front porch was lit, but not as brightly as before. Otherwise, the house was dark. The front porch light wasn't on, so Matthew assumed no cousins were imminently expected.

There was a knot in Matthew's stomach. He couldn't identify the reason he fought the urge to turn and run back to the SUV as they approached the front door. Danbury knocked loudly. Matthew's foot tapped on the boards of the small porch in anxious anticipation. There was no sound from within the house. Again, Danbury banged on the door, more loudly and insistently this time.

The door cracked open. This, thought Matthew, was the point in every horror flick where the whole audience cringed and screamed, "Don't go in there!" Maybe he was letting his imagination run away with him, but he didn't think so. Something was off. He could feel it.

Danbury moved in cautiously, weapon drawn.

"Jason Byrd?" he called out loudly. "Homicide Detective Warren Danbury. If you're here, answer me now!"

He hadn't motioned for Matthew to follow, and it would have made little difference. Matthew stepped to the side of the door, his back against the wall, listening intently. Danbury's footsteps grew quieter until they could no longer be heard. Danbury called out again from further inside the house. Nearby, a dog barked and another answered.

After a few moments hearing mostly his own breathing, which he tried to quiet, Matthew heard Danbury's returning footsteps, the cadence changed. He was climbing the stairs. Danbury's voice again called out to Byrd, identifying himself. Afterward, all was quiet within. Dogs barking in a nearby neighbor's yard sounded louder than they should. Matthew's heart thudded in his chest, until finally he heard Danbury summon him from inside.

"Hey, Doc! Can you come up? Second door on the right!" Danbury's voice was muffled, but it sounded urgent.

It wasn't what Matthew wanted to hear. He called back, "Is the house clear?"

"Of immediate threats, yes."

Not wanting to ask what that meant because he wasn't sure he wanted to know the answer, Matthew slunk through the doorway. Quietly, he made his way up the staircase with his back against the wall as he ascended. The staircase turned at a landing part way up. At the top, he made his way along the narrow hallway to the second door. Bending over a prone figure, Danbury looked up at Matthew in the doorway behind him.

"What do you make of this, Doc?" asked Danbury.

Splayed over a stool was Jason Byrd, his neck severed, with a pool of blood beneath the supine body.

"Somebody slit his throat," Matthew stated the obvious as he hovered in the doorway. "Did you touch the blood pool?"

"No. Why?"

"The blood isn't coagulating yet. This is recent. Is it warm?"

Danbury touched a gloved finger into the blood pool closest to the body.

"It's not warm. Or cold either. No obvious murder weapon. I'm calling it in," said Danbury reluctantly. "For whatever good that does."

"What has your precinct said about all of this?" asked Matthew.

"Not much," answered Danbury. "I've requested to work the old case. Now that it seems relevant. No response yet. I haven't been told no. But it hasn't been approved. They're not talking to me. If they're talking about it at all."

"I'll take some pictures from here and then get back downstairs so as not to contaminate the scene," offered Matthew. With his phone, he snapped pictures of the body and recorded a video of the surrounding room. Danbury joined him in the hallway. Pulling his gloves off inside out, he tapped his phone.

Descending the stairs together, carefully touching nothing, they stepped out onto the porch. Danbury provided the address and the details about finding the body to the dispatcher.

"Hey Doc," he said softly, looking all around them as they made their way to the sidewalk. Danbury pulled a bagged piece of paper from the pocket of his cargo pants and held it up for Matthew to examine. A chill ran down Matthew's spine. On a yellowed piece of paper, in the same blockish lettering as the note they'd found on the corpse in Jason Byrd's old house, was written:

YOU'VE A BAD BISHOP AND WE'RE NOT TO MIDDLE GAME.
I'VE GOT ALL THE COMBINATIONS. CALL ME MASTER.
PICK UP THE PACE, FISH, IT'S SUDDEN DEATH!
YOU'VE GOT 24 HOURS TO FORFEIT.

"What does that mean?" asked Matthew in nearly a whisper.

"Chess," said Danbury quietly. "The killer thinks this is a game. They're the master. I'm a fish."

"A fish?"

"A bad chess player. A novice. That much is true. My dad was teaching me to play. When I was a boy. I never played again. After he died."

"Oh," said Matthew. "This is personal."

"Apparently so. The killer is telling me I'll never catch him. At least that. And likely that he's after me."

"And the twenty-four hours to forfeit? That's a threat. At least he doesn't mention any more bodies dropping."

"Sudden death?"

"Oh. Yeah. Are you going to share that?" Matthew asked as Danbury stashed the note in the plastic sleeve back in the side pocket of his black cargo pants.

"I haven't decided. Maybe not. This was clearly meant for me. As you say, it's personal. I'm wondering who to trust."

"Why's that?"

"I'm being shut out. By my department. On the new investigation. The body dressed like my dad. It hasn't been assigned to me. And I'm not being looped in. I don't know where that is now."

"Speaking of, what about the physical evidence from the original case? Wasn't there something left of it?"

"I requested it. It can't be found. Suspiciously, it's missing. That was almost predictable."

"Because somebody doesn't want you seeing it," added Matthew.

"Right. The requisition is open. They'll notify me if it turns up," said Danbury sarcastically, making air quotes with his fingers.

"Any chance that'll happen?"

"Snowball in a microwave," he said. Thumbing his chin thoughtfully, Danbury added, "It depends on who's looking. Most of the officers are above board. Conscientious and all of that. I wish I knew which ones. It's rough thinking I can't rely on colleagues. People I should be able to trust with my life."

"Can you find out how the files and evidence disappeared? Or who might have tampered with them?" asked Matthew. "Is there a log of who accessed the files?"

"No," answered Danbury. "There should have been. Computerized records are recent. Paper files were easier to lose. Or alter. Without leaving a paper trail. People can 'lose' things—or be convinced to. Either by coercion or payoffs. Something like that had to have happened."

Matthew detected the hurt beneath the anger in Danbury's words. It must feel, Matthew thought, terribly defeating to know you're fighting a battle with enemies among your allies and not be able to determine which is which.

"You don't know who you can trust in your own precinct?"

"I don't," agreed Danbury. "I know a couple of guys well enough. But it's a huge department."

"What about this new note? Who might have known you played chess with your dad? That was a long time ago, but somebody remembered it."

"Conrad Manchester gave Dad the set. They played together some. Guys in their department probably knew."

"Maybe," said Matthew in a whisper, remembering Danbury's response to the carved chess set among his parents' belongings, "the killer saw the set in the storage unit and assumed."

"Doc, if you want out, I understand," said Danbury quietly. "You agreed to help with a cold case. It's far from cold. Somebody killed my parents or had them killed. And now somebody is after me. Too many parallels."

"Parallel lines don't cross."

"What?"

"If it's the same killer, now and over twenty years ago, there's a convergence point between your father's original investigation and your current one. The killer is at the center where your lines of inquiry meet, yours and your father's."

"OK," Danbury nodded, indicating he followed that logic so far.

"To get to that convergence point, we look for the things that the two investigations have in common."

"If we can determine what that is."

"If there are different killers and this is some sort of sick copycat, then the lines are parallel, yours and your father's. Either way, the killer, or killers, must be unhinged."

"Likely so, Doc," said Danbury. "Unhinged doesn't mean stupid. Probably the opposite."

"More like," said Matthew, and then added in his best evil voice, that sounded more like a goofy vampire than a deranged killer, "I want to take over the world!" It was getting late. Hungry and punchy, he attempted to relieve the stress tying him in knots.

Danbury couldn't help but chuckle at Matthew's attempt at levity. "Maybe not the whole world. Mine, apparently."

"Then we have to stop him. I agreed to help with this, and I keep my word. Here, I'll forward you the pictures I took inside," said Matthew softly, tapping his phone as the first emergency vehicles began to arrive on the scene.

"They'll want to talk to you. Eventually," said Danbury, meeting the first police cruiser and motioning to the house in apparent explanation to the officers who had slid out.

In no time, the street was alight with flashing red and blue lights. The following chaos made Matthew forget his stomach growling, though the lunches Penn had packed were gone hours ago. Chilly without his jacket, Matthew climbed into the SUV to wait. His foot tapping harder and faster than usual with frustration at his inactivity while a killer threatened, he watched.

Observing from the sidelines was frustrating. A uniformed officer began running yellow police tape around the perimeter. People gathered at the corners of the property along the sidewalk under street lights, all curiously slipping closer into loose groups.

As workers swarmed the house like a bee's nest full of honey, an unfamiliar ME's van pulled up. A medical examiner he'd seen before, and another person he hadn't, got out. Going to the back of the van, Tegan McFarland and a slender younger guy suited up and strode purposefully toward the house. Matthew wondered why the bug lady was on the scene. There had been no time for bugs to appear.

Danbury disappeared inside some time ago and hadn't reappeared when a uniformed officer tapped loudly on the SUV window beside Matthew's head. He opened the door to the officer waiting less than patiently. The guy's face seemed to be contorted into a permanent scowl. *Because I don't like the looks of him, doesn't make him a bad guy,* Matthew reminded himself.

16 ~ THE THIRD DEGREE

"How can I help you, Officer?" Matthew asked as he dropped onto the sidewalk and closed the SUV door soundly behind him.

"You're Doctor Matthew Paine?" the guy asked.

"I am," said Matthew when the guy waited for a reply, though it seemed a rhetorical question.

"You're here why?"

"Pardon?"

"You're here in what capacity? Do you have an official role?"

Initially unsure how to answer that question, Matthew said, "I'm a medical consultant with the police department."

"Were you expecting to consult? Medically?"

"I had no reason to think so. Today, I was mostly tagging along."

"Tell me, in your own words, what happened here," the officer instructed Matthew. "You arrived on the scene here with Detective Warren Danbury, right?"

Matthew refrained from asking how he'd respond in anyone else's words. Instead, he said politely, "That's correct, Officer. Danbury wanted to talk to Jason Byrd."

"About what?" asked the officer, staring hard at Matthew. It was a technique he'd seen Danbury use multiple times when questioning suspects.

"They were neighbors, years ago," said Matthew. "He lived across the street."

"And?" asked the officer when Matthew paused.

"And it was his former house, which now stands empty and is falling to shambles, where the first body was found," said Matthew bluntly.

"What did he want to talk to Byrd about?"

"He wanted to know if it was Byrd's unsigned statement that Danbury found in records from the initial investigation of his parents' death. In it, the witness stated that he was home all morning and saw no cars or foot traffic at the end of the street," answered Matthew with a partial truth.

"He wanted to ask Jason Byrd about a morning over twenty years ago?"

"That's right," said Matthew.

"OK," said the officer, looking unconvinced. "What else?"

"What do you mean, what else?"

"He wouldn't have come all the way up here just for that. There had to have been more."

Mentally reviewing the theories they'd postulated, Matthew chose the least likely, one they hadn't seriously considered recently.

"The airport expansion," he answered. "Somebody had been buying up the properties on the road where they lived. Jason Byrd moved away suddenly. Danbury wanted to ask him who bought the house and why he moved out abruptly, leaving everything behind."

"What time did you get here?" asked the officer, changing his line of questioning.

"That's a good question," said Matthew, checking the time on his phone. "It was mostly dark. Around eight, I think."

"What did you do when you got here?"

"We got out of the car, went up to the porch, and Danbury knocked."

"Was there an answer?"

Matthew looked at the guy as if that were the most ridiculous question he'd ever heard, but he drew a deep breath, and replied, "No. There was no answer."

"Was the door closed?"

"It looked to be at first."

"How did it get opened? Did one of you tamper with it?"

"No. Neither of us tampered with the door. Danbury knocked on it. When there was no answer, he knocked again, harder. When he did, the door opened."

"And then what happened?"

"Danbury inched inside, with his weapon drawn, calling out to Byrd and identifying himself."

"Did you follow him in?"

"No."

"Did Detective Danbury invite you in?"

"Not at first. I stood outside listening."

"What did he say?"

"He asked if Byrd was in there and identified himself."

"Warren Danbury, Homicide Detective?"

"Exactly."

"That's what he said?"

"It is."

"Then what?"

"I heard footsteps walking around the downstairs of the house, Danbury's I presumed. He called out again, asking Byrd if he was there, if he was OK, and identifying himself by name and title. Then I heard footsteps going up the stairs and Danbury called out one more time, upstairs saying the same thing."

"And then?"

"Then he called to me, asking me to come upstairs. He asked what I made of the murder scene."

"You went in the room?"

"No. I paused in the doorway and told Danbury to check the temperature of the blood because it hadn't coagulated yet. I assumed this murder was recent. The blood looked fresh. It could have drained from the body slowly, but it would have ceased after the heart stopped pumping. It had to have happened just before we got here."

"In your opinion, the murder had just happened when you got here?"

"Right. Very shortly before we arrived. But ask your ME. I'm sure she can get closer on the time and method of death than I can."

"Did Warren Danbury have a weapon in his possession?"

"Yes," said Matthew, losing patience with the questioning. "He drew it when he entered the house."

"A handgun?"

"Right."

"Did he have another weapon?"

"No."

"Let me rephrase the question, Doctor Paine. Is it possible that he had another weapon? Other than his handgun?"

"None that I saw or was aware of," Matthew responded, thinking this guy sounded more like a lawyer than a police officer.

"Did you see any weapons in the house?"

"I went straight to the room where the body was. I went in the front door and immediately up the stairs. . . ."

"And into the room?" the officer asked, pointedly.

"What? No. I observed the scene from the doorway. I never actually entered it."

"And you saw no weapons in the room?"

"No. I didn't see a weapon in the room with Byrd's body or anywhere on my way up to that room. Whatever caused that sort of damage must have been extremely sharp."

"Did you go through the rest of the house afterward?"

"No. We left after Danbury checked the blood temperature and I assessed the scene from the doorway."

"You left immediately after you saw the body?"

"Right."

"Did Detective Danbury linger in the house? Did he stay behind?"

"No, he went out ahead of me."

"Did he go back in the house?"

"Not until the other officers got here. He entered behind them."

"OK," said the officer, sounding annoyed. "I'll write up the report, and I'll need you to sign it."

"OK," said Matthew, mimicking the annoyance in the officer's voice and vowing to himself to read every word carefully before he signed anything. It felt like a witch hunt. The officer seemed to be questioning Danbury's involvement in the murder. That, Matthew thought, was ridiculous. But if it had worked with his father . . . he wouldn't allow himself to finish that thought.

Matthew waited, leaning on the SUV under the street light, watching the coming and going from the house. Finally, a stretcher with a body bag was wheeled and loaded into the medical examiner's van before it pulled away. Tegan McFarland gave Matthew a wave of recognition when she spotted him.

When Danbury returned, he was finishing a conversation on the phone. By his tone, Matthew knew it was with Penn. He looked haggard as he told her they'd be there in about twenty minutes.

"Hey, Doc. Did they rake you over the coals?"

"Me?" he asked in a whisper. "I'm fine. Looks like you had a rough time. Do they seriously think you had anything to do with this murder?"

"Not likely. More wish than actual thought."

"How so?"

"I've been ordered to stand down. Not to investigate this murder. Or the one at Byrd's house. Or the original one, my parents' murder. It's being closed. I've been threatened with administrative leave. If I don't comply."

"Oh," said Matthew quietly. "What are you going to do?"

"Take a little vacation time. Maybe go fishing."

"Fishing?"

"Do you like mountain trout?"

"Umm, sure," said Matthew hesitantly.

"Great. I know a place in Virginia. Mountain streams, lots of fish. We leave in the morning," said Danbury sliding behind the wheel. Circling the vehicle quickly, Matthew climbed in before Danbury all but peeled out.

Initially, Matthew was silent, weighing his words before he spoke. Finally, he said, "We might be walking into a killer's trap. Conrad Manchester could have killed your parents."

"Anything is possible. But I don't think so."

"Based on what?"

Blowing out a deep breath, Danbury said, "I've been considering that. It's more than a gut feeling. And not just because my father trusted him. There's something else. I can't quite identify it."

Leaning back into his seat, Matthew changed the subject. "Did you find a murder weapon in the house?"

"We did."

"Where was it?"

"In the downstairs trash."

"Oh! Not in a knife rack or drawer?"

"No. It was meant to be found."

"What sort? It had to be sharp to do that kind of damage."

"It is. A dagger. A short sword. Think Arabian Nights. Curved. Razor sharp. Deadly."

"The killer left that behind?"

"Yup. In the kitchen trashcan under the sink. He went out the back door. Left it standing open."

"That's pretty brazen."

"That depends."

"On what?"

"The motive for leaving it behind. They'll find no prints. I'm sure it's wiped clean."

"What are you saying?"

"They want to pin it on me. I was questioned. Ad nauseam. He got nowhere fast. Then he came out to talk to you. What did you tell him?"

"As little as possible. The guy was antagonistic and rubbed me all the wrong way. If anything, I gave them red herrings."

"Such as?"

"I told him we wanted to talk to Byrd about why he moved and who bought the house. We did, but I neglected to mention that we already had. And about the reason the properties were bought up in your old neighborhood. As if we still thought that the runway extension had anything to do with all of this."

"We're not sure it doesn't."

"Aren't we?"

Danbury shrugged. "I wish I knew. The more we learn, the more questions I have."

"Isn't that always the case?" asked Matthew.

"It is, but this is personal. And I'm being targeted. By a killer. And by my own department apparently."

"Did you show them the note?"

"No. And that's telling."

"How so?"

"Weren't you questioned relentlessly?"

"Yeah, I was."

"More stringently than before?"

"Well, except by you last year. When you thought I had something to do with killing a new patient I had seen exactly once."

"Touché," said Danbury. "But from other investigations."

"I was trying to make light of this. It's a coping mechanism," Matthew explained. "I agree this time was different. I was scrutinized more closely, and yes, I think the officer knew I was withholding something."

"Exactly. He knew I was too. How could he know that?"

"Ah," said Matthew, understanding. "Somebody knows about that note. And they know that you're not sharing it."

"Right. Somebody on the inside. Maybe they're behind it."

"Maybe they're following orders," said Matthew.

"They must know what's happening. And coming after me. Instead of going after the killer. A criminal mastermind with a badge. Or one who has control of badges. That's the worst kind. I'm being targeted to look guilty. Instead of being allowed to investigate. I am too close to this. That's valid. But administrative leave? That's harsh."

"Cases you've worked before were difficult and frustrating, but I see how this one is different."

"This is much more frustrating. Every time I think we have a direction," Danbury began, "we get sidetracked with something else. Either with pieces of a puzzle that we can't see how they fit. Or as red herrings that somebody is throwing at us. To get us off track."

17 ~ WINNER, WINNER

When they arrived at the Lingle Plantation, Matthew wasn't certain if he was more exhausted or famished. Penn warmed the chicken dumplings and side dishes. She insisted he had to eat, so he might as well stay for a very late dinner. Too tired and hungry to argue, Matthew agreed.

Penn looked quizzically at Matthew's shirt. She seemed to recognize it as Danbury's but wisely chose not to ask.

"Oh, Whattlesby!" said Matthew suddenly, swallowing his last forkful.

"What?" asked Penn. Winking at him, she added, "That's a new swear word I've never heard before."

"I forgot to tell you that Ogilvy came up with the name of the foreign diplomat that Iron Clad provided security for. That's one more thing we need to figure out."

"Whattlesby?" repeated Danbury.

"Does that mean something to you?" asked Penn.

"I'm not sure," said Danbury. "I think I've heard it before. But I can't place it."

"I did a quick search online before we left Ogilvy. I didn't find anything," said Matthew.

"Database access," muttered Danbury in frustration.

"What database?" asked Penn.

"Some I could search for that name. At the office. I've been told to take some time off. I'm sure I'm being watched. My actions are monitored. I wish I knew how closely."

"I know how to get that information," said Matthew.

"Let's hear it," said Danbury.

"Justin. He has access to resources that you don't right now."

"Yeah, OK," said Danbury reluctantly, before loading his plate with another helping.

"I saw the document you've been updating, but it sounds like I'm still missing a few things," said Penn, looking concerned. "Catch me up?"

As Danbury explained what happened that day, between bites, Matthew retrieved his cell phone to contact his lifelong best friend, Justin McMillian. They'd been friends since preschool. Though their careers were nothing alike, their basic personalities, likes and dislikes, were eerily similar.

Justin was in some branch of a military or government agency job that he couldn't talk about. Which agency, exactly, and what he did, precisely, Matthew didn't know.

"Hey, are you where you could help me with a database search?" Matthew texted.

To Danbury, he asked, "Anything I can't tell Justin about what we're working on, if he asks?"

"I guess not," said Danbury, who had worked with Justin in the past. Initially, Danbury had been suspicious of him. They'd come to an understanding, if not full appreciation, and mutual respect for each other. "You're right. He can do things I can't. Right now, probably a lot of them."

"What's in western Virginia?" Penn asked as Danbury filled her in on their plans for the following day. She served Matthew peach cobbler she insisted he should try.

"Hopefully, my father's friend, Conrad Manchester. Manchester and Ogilvy left the police force about the same time." Danbury explained what they'd learned from Brian Ogilvy.

"It's one more reason to find Manchester," he said. "His weapon killed my father. Ogilvy's fingerprints were on the bullets. That's documented in the files Ogilvy gave us. If any of that was true. A third person was at the house. The morning my parents were killed. Ogilvy swears it wasn't either of them. Neither he nor Manchester. We need Manchester's version of it. Maybe he didn't kill my parents, but he was a suspect."

"With no motive and an alibi," added Matthew.

"True," agreed Danbury. "One that he shouldn't have had. If his wife had been at work."

Matthew's phone dinged with Justin's response. "Sure. What do you need?"

Matthew summarized the situation as succinctly as possible. "Whattlesby. Anything you can find. He was a political figure in the late 1990s. Maybe Kenyan. There's nothing about him online."

"Give me a few minutes. I'll let you know."

"Thanks, Dude," texted Matthew, hoping to give Justin a smile. As kids, they'd tried to see how many times they could get the word "dude" into a sentence. Mostly, it was to annoy Matthew's older sister, Monica, and rarely failed to do so.

A laughing emoji from Justin told Matthew that he'd succeeded.

Matthew finished the peach cobbler and was saying his goodbyes when his phone dinged. "It's Justin," he said, pausing by the front door.

Matthew read Justin's texted response aloud, "Sorry, Man. A quick search didn't find much. See attached note."

Matthew texted back his thanks, opened the attached note, and read:

> *Lemako Whattlesby 1951 - ???. Kenyan political official from Samburu region. Current whereabouts unknown, potentially deceased. Friendly to US. Worked with US Ambassador Patricia Shrubpeal until his disappearance in*

1998. Supposed to have met her at the US embassy in Nairobi at 10 a.m. on the morning of August 7. Embassy was bombed at 10:30 a.m. that morning.

Shrubpeal was injured in the blast, survived, and toured the wreckage the following day. Sources are limited. some discrepancy as to whether Lemako Whattlesby was killed in the blast, or if he was in the building at the time. See news sources on the incident—trucks containing bombs pulled in front of the building, later blamed on twenty-one members of the Al Qaeda terrorist group, including Osama bin Laden. Whattlesby's name isn't included in those news reports, just Shrubpeal's.

Back then, embassies were on public streets, not behind protective fencing. There's some insinuation that Whattlesby was trying to warn the US embassy that there was a bomb being driven in by truck. No records exist on Whattlesby after August 7, 1998. Conclusion: either he was killed in the bombing or he went into hiding immediately afterward.

Matthew exclaimed aloud, "It was after August 7, 1998!"

"What was?" asked Penn.

"When Ogilvy provided security for Whattlesby. "Here," said Matthew, handing his phone to Danbury. "See for yourself."

After a moment of reading and rereading the note, Danbury looked over. "This guy isn't dead," he said at last.

"Nope. At least, he wasn't killed in the blast if Ogilvy is right about who he was providing security for afterward."

"Ogilvy's mind is still sharp. He wouldn't forget a name like that."

"He never saw the guy, though," said Matthew. "It might have been Whattlesby. But who knows? It could have been a cover up for his death. It could have been anybody. The security detail, and who knows who else, was told that they were guarding a guy named Whattlesby."

"That's possible," said Danbury, thumbing the stubble on his chin. "Entirely possible. To what end?"

"Using Whattlesby as bait maybe? Don't ask me for what. I have no idea. We don't know enough yet to speculate. Or if it's even related."

"True," said Danbury. "We need more information."

"We do," said Matthew. "We could really use Justin's help now. I can tell him what we know from Ogilvy and ask if he can find out anything about that specifically. About Iron Clad providing security for someone using the name Whattlesby after the bombing in Nairobi. If he has time to help, he could be working that angle, however that fits, while we look for Manchester."

Danbury hesitated, so Matthew continued, "We can trust Justin, you know that. He sent what he could find about Whattlesby, so he knows that much. We need to ask for his help and get him up to speed on all we know so far. See what he can find out about your parents' murder and whatever else we need help with. This is in his wheelhouse if there's something going on that involves the Kenyan embassy bombing. I'm guessing he's CIA because he travels internationally."

"NSA," said Danbury quietly.

"What?" asked Matthew. "How do you know?"

"Something he said in Miami last year. Or one of his buddies said it. He isn't CIA. My bet is NSA."

"OK, all the more reason to involve him. This could well involve a national security issue from 1998 that's resurfacing now. Maybe it's an older threat, but that doesn't mean that it isn't ongoing."

"Possibly," said Danbury, rubbing his thumb over his chin.

"Maybe he can track down Patricia Shrubpeal, the ambassador to Kenya who was there at the bombing. If she's still around."

"Hang on," said Penn, tapping her phone. After a moment, she announced, "She'd be in her late seventies now, but there's no date of death, at least according to this search."

Danbury replied softly, "Yeah, go ahead."

Matthew stepped out onto the porch as he tapped to text Justin asking if he could call.

"Give me five," Justin texted back.

"OK, call when you can," texted Matthew.

Danbury was quiet, which wasn't unusual. What was unusual for Danbury were the creased worry lines in his face that Matthew could see clearly in the dim light on the front porch.

"What's the plan for tomorrow?" asked Matthew.

"I'll rent a car. Leave early. Find the road where the coordinates cross. See what's around there. Wear or bring hiking gear. Who knows where we'll end up."

"Oh. You can't drive your SUV if its government issue and you've been taken off of the case, can you?" said Matthew, motioning to the black SUV parked at the end of the porch.

Danbury's expression was agonized. "No, I can't. But neither can I walk away. I know my parents were murdered. That's clear. I owe it to them to know why. And by whom. I owe it to myself. And now somebody is killing again. I don't know how much time we have. And no idea who they'll target next."

"What time do we leave? Are we meeting here?"

"Yeah, how does five work?"

Matthew grimaced as he checked his watch and saw it was nearly midnight.

"Six then?"

"Yeah, I'll be here at six. Maybe five thirty if we get breakfast on the road."

"Deal. It's a good four hours or more up there. Bring extra clothes, in case."

"Got it," agreed Matthew.

As he was about to step off the porch, Penn reached over and hugged him. She said softly in his ear, "Thank you, Matthew. I really appreciate you helping Warren, especially since you wanted nothing more to do with police work. You're a good friend."

Having agreed to meet Danbury at six the next morning for the trip to western Virginia, he was anxious to get home to what little sleep he could manage. His phone sounded from where he'd placed it on the dash, and he clicked to answer the incoming call.

"Hey, Man," said Justin. "What's going on?"

"I need your help," said Matthew, and then clarified. "Actually, Danbury needs your help."

"And he's admitting it?" asked Justin incredulously, chuckling.

"He is," answered Matthew.

"It must be bad then," said Justin seriously. "Tell me what's going on."

Starting from the beginning, Matthew described how Danbury's parents had been killed when he was twelve, the original case, and the things they'd learned since Danbury began unofficially investigating.

"You think it's the same person behind it all?" asked Justin.

"It's likely," said Matthew. "Otherwise, why would they care so much about what Danbury does? If the killer were smart, he'd have backed off and waited to see if anything potentially damaging turned up in Danbury's investigation. That first body was killed right after Danbury's grandmother died. They didn't wait around to see what he'd learn."

"Unless he had already found something important," said Justin. "Didn't you say he'd started looking into it just before his grandmother died?"

"I'm not clear on whether it was just before or just after her death. Somebody knows a lot about his family, though. They knew the storage unit was there before he did, and that it contained his parents' belongings. Pretty much everything from their house except clothing. Somebody knew the houses were still there, his parents and the one across the street, and they knew he'd start looking."

"Is it possible that it's this Conrad Manchester guy?"

"Anything is possible. Danbury doesn't think so. Maybe it's a gut feeling. Or it could be his confidence in his father's ability to assess people's character. Manchester's wife was killed a few months after Danbury's parents. At least, it looks like she was killed. The investigation details on her death are scant, and the case was closed quickly as a single-car accident. Why would Manchester kill his alibi if he had killed Danbury's parents? His rumored motive was that he had feelings for Danbury's mother. She was already dead by then, so why bother to kill his own wife after the fact?"

"None of that adds up," agreed Justin. "I'm sure we're missing a lot, so it makes no sense yet. I'll help out however I can, starting with finding Patricia Shrubpeal. She was there at the embassy bombing. She should know best who was and wasn't alive afterward. If he survived the blast, Lemako Whattlesby might still be alive. He would be slightly younger than Shrubpeal. By a few years, I think. Is there anything else you need?"

"A location on Conrad Manchester. The strings of letters that Ogilvy provided look like latitude and longitude coordinates. That could get us close. From the satellite earth view of the location, it's in the middle of nowhere, miles from the nearest town. We're going to check it out tomorrow morning."

"I don't have to tell you to be careful," said Justin thoughtfully. "I'd come with you if I could, but I'm tied up in DC until Monday."

"I wasn't going to ask," said Matthew. "We could be walking into a killer's trap, but Danbury doesn't think so. I'll mention the possibility again, though. Loudly."

"OK. I'll be in touch. And Matthew," said Justin, and paused. "You have weapons and a concealed carry license. I know you've taken an oath to do no harm, but it's probably a good idea to get them out and take them with you."

"Yeah, you're right. Thanks, Man."

Talking about weapons made Matthew wonder about the one that killed Danbury's parents. If the physical evidence from the investigation was missing, where was the gun now? Had Conrad Manchester gotten it back? Or was it truly misplaced somewhere in evidence lockup because the case had neither been solved nor officially closed?

The missing physical evidence seemed to be key to answering many of their questions.

Going through his usual evening routine at home, Matthew texted Cici telling her to contact him early in the morning, around five, if she was able. He set an alarm in case she still couldn't get a connection. Slumping into bed, exhausted, he removed Max from around his head and drifted off to sleep. Fitful dreams of missing things and people that he couldn't find ran through his head in the night.

18 ~ GO WEST

Matthew was relieved the annoying noise dredging him from troubled dreams was the sound of his phone and Cici requesting a video chat. After their morning greetings, Matthew decided to get right to the point and address what was bothering him.

"Are you getting cold feet about marrying me, Cees?"

"What? Why would you ask me that?"

"Because when you left in January, you didn't want to leave. You've been cautioning me to be careful ever since to come home and marry me. Until recently. You refused to come home before the world shut down and travel became impossible. Now you're stuck in London and we have no idea how to get you home. I wish you'd come home when you could have," he groused and immediately felt small for it.

He was cranky; he needed coffee.

"Me too. I can't begin to tell you how much I wish that now! But I was so close to being finished here. There were only a few remaining contracts to sign and one final detail to work out, and I could have come home, fait accompli."

Matthew blew out a deep breath, trying to reset and relax.

"I swear to you, it's the truth. I'm not getting cold feet," she added. "I want to build a life with you. And I do wish I'd come home when I could have. I mean, I believed you that the COVID virus could become a pandemic when you warned me a couple of months ago. What I didn't begin to comprehend was how quickly that would happen or how completely it would bring the world to a screeching halt. I'm sorry I didn't take it more seriously. I'd give anything to be home now, as planned, back in your arms where I belong."

That last statement sent a warm sensation through Matthew's body, and he smiled at her earnest face.

"I wish you were back here in my arms too, Cees."

"I'm trying not to think about it because I'm homesick for North Carolina and my life there, but mostly for you. I try to distract myself from thinking about it constantly."

"Me too. I'm trying. I haven't been very successful, though," Matthew confessed.

"Me neither. I have to try because I'd go crazy if I let myself dwell on how badly I want to be home with you." Then she added in the honied voice that was just for him, "I would give so much to be there with you right now, curled up between you and Max."

Max had settled in beside where he was propped in bed.

"You'd share the bed with my cat?" asked Matthew, incredulously.

"If it meant being there with you, I absolutely would."

"Wow, you really do miss me," teased Matthew.

"I do. With every fiber of my being, I long for you."

He agreed wholeheartedly. Changing the subject to ease the longing that couldn't be fulfilled, he told her he was going to the mountains for a few days with Danbury. His connection, he explained with a boyish grin, might be unreliable. Outlining how he was trying to help Danbury, he omitted the recent murders but explained why they needed to find Conrad Manchester.

"You're sure this guy isn't dangerous?" Cici asked, simply.

"Danbury trusts him. I trust Danbury," Matthew responded.

Knowing what her response would be to working with Danbury again, he also knew she had no grounds to lecture him now about being careful. Apparently knowing it too, she didn't.

Promising to stay in touch as best he could, they reluctantly said their goodbyes and Matthew went for coffee and a hot shower. Max, disturbed by the motion, jumped up looking offended. An overflowing bowl of food for his breakfast, and two extra bowls set out because Matthew had no idea when he'd be home, appeased the big cat. Matthew added extra bowls of water and figured he could call Mrs. Drewer, who had a key to his condo, and have her check on Max if he were gone more than a day or two.

Dressing casually, Matthew donned cargo pants he'd recently acquired, a short-sleeved T-shirt under a flannel shirt, and slip-on dock shoes. He packed his hiking boots, thick socks, and a change of clothes into a duffel bag. His jacket over the shirts should provide a layer against the wind and additional warmth in the still-cool mountain mornings and evenings.

Before he left his bedroom, he retrieved his Glock 19 and his Browning 1911 from the locked safe in the top of his closet. He added ammunition, holsters, his concealed carry permit, and magazines to a travel bag. That, he put in the duffel bag with his clothes. Scratching Max on the head one last time, he set out.

It was quarter to six when he arrived at the Lingle Plantation and Danbury waited for him, sitting on the porch with bags of lunch packed.

"I reserved an SUV like this one. Online. It's over near the airport. Penn's going to drop us off."

"She doesn't have to do that. We can take the Element to pick it up. Is there a place to leave it for a day or two?"

"Should be. It's a huge lot. If you're OK with that."

"No problem."

"I'll tell Penn," he said, handing over the lunch bags and a duffel. Matthew recognized it as the one usually in the back of his state-issued SUV.

Piling it all in the Element, they climbed in and headed west.

As if it pained him, Danbury asked, "What did Justin say?"

"He's going to find Patricia Shrubpeal. He'll ask about the

possibility that Lemako Whattlesby is still alive—or at least if he survived the explosion at the US Embassy in Nairobi in 1998. She was injured herself, but she would know—if anybody would."

"If she'll tell us," said Danbury.

"Good point," admitted Matthew.

When they arrived at the car rental agency, a dark green Chevrolet Tahoe SUV that looked like the black one Danbury usually drove waited for them. Danbury signed papers and slipped them through a slot. A tired-looking attendant reiterated that the car had been thoroughly cleaned and sanitized and wished them safe travels.

Danbury clicked the key to unlock the SUV and moved his duffel bag and their lunches into it while Matthew pulled out his bag and locked the Element. Chucking his bag in the back, Matthew climbed in, and they set off again.

Taking I-40 west and following it as it turned north, Danbury drove while Matthew searched his phone for his favorite biscuit fast-food drive through. It had originated two counties west of Peak and hadn't made it to Raleigh yet, but they would be going by several of them on interstate exits. Ignoring the navigation app on Danbury's phone mounted on the dash, Matthew directed them to the biscuits.

Back on the road, they made fast work of the biscuits and coffee—that even Danbury had to admit was great coffee—and settled in. Danbury tapped the stereo button, finding a pop station of music they could agree on, as they merged onto Highway 421 to head west before turning north into Virginia. When the radio station was out of range, Danbury turned it off, and they rode in silence.

Trusting a guy because Danbury trusted him, because his father had, felt hollow now. Danbury didn't know Manchester. On his way to who knew where, Matthew wondered if it was really that simple.

"What do you think we're going to find up there?" he asked.

"Hopefully Conrad Manchester. And some answers," said Danbury.

"Do you think Manchester is dangerous?"

"Depends on who you are," said Danbury after considering for a moment. "To me, no. To you with me, no. I think he'll be wary. He went into hiding for a reason."

"Meaning what?"

"Meaning we tread carefully. We don't rush in. We take things on his terms. If we can find him. No demands. He's doing us a favor. If he agrees to talk to us."

"Got it," said Matthew, and they lapsed into silence.

Eventually, they turned off the highway onto a two-lane road. The next turn was onto a narrow twisting road. It was paved, but there were no lines painted on it. Not that there could have been lines—it wasn't wide enough for two cars to pass in most places along it. Shoulders widened out occasionally, and Matthew assumed that's how you'd deal with meeting an oncoming car. One or both drivers would have to pull to the shoulder to pass.

After twisting around the mountain road for at least a half hour, Danbury slowed to a crawl, pulled over, and tapped the navigation app on his phone.

"We're close."

"We just passed a gravel road off to the right back there," Matthew said, thumbing over his shoulder. "It was probably less than a quarter of a mile back. It wound off uphill before that last curve."

"Yeah, I saw it. Let's go another half mile," said Danbury. "See if there's anything this way. If not, we'll double back. And check the dirt road."

No roads, paved or otherwise, presented themselves—merely two more turnouts for passing, one on either side of the road. A sheer rock face went straight up on their right, and trees dotted the drop to a valley below on the left.

"Back to the dirt road," said Danbury, absently thumbing his chin that had a days' worth of blond stubble on it. Making a three-point turn, he reversed direction and they scanned the roadsides again.

"There," said Matthew pointing.

"We'll see where it goes," said Danbury.

"It goes up," said Matthew, feeling the need to lighten the mood.

Danbury grunted unappreciatively in response.

The slope above the dirt road was steep but traversable with the large vehicle as it climbed, back and forth, wending upward. Four-wheel drive and lower gears got them to a plateau where a massive tree blocked the ascending path.

Another path descending was the only option. Danbury took the path down, winding and bumping slowly over the rutted trail until it ended at a river or wide creek. Rocks jutted out across the water, but too sporadically to cross.

Turning around was difficult. Managing that, Danbury maneuvered back the way they'd come. Scanning the tree lines and thick undergrowth on either side, they saw nothing resembling a pathway, even a foot trail. At the downed tree, Danbury stopped, got out, and paced the area. Climbing over the tree, his head and shoulders were all that was visible as he examined it from the other side.

"OK, Doc," said Danbury. "Here's where we get out. Got your hiking boots?"

"They're in the back," said Matthew. Alighting, he retrieved them with a pair of thick socks from his bag.

"So is our lunch," said Danbury. "Penn and I made sandwiches last night. Roast beef. Hope you like carrots. We have those and hummus."

Matthew prepared for the trek. Lacing his hiking boots and checking the Glock one last time, he strapped on the body holster over his soft T-shirt. Over that, he buttoned a flannel shirt for the still cool morning—cooler in the higher altitude. He stashed water bottles in each of the large side pockets of his new cargo pants. Shrugging into his jacket, he carefully placed the wrapped lunch into the pockets and figured he was ready.

19 ~ INTO THE WOODS

Following Danbury, Matthew climbed over the giant downed tree. They ascended a path that wound through the woods. It might have once been wide enough for a vehicle to traverse before saplings had begun to grow along the edges. Low-hanging branches with budding green leaves swiped at them as they passed. After each turn, Matthew expected to see something new, a house or a clearing, but the trail wound upward without interruption.

Trekking through dried leaves from the previous fall, Matthew saw new growth sprouting all around him. The winter had been a mild one, the early spring a wet one, and the world was coming to life again. Matthew was always up for a hike through the woods on a spring day, though he wished it were purely for enjoyment. Both sides of the trail were dotted in vibrant color. Against the backdrop of sprouting green leaves, grasses, and weeds were wildflowers and trees beginning to bloom in profusions of pinks, purples, whites, and yellows.

Matthew and Danbury were deep in conversation about the progress they'd made on the case and the things they still needed to learn. The first question was the number of murderers involved. Were they looking for two, one of Danbury's parents and a second copy-catting that crime over twenty years later? Or were there three, a different murderer at each scene? A single murderer could have committed all three crimes or hired hit men. A single murderer who had staged two scenes comparable to that of Danbury's father—one more so than the other—would do so to make a statement, they agreed.

"The forensic entomologist said the unidentified man in Jaber's house had been dead two days or less," Matthew summarized, breathing deeply as they climbed a steep bit of the path. "That sets the murder nearer to the middle of last week, probably Wednesday. The body was likely staged there on Thursday with the borrowed Ford Aerostar. That's not long to put all of that together. How did he or she know you'd be digging into the death of your parents before you started looking? Or had you already started before your grandmother died?"

"I had been poking around. A little bit. Not in obvious ways."

"It feels like it's been a lot longer," said Matthew.

"It does," Danbury agreed. "I thought she'd go faster. The Friday before. We nearly lost her then. But she rallied. And hung on three more days. She looked frail. She was tougher than she looked. More than anybody gave her credit for."

"I'm sorry you lost her," said Matthew.

"I lost her a long time ago," Danbury replied. "She hadn't known who I was for a while."

They climbed in silence until Matthew broke it by voicing his thoughts aloud. "The killer must have had the victim in his sights before, somebody who resembled your dad. But how did he know the right time to act? Was that the catalyst?"

"You mean my grandmother's death?"

"Right."

"Inside information. It had to have been. Somebody knew her condition. Knew I'd wait until she was gone. But then I'd begin the search. To learn what happened to my parents."

"Nobody had been to see her recently or asked about her at the facility where she was?"

"The manager asked the staff. Nobody knew of other visitors. Just me. And Penn checked on her a couple of times."

"There must be a tie. Maybe somebody who works there was paid off for information. Or bribed or blackmailed."

"That's all possible."

"How else could somebody know all of that, about her condition? I didn't know before last week," said Matthew. "It was all happening in tandem somehow. Her death, your questions, delving into the files from the investigation twenty-two years ago. Somebody knew you'd want to prove your father's innocence, but how did they know when?"

"My father is innocent. I know that. Beyond doubt."

Matthew didn't think this was an earth-shattering revelation. It was the assumption they'd been operating under all along, and one Danbury had definitively concluded the day before. He waited for him to continue.

"If he had been guilty, our investigation now would parallel somebody else's back then. But he wasn't guilty. He was investigating. Not being investigated. It's like you said. Our lines of inquiry are crossing, his and mine. The same killer has to be at that convergence point. I'd stake my reputation on it. The killer is a seasoned pro. With access to resources."

Matthew provided no immediate response to Danbury's assertion, except to think that the big detective's reputation was indeed on the line. Whether he was right or wrong might not matter. Before he had a chance to ponder that or discuss it further, Danbury stopped suddenly and stood completely still.

"Doc," said Danbury. "Hold up. Put your arms out. Away from your body."

Glancing over at the big detective, Matthew saw Danbury had done as he was instructing. "What is it?" he asked.

"We're not alone. Haven't been for a while. Now we're being joined."

"Joined?" asked Matthew. "By who?"

"By me," said a deep, resonant voice behind them that grew closer as its owner spoke. "You'd do well to take his advice. Keep your hands where I can see them. And don't move."

Matthew had frozen in place at the sound of the voice. Moving, even a twitch, wasn't on his agenda.

"Doc, meet Conrad Manchester," Danbury said. "The man we came to find. He's been following us. The past two miles."

Cuing off of the lack of alarm in Danbury's voice, Matthew simply said, "Almost since we got out of the SUV. How did you know?"

"The tree blocking the road. It didn't fall there. It was put there. On purpose. We were on camera."

"You might have told me," grumbled Matthew under his breath, but loudly enough for Danbury to hear.

"Couldn't. He'd have known you knew. Seen it in your behavior. I didn't want to scare him off."

"Stop talking and start walking," said the voice behind them. "Follow that path to your left. That's it. Keep your hands where I can see them and keep going. I'll tell you when to stop."

They'd trekked for what felt like the rest of the day but was probably an hour or so, in Matthew's estimation, back down the hill. The voice behind them suddenly said, "Hold up. Hand over your phones, slowly, no sudden motions."

"Our phones?" asked Matthew, surprised the demand hadn't been for their weapons. Matthew could feel the Glock 19 in the holster under his jacket. He knew Danbury likely had two concealed, one under his shirt at his waist and another strapped above his right ankle on the outside of his lower calf.

"That's what I said. You first," he said to Matthew. "Reach into your right pocket, and pull it out slowly. Then turn around and hand it over."

"OK," said Matthew, pulling out his phone. He held it aloft as he slowly turned around. Unsure if he was supposed to look at the man who still held a rifle on them, Matthew looked down at his phone, then held it out, with his eyes averted to the ground.

"Your turn, Erik's son," said the voice after he'd taken the phone.

Matthew didn't look up. In his peripheral vision, he saw Danbury hand over his phone as he said, "Warren. Warren Danbury."

"I know who you are, and I knew you'd be coming. You're just better at this than I'd hoped. You got here faster than I was ready for. Turn left and keep moving."

They'd left the dense tree cover and stepped out onto a gravel road that looked like the one they'd come in on. It was traveled enough to keep it clear, but nothing more. In another fifteen minutes, Matthew was proved correct in his assumption as Danbury's rented SUV came into view.

"We've determined that you can follow simple instructions," said the man. "Now here's what we're going to do. You're going to get in the SUV and drive out of here the same way you came in. You passed a gas station about three miles back. Drive back down to it and await my instructions."

"OK," said Danbury, clicking to unlock the doors and climbing in. Matthew followed suit, fastening his seat belt as Danbury maneuvered the big vehicle to turn it around on the narrow road.

"What was that?" asked Matthew.

"He's willing to meet with us. On his terms," answered Danbury. "I didn't expect less. I just hoped he'd agree. I need his help. Without it, we're stuck."

"How's he going to give us further instructions if we don't have phones?" asked Matthew practically.

"I have no idea, Doc. I'm just following instructions."

They were silent as they went back down the narrow road and pulled into the small gravel lot of a gas station that looked to be deserted.

"Now what?" asked Matthew.

"Now, we wait."

After another five minutes, they heard ringing.

"That sounds like a landline phone," said Matthew.

They climbed out and went in search of the sound. Rounding the side of the old brick building, they found a pay phone attached to the outer wall.

"I didn't know these still existed," said Matthew quietly.

Looking around him cautiously, Danbury picked up the receiver and put it to his ear but said nothing. Then, he said, "Yes. OK. Right. Got it."

Matthew waited impatiently for Danbury to replace the receiver and turn to explain. "We're waiting here."

"For what?"

"We'll know when we see it," said Danbury.

After another few minutes a hum approached. It wasn't the roar of an engine; it was difficult to hear. The motor was quieter than a lawnmower, Matthew thought, and definitely not a car or truck. From behind the building, a 4-wheel ATV emerged, and Conrad Manchester motioned them to approach.

As they did, he pulled both of their cell phones from his pocket, leaned over the ATV, and dropped them to the ground. While Matthew watched in disbelief, Manchester stomped vigorously on them with one booted foot. Matthew stood frozen, glaring at him. Having replaced that smart phone after his had been blown up two months earlier, he was beyond annoyed that he'd have to do it again.

"Keys," said Manchester.

Danbury reached into his pocket—as if moving in slow motion—retrieved the key fob, and handed it to him. Still, the guy didn't ask for the weapons, and he had to know they were carrying them. That, thought Matthew, was odder than any of the rest of it—right up until the guy reared back and tossed the keys into a thicket of underbrush behind the small brick store. OK, that was the oddest thing yet, Matthew amended his thoughts.

"Come with me," said Manchester as Danbury moved forward and Matthew reluctantly followed. "Faster. You have a limited window of time before I'm gone."

Up the hill behind the brick store they climbed, following behind the four-wheel ATV. After a brisk thirty-minute hike, they made a sharp right turn, and the ATV disappeared into the hillside. As they followed, Matthew realized it was a cave, of sorts, three-sided, and covered from the front with some sort of hanging vines used as a screen. It looked like a great bear cave to him.

Manchester dismounted. Pointing into the depths of the cave, he ushered them in with a small penlight. Outside, it would have made little impact. Inside, it lit the pathway directly in front of them, but little more. Water dripped from somewhere. Matthew imagined bats hanging overhead and shivered, though he couldn't see any in the darkness.

"Pick one," said Manchester, pointing to a row of three ATV vehicles similar to the one he had driven into the entrance of the cave. Danbury pulled one out, and Matthew dragged out another. Pushing them out was harder than walking in behind the dim pen light. Clumsily, they managed.

"Let's go," said Manchester, turning the key on his and starting it up. Glancing down, Matthew saw the key was in the ATV, and he climbed on. It was a dark green, Danbury's was brown, and the one Manchester rode looked like smoke. Fleetingly, he wondered if there was any significance in that as he started his and followed Manchester and Danbury out of the mouth of the cave.

Turning right and heading back up hill, Manchester said, over his shoulder, "Stay close."

In a few areas that widened out on plateaus, they could come alongside each other. As they climbed the steep terrain, most of the path was overgrown and narrow, necessitating single-file travel. Matthew wondered what time it was and wished he'd remembered to get his watch off of the charger beside his bed that morning. Looking up, he wasn't sure how high the sun was in the sky. The day had turned cloudy and a thick canopy of tree limbs obscured what he might have seen of it.

Descending steeply, they rounded a wide bend. To their right was a creek bed below. It was to this that they traversed, zigging and zagging back down the hill. At the bottom, Manchester led them a short distance along a narrow outcropping of the creek bank. At a flatter spot, they crossed the creek one at a time and began their climb up the other side. Throughout the trip, Manchester and Danbury's heads were turning constantly as they scanned the surrounding areas. Matthew felt like a gazelle at the back of a herd, vulnerable to be picked off first from behind if they were being followed.

Putting that thought aside, he concentrated on keeping all four tires of his ATV on the ground as they zigged up a steep incline, around a sharp curve, and down. As he was thinking he'd never walk straight again, they came to a wide but shallow creek, dropped into it, and drove along the pebbled bottom to a small clearing.

Up the hill in front of them, in the edge of what he first thought was a thick woodland forest, was a dilapidated log cabin. It looked to be barely standing. A tin roof covering the top seemed to be intact, all but the bit covering a long porch which leaned precariously on one side. Brush had grown up all around it, and the windows and front door were boarded up. To the left side of this cabin, they followed Manchester.

Looking up, Matthew saw rays of light filtering too brightly through the trees for them to be growing as thickly as he'd first thought. The light split, its rays penetrating the tree canopy in two distinct shafts. It was a fleeting realization that told him several things. He was facing west and the day was waning. Beginning to descend behind the cabin, the sun was dropping from its earlier higher position in the sky. The cabin was perched on the edge of a cliff, not surrounded by a thick forest.

Matthew had no idea where they were or how far from civilization. He felt as though he'd been transported from earth to some other dimension as he turned off the ATV and wheeled it, behind Manchester and Danbury, into another hole in the side of the mountain. This one wasn't as deep as the cave from which they'd pulled the vehicles, but they were equally well hidden from sight. Like the other cave, you'd have to know this one was there to find it.

Silently, they made their way, single file, to the back of the cabin. Manchester pushed something on the wall, swung a section of it open, and stepped through. The logs making up the panel weren't cut in the rectangular shape of a door. Instead, they overlapped back and forth to blend with the logs in the wall. Following Manchester through, Matthew was careful to step around the protruding logs. Somebody, he thought, had gone to a lot of trouble to make this section blend in. No hinges or hardware was visible from either side, but they must be huge because the logs couldn't be lightweight.

Dim lighting inside was mostly supplied by what little sunlight managed to seep through the cracks in the weathered gray logs. Broken wooden furniture, covered in dust and grime, was strewn around an interior that seemed to be divided into two rooms. The larger portion of the cabin was visible from where they'd entered. A huge, black, potbellied stove sat against the dividing interior wall atop half of a circular black plate in the floor that looked to be rusted iron. It was that wall which Manchester approached.

Pushing something beside the wood stove, he pulled a section of the interior wall behind the stove open. As the wall slid out, the round metal plate under the stove spun, and the stove met the wall on the other side.

"You first," said Manchester, motioning Danbury and Matthew in front of him. "Hold on to the railings." Danbury took a step forward and down. Matthew followed. As Manchester descended behind them, a scraping noise disrupted the silence. The dais on which the wood stove sat closed.

Holding tightly to a metal handrail with what felt like rock behind it, Matthew followed, step by tedious and uncertain step, around a gently curving staircase, a dark abyss beyond their feet. Then, Matthew's breath caught in his throat. As they rounded the final curve in the rock wall, an eerie light shone from below.

20 ~ DESCENT TO THE UNSEEN

Landing on the solid stone floor, Matthew looked around, taking it in. The far-right wall of the room beneath the cabin was covered with mounted computer monitors. Blue lights from some of them flickered with various scenes from carefully located security cameras. An amber glow emanated from others. There were tables full of electronic equipment beneath the wall of monitors and chairs tucked beneath. Two closed metal doors, one to the left and one directly in front of them, led off to who knew where.

"What is this place?" Matthew whispered under his breath.

"Somewhere you never were. Containing things you never saw," said Manchester. "Take a seat."

"Got it," said Matthew, pulling out a chair and dropping into it.

Manchester lowered a task light on a movable arm and shone it in Danbury's face before returning it to its spot above the table. Danbury didn't flinch; he merely stared into the light allowing their captor to get a good look at his face.

Captor? Matthew questioned. Had they been captured? Or could they leave any time they chose? He figured it was a moot point. He now understood this was exactly what Danbury had intended and anticipated.

Matthew assessed Conrad Manchester in the flickering light. The guy was a medium height with a wiry, muscular build, more like a long-distance runner than a body builder. Serious brown eyes peered from a tanned face beneath close cropped brown hair, with a touch of gray at the temples.

"Congratulations. You found me. And you brought a buddy. Hopefully, you weren't followed by anybody else. We'll deal with it if you were," he said, motioning to the monitors on the wall beside him. "Now, what do you want?"

"Answers," said Danbury simply. "I want to know about my parents. What really happened. And who killed them."

"Be careful what you ask for," said Manchester. "You could be talking to him."

"I doubt that," said Danbury mildly.

"What makes you sure?" asked Manchester, though he sounded amused this time.

"My father was a lot of things. Stupid was never one of them. Neither was he a bad judge of character."

"Nice assessment," said Manchester. "You're right. He was anything but stupid, and he wasn't at all naive. How he wasn't jaded, I'll never know."

"I'm guessing Mom helped."

"You're probably right. Now, what is it that you want to know? Or I guess we should start with what you already think that you know."

"Sometimes, it seems like a lot. Others, like a bunch of nothing."

"Tell me what you've learned. And then we can discuss what you need to know."

Danbury told Conrad Manchester about the body he'd found after his grandmother's death and the note that made it personal as well as the strong possibility that the uniform and decorations on it were actually his father's. He explained how the original police records contained very little information and that the physical evidence was reported as missing, though he didn't believe that. Finding Ogilvy, Danbury explained, had filled in some of the gaps. Getting shot at had convinced the guy to hand over the original police records and the very lightly encrypted location for Manchester.

"I figured that's how you found me. And that it must be important. Otherwise, Ogilvy would never have shared that information. It's why I trusted him, and him only, with it."

Danbury described how he'd also found Jason Byrd murdered and a second note on his body that was clearly meant for him.

"Ah, cleaning up loose ends," assessed Manchester.

"I've been all but accused of that murder. I was told to stand down. To take a vacation. Not to touch the cases. Any of them. Neither my dad's, the unknown body, nor Byrd's. We must have barely missed Byrd's killer. Doc assessed the blood. It hadn't begun to coagulate. It was still semi-warm."

"Ah," said Manchester, nodding at Matthew. "He's useful."

"Sometimes," said Matthew tersely, choosing not to take offense.

"If you've seen the complete police records," began Manchester, "then you already know a lot about what happened."

"Some of it makes sense," said Danbury, but then he described the files they'd found in his old childhood desk and the scribbled information about Kenya. Adding Ogilvy's recollection of guarding a Kenyan diplomat who was presumed dead in the terrorist attack on the embassy in Nairobi, he explained how none of that explained his parents' murder.

Manchester's eyebrows rose as he said, "Go on."

"You and dad worked for Iron Clad. As did Ogilvy. Though, that was later. After my dad had been killed. Ogilvy providing security for the foreign diplomat from Kenya. That seemed to connect with my father's notes. Iron Clad went out of business. Abruptly. Your wife died suddenly and inexplicably. Days after Iron Clad dissolved. That's it. I have no idea how it all fits. It must. Somehow. Were you and Dad planning a trip to Nairobi?"

"That's the tip of the iceberg," said Manchester. "Only because you're Erik's son, and you could already be in danger with what you know, I'll fill in some blanks and tell you what I can. Erik would want me to help you now."

"Thank you."

"If you're being accused of these murders, you'll want to lay low for a while. I had to go completely off the grid out here."

"This is impressive," Matthew chimed in. "How does all of this work?" he asked, indicating the computer equipment behind where he sat. "How do you power it?"

"Solar. From the top of the mountain to the left of the cabin. The lines feed off down the other side. There's a wealthy community over there wired for the power that's currently deserted. The owners believe that doomsday is imminent. They built houses on top of bunkers, with years' worth of food stored away. I tapped into the power source, ran lines down a ravine over here, and covered it all back over with rubble."

Leaning back, elbows on the table behind him, Manchester added, "This bunker was built surreptitiously by a company that built the others. The company owners don't believe any of it. They thought I was another 'doomsday whack job.' Their words that I overheard, not mine. They made a mint providing the rock excavation and construction services, so their lips are sealed about who built what where. That was part of the contract."

"What can you tell me about my parents' murder?" asked Danbury, returning Manchester to the subject he wanted to learn about.

"You already know that my gun was found on the scene and ballistics matched. It was the murder weapon."

Danbury nodded.

"I last saw it the night before your parents' murder. I left it in my locker at the station. I had that day off, which was public information. What nobody could have known was that Heather took the day off and called in sick. She got migraines sometimes. That day was one of the worst. She was dizzy, sick, and was seeing spots with a restricted field of vision. I was glad to be off and home to take care of her, though there wasn't much I could do. She had medication, but it had side effects she hated, so she was trying to tough it out."

"She testified to that," said Danbury. "They were rough on her."

"She did, and they were, extremely so," confirmed Manchester. "She was a tough woman, though. I guess she had to be to marry a Marine turned cop. Heather was petite. She might have looked fragile, but it was a facade. She was shrewd, street smart. She was well educated, book smart too. And sexy as hell. The perfect woman."

"Sounds like it," agreed Danbury.

"I haven't been the same since I lost her or your dad," said Manchester. "I don't expect ever to be again. I think about her every day. And I wonder what our life would be like now if she hadn't died."

"Was she killed?" asked Danbury pointedly.

"Yes," answered Manchester honestly. "I know she was murdered. I could never prove it."

"Why?" asked Matthew, unable to wait any longer for the rest of the story.

"I wish I knew who killed her and why," said Manchester, his face drooping. "There's no logical explanation. Her statement was already on file, clearing me of the murder. Anybody who wanted to prove that my unrequited love for your mother was reason for the murders was months too late because your parents had already also been killed."

"Why did you think her death wasn't an accident? You seem pretty certain," said Matthew.

"The police file is thin. There isn't much to go on. It was a single car accident," said Manchester. "It wasn't late. She wasn't a drinker, and she wasn't on any medication. The report showed drugs in her system. I don't know how they got there, but I've always been certain she didn't take them herself. I knew her too well to ever believe it."

"That wasn't in the police report. The drugs in her system," said Danbury. "Not the one I read."

"No, it wasn't," agreed Manchester.

"Why do you think that was?" asked Danbury.

"It certainly wasn't to spare me. I assume it was covering up a murder that couldn't neatly be pinned on me."

"What sort of drug was found in her system?" asked Matthew.

"A derivative of LSD," said Manchester sadly. "She'd never have taken anything like that on her own. Somebody had to have slipped it to her, either in a drink or food or something."

"I'm sorry," said Danbury meaningfully.

"But you want to know about your parents," Manchester said, turning his gaze to Danbury. "I was not in love with your mother, and I did not kill your parents. Let's start there. When I first saw your mother, your dad and I met her together. We both thought she was 'the one.' I thought so, and so did he. As we got to know her, it was pretty obvious that the two of them were meant for each other. I backed off completely, and they got married not too long after that."

"You were both still in the service then?" asked Matthew.

"Right. We'd been stationed together as much as we could manage. Erik was the brother I'd never had, and I think I filled that same role for him. And then I met Heather. After we met and married, the four of us did things together. Movies, card games, dinners, a couple of weekend trips, you know, the usual couple things," said Manchester. He hesitated, and then added, "That seems like another lifetime ago, doing normal things."

Swallowing hard, he continued, "Your mom and Heather got to be great friends, and they shared everything with each other. I don't know how much they withheld from your dad and me, but I'd guess there were things. I know they commiserated about their worry over the two of us, first in the military, and then on the police force. They bonded over that as much as anything else. They wanted us to leave the police force and join Iron Clad full time. That would have been out of a frying pan and into a fire."

"How so?" asked Danbury.

"Iron Clad got into some things they didn't mean to get involved in. I'm sure it's what shut them down. They were either under threat of exposure for lines they'd already crossed and being blackmailed to continue, or they were under personal threat for the things they knew about but refused to participate in. I was never sure which."

"What things?" asked Danbury.

"Your dad was the one who put it together, made sense of it all and understood what was happening," responded Manchester. "He approached them with what he'd figured out. He was brilliant. I always admired that about him. It's what made him an excellent police detective. He could see connections, draw conclusions, in disparate information that nobody else saw."

"That's what got him killed?"

"I believe so."

"What did he see?"

"It did have something to do with Kenya, but it went well beyond Nairobi."

"Samburu?"

"Right," said Manchester, looking at Danbury in surprise.

"Did you suspect Iron Clad? Of killing my parents. The owner maybe?"

"No. I knew the owner and the top tier of management. They were solid. They would never have been blackmailed into killing an innocent person. If I had believed that, I would have ceased employment with them immediately. I did think they knew more than they were admitting, though, and part of the reason I stayed on was to try to figure out what that was. My bridges were already burned on the police force. Things like suspected murder—even if it's unproven rumor—follow you. It's hard to change precincts, sometimes even in other states."

"You worked at Iron Clad full time," said Danbury.

"I did. Until they suddenly closed up shop. There was no warning. I tried to contact the owner directly, but the numbers were no longer in service, and he disappeared from the business entirely. I'm not sure what happened to him. I'll admit that when Heather died shortly after that, I didn't care anymore. I wanted to get away from everything and everybody."

"I asked Ogilvy about other companies I found in my dad's files," said Danbury. Then, he added pointedly, "I could access that list from my phone."

"Your phones could be tracked," answered Manchester. "It's why we doubled back and I destroyed them away from one of the paths to get up here. We needed it to look like you found nothing and went in another direction."

"Couldn't we have turned them off?" asked Matthew.

"No," said Manchester firmly.

"You didn't take our weapons," said Matthew, trying to understand the man.

"You might need those still," said Manchester. "You wouldn't use them on me. You wanted information from me. I couldn't provide it if I were dead."

"You assumed Danbury thought you were innocent of his parents' murder," said Matthew.

"I knew that," said Manchester quietly.

"There were multiple companies," said Danbury, "in the list my dad left. One sounded familiar to Ogilvy. Satellife."

"A competitor to Iron Clad," said Manchester nodding. "A heated competitor. I'm not sure what the past history was, but there was animosity on both sides."

"It isn't in business anymore," said Matthew. "What happened to it?"

"I have no idea. Whatever it was would have been after Iron Clad shut down."

"After you went into hiding?" asked Matthew.

"After I went off the grid," Manchester corrected. "I allow myself to be found when I want to be. Until now, I've seen no point. You might be able to help me clear my name along with Erik's. That hasn't mattered much to me before. Maybe it does now."

Instead of asking what he'd meant by that, Danbury asked, "Did you stay in touch with my grandmother?"

"Loosely. I kept tabs on you through her. Erik was the family I didn't have. As was Freya. I checked on her at the nursing home periodically until she no longer knew who I was. I was at her grave side service."

"You were there?" asked Matthew in surprise.

"I was," Manchester confirmed.

"Did you recognize anybody?" asked Danbury. Then he added, "Anybody who shouldn't have been there? Or who you wouldn't have expected to see?"

"No, and I was looking. It's one of the reasons I went, other than to pay my respects to Freya. She was an amazing woman."

"She was," Danbury agreed.

"There were people I didn't recognize, of course. I saw a couple of neighbors from her old neighborhood, where she raised you."

"Right," said Danbury.

"I recognized a group of the workers from the home where she lived after that," added Manchester. "There were people I didn't recognize. I have pictures, if you want to see. Maybe you know who they are."

Turning, Manchester tapped keys, then pointed up to a monitor. Simultaneously, a light on a panel to his left blinked, and they heard a beeping sound.

"Hang on," Manchester said, tapping and clicking to scrutinize one monitor in particular. "It's only a deer," he concluded. "Usually, the system recognizes the animals around here, but occasionally, a camera catches one at an odd angle. If it had recognized a human form, the alarm would have blared. Here are the pictures."

Matthew and Danbury leaned over and watched as pictures update every five seconds on the screen. They'd been captured themselves in many of them, Matthew noticed. There were two close-up pictures of Danbury's face. Struggling to recall the terrain, Matthew thought he remembered a mausoleum on the hill off to one side. Manchester must have been either behind it or Matthew considered the alternative and shuddered. Had he been inside it?

"I recognize all but the third frame," said Danbury. "Can you go back?"

"Sure."

"Do you know who they are?" asked Danbury, pointing to a group of three men. Two were huddled together at a little distance from the rest. They were tall and dark. The third stood farther off than both of them.

"I don't. I was curious too," Manchester responded. "I can blow them up to see their faces."

Tapping a few more keys, the picture zoomed in to the faces of the three, one at a time. The lone man was beneath a hat under an umbrella. Dark faces of the other two peered from beneath umbrellas that barely covered their bulk. They were huge men. The picture was clear, not pixelated as Matthew had expected it to be.

"That's the Mayor of Peak," said Matthew, pointing to the lone man in the hat. "But I have no idea who the other two are. They don't seem to be with him."

"Can you zoom back out?" asked Danbury. Squinting closer, he pointed to another man at the edge of the picture. "Isn't that the previous police chief? He was before my time. Was he there during yours?"

Leaning over, Manchester looked closer, then shook his head. "He must have been after I left. I don't recognize him."

"Tell me about Kenya," said Danbury. "How it fits."

"It has to do with the bombing of the US Embassy in Nairobi before it happened," said Manchester, slowly. "Your father believed Satellife had learned of the possibility. He thought that either they'd been informed by politicians or that they'd learned of it and reported it in Washington. Nobody seemed to want to hear it or act on it. Erik believed it was purposeful, as if condoning the action. He had some theories as to why that was. They weren't popular theories but dangerous ones. Accusing people in power of corruption always is."

"What did he do about it?"

"He went through the proper police channels, but he was told to drop it. Initially, he thought maybe it was because he was wrong. But then he was threatened."

"By who?"

"If I knew that, I'd have a better idea about who murdered him."

"You don't?"

"Not definitively. When Erik got the threat, he went to Iron Clad with it to see if they could help him determine what was happening, by whom, and at what level of government bureaucracy. He didn't know who he could trust in his own department or where the order for him to drop it had come from, how high up, or for what reason."

"Did Iron Clad agree?"

"They agreed to look into it. What they were finding, they apparently didn't like. They backed off eventually too. Your dad was ready to go to Kenya and poke around. There was a church there he was working through. The founders are Americans, out of Texas if I remember correctly. He'd gotten in touch with them. They were able to confirm some of what he suspected, but not enough for him to build a case. What he planned to do with that information I have no idea."

"You weren't involved?"

"To a degree because your father was. We were planning a trip to Kenya."

"Tell me what he suspected."

"Are you sure, Warren? If some of this knowledge is what got your father killed and the killer is still on the loose, are you certain you want to know?"

"I am. The killer is already aware. I've been ordered to 'drop it' too. Somebody is still protecting the killer."

"Or killers," said Manchester. "Somebody is taunting you with your parents' murder. Maybe threatening you to get you to stop probing into their deaths. It's pointed. It might be the same killer. Or somebody who knows about the original murders and also has something to lose if you figure out who committed them and why. So, I'll ask you. Is it worth the risks to know, to pursue this?"

Matthew's foot was tapping at a frantic pace, he realized. He pushed down on his thigh to stop it. With one eyebrow raised, he held his breath and waited for Danbury's response.

21 ~ THE COST OF KNOWLEDGE

Without hesitation, Danbury responded, "It is worth it. I intend to pursue. I have to know who killed my parents. To prove my dad didn't do it. I need him vindicated."

"And your buddy here?" asked Manchester. "Doctor Paine, are you also willing to take the risk?"

"Danbury asked me that once, and I told him I was still in," said Matthew, blowing out the breath of air he'd held. "I'm afraid that was the last chance I had to back out. I'm in way too deep now. Whoever knows he's on their trail knows I am too. I'm already in danger by association, whether I move forward with this or not."

"OK," said Manchester. Turning to Danbury, he explained, "Your father believed that there was human trafficking out of Kenya into the US. What do you know about Maasai warriors?"

"They're fierce," said Matthew, and he reiterated the story about the British being unable to subdue them with troop invasions of their territory in the previous century. He'd looked it up and been right about that. It was the territory in Samburu that was the no-go zone for the British.

"They're well-trained," agreed Manchester. "Or at least they were back in the nineties. They were ignored by most of the rest of Kenya, struggling to recover from a drought the decade before and the resulting widespread starvation."

"Desperation," summarized Danbury.

"Desperate people do desperate things, like selling their warriors to the highest bidders. Mercantiles of some description."

"For what purpose? Why?"

"That's where it gets hazy. Erik wasn't able to determine where the warriors were being taken, just that it was out of that region of Africa. Why they were wanted, for what purpose, was merely a guess. Erik believed that somebody here was involved. He was convinced that the US knew and turned a blind eye when they were warned that the embassy in Nairobi would be attacked. Erik vacillated between thinking that the US Ambassador to Kenya was either involved or needed to be warned. I'm not sure where he landed on that when he was killed. The bombing he feared happened a month later."

"Either way, the conclusion being that somebody here didn't want somebody there to be warned about the pending bombing or the warriors leaving the country," said Matthew.

"It's what we concluded," said Manchester. "The bombing was likely allowed to cover up the mercantile operation, anyone at the embassy who knew about it and might have opposed to it."

"Wasn't a terrorist group responsible for that bombing?" asked Matthew.

"That was who took credit for it after the fact. If that's true, they had motives of their own, but they could have been stopped. Erik was certain that somebody here had other motives to allow the embassy, and the people there, to be destroyed. He didn't think we were going to bomb it ourselves. But there was chatter about the impending attack. He suspected that the US had knowledge of it but wasn't taking steps to prevent it. He wanted to warn the embassy."

"What was he planning?" asked Danbury.

"There wasn't sufficient evidence, yet, to prove that an attack was in the works. He was making plans to go to Nairobi. I was going with him. The embassy, back then, was out on the street with local businesses. Their security wasn't adequate. He literally could have walked in and told them. The bombers, a month later, drove up in front and detonated car bombs. It was accessible to the public."

"You think that's why he was killed?" asked Danbury. "To stop him?"

"I don't have a better answer. It's what he was investigating, what he was told to drop. He didn't drop it but stopped talking to anyone else about it but me. He was still digging. I don't know how he got his information or from what sources. After the fact, I wished I'd asked more questions and been more involved. Then again, maybe I don't. Whatever that was got your parents killed, and probably Heather, as a result, when I wouldn't take the fall for their murders."

"Thank you," said Danbury. "You've given me a lot to think about. And a direction to pursue."

"Even if it leads you straight to a killer? Or several?"

"Even if," said Danbury. "I can't let this go. Sorry, Doc. I wish I hadn't asked you to help. I had no idea what I'd uncover. I still don't. It's a lot bigger than I thought. Beyond somebody disgruntled with Dad."

Matthew was incredulous with Danbury's continued apologies. Merited, though they might be, it wasn't the norm for the big detective.

"Likely not," said Manchester. "I can point you in a few directions, and I can watch remotely. After that, I'm not very helpful."

"Thanks," said Danbury. His whole countenance appeared heavy. "Point away."

Manchester had merely opened his mouth when an alarm sounded loudly and insistently behind him. Turning, he tapped a keyboard and then rearranged the views on the screens to pull one into the center and largest screen. "Shit!" he yelled. "Those ARE human! Let's go! We've got maybe fifteen minutes before breach!"

Jumping up, Matthew felt his adrenaline surge. "Go where?" he asked and then watched in amazement at the scene that unfolded.

Manchester flipped switches turning off the electronics and sending the three men into near darkness. Two wall sconces on either side of the room provided dim lighting. Manchester clicked latches and pushed buttons that flipped down a solid metal sheet walling off the technology. After it was in place, a rock wall dropped from above, completely obscuring it.

"They shouldn't be able to get down here," said Manchester. "If they do, they can't find that. I won't be able to come back any time soon, though." Jogging to the metal door in the side of the room, he tapped something, pulled something else, and swung the heavy door out. It protested noisily on unseen hinges.

"Here," said Manchester, handing each of them a large backpack and taking two for himself. Inside the room, Matthew saw a bedroom set up on one side. On the other was an arsenal of weaponry like he'd never seen in one place before. Returning the door to its place and dropping a rock wall in front of it, Manchester darted to the remaining metal door. He went through a similar procedure to open it. Matthew felt a sudden rush of air and looked out into nothingness.

"Time to go," said Manchester. "It's like the airline. Pull the inflatable rafts out of your bags!"

Danbury and Matthew fumbled with them as Manchester demonstrated.

"You're going first," he told Danbury. "Then, the good doctor here. I'm bringing up the rear and locking up behind. Here," he said, sliding the plastic raft onto the narrow ledge outside the door sideways and holding it in place. "On your stomach. Hang on to the handles."

Danbury flopped onto the plastic raft that had inflated under him and disappeared. Matthew hoped he knew what he was doing as he prepared to follow suit.

"OK, now!" said Manchester, repeating the maneuver for Matthew.

His breath caught in his throat as he slid down the mountain, in a winding pattern, into the gathering dusk at a speed he'd have feared to calculate. He clenched the handles on the sides of the raft with white knuckles. Never had he been on a snow sled or a roller coaster ride like this one. In that moment, he was thankful he hadn't been afraid of them, for what little good that did him now. This would be a thrill for a luge team and terrifying for nearly everyone else, he concluded.

What seemed like hours, but was probably a mere minute later, he felt his momentum slow, and he landed in a pile of gravel. Releasing the breath he'd held, he looked around briefly before Danbury pulled him and the raft from the bottom.

"Doc, this way!"

A chute, of sorts, that still looked to be covered in leaves and debris disappeared up the hill behind them. Before Matthew could get his bearings, Manchester landed at the bottom where he himself had been seconds before.

"Push here," said Manchester, and his raft instantly deflated. Matthew fumbled to find the button. Both he and Danbury deflated their rafts and, following Manchester's lead, stowed them in the outer compartment of the backpacks they carried.

"This way," said Manchester as he sprinted through the woods.

Danbury was more agile than a guy his size ought to be, but he wasn't built as a distance runner. He struggled over branches and brambles to keep up. Manchester paused to wait for them only momentarily before darting off again. Around a curve in the wooded valley and into the side of a hill they followed. It was another of the caves that you wouldn't find if you didn't know it was there. At the back of it sat a row of five ATVs. Why did one guy need so many? Matthew wondered without pausing to consider a possible answer.

"This is where we part," Manchester said. "Head northwest, twenty-six clicks. Follow the creek for the first twenty. When the creek veers sharply north, go over the short ridge to the west and keep going. It'll get you to a road. Head west on that, and it'll take you to a town. Call for help if you think that's best. You were never here, and you didn't see me," he admonished.

"Where are you going?" asked Matthew and felt immediately stupid as soon as the words flew, unchecked, from his mouth.

"Think raccoon and fox, not groundhog," Manchester said as he tore off on an ATV and left them there in the cave.

"Better get moving," said Danbury.

"Where? And how far?" asked Matthew, still stunned.

"A little over sixteen miles. That way," he added pointing.

Remaining daylight was waning, but they didn't dare turn on lights as they pulled the ATVs out of the cave and started them. Matthew was relieved they were relatively quiet. They hummed; they didn't rev loudly.

Following Danbury out uncertainly, Matthew started along the winding valley. Through underbrush that reached out to grab their legs and low tree branches that swatted occasionally at their faces, they made their way as quickly as they could travel. Forced by the terrain to cross the creek, they maneuvered the ATVs over stones through the shallow water. They hadn't gone far along the other side of the creek when a deafening roar crashed through the woods behind them, causing them to duck and then look over their shoulders. A fireball lit the darkening sky.

Turning back to the path, they needed no further incentive to get as far away as possible. They rode on for the next hour. Skirting the creek bed, they traveled over downed saplings and made their way, painfully, around bigger trees until they could cross them and return to follow the creek.

Matthew's brain was on overload. Had the interlopers blown up the cabin believing Manchester to be inside it? Had Manchester remotely detonated an explosive? Had he put out trip wires so that trespassers would detonate it themselves? There were none that Matthew had seen—but he'd been with Manchester, who would have avoided them. The question his mind had skirted presented itself first and foremost. Had anyone been killed in that explosion?

Pondering that question for a moment, Matthew's mind raced faster than the ATV to the second one. Had anyone survived? And were they in pursuit now? Looking back over his shoulder, Matthew couldn't see much through the trees. Acrid smoke drifted on the breeze, and a distinct glow lit the mountain range, growing distant behind him. Turning to navigate a downed tree, he realized he'd dropped back and raced to catch up with Danbury.

Feeling the pit of his stomach lurch, Matthew also realized his lunch was still in the pockets of his jacket. They hadn't taken time to eat. It was probably squished beyond recognition. There was no time to stop and find out. One of the two water bottles was still in the side pocket of his cargo pants. That, too, would be welcome now. He pressed on, determined to keep up with Danbury and get as far away from whatever they'd just escaped as possible.

"We're close," said Danbury, finally stopping as Matthew pulled alongside him. "Here's Manchester's landmark. The creek turns sharply north. We go west over that ridge to find the road. In nearly four more miles. It leads to a town. We'll decide what to do when we get there."

Before Matthew could respond, Danbury took off, heading up a sparsely shrubbed incline to go over the ridge. If he had his cell phone, Matthew knew what he'd do when they reached the town— something he'd already have done by now if he had a cell signal. He'd contact Justin without involving any of his other friends or family.

The squished roast beef sandwich presented itself to the forefront of Matthew's mind with far more appeal than it should. Would a hotel be safe? Would there be one in the town? His thoughts were muddled as his ATV climbed behind Danbury.

Suddenly, Danbury veered wide into the tree line, motioning wildly for Matthew to follow. Zipping in and out of trees, Matthew heard Danbury yell, "AMBUSH!"

Leaning abruptly forward on the ATV, as if he could will it to go faster that way, Matthew saw and heard nothing more.

22 ~ LOST IN THE WOODS

Pinpoints of light were spinning. Or was it light? Something was spinning, and he was heavy. And cold, an invasive, damp cold. Something screeched nearby. What was it? Matthew wondered before it all faded into oblivion.

The weighty, chilled sensation returned with a persistent vengeance. Forcing himself to squint his eyes open and look around, Matthew surveyed his surroundings. On his back, flung there like a rag doll, he lay on the damp ground. Above him, tree limbs laced the night sky—small leaves budding—against a partial moon, more than half but less than full.

Nearly silent wings whispered above him, and he heard the hoot of an owl. That was followed by a screech that sounded almost like a human scream. That jolted him awake, and he listened for the sound again. When it finally came, it was more distant, and he recognized the call of a fox. Deprived of the light of the moon when clouds obscured it, the darkness was complete. There was no light pollution on the horizon in any direction he could see.

He was cold, but not freezing, he assessed, though he wondered how much difference it made. Drawing his knees to his chest, he rolled over in a fetal position and tried to get warm. Where he was and how he'd gotten there began to break the surface of his mind. He'd been on an ATV, following Danbury, trying to get to a road and then a town. Where was the ATV? With an effort, he lifted himself onto an elbow and looked around. Something glinted in the moonlight just beyond the next tree.

The more important question was where was Danbury? Sliding his body into the shelter of the nearest tree, he pulled himself up and propped there. Nothing and nobody moved around him. Reaching for his pocket, he remembered his cell phone was all but dust, crushed under the boot of Conrad Manchester. How long ago had that been? He wasn't sure. It seemed like days, but that couldn't be right.

He dared not call out in case whoever had attacked him was still around. In that moment, he was certain somebody had hit him from behind and knocked him off the ATV. If he could get upright, he'd search for Danbury. Maybe he was nearby in a similar state. If that were the case, he could be worse off, thought Matthew, cringing at the thought. He would search, he vowed, as soon as he felt able to move.

His jacket was tied around his waist, he realized. With an effort, he untied it and lifted himself enough to get it out from under his body. Pulling it on helped somewhat with the cold. Why had he been hit?

Bits of hazy memory flitted through his mind. Danbury had made a dash for the tree line and he'd yelled something. What it was, Matthew couldn't quite recall. Reaching up because the back of his head throbbed and sparked in intermittent pain, he realized it was also wet. Blood, he saw, by the moonlight as he pulled his hand around to his face. Did he have a concussion? How much blood had he lost? Had he been shot? He didn't think so.

Surveying the rest of his body clumsily, he realized the holster containing his Glock 19 was no longer strapped in place. Angry bruises would be inevitable, but he found nothing broken. His head throbbed and his right arm was banged up, but he was thankful he seemed to be otherwise intact. Reaching behind his head, he gritted his teeth and tried to assess the damage. The cut felt wider than deep, which he hoped meant his skull had not fractured with the impact of whatever had hit him.

There had been a backpack too, he remembered, one Conrad Manchester had thrust at him. He had no idea what it contained. There'd been no chance to look. What he didn't find, as he patted his pockets with a sinking feeling, was his wallet. Maybe he hadn't awakened in the spot he'd landed from the ATV. He'd been searched and stripped of the Glock and anything identifying. Had he been left for dead? That was entirely possible, he concluded, the heaviness in his inner being overwhelming.

Water. That would help his throbbing head. He was likely dehydrated, and he had no idea how much blood he'd lost. There was a water bottle, he remembered, that he hadn't opened yet. Sliding the somewhat mangled bottle up and out of the side pocket of his cargo pants, he was relieved to see it was still full of water. Sipping slowly, he fought the urge to guzzle it. He felt weak and slightly nauseated, but that was to be expected, he reasoned.

Food. He had sandwiches, carrots, and hummus in his jacket pocket, he remembered. Was it safe to eat? Was the backpack still around? Wishing he had the light from his phone, he returned the lid to the water bottle and circled on his hands and knees surveying the area. Near the overturned ATV glowing in the moonlight, he spotted the backpack and made his way to it.

While he was there, he surveyed the vehicle. Pushing it upright, he wondered if it was still serviceable. More importantly, was he himself still able to ride it? His inner thighs were chaffed and sore from being on it for so long over rough terrain. Cowboys would be in awe, he thought. His legs hurt nearly as much as his head. Not ready to try that yet, he returned to his spot under the tree to sift through the backpack.

A first-aid kit was the first thing he pulled out. It contained what he needed except that he couldn't see behind his head. Wrapping a bandage around it would be impossible. His head would need to be shaved, the area numbed, stitches administered, and bandages taped in place. He'd need help to do that. Laying the first-aid kit aside, he reached back into the backpack.

A solar battery bank with a tiny compass attached was the next thing he discovered. That wouldn't help much without a cell phone. Or would it? It had a light. In dismay, he realized it hadn't been charged recently, and there was no sunlight to do so now. Verifying which way was west, he clipped it to the outside of the backpack. Returning to his search, he pulled out seven protein bars, one water purification system, and three small shrink-wrapped packages.

What he could see of the packaging indicated they were lightweight thermal blankets, though he was dubious that what felt like thin plastic would be of much help. Unwrapping the end of the packaging, he examined one. Silvery in the moonlight, it wasn't colored but camouflaged. A small ball of twine fell out next, along with a Swiss army knife and a bundle of stick matches.

A fire would draw attention—possibly the wrong sort—if anybody was still around. If he'd been an Eagle Scout like his dad, he'd have a far better idea about what to do now. Pausing, he considered the myriad other ways his dad had affected his life and wished he could talk to him.

Always encouraging, Joc had chosen to focus his attention on the positives in any given situation. Matthew tried to imagine what his life might have turned out like if his dad hadn't been there through all of it, as Danbury's hadn't. Unable to grasp that concept, he decided to be thankful he'd never have to know.

Shifting his focus back to his current situation, Matthew stuffed the items back in the bag. In any other circumstance, his first move would be to seek medical attention. That was out of reach for the foreseeable future. If he could get to a phone, Justin would be his first call. Manchester could help if he would show himself. And what did he mean by raccoons and foxes not groundhogs? Matthew pondered. They have multiple dens, he concluded. That must have been what he was saying.

Conrad Manchester was an enigma. Having met the man didn't help at all in understanding what was happening. Manchester had a soft spot for Danbury, obviously—as well he should have. The son of the best friend he called his brother deserved that privilege.

Matthew reviewed what he'd learned the previous day, which he assumed was mere hours ago. In the underground bunker—or at least underground from the front, as the back seemed to hang on the edge of a cliff—he'd caught a glimpse of people on cameras some distance away. How many had there been? Matthew could remember seeing three—two men caught on one camera and another man on a separate monitor. Had there been more?

Were the approaching men the same people who knocked him off the ATV? And what about Danbury? Where was he? The things he didn't know could get him killed. Danbury might already have been, for all he knew. That saddened him beyond what he could bear. He couldn't return to Peak without Danbury and tell Penn her fiancé was dead. He thought he'd felt truly alone before, but this was a whole new level of isolation.

But he wasn't alone, was he? Not ever. Though he recognized that bargaining with God wasn't wise, thoughts like "Get me safely out of this alive and I'll sign up for the next survivalist expedition or join the praise and worship team at church" still ran rampant through his mind. God didn't operate that way, he well knew.

As he looked up through the tree limbs at the moon, begging for help, he felt a sense of calm wash over him. Plans began to formulate in his mind in place of the circling churning chaos. Rest. He needed rest. Dawn would come shortly before seven in the morning in April. The sky would lighten before that, but he had no idea what the current time was. How far had Danbury said the road was from here? "Nearly four miles," he heard the answer in his mind.

And then what? There was a road he should take west, and it went to the nearest town, he recalled. How far was that? That distance wasn't included in the nearly four miles, was it? Would it be safe to hitch a ride, if one came along, or would he do best to stay out of sight and get there himself? Feeling his mind and body begin to wind up in trepidation again, he knew that wouldn't help. Slowly drawing and releasing three deep breaths, he prayed for direction. Rest. The overwhelming knowledge he needed rest came again. With it was a further understanding that he needed to eat. He had food, both his leftover lunch and the protein bars.

Pulling the plastic bag containing the unrecognizably mangled roast beef sandwich from his zipped jacket pocket, he ripped open the wrapping. It didn't matter at all what it looked like. He paused for a blessing, then tore into it. In that moment, it was the best roast beef sandwich he could ever remember eating. After downing it and rationing a bit more of his water, he managed to get to his feet.

"Please give me strength," he said aloud. Carefully walking

concentric circles around the tree he'd been leaning on, he expanded outward as he went. Stepping over branches and brambles, trying not to trip over any of them, he broadened out further and further from his tree. All the while, he had the assurance that Danbury wasn't there. He had to know that for certain. Past the ATV, he went twice, continuing to widen his circles in the moonlight.

No trace of Danbury could he find – neither bodily, the other ATV, nor the backpack. Danbury, he concluded, couldn't have been bashed on the head at the same time in the same place. Unless. Matthew stopped and stood still. Danbury would never have left him alone out here of his own volition. If he wasn't here, then somebody had forced him to leave. The realization sent a fresh batch of chills through Matthew's body. Danbury wasn't here, injured and bleeding. He wasn't here at all.

"You've got this," he confessed to God aloud, returning to his tree and sliding down the trunk to sit beneath it again. "And me. You're telling me to rest. I'll rest. I trust you."

From the backpack, he retrieved the first-aid kit. Sifting through it, he took stock of its contents. Retrieving a little packet, he tore it open and pulled out two acetaminophen tablets. That was far better than aspirin, he thought.

Unlike aspirin and the other nonsteroidal anti-inflammatory drugs, more commonly referred to as NSAIDs, it wouldn't thin his blood. It wasn't an anticoagulant. He needed the blood on the back of his head to clot. There were other little blister packs of pills, including diphenhydramine, a useful antihistamine in case of bee stings or anything else that could cause a severe allergic reaction.

Reassembling the first-aid kit, he put it back in the backpack and swallowed the tablets with a small swig of water. Securing the lid on the partially consumed water bottle, he stuffed it in the backpack and retrieved the shrink-wrapped thermal blankets. He unwrapped two, stuffing the third one back in the bag. One he laid on the ground under him, and the other he pulled over himself as he curled up beneath the spreading branches of the huge tree.

The thermal blanket, he realized as he rolled on his side unable to lay on the back of his head, was incredibly warm. The ground, atop last years' dried leaves and the new growth of early spring, wasn't so bad either.

*****

Warm and hazy, Matthew stretched his arms in front of him. Feeling the cold, he pulled them back next to his body under the covers.

"Max?" he muttered, feeling around for his cat and wondering why the light was so bright this morning. As the last wispy fingers of the sleep world released their grasp on him, Matthew sat painfully upright, remembering where he was.

This wasn't his comfortable bed or his soft blanket, and his cat wasn't here. His body ached in various places. He'd spent the night under a tree in the woods with no idea where he was and only a general idea about where he was going. Though it wasn't throbbing anymore, his head still hurt. He took that as a good sign.

The morning had dawned without him. The sun wasn't high in the sky, but it was up and shining more brightly than it had been the day before. Without his cell phone to have his usual morning video chat with Cici, he worried what she'd think when she found him unreachable. She knew he was going into a remote area with Danbury to search for Manchester. Likely, she wouldn't worry—yet. Instead, she'd probably think he didn't have an available cell connection.

Trying to stifle the rising panic, Matthew instead paused to be thankful he'd survived the night and whatever had happened the evening before and to ask for guidance in getting back to civilization. The inexplicable feeling of calm washed through him again. Thanking God for that peace which he knew wasn't his own, he sat up and pulled the backpack to him. From it, he retrieved one of the power bars. Normally, it would have been mediocre at best, but the seasoning of hunger made a delicious breakfast of it.

After a swig of rationed water, Matthew repacked the backpack with all but one of the thermal blankets. That one he kept wrapped around his shoulders against the chill of the April mountain morning. It was amazingly warm, he assumed because it trapped his body heat and radiated it back to him. Pausing to appreciate the beauty of the nature around him, he realized he'd have enjoyed being here camping under the partial moon if it were under different circumstances.

That thought spurred him on. Getting slowly to his feet, he reassessed himself. Reassuring himself nothing was broken and that his head had stopped bleeding, he stretched and started walking to get rid of the stiffness. Sweeping the area in wider concentric circles, he confirmed by daylight that there was no sign of Danbury. He had gotten the message clearly enough the night before that Danbury wasn't here, but he couldn't move on without searching one last time. What was the Marine's motto about not leaving anybody behind? He couldn't remember exactly.

Finding nothing, he returned to his tree and slung on the backpack—albeit with difficulty getting it over the thermal wrap. His arm was unhappy with the effort. Pushing his sleeve up, he saw the angry bruising and abrasions. Through gritted teeth, he sighed, dropped the sleeve, and got to work on the ATV. It seemed to be intact, but the key was missing. Was there a way to hotwire an ATV?

In a moment of frustration, Matthew wished he had his cell phone to search for that information. Being a bit of a self-professed motorhead helped. Thinking through what it would take to hotwire a car, he looked over the ATV. If he had the proper tools, he could attempt it. Digging through the backpack again, he pulled the Swiss army knife out and flipped through the options it provided.

As he was about to conclude, after working on it for some time, that he'd have to walk the nearly four miles plus whatever distance down the road to the town, it started. Grinning broadly, he chided himself for worrying about four measly miles. Those he could easily do at home on mostly level ground in an hour or less. It was with a feeling of accomplishment that he carefully threw one sore leg over and climbed on.

Cringing from the pain in his inner thighs and the chaffing ahead, he started out slowly. Purring along, it took him over the hill as he hugged the tree line, scouting for potential trouble. Seeing nothing and nobody, he descended a short way down the ridge, dodging rocks in a wash area, and continued in the direction the compass said was west.

Judging from the direction the sun was coming up through the tree line, he figured he knew which way was east, and he was headed in the right direction. What he couldn't remember was how far the town was. His mind raced trying to remember exactly what Conrad Manchester had told them. West, then west again, he repeated, muttering under his breath as if afraid he'd forget.

His arm ached, his inner thighs felt raw, and his head began throbbing again as he bumped and bounced over the rough terrain. Stopping in the edge of the tree line, he pulled the first-aid kit from his backpack and broke open another blister pack of acetaminophen. His tall water bottle, he saw with dismay, was down to a third full. He sipped cautiously to swallow the two white pills before continuing more slowly on his way.

Any exultation he'd felt at starting the vehicle without a key faded when the ATV lurched, shuttered, spluttered, and then stopped entirely. That was it, he concluded. It was out of juice to go any further. Well, three miles on foot isn't so bad, he told himself. Refusing to wonder if he were on the most direct route to the road or to think about how much farther he'd have to go after he reached it, he slid gingerly off of the ATV and set out on foot.

Every step was painful. Humming some of the praise and worship songs he'd heard during the church service he'd watched last Sunday, Matthew tried to refocus his mind. The more he praised, the less discomfort he felt. His old leather hiking boots, thick and heavy, held up well as he crossed a creek and laboriously climbed another ridge.

This ridge was higher than the last, the view from the top spectacular. He considered it a reward for the painful climb. If he'd had his cell phone, he would have captured an image of it to share with Cici later. The sun was climbing with him. That and the exertion was warming him nicely. He paused to fold the thermal blanket and stow it in the backpack. A sip of water would be wonderful, he thought, but his supply was below a quarter of the bottle now. He decided to wait, at least until he found the road, to deplete it completely.

If his head, arm, and thighs weren't so painful, he could perhaps forget the dire straits he'd found himself in and enjoy the beautiful day. Even so, he tried. The next ridge was more challenging because it was rockier. Zig-zagging, he went around the side of it to the left. Breathing hard, he finally reached the top and felt like he'd run a marathon. With his body in less-than-optimal shape, the exertion level was probably about the same, he thought. In and out of the tree lines, his jacket was on and off multiple times. In the warm sun, he got hot. Out of it, the breeze was chilling.

Matthew sat down on a rocky outcropping to rest. How much farther could it be, he wondered. He must be getting close. Without a definitive way to gauge time, he wasn't certain, but his guess was it had been well over an hour, and closer to two, since he set out. This wasn't home, it wasn't flat ground, and he couldn't do it in this shape in an hour, he bemoaned. But he could do it, he told himself, standing up and heading down the hill.

The going was rough down the rocky side of the mountain, and he was having to take the descent slowly to keep from slipping on the rocks or stepping in holes along the way. Birds called to each other, a blue jay cawing noisily, and unseen small creatures scurried for cover into the underbrush of rhododendron as he approached. Around bends, into woods, and back out again, he made his winding way down the steep hill.

Just as he thought his body couldn't take much more, particularly without water, he saw it. Beneath him was the snaking ribbon of a narrow road. "West," he said aloud. Looking up, located the sun that wasn't yet overhead. It was off to his left, more or less. Checking the compass when he hit the rocky pavement below, he turned right. He seemed to be heading south. That was concerning until the road made a sharp hair-pin turn to the right, then curved back gently to the left, which put him heading mostly west.

Past the point of exhaustion with the effort it had taken to get him this far, he was pleading with God, aloud, to get him quickly to the town and to help. Almost audibly, he knew he was being told to finish the water in his bottle. That was encouraging, he thought. Maybe it wasn't much further. He squashed the empty water bottle, capped it, and shoved it in an outer pocket of the backpack.

Returning to his trek, a distant rumble caught his attention, and he paused in fight or flight mode as it grew louder. A vehicle was approaching that could be helpful, or it could be the return of whoever had whacked him in the head. It was, at least, coming from the right direction to be heading west. Darting off the road and behind a tree, he figured he had a few quick moments to determine his response.

"Be he friend or be he foe?" circled Matthew's tired brain as he pondered the origin of the question. Shakespeare, maybe? Maybe not, he thought, in annoyance. History buff that he was, he should know where that came from. It was a fleeting thought as his focus was the source of the noise.

An old pickup truck that looked less than roadworthy rattled into view. The windows were down, and it was kicking up dust. Behind the wheel was a grizzled older man with a long gray beard flying in the breeze. Matthew caught a distant glimpse of the guy's face and stepped from behind the tree.

He might not be friendly, Matthew assessed, but this man wouldn't likely have been one of his attackers. Waving his arms as best he could, the right one still angrily sore and screaming at him from the effort, he made eye contact with the driver as the old rattletrap truck approached and slowed to a stop just beyond him.

The guy was wiry and wary as he stared out at Matthew. "What are you doin' out here, young man?"

"I was riding an ATV and had an accident," he said truthfully. "I need to get to a hospital and get checked out and stitched up."

"You out here all alone?"

"I didn't start out that way, but I got separated from my buddy who I came up here with. I hope he's OK, but I don't know where he is."

"Is that right?" the guy asked, looking Matthew over. "All right, then, you can hop in the back, if you want to. I'm goin' almost into town."

The guy erupted into laughter, his face in a plethora of crease lines, when Matthew said, "Thank you, Sir."

"On second thought," the guy said, "jump on up front. My granny would have reached up out of her grave and smacked me silly if I hadn't stopped for you. She always said that good manners get you places in life."

"Thank you!" said Matthew, relief washing through his banged up and exhausted body. He'd have to remember to thank his mother, who had always told him that manners paid off. They certainly had today. "Thank you," he said again as he stashed the backpack on the floorboard and climbed in.

"Don't you have one of those fancy smartie phones?" asked the guy as Matthew searched for a seat belt that apparently wasn't there.

"I did have one," said Matthew, hiding his amusement at the guy's reference to his phone. "It got crushed," he said, thinking that was also a true statement. He wasn't going to provide further information about how that happened if he wasn't asked, nor would he be likely to admit to it if he was asked, he realized.

"I see," said the older man, tugging on the bottom of his beard. "I got one of these here cell phones if you need to call somebody to come and git you."

Matthew felt sweet relief wash through his whole body as the man reached over and handed him an ancient flip phone.

"You might want to wait 'til we get around that next curve, though. The signal is better over there."

"Thank you," Matthew said simply, and silently thanked God too. It had never occurred to him that angels could show up in ancient pickup trucks as grizzled old mountain men. "Thank you, Sir."

There were several numbers that Matthew knew from memory, but if he could get an answer from the first one, he didn't need any of the others.

23 ~ ASK AND RECEIVE

After the third try without getting an answer, Matthew was disheartened. Clicking the old flip phone to redial, he decided to attempted it one final time before giving up and moving to the next number. He could have shouted for joy when Justin McMillian answered.

"This is Matthew; don't disconnect!" he said.

"Why would I disconnect?" asked Justin. "Where are you?"

Matthew realized, in that moment, he had no idea where he was or where he was headed.

"I'm in the mountains of Virginia, and I need your help."

"What happened?"

"I had an ATV accident," he said looking over at his rescuer behind the wheel of the old truck. "My cell phone is crushed. I lost the rest of my party," he said discreetly, not wanting to call Danbury by name in the off chance he was wrong about the rescuer. "I got out to the road and was picked up by . . ." he hesitated.

"My name's Clarence," said the man.

"By a nice man in a pickup truck named Clarence. I'm headed into . . ." again, he paused and looked over at Clarence.

"The town?" the guy asked. When Matthew nodded, he answered, "You're headed to Coalglow, Virginia, but there ain't much there. You need to go to the community clinic. There ain't no hospital. Now there's a VA hospital in the next town over. Did you serve, Son?"

"No, Sir," he said to Clarence, and then gave Justin the information about the town and where he was going when he got there.

"It'll take me a few hours to fly in and then get there. I'm on my way," said Justin. "I can bring you a cell phone. We just replaced that one, like, a month ago."

"Two months ago, but I know," groaned Matthew.

"We can replace it again," said Justin. "You were onto something, and I can use your help now. I'll tell you all about it when I get there. How do you keep stumbling into these things?"

"I didn't," said Matthew. "Our buddy did. Or his dad did."

After Justin had verified the cell carrier and cryptically gotten Matthew's login information, he said they'd meet up in Coalglow in a few hours and disconnected. Matthew hadn't mentioned his wallet and Glock were also missing, but he figured those weren't of immediate concern.

After handing the phone back and thanking Clarence profusely for the use of it, he settled in for the rest of the ride. Leaning the side of his face against the door frame, he promptly fell asleep.

"Son, hey, Sonny," was the next thing Matthew heard. He jolted awake as the grizzled gray mountain man was shaking his left arm gently. "We're here."

"Oh, thank you," said Matthew, looking up and seeing low buildings fronting a narrow street. "We're where?" he asked, looking around and growing concerned.

"We're at the community clinic in Coalglow. I didn't have the heart to wake you up and put you out before."

Whatever his story, the man was kind. That much Matthew knew for certain. He'd have loved to have paid the man for gas to thank him for the ride, but when he offered to find him later to do so, the man shook his head sagely and refused. "Just pay it forward, Son. You already do that anyhow, don't you?"

"Sir?" asked Matthew as he climbed out.

"You take care of other people. Now take care of yourself," said the man, waving as he pulled away, leaving a plume of smoke and dust in his wake.

That, thought Matthew, was remarkable. He hadn't told the man he was a doctor. He hadn't told him much of anything personal, yet Clarence seemed to have known. It was one more inexplicable thing to add to the long list of strange things that had happened to him over the past twenty-four hours. Brushing the dust and dirt from his clothing as best he could, he opened the door and entered the clinic.

A baby screamed inconsolably in a young woman's arms in one corner of the room. She was trying to keep a mask on the baby, who was having none of it. Two older women—who were huddled along the other wall—fussed over a younger man whose finger was wrapped and bleeding. It was difficult to tell peoples' ages under their masks. This clinic had apparently not adopted the same methods to handle the COVID virus as his practice, Matthew thought, surprised there were people in the waiting room.

Taking a paper mask from the dispenser by the front desk under the sign that said "Masks required. No exceptions," Matthew felt at home amidst the permeating antiseptic smells as he stepped up to the receptionist. This would be interesting, he thought.

"Hi, Ma'am," he said as she slid open a glass panel. Her PPE was more complete than most he'd seen. She wore a K-95 mask beneath a clear plastic flip-down face shield. Her hands, on the keyboard, were gloved.

"How can I help you, Sir?" she asked. "We're about an hour behind on appointments this afternoon, I should warn you. Only one of our doctors is here on Sundays."

"I'm Matthew Paine," he told her. "I'm visiting the area, and I was in an ATV accident up on the mountain. My cell phone was crushed, and I lost my wallet."

Before she could object, he added, "I have a friend on the way here now. Paying the deductible today won't be a problem. I have mostly bruising on my arm, with a few lacerations there, and I'm dehydrated. The worst, though, is the back of my head. I hit it on something hard and was knocked unconscious. I don't know for how long or how much blood I lost, but it'll require sutures. I don't have my insurance card, but I can call my office back home and give you that information if I can use your phone."

"Lacerations, sutures," she repeated nodding. "Are you in the healthcare profession?"

"I'm a general practitioner near Raleigh, North Carolina."

"Oh," she said, and she sounded like her mouth made a complete circle as she said it, though he couldn't see it.

"Please, Sir, have a seat. We'll collect that information in a minute. I'll send somebody right out with some water and get you back quickly," she said, waving him toward a chair. "Charity," she called through a speaker phone, "I need you up front."

Almost immediately, a younger woman appeared through a door behind the front counter. "Is the third room clean and available?" asked the woman at the desk.

"It can be in about five minutes," said the young woman, whose name, Matthew figured, must be Charity.

"We have a head injury," the receptionist gestured to Matthew. "Bring him a bottle of water and call him straight back as soon as the room is ready."

"Yes, Ma'am," said Charity and glanced over at Matthew before she disappeared through the door behind the desk. She looked to be in her early twenties, maybe a college student, Matthew assessed. Clad in scrubs, she was a medium height and build with dirty blonde hair pulled back in a low ponytail. Her most striking feature was her huge brown eyes. She looked like a young fawn when she glanced his way.

Leaning his head against the wall to wait wasn't an option. His head had begun to throb again, and he couldn't put pressure on any part of it. Matthew placed the backpack on his lap, leaned his elbows on it, and tried to think through all that had happened in the past day. It was merely a day, wasn't it? Looking around, he noticed an old-fashioned calendar from a local insurance agency on the counter. Craning forward, he saw that the day was Sunday, as the receptionist had said, and it was April the twelfth. Twenty-four hours had made an unbelievable difference in his life.

He would need to call his office. He was due back in the office to see the few patients who came in person tomorrow. He had no intention of going home without Danbury unless Justin told him to.

He wondered for at least the hundredth time where Danbury was, what had happened to him, and prayed he was still alive and would be well. Before he could think much more about that, Charity appeared beside him, handing him a water bottle and holding out her hands as if to steady him if he shouldn't be able to stand.

"This way, Sir," she said.

He stood, opened the water bottle, and downed half of it. She led him through a doorway to the left of the reception desk and down a short hallway to the last room on the right.

"Or did I hear that it's actually Doctor?" she asked.

"That's right," he said. "I'm a physician in a family practice in a little town outside of Raleigh, North Carolina."

"I want to go to North Carolina!" she said, and then looked embarrassed as she ushered him into the room. "There are excellent medical schools there."

"There are," said Matthew, downing the rest of the water bottle. "You want to go to med school?"

"I do! My grades aren't good enough to get into Duke," she confessed. "My MCAT is good, but I want to take it again. There's a great med school in Deacon Grove and another in Welton Simons. Which did you go to? Are you originally from North Carolina?"

Before he could answer, she said, "I'm sorry, I'm asking too many questions. Have a seat up here," she said, patting the patient table. "We only have one medical assistant and one doctor here today, but you've been flagged as a priority. Our MA should be right in."

"It's OK," he said, smiling at her reassuringly. He hoped she could see it in his eyes above the mask as he dropped the backpack on the floor and climbed onto the exam table. "Asking questions is how you learn things. I didn't go to either of those, though they're great schools. I opted for an osteopathic medical degree and went to a smaller private university in Mallard's Creek, a little town that nobody outside the immediate area has ever heard of."

"I have heard of that one. It sounds like a great program."

"I thought it was. I wanted a holistic approach to medicine. The problem with specializing is the pillarization. More classically trained physicians know a wealth and depth of information about their specialty. Many of them can't see outside of it to find systemic issues or interactions with other systems or functions. It's not their fault; it's how they're trained. That can be limiting in fully treating patients, though."

"That makes sense." She nodded.

"I'd be happy to help you tour any of those schools if you decide you want to apply. What's your timeframe?"

"Oh, thank you! That would be great. I just finished my undergraduate degree, a bachelor of science at Radfolk University. I moved back home to work and save up some money while I'm studying to retake the MCAT in September."

"Let me know when you're ready. I don't have my business card on me, but you can reach me at the phone number I'll list in my paperwork here. Put it in your phone and contact me when you're ready to visit."

Her face lit with a genuine smile that he saw in her eyes as she reached for the empty water bottle. "I can take that for you," she said. "Would you like another one now? Or do you want to wait to see if you need an IV?"

"Thanks," he said, handing her the empty bottle. As she opened a cabinet under the counter and threw it into a trash bin, he added, "And yes, another one now would be great. My headache is a little better after that one."

"Sure, Doctor. I'll be right back. In the meantime, if you can fill this out, that would be so helpful," she said, handing him a clipboard he hadn't realized she held.

Matthew slid off the table to examine himself in a mirror over the sink in the room as the door clicked closed behind her. He looked rough, but his pupils seemed normal, so that was a good sign. His face was scratched in a couple of places, which he hadn't noticed. Rolling up his sleeves, he carefully but thoroughly washed his hands and arms and then his face as best he could, drying off with paper towels.

Climbing back onto the table, he slumped there wanting to curl up and sleep for a week. He knew he needed to fill out the intake forms. Then he'd have his head tended to, get thoroughly checked out, and wait for Justin before he could settle his bill and find a place where he could rest. And then what? Maybe there was a local hotel, he thought, as he unclipped a pen and began filling out the form.

Charity returned with another water bottle before he was through the forms, though he had completed the initial information on the intake form.

"I lost my wallet and my cell phone was crushed," said Matthew. "We'll need to call my office for the insurance information and leave a message with the answering service. Our senior partner is on call this weekend. He'll get back to you quickly with that information. I've filled this first form with the information I know."

"You were in an ATV accident?" Charity asked, handing him the water bottle.

"I was," he said, opening the bottle and drinking half of it before returning to the form.

"I can take that top form and get you in the system."

Nodding, he pulled the intake page from the clipboard and handed it to her.

"They'll be right in," she said and slipped quietly out.

He'd finished the remaining forms—all of the detailed information about his medical history—and the water bottle when a crisply dressed medical assistant, wearing purple scrubs, swooshed into the room and began briskly plying him with questions. The guy was calm and efficient, but not warm and fuzzy, as he took vitals and tapped the information into a tablet.

"Let me see this injury," said the guy after he'd checked Matthew's pupils and seemed satisfied with the results.

Matthew spun on the table to reveal the back of his head, which he knew was matted and caked with blood and dirt.

"That is a nasty one," said the guy, probing the area with a gloved hand. "I'll clean and shave around it. Then we can stitch it up. The doc will likely ask for x-rays to be sure there isn't a skull fracture."

"OK," Matthew nodded agreement. "That's reasonable."

A couple of hours later, the back of Matthew's head had been shaved, cleaned, sutured, and x-rayed. While waiting in the exam room for the results of the x-ray, he pulled out a protein bar and ate it, downing another bottle of water. He'd adjusted the exam table to lean comfortably, partially raised on his side.

When the tap at the door came, Matthew awoke, startled. He expected the doctor to walk in, when he realized where he was. Through the door, instead, came the best sight he'd seen in two days – Justin McMillian. His dirty blond hair long and shaggy, he sported at least two weeks' worth of facial hair growth. There was no telling where he'd been recently or under what cover.

"Justin!" said Matthew, rising slowly from the table. "Thank God."

"Got yourself in it again, huh?" asked Justin jovially, returning Matthew's brotherly hug.

"Not purposefully. I agreed to help work on a cold case that was over twenty years old. That was it."

"And you poked a hornet's nest. You have no idea what you've gotten into. I don't either entirely, but whatever it is, it isn't good."

"Well then, enlighten me," said Matthew.

"I will. But not here," Justin said, taking a seat across from Matthew. "They'll be in to check you out in just a minute. Your office provided your insurance information. I paid the deductible, which was minor. Professional courtesy, they called it. The x-rays look good. Apparently, your head is too hard to be fractured," he joked.

"Oh, and here," Justin added, reaching into his pocket and handing

Matthew a cell phone. "I took the liberty of having your cloud content downloaded. I put this one in an indestructible case, at least according to the packaging."

"How did you manage all of that?"

"Called in a few favors. I had a buddy working on your phone while I was working on my flight and car rental. I had to drive in from about an hour away."

"Really?" asked Matthew. "How long have I been in here?" The interior room was windowless. He had no idea how long he'd been asleep.

"All afternoon. It's after six now. The clinic is technically closed. After they called your office, I guess they decided to let you stay and rest until I could get here. They told me to take you out the back door. I circled the block and parked back there."

Matthew looked at Justin oddly.

"You listed me as your emergency contact," said Justin. "They called me to be sure everything was OK. Sounds like they were skeptical of your ATV 'accident.'"

"Oh! How'd you convince them that's all it was?"

"I told them we'd been friends since childhood, that you'd always been clumsy and seemed to decide to be a daredevil at all the wrong times."

"What?" asked Matthew.

"OK, maybe that daredevil part was more me, but you were clumsy as a kid. Is that really what happened? An ATV 'accident?' And where's Danbury? How'd you get separated?"

"Sort of," said Matthew. "And I wish I knew where Danbury is. I got whacked in the back of the head. When I came to, he and the ATV he'd been riding were gone. There was no trace of him. I looked."

A young man Matthew hadn't seen before brought in the final paperwork for the visit. The guy had him sign it, then handed Matthew a small bag of bandages and supplies.

"You're free to go out the back exit," the guy told him, pointing across the short hallway before he left them alone again.

"Let's get out of here. We can talk on the way," said Justin standing. "When have you eaten?"

"I've had two protein bars today, and I could really go for a steak with all the trimmings."

"Sounds good. I'm glad you haven't lost your appetite," said Justin grinning. "I saw a place just down the road that had an *Open for Takeout* sign in the window. And there's a hotel here that has an open sign too." Lowering his voice, he added, so quietly that Matthew had to lean in to hear him, "If Danbury is MIA, then I assume we're staying close. Unless you think he's been taken somewhere else."

"If he has, I have no idea where," Matthew answered equally as quietly. "Conrad Manchester said this was the closest town. He gave us general directions before he disappeared heading the other way."

Checking the small bag that contained bandages, tape, ointment, and Tylenol, Matthew added it to his backpack and followed Justin out the back exit. They headed for the restaurant a mere four blocks down the street and parked in the gravel lot beside it. A wall of dust rolled up behind them, and Matthew was happy to have the windows up until it settled.

Leaving the backpack but taking the new phone he didn't want out of his sight, Matthew slid out and walked like a bow-legged cowboy on sore legs to the door of what turned out to be a steak and seafood restaurant. The view from the doorway indicated the atmosphere inside was lacking, but the food, he soon learned, more than made up for it. They placed their order with a teenager who sat on the other side of a kiosk table positioned at the door blocking entry.

That the pandemic had necessitated the takeout-only policy was fine with Matthew. It wasn't as if he were dressed to eat out anyway. Brushing himself off again, as if that would help with clothing that had been through rough terrain and then slept in the woods in, he chided himself.

They placed their orders and returned to the rented car where they lingered, waiting for their food to be brought out. Starting from the beginning of the day before, Matthew began explaining all that had happened. As his stomach rumbled loudly, a tiny woman, whose age was impossible to determine, delivered their food in bags.

"Let's go check into that hotel. We can eat there, and you can tell me the rest," said Justin, starting the car and driving five blocks to a hotel at the edge of the small town.

"The first thing I want is food," agreed Matthew. "The second is a shower. I could use your help rebandaging my head, if you're up for it."

Justin checked them in, procuring two rooms with king-sized beds and an adjoining door. After they hauled their meager possessions up to the second floor, Matthew opened his door and dumped the backpack and his jacket on a long desk. Removing his heavy hiking boots, he put those beside the backpack and washed his hands before tearing into the bags of food.

Polishing off a steak, baked potato, broccoli, and side salad, Matthew explained, between bites, all that had happened. Staring down at a melting chocolate brownie sundae and a cup of decaf coffee, he asked, "Want to split this?"

"We used to share those huge ones downtown as kids," said Justin. "Remember?"

"Yeah, it's just like that. This one looks smaller, but to kids everything looked bigger."

Chuckling, Justin picked up a plastic spork and dug in on the other side.

Sated, Matthew leaned back in the office chair at the little desk in his hotel room, happy he could finally put his bandaged head on the headrest somewhat comfortably.

"Now tell me what hornet's nest we've poked," he said.

"Didn't you want a shower first? You need clothes. No offense, but you reek, Man."

"I had a bag in the back of the SUV Danbury rented, but I can't go back there. It's likely being watched, if it's still there. I'm OK on clothes for tonight. I can wash some things out in the sink and hang them in front of the radiator o dry by morning. I do need more Tylenol, though."

"There's some in the bag the doctor's office gave you, right?"

"Yeah, and there's still a generic brand in the backpack. The one Manchester tossed at me when we were leaving the underground bunker at the cabin."

"That guy sounds like he's got plans on top of plans. And multiple places to hide. Like you said, he's thinking like raccoons and foxes. He must have multiple dens."

"I wonder if he knows where Danbury is or at least who snatched him."

"Think you can find him to ask if he does?"

Pondering a moment, he responded, "I wouldn't begin to know where to look for him. But there is somebody who might be able to find him again." Matthew told Justin about Ogilvy and the conversation they'd had after he'd been shot at by the lake.

"Sounds like he told you all he knows," said Justin.

"If that's true, then I have no idea how to find Manchester. He's the kind of guy who isn't found unless he wants to be. He'd be more likely to find us."

24 ~ COMPARING NOTES

Justin went through the door to his adjoining room, leaving Matthew to shower. Dumping the contents of the backpack, Matthew sorted through it. Toiletries were not included in the bag, but he'd asked for a toothbrush and toothpaste when they checked in. Shampoo and soap were in dispensers mounted on the shower wall, so he figured he was set.

Carefully, he removed the bandage and washed his hair, gingerly around the sutures as he showered. The back of his head was tender, and he was sure it was badly bruised. It wasn't the best plan. Ordinarily, he'd wait a couple of days before disturbing it, were he not so filthy from his ordeal.

He washed his T-shirt and boxer briefs in the sink, wringing them out thoroughly, and hung them over the luggage stand in front of the old-fashioned radiator to dry. Initially, he felt ridiculous in the soft, white, terrycloth robe he'd found in the closet in his room. Catching sight of himself in the mirror, he thought he looked like a giant fluffy chicken. The robe was soft, warm, and cozy, a much-needed respite after the night before. Chicken or not, it was nice.

Peeking discreetly out of the window, he realized it opened. Not that he wanted it open to let the chilly night air in, but it was surprising because they were on the second floor. Some sort of decorative railing was on the bottom half of the window, likely to keep toddlers from falling out. The partial moon glinted on the few cars parked beneath him in front of the three-story building.

"This robe is humbling," said Matthew when Justin came in to bandage his head.

"You're just having a spa day, Man," Justin joked. "Relax and enjoy it while you can."

"I'd leave the bandage off, but I want to sleep and not disturb the sutures. I'm not sure the medicated ointment the clinic gave me does much good, but it will provide an occlusive layer and prevent drying."

"OK, ointment it is," said Justin. "I'll do my best on the bandaging," he added, looking dubiously at the supplies.

After Matthew's head was bandaged reasonably well, Justin said, "I'll show you what I've learned. And explain what I know so far. Then we'll swap."

"Deal," said Matthew.

Pulling out his new smart phone, he tapped to log into the app and shared the document he and Danbury had been compiling.

"There, that's what we'd learned up until yesterday, who we've talked to, and what Danbury did before I got involved."

Retrieving a tablet from his room, Justin held it out. "This is from my interview with Patricia Shrubpeal. She agreed to talk to me. It started out well. She was telling me about her days as a US ambassador. There wasn't anything new or exciting in the first part of the conversation. It was simple introductory questions and answers. When I asked about the bombing, and particularly about Whattlesby, she got thoroughly agitated."

Matthew looked over Justin's shoulder as he ran a video clip forward on the tablet. An elderly woman, classically clad, sat in a tall leather chair. Stopping, restarting, and trying again, Justin said, "Here it is."

In the video, Justin's voice asked, "What can you tell me about the embassy bombing in Nairobi?"

"That it was the worst day of my career and, indeed, my life!" she replied. "It was horrific."

"I'm sure it was beyond what most people can begin to imagine," Justin commiserated. "What can you tell me about Lemako

Whattlesby, and what happened to him that day?"

Matthew noted how Whattlesby's first name rolled effortlessly out of Justin's mouth. The woman's face moved quickly from placid peace to alarm after the first question, then registered abject horror at the second question.

"Turn that thing off!" she exclaimed, obviously distraught. "If you don't turn it off, we're finished here. I escaped with my life, and I counted myself fortunate. Don't dredge all of this up again. Please, don't do it. Turn it off," she pleaded with Justin.

"People died that day," said Justin's voice, softly. "More people are potentially in danger now as a result of whatever happened back then. It's connected. You can help to prevent more needless deaths if you'll talk to me about this."

"Turn it off!" she said, her face clearly depicting the terror she felt and her voice sounding near hysteria.

The video ended, and Justin leaned back in the office chair at the desk in Matthew's hotel room.

"What do you make of that?" asked Justin.

"Something traumatic happened to her, probably beyond the bombing, involving Whattlesby."

"I agree. She was agitated when I asked about the bombing, but she completely lost it when I asked about Whattlesby. And there's this," he added, tapping the tablet. "I coaxed her into a voice recording, without the video, about the events leading up to the bombing."

"That's right," said the woman's voice. "I was contacted by someone who said they were from Iron Clad security."

"Iron Clad," said Justin. "What do you know about the company?"

"It was one of a handful of security companies contracting with the government during that time," she answered. "One of the smaller ones, one of the few I fully trusted."

"And they went out of business abruptly in January of 1999, right?"

"That sounds about right," she answered. "It was after I'd come home to recuperate and recover. It's like my life was partitioned in two. Things in the sequence of my life were either before that event or after it."

"Traumatic experiences can have that effect," Justin's voice commiserated. "Do you know why Iron Clad went out of business?"

"I don't. I never did know. Honestly, I didn't question it. Those companies came and went from favor with administrative changes. Some lasted longer than others."

"Let's go back to the phone call you received, before the event in Nairobi. You were contacted directly by someone at that company, you said?"

"I was," she responded.

"When was that, and what did they say?"

"It was the summer of 1998. July, perhaps. The man told me he needed to speak to me urgently, as a matter of national security, but that he couldn't do it by phone. He asked to meet with me."

"Where were you when he contacted you?"

"I was still in Washington at the time, preparing to fly out to Nairobi a few days later. He told me to postpone my trip and meet with him. I told him I couldn't postpone the trip, but that I'd make time to talk to him before I left. National security, that sounded important. I asked why he came directly to me. It was unusual. He didn't answer. He reiterated how critical it was that we meet because he had crucial information for me."

"Did you meet with him?"

"I didn't. We set the time and location to meet, but I was late arriving. He was either already gone, assuming I wouldn't show, or he didn't make it at all. I did ponder which it was at the time. I figured I'd never know for certain."

"Do you remember who that was, the person you were supposed to meet?"

"I don't. I should have asked him for a physical description to know him when I saw him, but I was engrossed in my plans to return to

Kenya. I assumed he'd know me on sight. I wondered, later, if it had anything to do with the bombing. But I assumed that US Intelligence surely would have acted, had they known. And they should have known. If somebody from Iron Clad knew about it, they'd have worked with Homeland Security, not me."

"How specific was the location to meet? Would he have had to know you by sight to meet you there?"

"No, I guess not. It was a specific table in the front corner of a coffee shop in Washington. When I got there, the table was clean and empty. I sat down and waited about fifteen minutes, but that's all the time I had to spare. I had far too many things to do preparing to fly out a few days later."

"Can you try to remember exactly when it was? It's important, or I wouldn't be bothering you with all of this."

"Oh, I haven't thought about this in so many years! It must have been early July. No, it had to have been more mid-July. I had been in Nairobi a couple of weeks when the unspeakable happened, the bombing on August seventh, and the phone call came a couple of days before I left to go."

"Let's try this. I'll name some of the people who worked for Iron Clad during that time. You tell me if any of them sound familiar, OK?"

"I'll do my best," she said.

Justin began calling out names that were unfamiliar to Matthew.

Pausing the recording, Justin said, "The first was the owner of the company, the other three were directors who reported to him. The owner started the company about ten years prior. Two of the three directors he knew from previous employment. The other one he'd recently hired, but he'd known the guy since college."

"Interesting," said Matthew. "A tight-knit group. They hired people they thought they could trust. But for what?"

"Good question," agreed Justin, then tapped to continue playing the recording.

"I knew them," Shrubpeal said. "It was neither the owner nor the upper management tier you named. That's another reason the call was odd."

"Erik Danbury," said Justin.

"His name sounds familiar," she paused. "But I'm not certain it was him."

"But it's possible?"

"Perhaps. I do remember the name, but I don't think that's who it was."

"OK, how about Brian Ogilvy?"

"That name isn't familiar at all."

"Conrad Manchester."

"Oh! Now that one sounds right. It might have been him," she said, sounding excited.

"I know it's been nearly twenty-two years, but can you remember anything about the conversation on the phone? Anything might be helpful."

"I really can't remember any more than I've told you. I did think it odd that he'd come directly to me with a national security issue. That wasn't in my wheelhouse. As an ambassador, of course I was concerned with security issues. I knew there was risk involved, but I never dreamed," her voice tapered off and Justin stopped the recording.

"That's all I got out of her," said Justin. "If you think about the timeline she provided, she went back to Nairobi a couple of weeks before the bombing. Erik Danbury would have been dead by then. It could have been Manchester who called to warn her after Erik had been murdered."

"Why wouldn't he have met her, though? Unless he got spooked."

"That's possible."

"Wouldn't he have tried again, if that were the case?"

"It depends on what spooked him. If the call was intercepted or he was tailed, he might have realized that it wasn't safe to talk to her," answered Justin.

"For who? Him or her?"

"Potentially both of them."

"That's all possible," said Matthew, one eyebrow raised and his foot tapping in concentration. "If Erik Danbury had heard chatter about plans for the bombing and shared that with Manchester, then he'd been killed, Manchester would be wary of trying to get that information through. Whoever it was that Erik Danbury didn't trust with that information would be telling. Iron Clad? US Homeland Security?"

"That's what I thought too," said Justin. "He wanted to warn her without sticking his neck out too far."

"And then Manchester's wife was killed a few months after the bombing and immediately after Iron Clad went out of business. We've thought that was about her alibi for the Danburys' murder. What if that wasn't it? What if it was to shut him up? Maybe that's also why Iron Clad closed their doors so abruptly."

"That's logical. If Erik Danbury, and later Conrad Manchester, had gone to Iron Clad with whatever it was that they knew, maybe his wife's murder wasn't about the Danbury murders. If they all had prior knowledge of the bombing and somebody didn't want to stop it for whatever reason, then Iron Clad had to be shut down alongside Manchester."

"Makes sense to me," said Matthew. After pondering for a moment, he asked, "What if it wasn't Conrad Manchester or anyone actually from Iron Clad who called her?"

"What are you getting at?"

"What if they wanted to draw her out for some reason. Her picture would have been readily available back in 1998, right? They wouldn't likely have drawn her out just to see her. Maybe the caller was drawing her away from something instead of to something else."

"That's a possibility."

"Could they have planted something in her luggage for transport to Kenya? Or tried to? Airport security, private and public, would have been laxer before September of 2001. We still thought we were invincible and impenetrable in 1998. We found out on 9/11 that wasn't true, but who knows who had been in the country before that and for what nefarious purpose."

"True."

"It all makes my head hurt worse. We've had so many theories. Danbury's parents' death could have been about the airport runway expansion project, or it might have been about what his father learned of the impending bombing in Kenya. We've thought that Manchester's wife being murdered and his subsequent disappearance was about being accused of the Danburys' murders. It makes sense that it was because of what he knew about the bombing in Nairobi instead."

"Likely, it's all related. We just don't know how yet."

"Manchester was set up as the fall guy for the Danburys' murder. That seems pretty clear. Why that was or who actually murdered them seems as far out of reach as it ever has. And why would somebody now snatch Danbury or—" Matthew broke off. He was not wanting to admit that they could have killed him. "I mean, he knows nothing more than we know. Are we that close on the trail and we don't realize it yet?"

"It's possible," said Justin as he scrolled through the document Matthew had shared on his tablet. "Somebody didn't want you finding this Ogilvy guy."

"But is it the same 'somebody' who tried to kill me and snatched Danbury? Or did they try to kill me?"

"What do you mean?"

"Wouldn't they have shot me if killing me was their goal? It would have been surer and easier."

"Maybe. Unless they wanted it to look like an accident. A bash on the head looks like an ATV accident—at least on the surface if nobody probes any deeper. A bullet hole, not so much. Shots can be heard for long distances too."

"I doubt there were people around to hear it. Maybe there are houses around the area that I didn't see. Except for the time of day, shots could be attributed to hunters. But it was dark out," said Matthew pensively. After a moment of contemplation, he asked, "What do we do next?"

"First is finding Danbury. With that might come a lot of the information we need to know. This town is the closest one to where you were when Danbury disappeared. There are a few others farther away. I'd say we start here. As outsiders, it might be hard to get information. The locals might not talk to us. We'll start here and see how it goes."

"Let's start at the local clothing store, or thrift shop, wherever I can find some clean clothes."

"Sure. Barber shops, diners, bars," added Justin. "Sometimes the post office. Those are all great places to strike up conversations. Sometimes people give away more than they meant to or that they know is important information. You need a haircut, right?" he teased Matthew. "So that it's all the same length?"

"We're not shaving my head, Man."

"You wouldn't shave your head for a buddy?"

"I would if I had to. I can get the rest cut shorter while the shaved part grows back out."

"I need a trim, but I was planning to do it myself," said Justin. "I guess there's not much else you can do tonight, dressed in your fluffy chicken robe."

Matthew grimaced at the comment but then laughed. He hadn't shared his chicken analogy with Justin, but as was often the case, their minds were on the same wavelength.

"I could go out tonight to the local bar, if there's one open. Some of them have outdoor seating with radiant heaters. I'll see what I can find."

"I'll do whatever we need to do in the morning. Tonight, I'm going to bed. I'm so exhausted I'm no good to anybody."

"I was going to tell you not to wait up, Dad," Justin joked. "Just leave the adjoining door cracked in case I learn anything interesting."

"Can't you get through that lock? Child's play!" jeered Matthew, chuckling.

"I mean, I could, but you could leave it open and save me the trouble," Justin answered, grinning.

"OK, be careful. Ugh," said Matthew, laughing. "I sounded like my dad just then. But seriously, Man, I don't know if they left me for dead or just wanted me temporarily disabled. Whoever 'they' are, they've seen me, and they took my ID. They know everything about me. If they've been around since you got here, they've seen you with me."

"Duly noted," said Justin. "You'll need to cancel credit cards and all of that tomorrow."

"Yeah, I know. I figured I'd call my neighbor and talk her through getting into my lockbox and pulling out the photocopies of all of that, then ask her to read it all out to me. I'd call Penn, but I don't want to tell her that Danbury is missing. She'll contact me soon enough when she hasn't heard from him," Matthew added wryly.

After they'd made plans to get out by six, grab breakfast, and start canvassing the town, Justin went back to his room. The outer door clicked quietly behind him. Matthew slipped between cool sheets under a soft fluffy blanket and thanked God silently before sinking into a deep, sound sleep.

Looking around and trying to get his bearings, Matthew was forcefully yanked from the depths of the dreamworld by an insistent voice. "Doc, get up! Now! Get dressed! We have to go!"

"Danbury?" he asked, his mind fuzzy but alert enough to know that Danbury was the only person who called him Doc. Somehow, the voice wasn't right.

"No, they have Warren. And they're coming for you. Get up! We've got to get out now!"

Bolting upright into a fight stance, Matthew realized three things.

His black belt training in Tae Kwando from childhood was still an instinct. He'd gone to bed buck naked because he had no sleep clothing with him—what clothing he did have was drying—and it was Conrad Manchester who had abruptly ended his tranquil dreamworld.

Manchester was found only when he wanted to be. This must be important, or he wouldn't have resurfaced now, Matthew reasoned through the sleepy fog in his brain.

"Let's go!" Manchester said again. "Now!"

Manchester seemed unfazed as Matthew bounced across the bed and pulled on damp clothing—boxer briefs and a T-shirt under his other clothing. His left arm and inner thighs still objected as clothing rubbed over them, and the dampness wasn't welcome. Stuffing the contents of the bag from the clinic into the backpack, he added the toiletries the hotel had provided. He snatched his phone off the charger, stowed the charger, and quickly stuffed his feet into damp socks and into his hiking boots and laced them.

"Turn it off," said Manchester.

"What?" asked Matthew, his mind still hazy with sleep.

"The phone. Turn it off or—" began Manchester.

Pulling it quickly from his pocket, Matthew turned it off. "See?" he held it up before stuffing it safely back into his pocket. He wasn't giving the guy a shot at destroying yet another new smart phone. "Ready. I'll get Justin."

"No," said Manchester. "I don't trust him; he's government. Just you. Let's go."

"No! You trust me because Danbury does. I trust Justin with my life. Danbury trusted him too, but he's not here to tell you. I'm not going without him," said Matthew, darting to the adjoining door.

He need not have bothered. Justin stood in the doorway, fully clothed. His backpack was over his shoulder, his hair buzz cut, his face shaved. In his hand he held a baseball cap.

"Let's roll," said Justin. "Which way are they coming from?"

"East. The front. Any minute now. They won't stay there. Out now, or we'll be surrounded," said Manchester, leading the way across the hall. In one fluid motion, he flipped something at the door across the hallway, flung the door open, and darted to the window with Matthew and Justin close on his heels.

25 ~ RUN FOR THE HILLS

Disassembling the window of the hotel room across the hall in mere seconds, Manchester crawled through. Holding on to the decorative railing outside, he slid down it, and dropped out of sight. Justin followed and Matthew brought up the rear. Normally, he'd have paused to consider the safety of the maneuver, but a worse threat was arriving behind him. He dropped to the ground without hesitation, thankful to have landed softly on thick grass below.

"Why not the back door?" asked Matthew, surprised by the ease of the exercise.

"Cameras," said Manchester as he darted into the woods behind the hotel. There was nothing to do but follow. Matthew figured he'd eventually be able to rest and stop running. It seemed he'd done nothing but run toward and then away from things for far too long. Maybe the other two were used to that, but he never had been, nor did he want to be now.

Through the woods, over logs, around bushes, up a ridge, down the other side, and over a creek they ran before Manchester slowed. How he managed to run in near darkness with a mere partial moon lighting the way was a mystery, but with him leading, it was easier to follow. The sky was clear, which made the moon brighter. Was that a hunter's moon or hunted moon, Matthew pondered. He wasn't sure.

"We go two ridges over heading west, then turn slightly north. We'll regroup there," Manchester instructed. "We'll have vehicles after that second ridge."

"What's there?" asked Justin.

"Another den," said Matthew flatly.

Manchester turned to him. "Useful," was all he said, before he darted off again.

Following Manchester had been difficult the first time because the guy was built for speed. Another inhibitor, Matthew already knew, had been his hiking boots. While they were built for rough terrain and they'd protected his ankles from turning multiple times, they were a hindrance. An added problem, he soon discovered, was he hadn't taken the time to tighten the laces properly when he put them on. He felt blisters rubbing and bursting on both heels.

Wishing for moleskin he knew would be a luxury, he muttered under his breath as it came in gasps, "Add that to the chaffed inner thighs, bruised arm, and bashed head."

"What?" asked Justin, who was just ahead of him.

"Nothing. I'm right behind you."

Matthew's lungs burned and felt like they would explode as he gasped in the cool night air. They stopped, briefly, to catch their breath beside a rock formation. Since the COVID virus had hit, Matthew had been jogging more because Penn's gym was forced to close. For that, he was now thankful. He heard Justin's breath coming in similar gulps beside him. Only Conrad Manchester seemed unfazed by the exertion.

"One more ridge, then we ride," said Manchester, darting off again.

Arriving at yet another of the caves with stashed ATVs, Matthew wasn't sure if riding it on the rough terrain or running over it would be more painful at this point. Two of the three vehicles started easily, but the third refused.

"We'll double," said Justin, shifting his backpack to the front. Matthew jumped on behind him and held on as they peeled out behind Manchester. How, he wondered again, did the guy have so many stashes and why, in each one, were there multiple ATVs for one person? He had so many questions. What had happened to the underground room at the cabin that had blown up? If they ever paused long enough, he determined to ask.

Leaning around Justin, he tried to get his bearings. It became easier about an hour later when the sun came up behind them. They were headed, as Manchester had said, due west.

Pulling up short, Manchester dismounted and moved tangled vines in front of a cave. He rolled the ATV in. Matthew and Justin climbed off behind him and Matthew stood, frozen in place as Justin stowed the ATV. How was Manchester unbothered by hanging on with his inner thighs? The guy seemed to be made of flexible steel, Matthew concluded.

"A mile and a half to go, on foot, northwest. We do the final half mile approach slowly and silently."

"Got it," said Justin. Matthew nodded in the dimly appearing light before setting off again at a breakneck pace through the woods. At least, with the sun coming up over the mountain behind them, he could see where he was going—mostly.

Slowing, Manchester led the way along a path inside of a thick hedge of rhododendron. Something nearby was blooming, and it smelled wonderful. Manchester turned to glare at Matthew when he stepped on a branch and it snapped, making a loud noise.

Pausing, they waited for Manchester to be satisfied before moving on. Justin, their rear guard, was far more adept at this sort of thing. Matthew matched his steps into those of Manchester and realized it was something he should have thought to do earlier.

They approached a small cabin that appeared to be in about the same shape as the one they'd been in before. There was no clearing around this one. Trees had grown all around its foundation, then shot up at least twenty feet into the air, Matthew estimated. Brambles, vines, and briers were taking it over so that there appeared to be no way in.

After circling the perimeter, Manchester approached the back of the cabin and went through a series of taps, pulls, and prods to open what appeared to be a cellar door. It, too, was overgrown with brambles and covered in dried leaves that didn't move as he opened it. Instead of entering the cabin, as Matthew had presumed, they descended steep steps carved into the rock by the light of a single beam that Manchester held.

When they reached the bottom, Manchester tapped, prodded, and pulled a wall until it, too, opened to them. After they were through and the wall closed behind them, Manchester pushed a button to dimly light the rocky room. Turning to them, he said menacingly, "You were never here."

"Never where?" asked Matthew. "I literally have no idea where I am right now."

"Got it," said Justin. "You decided to trust me?"

"Didn't have a choice," grunted Manchester. "Don't make me regret it."

"Hey, all I want to do is find Danbury and figure out what's going on. I was doing him a favor gathering information," said Justin, holding out his hands. "Do you know where he is?"

"I have an idea."

"Alive?"

"I believe so," said Manchester, to Matthew's relief.

"Any thoughts on extraction?"

"A few."

As they sized each other up, Matthew took in his surroundings. The interior was rock, like that of the excavated cavern beneath the earlier cabin, though this one looked to have been naturally carved. Passageways led off in two directions, and the cool dampness was eerie.

"Let's hear it," said Justin.

"This way," said Manchester, ducking to make his way through one of the passages.

Matthew had to bend nearly at the waist as he and Justin ducked and followed Manchester. The passageway was short, and it opened into another cavernous space; this one had added rock walls built around it. Tapping and flipping something Matthew never saw in the wall, Manchester caused the room to light. The wall flipped open, revealing panels of monitors and equipment.

"Give me a minute," said Manchester, seating himself on a bench in front of the controls, "to get it all up and running."

As one monitor after another came to life, Manchester pointed to one of them. "There," he said.

"What are we looking at?" asked Matthew, leaning in on one side with Justin on the other.

"Infrared images," answered Justin. "A heating or cooling system or something else big and boxy, there," he pointed, "and people there."

"Right," said Manchester. "I believe that's where they have Warren."

"How did you find them? And why do you think he's there?"

"Tracking devices. On two of their vehicles. They both stopped first at the road I told you to take to get into Coalglow, near the place where you and Warren should have come across the ridge on the ATVs. They stayed there over an hour. Then, they led me to this location, and I searched it to determine what was here."

"When did you put tracking devices on their vehicles?" asked Matthew, thinking the guy hadn't had time to accomplish so much since he'd seen him last.

"I circled back and planted them after the cabin blew," said Manchester. "They were too distracted to notice at first. They figured out we were gone, though. They were in pursuit before the smoke cleared."

"You knew they were coming after us?"

"I figured they were and hoped you had a good enough head start. I couldn't stop them then and there. I had the escape route and the cover for the cave, but the arsenal is in that bunker. My oversight. That won't happen again."

Matthew thought slit tires would have worked, but maybe there wasn't time.

"Back to Danbury," said Justin. "Where are they holding him? And why they didn't kill him?"

"They will. When they're done with him," said Manchester. "We need to get him out first. It's why I came for you."

"And I thought you were just being nice," said Matthew acidly. "How did you know where we were and that they were coming for us?"

"You," corrected Manchester. "They were coming for you. Your buddy was just icing on that cake."

"Why?" asked Matthew.

"Because they know what you know. And they'll leave nobody alive to know that if they can help it."

"I wish I knew which 'what' that was," said Matthew, realizing the confusing sentence he'd just uttered but vindicated when both of the others nodded. Then, he added, "It still doesn't make sense. How did you find me?"

"Charity."

"Charity?" asked Matthew, the word sounding familiar to him. "You mean the young woman at the community clinic?"

"Right."

"Did she contact you?"

Manchester nodded.

"How? Why? When?" Matthew asked, trying to make sense of it all.

"She's my goddaughter. Erik Danbury's too. She's the daughter of a buddy of ours from the Corp. He died when she was little."

"And she contacted you, why?" asked Matthew, incredulous that anybody knew how to reach the elusive Conrad Manchester.

"She wanted my advice."

"About what?"

"She asks for my advice. Regularly," said Manchester, clearly annoyed. "I've been a stand-in dad for years. It's why I moved up here. When her mom got sick with cancer, she was in college. I made sure she could always reach me. She thought you were a nice man, she liked you, and she pulled a Rahab when two huge rough-looking men came in asking for you. She said they looked like they meant business. Her words. And before you ask, no she hadn't seen them before."

"A Rahab?" asked Matthew.

"Like in the Bible," said Manchester, sounding thoroughly exasperated.

"Oh!" said Matthew. "At Jericho." He knew the story of Rahab hiding the Israelite spies, but he was surprised Manchester did.

"Exactly. She told them you had been there but that you'd already gone," explained Manchester when Justin looked confused. "Charity is both smart and intuitive. She made sure they believed her and they'd left. She called me and asked if she'd done the right thing and what to do next. I reassured her you were OK, she'd done the right thing, and I'd take it from there. I need the extra manpower to extract Erik's son. I followed them, listened in remotely, learned that they knew where you were, and made sure I got to you before they did. No more questions. We get to work."

"OK," said Matthew, less confused in some ways and more so in others. "What do we need to do?"

"There's what looks like a warehouse, likely containing a bunker. You can see the heat signatures come and go from an internal space where they aren't detected."

"Where is it?" asked Justin. "And what's surrounding it?"

"It's an old mine. Near a mining town. North and east of here. About an hour by car. Just west of Clinch Mountain."

"Population?" asked Justin.

"Abandoned," answered Manchester.

"Nearest populated town?"

"Nothing, except a few rural houses within nearly fifty clicks. There's a small church about eight clicks east, with an old family cemetery. That's it. The mining town was on the historic register and in line to get revamped and opened as a historic site. But that listing was mysteriously removed when it changed ownership a few years back. There's no information about the new owner."

"That's about thirty miles, give or take, away from the next town and five miles from the old church," Justin translated for Matthew. "The old mining town is presumed deserted?"

"Right."

"Obviously, it isn't," said Justin. "We need eyes on it. Closer and more detailed than this image can show us."

"Exactly. I'm thinking drones first. Then we plan from there, depending on what we see," said Manchester.

"What do you know about them? Who are they? What's the end goal?" asked Justin.

"Who's in charge, I don't know. Mercenaries. That's all I can tell you, so far. They obviously have support from somewhere, but I don't know how deep the pockets are or how limitless the resources. I wish I did. The goal is also unknown. Whoever this is holds his cards close to his chest."

"How long do you think Danbury has?" Matthew asked. "As in, how long do we have to plan before we need to act?"

"I'm hoping days," said Manchester. "My guess? They're setting him up to take the fall for whatever it is that they're up to. Just like somebody did with Erik and me. They wanted Erik out of the way and set me up. It backfired because my wife was home that day. If I knew their end game, what that goal is, I'd have a better estimate."

Matthew cringed as Justin said, "Makes sense. It's a logical reason to hold him and keep him alive until they're ready to dispose of him."

"We need to pack up and head out quickly. With vehicles for mountain terrain. I can get those."

"ATVs?" asked Matthew skeptically.

"Humvees," said Manchester. "Real ones."

"You've got those?" asked Justin.

"I can get them. You OK driving one?" he asked.

"Sure," said Matthew as Justin was answering, "Oh yeah."

"OK, we'll load supplies from here. Bring in one vehicle, load up, go get the other two, and pick up whatever else we need. Speed is critical. I don't know how much time Warren has. I owe it to Erik to extract him. My godson deserves better than his father and I got."

Matthew nodded, finally understanding why Manchester was so invested and knowing that he owed the big detective a lot too, not just because he was a friend. He was all in on getting Danbury safely out from wherever he was.

"Do we need reinforcements?" asked Justin.

"I don't know who else to trust," said Manchester. "Some of this, particularly earlier, smacks of governmental involvement. Dirty politicians who were bought."

"The bombing in Kenya?" asked Justin.

"Right," said Manchester. "People disappearing. Others killed. No known motive, seemingly unrelated events."

"Somebody had a motive then; maybe it's the same now," said Matthew. "Shutting us up."

"They thought they'd shut you up," said Manchester. "It was when they went back for the body that they realized they'd missed."

"They left me for dead," said Matthew with a shiver.

"They did," confirmed Manchester. "I overheard them arguing about it, one guy blaming the other for leaving your body behind the night before."

It wasn't that Matthew needed more reason to go after the goons who held Danbury, but the shiver down his spine was quickly turning to a jolt of anger back up it. This time, he had no intention of squelching that vehemence. His fury, properly controlled and aimed in the right direction, would help.

"We need food," said Justin.

"Protein," Matthew chimed in, thinking of Danbury's credo to eat when you could and sleep when you could because you didn't know when you'd be able to do either one again. Sleep had been elusive, but food would help. "And coffee," he added.

"I'm still considering reinforcements," said Justin. "I know people I can trust. I haven't looped anybody in on any of this yet. What I've researched and learned, I've done on my own. But we could have backup within hours of a couple of phone calls."

"Table it for now," said Manchester. "Let's get going and see what we're up against first."

"Copy that."

26 ~ GET READY

Supplies were loaded through a back exit in the caves—a hidden rock-faced door. The technology stash made Justin drool and Matthew shake his head in amazement. How had one man managed to stockpile all of this? Granted, he'd had nearly twenty-two years to do it, and he had assumed someday somebody would come after him.

Matthew helped load weaponry, explosives, listening devices, night-vision goggles, drones, and other technical gadgetry he wasn't entirely certain what its function was. They pulled it all out of a back cave and packed it tightly into a Humvee. The cost must have been exorbitant.

Where had that funding come from? Belatedly, Matthew realized how little he knew about Conrad Manchester. The guy had rescued him and Justin in the early morning hours, or it was the story they'd been told. Was he leading them into an ambush instead of helping them to plan one? Matthew had cause to pause and wonder but no time to do so as he climbed into the Humvee and they raced off.

Twenty minutes later, Matthew had downed two egg, sausage, cheese biscuits, and enough coffee to make him regret having had so much, sooner or later. Under the cover of a baseball hat, Justin procured moleskin, thick socks, boxer briefs, and two *Virginia is for Lovers* T-shirts from a dollar store on the outskirts of a smaller town than Coalglow.

Matthew applied the moleskin, changed his socks and T-shirt, and figured he'd have to live with the boxer briefs a little longer. Tightening the laces on his hiking boots, he thought if he ever got them off, he might never wear them again. As Matthew turned to climb into the Humvee he'd be transporting, Manchester handed both him and Justin secure satellite phones.

Uncertain he wanted to know how the gadgetry was acquired, Matthew was relatively sure he wouldn't get an answer anyway. He listened instead of asking.

"We're going to the old church. It's deserted except for seasonal services. There's a basement, mostly below grade, with small windows. We'll black those, set up surveillance, and plan the extraction from there."

"We'll need eyes on that compound," agreed Justin, "to know what we're up against. Satellite images get you so far. Drones could be detected."

Manchester nodded grudging agreement.

"We need to get closer. Do you have any temporary injectable sedatives? Stun guns?"

"You have to get too close to use those," objected Manchester.

"You have to use those to get close," countered Justin. "Granted, under the cover of darkness. If you blast your way in, you let them know you're coming. They have time to respond. That could be to Danbury's detriment. If there are reinforcements, they show up. A little more finesse enables you to get in and out without anybody immediately knowing that you were there. Not to mention the unsanctioned collateral damage that I can't take part in. Neither can Matthew."

Matthew paused to consider that statement. Would he blow up the people who had bashed him on the head, left him for dead, and taken Danbury, likely planning to set him up and then kill him too? The fact that he didn't have an immediate answer to that was disturbing.

Frowning, Manchester conceded, "Point taken. I don't have it, but I can get it. It'll take additional time that we don't have much of."

"I can get my hands on it within hours," said Justin. "It'll take a couple of phone calls. And a minor detour after we get set up."

"Use the secure phone," barked Manchester, nodding curtly. "Let's roll."

"To the church?" asked Matthew.

"Right," said Manchester. "Stay with me. That's not hard. These roads are narrow and winding, but there won't be traffic."

"Got it," said Matthew. As he climbed into the Humvee, he saw Justin busily tapping the sat phone. They pulled out with Manchester in the lead, Matthew in the middle, and Justin bringing up the rear. It felt like a military convoy. At least, Matthew assumed it would be like this. He was the one member of their three-man group who'd never served in the armed forces.

The drive was picturesque, winding and wending along narrow mountain roads with the sun streaking through the tree canopy overhead. Despite a couple of occasions when the road appeared to be little more than a path along the edge of a precipice, the scenery was breathtaking. The mountain ridges were a lovely yellow-green with new spring growth. Trees, shrubs, grasses, and weeds sprouted in profusion along the edge of the roadway and in the valleys below.

Sloshing through puddles, Matthew realized it had rained in this area recently. He lowered his window to enjoy the cool mountain air. Gone were the dust clouds from the little towns. The freshness of the breeze on his face was simultaneously soothing and stimulating. He had no idea what lay ahead, but he determined to enjoy the journey.

Forty minutes later, they began to wind down the edge of a ridge. Around a hairpin bend in the road, the valley beneath came into view. Matthew caught his breath at the beauty of it—like a postcard or painting—too pristine to be real. At the head of the valley, a white clapboard church sparkled dazzlingly in the sunlight, its steeple bright against the deep hues of the evergreen trees behind it.

A creek rippled, refracting diamonds of light, alongside it and down the valley through lush green grasses on either side. Had he been approaching it for any other reason, Matthew would have reveled in the idyllic scenery. Despite the reason he was there, he tried to soak it in and relish it.

Into the edge of the woods behind the church they plunged, parking in a neat row under the tree cover. Before his boots hit the ground, Manchester was barking orders.

The lock on the back door—which was down a sunken set of stone steps with rock walls on either side—was laughable. Matthew could have jimmied it open without any special training or tools. The door opened onto a landing from which a short flight of stairs ascended and another descended. Justin went up to survey the upstairs while Matthew and Manchester went to the basement.

The musty dampness of the large room, that Matthew assumed to be an old-fashioned fellowship hall beneath the church, assaulted his nostrils. The church he'd grown up in didn't have such a room, but he'd seen them in others. A chill ran through him, and he pulled his jacket tighter and fastened it. Beneath grade, it was cool and dank. Manchester immediately began mapping out the room.

Folding tables were stacked against the back wall. Accordion partitions partially divided the right end of the large rectangular room. It had probably been used for Sunday school classes or other smaller gatherings, Matthew assessed. A kitchen with a pass-through counter was beyond the right side of the long room closest to the steps. Restrooms were to the left. There was no electricity to pump water in initially, until Matthew found a fuse box in a back storage room behind the restrooms and began flipping breakers.

"Be sure there are no lights on upstairs. None. No power indicators or anything," ordered Manchester.

"OK," said Matthew, climbing the steps and joining Justin in a lovely chapel with stained-glass windows.

After surveying every inch of the upstairs, including what seemed to be a choir room and robing area behind the pulpit, Matthew made his way back down the stairs. The restroom, though chilly, was most welcome. It enabled him to be free of the still-damp boxer briefs. He should have gone commando to begin with, he thought, but he had been abruptly awakened from a deep sleep. When he returned to the long underground room, Manchester had disappeared.

"Where'd he go?" asked Matthew.

"To cover our tracks," answered Justin. "Literally. He's pulling camouflage covers over the vehicles and obliterating our tire treads in. Moving in dry conditions is better than mud. Tracks don't show."

"Oh," was all that Matthew could think to say. As much as he'd enjoyed the fresh air, he hadn't considered they were leaving tire tracks on the muddied, rutted road.

When Manchester returned, they began blacking out the windows to use the space after dark without detection. After the vehicles were unloaded and the contents stacked against one wall in the basement of the church, setting up a command center began in earnest. Flipping out the legs on the tables, they set them up in a U formation. Running cords and cables to power strips, they began placing monitors and equipment as Manchester directed and Justin advised.

"Justin is a techno-geek," explained Matthew. "I'm not sure what else his job entails, but I know he's a wizard with all of this stuff."

Manchester grunted and grudgingly made a few adjustments Justin recommended.

"I'm not going to ask where you got all of this equipment or how you've hacked into some of the systems I see here," said Justin, shaking his head. When he was happy with the setup, he announced, "I'm going to hit the road. I'll be back in a couple of hours. With supplies and backup standing ready."

"What backup?" demanded Manchester.

"Friends. Off-duty buddies. They're bringing us supplies. Approaching from the east, the opposite direction from the compound we're monitoring to infiltrate. I can bring them in or direct them in. You'd gain three extra sets of hands, eyes, and ears. And years of experience in special ops."

Manchester scowled at Justin. "Son, I haven't had the leisure to trust anybody in over twenty years. It's served me well. I'm still kicking."

"I understand," answered Matthew. "But it's not about you anymore. Erik's son needs you now to use whatever means at your disposal to get him away from whoever is holding him."

"He's right," agreed Justin. "We stand a better chance of extracting your godson with the extra help. They're pros. Matthew met a couple of them down in Miami last year. They helped rescue a colleague of his and the guy's daughter."

"That was official business, right?" asked Manchester.

Justin nodded. "It was."

"They had orders, and they followed them."

"They did."

"I don't know exactly who's behind all of this, but think about it for a half second before you do something stupid. If this was about the bombing of the US embassy in Nairobi to begin with, then there were government officials at some higher-up level involved in covering up their knowledge of it. If it's about keeping whatever happened back then under wraps now, there still are."

"You're worried my friends will turn on you?" asked Justin.

"Hell, I'm worried you'll turn on me!" said Manchester in disgust.

"Why would I do that?"

"If you got orders, you would fast enough."

"And allow Danbury to be set up and killed? No. I wouldn't."

"You'd kiss your career goodbye."

"I'll take the chance. I know Warren Danbury well enough. He's not a traitor or a killer or on the take. He's a friend and ally in whatever this is we're dealing with."

Matthew felt like he was watching a tennis match, or maybe a ping-pong tournament, he amended his thought, as the lobbed exchanges were closer than on a tennis court. Finally, he stepped forward.

"Look," Matthew said. "I understand your hesitation. I do. But we need the help. Whoever we're up against won't have left Danbury half-guarded. You said it yourself. This goes deep and high to garner this sort of reaction from somebody because Danbury was looking into his parents' death. It's not to make an example of him. It's to silence him, and anybody else who might be prying into it to bury whatever happened for once and for all. If they have him, draw you out, and silence us, who's left to dredge it up?"

Narrowing his eyes to slits and glaring at Matthew, Manchester finally conceded, "You have a point."

"I can read them in," said Justin. "Let them know what we're up against. Six of us. And an unknown and unknowable quantity on the other side if they're coming and going from a bunker."

"At the very least," added Matthew, "three more people would know what we know. Police officers in a little town in the northern part of North Carolina have files on some of it. Mainly, information about the Danburys' murders that Ogilvy provided. Not about the embassy bombing in Nairobi."

The internal struggle Manchester underwent showed, for once, clearly on his face. Absent was the detached lack of expression Matthew had witnessed so far. Finally, he seemed to arrive at a conclusion.

"Get them here," he said. "Sat phone only. Drive about two clicks over that next ridge. Away from cell signals and listening devices. We're playing it safe, then fast. We don't have a lot of time. They've had him for two days. Whatever they're up to, they had ample time to have planned thoroughly. Before they grabbed him."

"For them to have an established compound up here is telling," Matthew agreed. "They had to have known where you were, and that Danbury would come looking for you eventually. It's more likely they were waiting for us here than that they followed us."

"That's what I've come to conclude," said Manchester grudgingly. "I've had little to lose since I've lived up here. I've got no family except Charity and her older sister, who moved out to Colorado some years back."

As if to prevent anything sappy from coming from his mouth, Manchester turned to Justin. "Aren't you back yet, Son?" he asked. "And don't forget to cover your tracks!"

"On it. I'll cover them back to where you stopped covering. Then it looks like whatever came this way kept going," answered Justin, shaking his head at Manchester as he slipped out the back door and into the tree line behind the chapel.

The fact that Manchester had called Justin "son" darted around Matthew's mind momentarily like a pinball in an arcade game that wouldn't land. Was that a good thing, in that he'd decided to trust him? Or was that a derogatory statement slightly shy of "sonny boy?" Before he could contemplate further, Manchester began barking orders to connect this, turn that on, shift some other thing.

"Take a seat," said Manchester, pulling up two folding chairs in front of a bank of monitors. "And learn things from surveillance before we go busting in there. We need to go tonight. Under the cover of darkness. The moon is still half-full, but there will be cloud cover. That'll help us. By daylight, you can see the perimeter of the place is cleared," he added, pointing.

Matthew nodded.

"That's to our detriment," continued Manchester. "They'll have their own surveillance, and they can see us coming. We need careful planning and critically timed execution." After a momentary pause, he turned to Matthew. "What do you know about Justin and his 'buddies'?"

"I've known Justin my entire life. We grew up together. It's a lot like you and Erik Danbury. You trusted each other with your lives, didn't you?"

Manchester nodded.

"And you had each other's backs?"

"He had mine. I should have had his," Manchester answered, dropping his eyes to the table.

"Justin has my back," said Matthew firmly. "You couldn't have known somebody would murder Erik Danbury in cold blood. You can have his back now by getting his son out of this compound. I haven't known him nearly as long, but I also trust Danbury to have my back. And I'll do what it takes to have his."

"Let's get to work," said Manchester.

27 ~ GET SET

As they monitored the activity, the coming and going from the bunker, Matthew pondered the loyalty of the people there. Were they guns for hire? Thugs who were merely doing a job for a paycheck? Or did they have a shared cause, a higher purpose they thought they were fulfilling? Was their purpose something that united them?

Answers to those questions would be helpful. It would make their response to invasion more predictable. Trust and loyalty were funny things. They were hard earned. He hoped they weren't easily discarded in Manchester's case.

"Four more out, one in," said Manchester, pointing to the monitor. "Wonder where they're going?"

"Can you zoom out and watch?"

"Don't have to watch these four," he said with a grin. "They just took the vehicles with the tracking devices. That's careless, not to check for those from time to time. Both are moving. In opposite directions."

"Huh," said Matthew. "That's a good point. Either they think they're invincible or they're careless. Which do you think?"

"I think," began Manchester, "they've seriously underestimated their opponent. It's probable, as we discussed, somebody knew where I was and set up nearby figuring Danbury would eventually come in search of me. All they had to do was wait and set the trap for when he did."

"That's logical, but expensive."

"They had to be somewhere. Here worked as well as any. What they don't know is how well I've prepared for something like this for the past twenty years."

"Or that you'd have help." Curiosity got the better of him and Matthew had to ask, "Your first cabin, did you blow it up or did they?"

"Yes," said Manchester as Matthew looked at him quizzically. "They tripped two wires. The first set off alarms. We were too far away by then to hear those. They apparently ignored them. The second set off explosives."

"To what end? To kill intruders?"

"No. They'd have been close enough to be temporarily blinded and deafened, potentially, and maybe injured, but not killed. The purpose was to do exactly what it did—give us the chance to escape through the back exit and remove all trace evidence that we were ever there."

"They couldn't get underneath to the bunker?"

"No. It wasn't directly under the cabin." Manchester confirmed what Matthew had thought. "It was behind it. The cabin is gone. Nothing left of it now. The passage is sealed off."

"What about the metal dais the wood stove was sitting on that spun to expose the steps?"

"It's under a heap of rubble from the wall. They'd have had to work for a while to uncover it and know that it's there. They didn't. They doubled back to pursue you and Warren."

"How have you managed to stockpile all of the equipment and weaponry?"

"You can get this stuff easily enough without a lot of questions asked, if you know where to look," Manchester replied cryptically.

"It must have cost a mint," said Matthew, without quite meaning to. He watched Manchester in his peripheral vision to gauge the reaction.

"I guess you don't know everything, Doc," replied Manchester.

"I don't claim to," answered Matthew honestly.

"It's common knowledge now. No harm telling you. We tried to keep it private back then. Not that it worked. It was the biggest reason that I was suspected of killing my wife by anybody who thought it was something other than an accident. I loved Heather. I spent my married life protecting her because she wanted a normal life."

"A normal life?" Matthew repeated. "As opposed to what?"

"A privileged one. She was an heiress, but she didn't want to live like that. She wanted to be out of that bubble she grew up in. We both worked, had a modest house, and good friends that we knew were real friends, not leaches after her money. After Erik and Gayle died, that all came out as a theory, a reason why I'd have married her but still had feelings for Gayle. That logic didn't hold because Gayle's murder preceded Heather's."

"Nobody knew Heather had that kind of money?" asked Matthew.

"It wasn't common knowledge. I didn't know it until after I'd proposed to her. Eventually, Erik and Gayle knew. They were sworn to secrecy and respected the reasons that Heather didn't want anybody else to know. We set up a foundation to make charitable contributions that didn't connect to Heather or to us. The Danburys helped us to figure out where money should go—to worthy nonprofit organizations doing good work. Mostly, they were for children, impoverished women, and to feed the hungry."

"That foundation still exists?"

"It still does lot of good globally," said Manchester nodding. "Charity's college tuition for her undergraduate program came from the foundation. So did her older sister's. Charity's medical school will too."

"Could Charity somehow have tipped them off?"

"That I was living up here? Not likely. She has a sat phone with direct access to me. She hasn't contacted me in any other way. I haven't physically seen her in several months. I don't see her regularly. I didn't want to put her in danger. I've told her to take cover now. She'll be out of work 'for a family issue' for a week or so, depending on what we do up here and how fast. She's hidden away. I saw to it."

"Good," said Matthew. "I'm happy to hear it."

"The foundation technically owns everything I own," Manchester continued, "with layers of shell corporations between that I thought nobody could figure out. I might have been wrong. These goons found me somehow."

"If they don't know, it could give us an advantage," said Matthew.

"Maybe," Manchester answered, his eyebrows meeting in the middle as he knit them in concentration. Resigned, he added, "That and the reinforcements coming. They probably figure you and your buddy are with me somewhere. Maybe having the extra three will help. It's something they won't be expecting. We can hit them from multiple directions at once."

While the guy was feeling chatty and answering questions, Matthew decided to ask a few more. "Any idea how Erik Danbury learned about the impending bombing in Nairobi all those years ago? He shared his suspicion with you. Did he share the source of the information?"

"I wish he'd told me. Or I'd asked, probed more. I thought it sounded far-fetched to begin with. Why would anybody want to bomb the embassy in Kenya? What was to gain from it?"

"That's what I was wondering. What Erik Danbury was onto, if he knew the motive, or who was behind it."

"At the time, I thought he'd picked up chatter about it. Maybe trying to report that through the proper channels was enough to get him killed. After Erik was murdered, nothing was done to prevent the bombing or evacuate the building. I've always thought somebody in our government didn't want it known—that Erik wasn't the only one who knew it was coming."

"Some sort of conspiracy?"

"It sounds crazy, particularly from a guy who's been living off the grid for over twenty years. But, yes, that's exactly what I thought. I still do. It makes too much sense. What else could it be?"

"Maybe Erik knew what the motive was—who or what was driving it all."

"Maybe. After the fact, Al Qaeda operatives were blamed for the bombing. I've wondered more times than I can tell you if that was true. If they were behind it, did they have help? If Erik learned about the plans, he wouldn't likely have been alone in that, would he?"

"Apparently not," agreed Matthew. "Did the name Lemako Whattlesby mean anything to you?"

"It sounded familiar when Warren mentioned it, but I wouldn't have been able to place it without the context you provided."

"What we didn't know then was how agitated former US Ambassador Patricia Shrubpeal would get when asked about him."

"In the context of the bombing in Nairobi?"

"Right."

"Who asked her?"

"Justin. He located her and went to talk to her, to see what he could learn. He recorded their conversation. She became agitated when he asked about the bombing, which makes sense. That was a horrific event in her life. But when Justin asked her about Whattlesby, she was over the top upset and demanded that he turn off the recording. She refused to discuss Lemako Whattlesby."

"What's the tie? How did you learn about him?"

"It was something Brian Ogilvy said. He was providing security for a foreign dignitary when he worked for Iron Clad. It was near the end of his employment with them—one of his last jobs before they closed up shop. He remembered the name Whattlesby. I looked him up, but there's no information online about him, so I asked Justin. He dug up some information just prior to the bombing. According to his sources, Whattlesby was to have met with Shrubpeal at the embassy the morning of August seventh of 1998 at ten that morning. The bombing happened at ten thirty."

Manchester nodded, without commenting.

"There's no information on either Whattlesby's death or his life after that point," continued Matthew. "Nothing. It's like he disappeared, as if he'd never existed. Ogilvy provided security for him, or somebody using his name, shortly before Iron Clad closed their doors at the end of January of 1999. Ogilvy said he never met him. It might have been a ruse. Somebody could have used Lemako Whattlesby's name."

"Lemako Whattlesby," Manchester repeated contemplatively as he sat staring at the screens in front of him. Matthew wondered if he was actually seeing the monitors or if his mind had traveled back in time as he tried to remember when he'd heard the name and in what context.

"It's a blank," he said a few minutes later. "The name is familiar but I can't remember why. I'll keep trying. Meanwhile, let's get back to planning. We need a surprise attack that effectively catches them off guard and prevents loss of life, at least on our side. The primary goal is to get Warren out safely. What happens to any of them in the process is between them and their god, if they have one."

Had the guy said anything other than God, Matthew might have heartily agreed. That one word gave him pause. He had no time to reconsider as Justin returned. With him were three guys, two of whom Matthew recognized. They carried huge black cases, which they set down inside and went back out for more.

"Change of plan," said Justin. "This just became an official operation."

"What happened?" asked Matthew as Manchester was objecting.

"This is not your op!" roared Manchester. "I will not stand down and allow you to run amok here. This is personal to me on levels you will never understand."

"You don't know what you're up against," said Justin. "I don't fully either yet. We're here to help, not hinder."

"What changed?" asked Matthew.

28 ~ GATHERING INTELLIGENCE

"Patricia Shrubpeal," said Justin, then added for Manchester's benefit, "The former ambassador to Kenya. I wasn't the only one who contacted her about all of this. She was already worried when I showed up."

"Maybe it's why she got agitated when you started asking her about the bombing and Whattlesby," said Matthew.

"Probably one reason. It's likely also why she agreed to meet with me so quickly. An administrative assistant to somebody in the political arena had contacted her first. A guy named Otto Edwards. He worked for Arthur Maynard, a high-powered advisor to the Secretary of State. After my visit, she tried to reach him again. She was told that he'd been fired, escorted out, and nobody has seen him since. That, along with me questioning her, made her decide to make a few calls of her own."

"That was fast," said Matthew admiringly.

"It was. She had Arthur Maynard checked out, perfunctorily. The guy was squeaky clean until about nine months ago. He acquired a gambling habit and was losing everything. Then, suddenly, the creditors were paid, and life went on as usual for him. There's something going on there that's now under investigation. No telling what else they'll dig up on Maynard."

Teddy, Rex, and the guy Matthew didn't know brought in more cases.

"I'll be right back after I finish covering our tracks in," said Justin, slipping out.

"Silkies!" said Teddy as Matthew stood up and went to greet them. Teddy, Matthew had learned, was no more this guy's name than "Silkies" was his. They were nicknames given to comrades who had worked together in special operations as best he could determine. Danbury told him it meant he was being included in the group and to go with it, so he had.

How he'd acquired the nickname was a bit embarrassing to recall. In Miami the year before, he'd had to resort to wearing red silk boxers because that's all the gift shop in the hotel had. Then, like now, he'd been unable to get to his own spare clothes.

"Teddy! Rex! Good to see you. We can use your help, but it sounds like in an official capacity from what Justin explained."

"Right," answered Rex. "Justin read us in. That's why we're here. I remember Danbury. Big, broad guy who didn't say much. Good guy."

"That's him," said Matthew and introduced them to Conrad Manchester, who hadn't gotten out of his chair to greet them but looked on warily. The third guy was introduced as Stoney, though Matthew was sure that wasn't his name either.

Their names didn't suit them, Matthew thought. Stoney, the tallest of the three, was slender with soft, big, brown eyes, golden tanned skin, and longish, wavy, brown hair. Teddy looked nothing like the bear he was named for. Shorter, with an average build, he had close cropped light hair and blue eyes that squinted nearly shut when he smiled. Rex, height-wise was between the other two, his build broad and solid. His facial features looked to have been carved from granite.

"Manchester is driving this one," said Matthew. "Or somebody else is. I'm here to help get Danbury out of the compound where we think he's being held. Here, have a look," he added, moving aside for the newcomers to see the bank of monitors.

"There's a bunker there," Matthew pointed at a screen. "We can see heat signatures coming and going from it. This satellite image," he added, pointing to another monitor, "is a real-time view of the compound. It's grainy, but we can see movement sometimes. Here's one showing the topology of the area."

"What's that moving?" asked Stoney, pointing to a dot making its way across one of the other screens.

"That's one of the vehicles that left the compound a little while ago," answered Matthew, wishing Manchester would jump into this conversation with his expertise.

"How do you have eyes on it?"

"Manchester put tracking devices on two of the vehicles. The other one left the compound and headed in the other direction. It's on this monitor," said Matthew, pointing across at it.

"Who are they?"

"The thugs who tried to kill me. We're pretty sure they have Danbury."

"They don't know the tracking devices are there?"

"We were wondering," answered Matthew. "We're assuming they haven't bothered to look and they aren't as well trained as we assumed they were."

"There's another possibility," said Rex.

"They're aware of it and they want you to know where they are," said Teddy. "That one is headed this way."

"I've been watching it," said Manchester calmly. "Prepare to intercept if they turn this way."

A surge of motion followed. Matthew was the only member of the group who didn't immediately bolt into the controlled chaos retrieving weapons. Manchester pulled a large one Matthew thought looked like a cannon from a case. He assembled, inspected, and loaded it in mere seconds.

Turning to Matthew, Manchester said, "Glock 19, right?" and handed him one, a holster, two magazines, and a box of ammunition before Matthew could answer. "Magazines are loaded. It's not registered, but try not to lose this one," he added sarcastically.

"Thanks," said Matthew, at a loss for words.

"Do you want a second one?" asked Manchester.

"No. I'm hoping not to need this one," Matthew answered honestly.

Poised for action, they intently watched the dot representing the vehicle make its way slowly toward them up the road running by the turnoff to the church they inhabited. Tensed, ready, and silent as it approached, they released a collective breath when it kept going.

"I have an idea," said Stoney.

"Ambush?" asked Teddy.

"Right," said Stoney. "They're likely to come back this way. Unless they're planning their own ambush and trying to lure us out, but I doubt that. More likely, they're scouting. We intercept on the return."

"Hostages?" asked Rex.

"Right," said Stoney again. "No fatalities, maximizing the element of surprise. Taking them alive for questioning is key. We'll convince them to tell us about the compound they came from. And whatever other information we can pry out of them."

"What's the incentive?" asked Justin, who had returned during the flurry of preparation. "What leverage?"

"Cutting a deal with them," said Stoney.

"We aren't authorized to make deals," said Rex.

"They don't know that," said Stoney as the other three heads nodded agreement. "Let us know when they're headed back and about here," he pointed to the monitor tracking the vehicle. "We'll go set up. If they take another route, let us know that too."

"There is no other route," said Manchester. "Not around the mountain heading back west. That's it."

The three newcomers quickly solidified their plan, then disappeared through the back door.

"We were discussing going in tonight," said Matthew to Justin. "To get Danbury out." He refrained from adding "alive." Admitting the possibilities, either that Danbury wasn't alive or that he might not stay that way much longer, dissuaded him.

"We'll learn what we can from the hostages, if they'll talk to us," said Justin, "and plan from there."

"Assuming they take any," said Manchester from the controls in front of the monitors at which he sat staring intently.

"They'll get them," assured Justin. "They're pros. It's a matter of when, not if. We'll watch and learn all we can from surveillance in the meantime."

Watching the dot on the screen veer from the road onto multiple side roads—some of which appeared to be logging roads or something similar, narrow and nearly invisible—the wait seemed interminable. Matthew's foot tapped out the rhythms in his head until Manchester glared at him.

"Son, do you have to do that?"

"Do what?" asked Matthew as Justin chuckled.

"You're tapping your foot again," said Justin.

"Oh, that," said Matthew. "I've always done it, though not purposefully."

"He has," agreed Justin. "It's a subconscious habit with him."

"It helps me to focus. Or sometimes it's because I'm highly focused," said Matthew.

"Or you're bored," added Justin, grinning.

"This isn't tapping from boredom," said Matthew. "It's from nervous energy, anticipation. My foot tapping is what's holding me in this chair watching that monitor and preventing me from pacing the room."

Manchester pointed at the screen, and they watched as the dot began moving back around the mountain headed in their direction. Justin called Stoney on the sat phone to give him a location update and an estimate on time to return.

"Leave the line open," said Justin. "I'm muting this end unless something changes. If it does, I'll notify."

"Copy that," Matthew heard somebody say. There was a slight

scuffling noise and then all was quiet, including Matthew's foot. He stilled it with great effort. Suddenly, everything erupted at once. The dot on the screen stopped abruptly and the sat phone was robust with noise, some of it yelling, shots fired, and then more scuffling noises.

"Heading back," said one of the voices that sounded like Teddy's. As Matthew blew out a breath he'd been holding, the voice continued, "Relocating the vehicle. We likely aren't the only ones watching it."

Fifteen minutes later, Justin opened the door to Rex and Stoney. They ushered in two huge men whose hands were tied behind their backs. The men looked dazed, as if they weren't fully conscious. Hauling them over to the corner and pushing them to the floor, side by side, Justin tied their ankles. Their knees, he tethered to each other. Both men were gagged.

Draping two extra-large black jackets across the table, Stoney pulled electronics and weapons from the pockets. "They were loaded," he said as he dumped the items into a heap on the edge of the table.

Justin stepped clear of them as the two men became more aware of their surroundings. In contrast to their dark faces, the whites of their astonished eyes showed clearly. Their expressions changed from surprise—like they were shocked to find themselves in this predicament—to menacing anger.

"We're not going to kill you," said Justin. "Unless . . ." He stepped forward staring down at them.

As he let that statement linger, both men strained against their bindings, grunting loudly through the gags. As arm muscles bulged under tight T-shirts, Matthew was thankful they were bound tightly. Neither of them would he want to encounter otherwise.

"One at a time," said Rex, kneeling beside the guy on the left. His foot on the guy's leg, he leaned back out of head-butting range. "We're going to ask you some questions. If you answer them helpfully, you have options. If you don't, your options get severely limited. Understand?"

As Rex released the guy's gag, his angry voice spewed rhythmic sounds, but nothing that Matthew understood. Stoney moved forward, staring intently at the guy.

"English?" Rex asked. The stream of emphatic words continued. "No? Let's see what your buddy here has to say." Carefully returning the gag to the guy's mouth and face, despite multiple attempts to bite him, Rex moved to the guy on the right.

Removing the guy's gag, he asked, "Are you willing and able to speak to us in English?"

The response was another eruption of unintelligible words, seemingly aimed at the guy beside him.

"We're not getting anywhere like this," said Rex.

As he reached to return the gag and held out a syringe, the guy suddenly shouted, "No! I will talk to you. In English. What do you want?"

"Tell us where you came from, what's happening there, and why you came looking for us."

"We were not looking for you," the guy responded. Sullenly, he added, "We did not know you were here. Who are you?"

"I ask the questions," said Rex. "You provide the answers."

"I cannot," replied the guy.

"Why not?"

"They will kill me."

"Not if I do it first," said Rex.

"Go ahead," said the guy matter-of-factly. It wasn't a challenge, nor was it sarcastic. The man seemed fully resigned to his fate.

"Why would you rather I kill you?" asked Rex.

He hesitated until Rex held the syringe up again. As the guy drew in a breath and began to answer, the one beside him yanked on his bindings and frantically, but still angrily, tried to talk beneath the gag.

"You have something to say about that?" asked Stoney when the first guy hesitated and grew quiet.

The guy nodded vehemently, still glaring at them. Stoney made his way clear of the sprawled legs to remove the gag.

"Don't take them both off!" yelled Manchester. "They can corroborate their story. In whatever language that is. It's not one I know."

Rex and Stoney exchanged a glance. Ignoring Manchester, Stoney removed the guy's gag. A string of emphatic sounds poured out.

Stepping back and scrutinizing them both, Stoney waited them out while they exchanged unintelligible conversation. Manchester, again, protested. Holding his hand up to silence Manchester, Stoney studied the two men as only their voices could be heard.

Turning to the monitors, Manchester announced, "Their vehicle stopped again."

"That's Teddy putting it somewhere that makes sense for it to be for a while," answered Rex over the din. "Far enough from here where there are possible places to explore. He'll jog back in a minute."

The voices of the two men reached a harsh crescendo, then died down. They stopped talking entirely. Stoney, still staring intently at them, answered in something other than English. Two astonished faces looked up, staring back at him, and the room grew eerily quiet. When Stoney spoke again, it was softly. The two men looked at each other, neither one answering. A more forceful attempt from Stoney yielded a flood of unintelligible words in response.

"You know that language?" Manchester asked, incredulous, after several minutes of multiple exchanges. "What is it, and what did they say?"

"It's Kiswahili," said Stoney. "They were saying, before I interrupted, that they're afraid for their families if they talk to us. They were making a pact not to. I pointed out that when the people they're working for realize we have them, it won't matter whether they've actually told us anything important or not. The end result for their families will be the same. I explained that their families' chances would be better if they helped us to take down whoever is running their operation. I convinced them that they might as well cooperate."

"And they agreed?" asked Matthew, from his seat across the room.

"Grudgingly, under duress. They claim not to know who is running the operation, merely who they take orders from. Obviously, they speak English. They chose not to. Discuss nothing in front of them you don't want them to hear."

"Did you ask them about Danbury?" asked Matthew.

"I did. They think he's being held at the compound. For now."

Matthew felt relief wash through him.

"Two other men are being held there, one was brought yesterday. They don't know the identities of either. The man brought in yesterday is also from Kenya, where they're from, but they haven't been allowed to talk to him. He's an older man who speaks their native language. From the glimpse they caught of him, they say he's in pretty bad shape, far worse than Warren Danbury. Another man has been there longer. They say he's mzungu, a white man, whose nationality they don't know."

"Do they know what's being planned?" asked Manchester. "Why they're holding Warren?"

"He's being set up to take the blame for something. They think maybe it's the murder of the other men, though they can't understand why their deaths would matter," Stoney answered.

"Interesting," said Justin, who had been intently listening to the exchange. "Unless they're important people somehow. One of them is Kenyan, they think. What did they tell you about the other one?"

"He's been there two days longer, before Danbury arrived. They haven't seen or heard him after he was brought in by plane. There's a short airstrip behind the buildings."

"Yeah, you can see that there," said Rex, indicating the monitor of the compound. "And what looks like a hangar on the other side of the runway from the main building."

"They don't know where the man was taken," continued Stoney. "It's possible he's been killed."

"Are they certain the other hostage speaks Kiswahili and is from

Kenya?" asked Rex.

"Yes," the man seated on the left spoke up. He had apparently decided Kiswahili was no longer necessary since it could be understood. "I heard his voice. He was pleading for help, yelling in our language. I could not respond to him. I wanted to, but they would not allow it. I would be tortured too."

"How do you know he's from Kenya?" asked Stoney, also now in English.

"He offered money to anyone who would help him. It was a large sum in shillings. In American dollars, not as much. He said it was hidden in Samburu Kenya. Only he knows where. It is a large territory. He promised it all to anyone who would help him. I think he is desperate. He does not care what he has to give up to be freed."

"Did anybody answer him?"

"Not in words," said the man on the right.

"What do you mean?"

"There was a loud noise. The man screamed, shouted out in pain. Then he was silent again."

29 ~ FRENEMIES

"Here's what we're going to do," said Stoney. "We have their comms. They're out of range here. I checked. We'll move these," he said, holding up the communication devices. "And them," he indicated the two men. "We'll get them in range and have these guys radio in to ask for help searching an area that looks promising."

"Who will respond to that request?" Justin asked the guys on the floor.

"Wasaki and Waruhiu," said the guy on the left.

"What are your names?" asked Matthew in an attempt to create a bond with them, standing so that they could see him.

"You!" exclaimed the guy on the left. "You are alive!"

"You tried to kill me?" asked Matthew, stepping forward menacingly, the anger rising like bile in the back of his throat.

"No! I am Gacoki. We were there, but we did not try to kill anyone. Waruhiu hit you from behind. I saw your face when they rolled you over and searched you. He said you were dead. But when we went back to find your body the next morning, you were gone."

"But you found me in town? And planned to attack in the night?"

"No! Wasaki and Waruhiu planned to kill you. We are trackers, not assassins. We have located and tracked you previously, before you arrived here, but we did not kill anyone."

That confirmed one important question that had still lingered, tugging at the corners of Matthew's mind, but it raised another.

Manchester had indeed overheard plans to attack and kill him at the hotel in the middle of the night. A shiver made its way up his spine, and he felt his scalp tingle in response.

"When did you track me before?" Matthew asked the other question.

"You were there, but it was not you we were sent to follow," said Gacoki.

"Who were you tracking?"

"Detective Warren Danbury."

"When was this?" asked Matthew.

"Two weeks ago," answered Gacoki.

As Matthew paused to work his way backward through time and associate that timeframe with the death of Danbury's grandmother, he was amazed at everything that had happened in the interim.

"What did you report about tracking Danbury and to whom?"

"Everywhere he went for three days. It was not far. We sent secure messages, pictures, and videos. Through an email address we do not have anymore."

"Who did you send them to?"

"We did not know."

"Do you know where Detective Danbury is now?" asked Matthew.

"No. We told your friend we do not know."

"But you think he's still alive and being held near here?"

"Yes, that is what we believe."

"What happened after Waruhiu hit me?"

"Wasaki used a stun gun on your friend. We helped to bind him and bring him back. It was not an easy job. We have not seen him since. Another guard takes food to him."

Before Matthew had a chance to ask them anything further, Manchester interrupted, "Who are Wasaki and Waruhiu?"

"Our cousins. We were Maasai Warriors from our youth."

"You're all South African?"

"Yes. Kenyan."

"Why are you here?"

"There was drought and much famine in Samburu. We were offered large sums of money to come and work here. We sent money to our families to keep them alive. Still, we send it."

Samburu, Matthew remembered, was one of the words Danbury's father had written on the paper they'd found in Danbury's childhood desk. It was both a place and a people group.

"Who offered you money?" asked Justin.

"A security company."

"Does it have a name?"

"Yes, but it has changed many times over years."

"How many years? When did you get here?"

"It was 2005," answered the other guy.

"After we got here, the promises became threats. They are not false. We fear for our families," said Gacoki. "We see our families once a year. At no other time can we go home. If we try to run and not return, our families are in grave danger. If we fail in our work here, they are in danger. We do not have a choice but to guard and track as we are directed."

"What's your name?" Matthew asked the other man.

"I am Tumaini. I hope to return to my family in Samburu. I will do all I can to help you if you will protect my family and reunite us."

"Who were you tracking just now?" asked Matthew.

"You," said Tumaini simply. "Someone in a town you passed through saw you and reported your location and direction."

"You found me. What were you supposed to do with me if you're not assassins?"

"We were to subdue you and your friend and bring you back to be questioned."

"Questioned about what?" asked Matthew as he heard somebody behind him laugh, and he turned to see Manchester guffawing at the two men.

"That's rich," said Manchester. "Since that's what just happened to you. The trackers were tracked and apprehended."

Matthew turned to glare at Manchester. These men were, for the moment at least, cooperating and answering questions. Antagonizing them and changing that would not be in anybody's best interest.

"We do not know what questions," said Tumaini.

"Tell us about Wasaki and Waruhiu," said Justin.

"They are brothers. They will not join you," replied Tumaini.

"You mean they won't help us in exchange for protecting their families?" asked Justin pointedly.

"That is correct," said Gacoki. "They will kill you on sight. Unless they are ordered to do otherwise."

"Why won't they help us?" asked Matthew.

"It is simple. They are angry. They have nothing left to lose."

"No family to protect back in Kenya?" asked Justin.

"Their families have already been killed. It is why they became assassins. They no longer care who they kill because they no longer value life, including their own."

"Then why do they stay here working?" asked Manchester.

The two men looked at each other, then Gacoki responded, "To find out who killed their families and take revenge. They learned that the murder of their community was ordered from here. It was carried out by assassins sent to wait in Nanyuki." When met with confused looks, Gacoki explained. "Nanyuki is a town between Nairobi and Samburu that is near Mount Kenya. It is a central location on the edge of Samburu territory large enough to hide in."

Matthew nodded as heads bobbed around him.

Gacoki insisted, "Though the tribes often fight among themselves, Samburu were not involved in their families' deaths. Wasaki and Waruhiu know this."

"What would happen if they were to discover that the people you're working for—whatever 'security company' that is—had their families killed? Would they turn on them?" asked Justin.

Gacoki nodded, and Tumaini responded, "They would. They do not believe our employer is responsible. They believe it is an enemy of those we work for. They are powerful and have made many enemies."

"You don't know who you work for?" Stoney prodded.

"We have never seen them or spoken directly. We have heard others talking to someone giving orders not to be questioned."

Teddy returned to the church through the back door. "All is clear as of now. I came along the edge of the tree line, watching," he said. "How's it going in here?"

"They can be persuaded to see things our way," answered Manchester. "And they speak nearly flawless English. Be careful what you say."

"Here's what we're thinking," said Justin and explained general logistics of another ambush using the two men they'd captured, Gacoki and Tumaini, to lure in the other two former Samburu warriors.

"You said Wasaki and Waruhiu would be coming," Manchester stumbled over the names as he addressed the two men still bound on the floor. "Were they up at my cabin when it blew up?"

"Yes."

"And you're sure they'll be the ones to respond if you ask for help searching an area?"

"Yes," they replied in unison.

"They would not hesitate to kill if ordered to do so," said Tumaini. "Nobody else would be sent away from guarding prisoners."

"Then we can see them coming," said Manchester meaningfully.

"If there's somebody here watching," said Justin.

"We need to move now. Before their silence and stillness is noticed," Manchester added, nodding at the two men. "It's nearly dark. That's a good reason to call for help searching. Let's get organized to keep going after we take out the other two. No prisoners."

"We're not killing them," said Justin emphatically. "We'll be disabling them."

"I have no such intention, no reason to spare lives," said Manchester.

The eyes of the two men on the floor widened, both of their mouths opened, and they began talking at once. The gist of their commentary was about how they'd cooperated and would continue to do so.

"If you untie us, we will help you," said Tumaini.

"In your dreams," said Manchester. "Not until this is over. And not by me then, if I live to tell about it."

That last comment made Matthew shudder, though he struggled to keep the inclination in check.

"What's in the surrounding area where you parked their vehicle?" asked Manchester of Teddy as he pointed to the dot on one of the monitors. "It's harder to see the terrain from this view as the sun sets."

"The gravel road comes in here," said Teddy pointing to the monitor as he spoke. "There's a rock formation. And a shallow rocky creek bed. I pulled their Jeep across the creek and parked it on the opposite side to look like they're busily searching. The bank is much steeper on the far side of the creek. Trees surround it and overhang both sides."

"How far to the compound from there?" asked Justin. "We need to get our bearings to approach in the dark."

Moving to another monitor, they began discussing the angles and approach to the compound where Danbury was being held.

"I can't function like this," Matthew muttered, watching them move back and forth between monitors. "I need to see it all together."

He had spotted a whiteboard on a wheeled stand against a wall earlier. Finding it behind the partial accordion wall, he checked the markers, found three still functional, and wheeled it into the main room. Parking it beside the U-shaped table, he marked a north, south, east, and west compass in the upper right corner.

Matthew spun the images from the monitors in his mind and began marking out the building and the surrounding compound to the west as it was being discussed by the others.

Rough-sketching the area where the Jeep that Gacoki and Tumaini had been driving was parked in the center, it fell beneath a curvy line across the whiteboard to denote the narrow main road. At the top to the far right, in the northeastern-most location, he put a box with a cross to mark the church steeple of the building they occupied.

"The creek, the rock outcropping, the high bank," he muttered as he sketched those in at the bottom of the middle section.

"Useful," said Manchester, evaluating Matthew's efforts.

"Gacoki and Tumaini could be helpful in mapping this out," said Matthew softly over Justin's shoulder. "Could we trust them if we're trying to reunite them to their families? Can we offer that help?"

"Maybe so," said Justin. "I'll do my best to get them help if they're telling the truth."

Matthew heard Gacoki mutter something under his breath that sounded like "*Washungoo*" and then something quieter.

"What did he say?" Matthew asked Stoney.

"'Wazungu hawapaswi kuwadharau adui zao,'" Stoney answered, with a smirk.

"In English?" Matthew persisted, annoyed. Normally, that would have been funny. Edgy, worrying about Danbury and how all of the ways to extract him could go horribly wrong, his usual sense of humor was lacking.

He wished he hadn't asked when Stoney answered, "It's roughly, 'White people shouldn't underestimate their opponent.'"

30 ~ PLAN OF ATTACK

"Will you help us?" Matthew addressed Gacoki directly, including Tumaini in his glance. "Or was that a threat?"

"I will help you," answered Gacoki quickly and earnestly. "You will need it. Your enemies are fierce."

"We can't trust them," objected Manchester. "They'll deliver us straight into the hands of their cousins!"

"We'll have to," said Justin. "We need to know what they know."

"This can't be a NIMSU situation," agreed Stoney. "We can filter their feedback, glean what we can from it, and use them in a limited way in capturing their cousins."

"NIMSU?" asked Matthew, wondering what he'd missed. "Is that a military term?"

Rex chuckled as he answered, "No, I think it's from the business world. It means when you don't have the information you need, you make things up. We can't do that. Going in with misconceptions means coming out in body bags. We need all the information we can gather. No assumptions, no misunderstanding, no room for surprises or mistakes."

"I, too, will help. I will do whatever you ask if you will protect my family. I have five children, three sisters, and my wife. There are twenty-one souls in my village that I am responsible for," Tumaini spoke up in the momentary awkward break in conversation.

"We'll do our best," answered Justin. "After we extract Warren Danbury and find whoever is behind this, we'll be better able to help."

"Disabling Wasaki and Waruhiu will be difficult. They are like the rock wall."

"Impenetrable?" asked Teddy.

Nodding, Gacoki answered, "Exactly so. It will not be a simple task. They will fight ferociously. With the weapons they carry."

"What weapons do they carry?" asked Justin.

"They are deadly with knives and spears," said Gacoki. He continued to describe fire arms and larger weapons they transported in their Jeep, including powerful and technologically advanced explosives.

"Great," said Matthew under his breath. Step one wouldn't be easy, and he wondered if they'd get to step two—raiding the compound and freeing Danbury.

Using the whiteboard, they drew out their plan to approach and surround the site where the Jeep was parked.

"There's a back path in from this direction that crosses the creek here," explained Teddy, pointing, from the line of the narrow main road to the creek and rock outcropping. "I came out that way."

Matthew sketched in a small winding line where Teddy had indicated between the main road and the creek near the rock outcropping at the bottom center of the whiteboard.

"We can drive in that far. There's a high bank under tree cover off the path where visibility should be good," Teddy continued, pointing to Matthew's sketches. "Gacoki will use his cell to call Wasaki and Waruhiu."

"Silkies stays here, watching the monitors where he can see all of them at once," said Manchester as if Matthew weren't standing in front of them. "Gacoki comes with us so that Stoney can hear what he says when he calls. To ensure it's exactly what we tell him to say. Nothing more, nothing less."

"We'll have the comm packs with ear wigs," added Rex. "We can mute ourselves but leave the incoming line open so that Silkies can alert us of any significant changes."

"Makes sense," Teddy agreed. Then, as if he were seeing it all fresh in his mind, he turned back to the rough map on the whiteboard. "They'll likely come in from the main road on the path by the big rock here. It's the way I took the Jeep in, the most obvious route."

Beneath the main road between the compound on the left and the creek in the bottom center, Matthew drew in a lump to represent the rock and a squiggly line approaching the creek from that western direction.

"If they have eyes on the Jeep, they already know that," said Teddy. "I came out on foot this way to scout that overlook." He pointed to the sketch indicating the rock outcropping south of the creek on the bottom of the whiteboard.

"I'll take that spot above the creek," said Justin. "I can go in on foot, camouflage there, and watch the area below. I'll communicate with Matthew until Wasaki and Waruhiu approach and be ready to move in if anything goes sideways."

Planning for the first phase continued in earnest so quickly that it made Matthew's head spin. After summoning Wasaki and Waruhiu, they'd catch them by surprise, overpowering them by outnumbering them. Each man had a camouflaged position around the parked Jeep, two from the north and two from the south, with a vantage point allowing them to keep it in view with night goggles.

They'd get into those positions and Gacoki would summon Wasaki and Waruhiu. Matthew, from the church, would enable Tumaini to see the monitors and advise logistically. The unspoken agreement was that this gave both Gacoki and Tumaini limited roles in the first phase to determine if they were trustworthy for the second.

Justin, Teddy, Stoney, and Rex would be equipped with syringes and stun guns in addition to the high-powered weapons. Manchester refused to carry anything but weaponry.

Injecting Wasaki and Waruhiu with a sedative would be the easy part. Getting close enough to the warriors to do so was another matter, Matthew thought. Stun guns, too, had a range that put them closer than he thought was a safe distance.

"After we put them, ah, out of commission," Manchester said, "we approach the compound in their Jeeps. Familiar incoming vehicles."

"This is the main gate?" Stoney asked the Kenyans, pointing to lines marked on the southern, longer, side of the rectangular compound drawing on the whiteboard.

"It is," said Gacoki.

"What are we facing when we get there?" asked Stoney.

"The wall on the eastern side," Gacoki indicated the shorter right side of the rectangle, "is high cement. Fencing at the gate on the south side is guarded, but it is not electrified like the fencing on the north side."

"We can get this far without detection?" asked Manchester, pointing at the line indicating where the road curved before approaching the southern main gate of the compound. "Could our faces be seen from that distance? Are there cameras here?"

"Cameras up high. Checking vehicles, not faces," Tumaini spoke up. "I have been in the control room and seen the monitors. Lean back until you are at the gate, and your face cannot be seen in the dark."

"The control room contains all surveillance monitors?" asked Gacoki, turning to him.

"I believe that is true," answered Tumaini.

"We vacate the vehicles, lights on, here," said Manchester, pointing at the last curve in the road sketched on the whiteboard before a straight stretch north approached the gate. "We don't go all the way to the gate where we can be seen exiting vehicles from above."

"Makes sense," said Rex. "When they come to see why our Kenyan friends aren't pulling into the compound, we disable them as they approach."

"If they approach," said Justin, who had been quietly watching through most of the discussion.

"He's right," said Stoney. "We need to be prepared if they start shooting or rush us all at once."

"No problem," said Manchester.

"You can circle downhill through the trees and approach from the west to not be seen," said Gacoki. "Can you climb?"

"Climb what?" asked Rex.

"Rock," answered Tumaini. "If you circle downhill to the west, then you climb to the compound. It is not high, maybe fifty meters. That is the only blind spot. The one direction they do not monitor closely. There is no fence. You should see it on your satellite image."

"I did. It's there," confirmed Manchester. "It looks like a sheer rock face. There are treetops beyond the west end of the compound."

Fifty meters, Matthew thought and did the calculations in his head, multiplying roughly by 3.3. If he was right, that was over 160 feet. In the cramped space he hadn't allowed to the left of the compound rectangle, he sketched squiggles to represent the tree tops that a kindergartener might be proud of.

"I can climb," answered Stoney, to Matthew's amusement. He refrained from pointing out the appropriateness of Stoney scaling a rock face.

"Me too," said Rex.

"I'm decent at climbing," said Teddy.

"Yeah, I'm in," said Justin.

"I could climb it in my sleep," said Manchester.

"Where do we need Silkies?" asked Teddy. "He's not joining this party?"

"No," said Matthew, though he realized that, again, Teddy was talking about him instead of to him. "I'm not a climber."

"You should be close," said Rex. "In case your medical skills are needed. If you follow, wait at a safe distance, like maybe here," he added, pointing to a bend in the narrow road further from the gate. "And be ready if you're needed."

"No medical assistance for any but ours. Casualties on that side are collateral damage," said Manchester insistently. "We take no prisoners. We get in, get Warren, get out."

Matthew watched the others gear up and leave.

Stoney led Gacoki out, his hands still bound but in front of him. His feet, of necessity, were free. It was a concession to his promise of help. Tumaini was settled in a chair on the other side of the table from Matthew, hands and feet still bound. Matthew wondered if he was being naively trusting. It would be a simple task for Tumaini to flip the table over on him and wreak havoc with the technical set up if he chose to.

Warily, Matthew sat half watching the monitors while watching Tumaini in his peripheral vision for any slight movement that could indicate aggression. Chatter on the comm packs turned Matthew's attention momentarily to the screens, one of which had been set to thermal satellite images of the area where they were headed.

"Heading in," said a voice Matthew thought belonged to Rex. "Going dark."

What followed was thick silence. As he watched, Matthew saw two heat signatures appear on the edge of the screen in front of him. "They're already there," he mumbled. "That was fast. They must have sprinted in the dark."

As he watched the figures move around, as if searching for something, he had a much more chilling realization. Those weren't members of his team, Matthew realized, standing so abruptly his chair fell to the floor, sounding with a hollow thud behind him.

31 ~ BEST-LAID PLANS

"That's not our team!" Matthew exclaimed aloud, watching the screen in alarm not knowing exactly what to do. Where were Justin and the others? His question was answered for him. Two more figures moved into the screen from the left, coming from the northeast, and then two more below from the southeast moved into place. How close was Justin to the others? Would he be able to see what was unfolding from his higher vantage point?

Fumbling with the controls, he alerted them, "Heads up! You have company. Two from the west. Stoney and Gacoki, you're in their path to the north. They're headed straight for you, coming along the north side of the creek headed east. I repeat," he said, and had just gotten the warning repeated when sound erupted from the console speakers in front of him.

He heard exclamations in something other than English. Turning to Tumaini, he knew he had no option but to trust the huge man now. "What are they saying?" he asked.

"It is Waruhiu's voice accusing Gacoki of being a traitor. Gacoki protests that his hands are bound and he's not acting on his own. Waruhiu is demanding that he prove it."

A loud thud reverberated through the sound system, and the distant voice, now much closer, said something unintelligible. Another voice responded in something other than English, and Matthew's brain whirred almost audibly making sense of it all and putting the pieces together.

"They've hit Stoney!" he exclaimed, turning off his microphone, jumping up, and pulling his Glock on Tumaini.

"Wait! You do not know that he is dead or who hit him!" insisted Tumaini. "Gacoki has given nothing away. Waruhiu asked how many others, where I am, and where the men they call Manchester and Paine are now. Gacoki told Waruhiu that he doesn't know where either of us are! He said he was separated from me hours ago, and he does not know if I am still alive."

"The others could all hear that but not understand it," said Matthew, choosing in that mere fraction of a second to believe Tumaini. Indeed, he had little choice. "Where is Wasaki?" he asked, putting the weapon on the table and turning his attention to the screen. He'd lost track of which figure was which on the satellite image, he realized, alarmed.

Into the microphone, Matthew urgently explained what he was piecing together of what had just happened below Justin's perch. "We think Waruhiu hit Stoney and threatened Gacoki."

"I'm going in," said Justin quietly across the comms.

"Like hell you are!" an angry voice with a lilting dialect hissed in reply.

"That's Waruhiu," informed Tumaini.

"He has Stoney's communication device," said Matthew, stating what was now obvious. There was something else about the fact that Tumaini knew Waruhiu's voice that was tugging at the edges of Matthew's mind, but he didn't have time to stop and consider that.

"They can't communicate with each other or with me now without giving themselves away. I'm not sure who's where. I lost track of them," he said in exasperation.

"Justin," he said, connecting only to his earwig, "I know you can't answer me, but here's what I know." Explaining the last known location of everyone as best he could, he added, "Tumaini and I are coming in to get Stoney."

"Let's go," he said to Tumaini as he picked up a knife. Darting around the table, he slit the cable ties securing the Kenyan's huge calves to the chair legs. Tumaini rose from his chair. Eye to eye with Matthew, his shoulders and arms were much thicker, his entire build broad and powerful. Matthew felt like a greyhound standing beside a pit bull.

Silently praying he was making the right decision, Matthew felt a peace wash through him as he sliced the bindings from Tumaini's proffered hands. Grabbing his jacket and two of the prepacked supply satchels—containing syringes, stun guns, night-vision goggles, sat phones, and weapons—Matthew scooped up the keys to one of the Humvees and dashed out into the night.

Silently, Tumaini appeared at his elbow as Matthew found which of the remaining vehicles the key matched. That was scary, he thought. Though they were huge hulking men, this provided credence to their claim to be trackers. The dome light in the interior had been switched off on all of the vehicles earlier, so Matthew climbed in and started it. So far so good on his decision to trust the guy, he thought as Tumaini had slipped into the seat beside him.

Donning the night-vision goggles, Matthew drove through the dark without headlights. The moon was up there somewhere, but it was behind the cover of clouds. He turned off the road, followed the narrow path in, and stopped short of the high bank.

Matthew remained in the Humvee momentarily, watching through night-vision goggles for any motion. The night was eerily silent. There were no discernible owls calling out, crickets chirping, or rustlings in the underbrush nearby. Grabbing one of the satchels, he handed Tumaini the other. Stocking his pockets and strapping on equipment, he drew a deep breath, nodded to the Kenyan who all but disappeared in the dark night, and slipped out of the vehicle.

His own boots made a slight noise as they connected with brittle sticks beneath him. He heard nothing from the other side of the Humvee. Striding as quietly as he could manage away from it in the direction of the high creek bank, he was startled by Tumaini, who silently materialized at his elbow. If he hadn't been convinced that the guy was on his side, that would have been entirely creepy.

As they climbed an incline to the vantage point above the creek bed, he heard his own breathing but nothing more. Turning once, he saw Tumaini close behind him. Reaching the top of the embankment, Matthew was about to turn to Tumaini again when he stopped up short and froze in his tracks, fear coursing through him.

"That's right, don't move until I tell you to! You will tell me where the others are," whispered a lilting dialect in his left ear as he felt the pressure of cold metal pressed against his temple.

His mind raced ahead, though his body remained frozen. Was this Tumaini who had turned on him and was now going to shoot him through the head? Before he could decide what to think, a shot rang out, and he dropped painfully to his knees. A warm mist blew across his outstretched hands and face as he fell. Had he just been shot?

After a panicked gulp of air, he took stock from where he'd fallen to the ground. Arms, legs, head, to his amazement, were all still intact. Looking up and pulling the night goggles back into place over his eyes, Matthew saw Tumaini holstering a Glock. A large body was sprawled beside him.

"We go now!" hissed Tumaini as he flipped the body over and removed weapons from it. Shoving it a little further, he pushed it over the backside of the ridge. It tumbled downhill away from the creek as Matthew scrambled to his feet on wobbly knees.

Tumaini led the way. Matthew couldn't think straight enough to do anything but follow, haltingly, through trees, under branches, and over brambles. Who had he just shot? Was it Gacoki? Surely, it must have been one of the others. Eventually, they came to a rock formation and stopped. Tumaini cocked his head, listening intently as Matthew tried to slow his breathing and quiet his pulse. That was an impossibility as he was slightly winded and shaking from the ordeal he still didn't fully understand, but he had no time to contemplate.

"Your friend lies there," Tumaini whispered in his ear, and pointed. "Crouch, but don't crawl. Quietly. If he is alive, motion to me."

Matthew followed those instructions, bending over, and tracking a line in the direction Tumaini had pointed. Even with the night goggles, he nearly tripped over Stoney's prone body. Reaching down, he found a pulse in his neck and gently rolled him over. It wasn't ideal. He'd have preferred not to move an injured person, but he had little choice given the predicament they were in. He saw no bullet wounds, nor was there bruising on Stoney's face.

He motioned for Tumaini.

As Matthew helped to lift Stoney's limp form, Tumaini whispered, "I have him. Follow me." Tumaini hoisted him easily over his shoulder as if Stoney were either helping him or weighed very little. Matthew figured he'd add that to the growing list of things to marvel over later as he followed, veering off through thicker underbrush.

A twig snapped loudly under Matthew's foot and Tumaini paused to listen before continuing on. Arriving at the edge of the path, Matthew saw the Humvee ahead. Turning a complete circle slowly and silently, Tumaini surveyed their surroundings before slipping noiselessly alongside the vehicle, opening the door, and gently laying Stoney across the back.

Stoney groaned, stirring slightly, which Matthew took as a good sign.

"Get him out," whispered Tumaini. "Back to the church. You need help?"

"Yes," said Matthew as he climbed in.

Back at the church building, Tumaini laid Stoney gently on a table and Matthew checked his vitals. While Tumaini stood by, Matthew searched the facility and found an ammonia solvent in the restroom. He held a tissue saturated in it under Stoney's nose until he opened his eyes fully and looked around. Tumaini turned to leave.

"Where are you going?"

"To find Waruhiu. Unless Gacoki has already killed him. He might not until he knows Wasaki is already dead."

"You shot Wasaki?"

"I did."

"And you're going to kill Waruhiu too?"

"I am."

Matthew's understanding was nil in that moment as he stood, mouth agape. "Aren't you related to them?" he finally spluttered. "We planned to take them alive."

"Cousins in blood only. They are no relatives of mine. They are traitors. The worst kind."

"How so?" Matthew asked as he worked.

Digging a thermal blanket from one of the backpacks, he placed it over Stoney. Adding a cool compress, in the form of a wet paper towel to his forehead, he struggled to understand. He couldn't fathom any reason to shoot his relatives.

"They helped plan an attack on Maralal, providing strategic guidance with their knowledge of the area. Our families are there. Wasaki and Waruhiu know our families are the targets, yet they helped. They value no life. They would take mine or Gacoki's without remorse."

"Oh," said Matthew, realizing the treachery involved in turning on your own family, slightly extended though they might be.

"We tried to send word of warning with missionaries. They were not able to reach my family. To tell them to get out. Neither has Gacoki reached his. There have been others."

"Others of your relatives?" asked Matthew, still confused.

"Yes," answered Tumaini. "Including my sister's husband."

"I don't understand," said Matthew, monitoring Stoney's vitals and shining a light in his eyes to check the size of his pupils as he questioned Tumaini.

"They were ordered to kill others of us who were brought here. We were all Maasai Warriors of the same age. Like your high school graduation here," Tumaini added, trying to explain in terms that Matthew could understand. "It is a different sort of brotherhood. They turned on the others when ordered to do so. We were next. Wasaki would have killed you and then me. Gacoki needs my help. Waruhiu will kill him if he thinks he is no longer useful."

"Oh," Matthew said, mostly to himself as Tumaini slipped out and

Stoney tried to lift his head.

"I'm pretty sure you have a concussion," said Matthew. "Do you remember what happened?"

"Gacoki hit me from behind," said Stoney, rolling onto his side and wincing.

"Are you sure it was Gacoki?" asked Matthew.

"I am. I was in the crosshairs of a rifle at close range. There was a heated conversation between Gacoki and the guy holding the gun."

"Waruhiu," Matthew supplied.

"I'll take your word for it, Silkies," said Stoney, with a crooked smile. "We weren't formally introduced."

That, thought Matthew, was a good sign. The guy's sense of humor was still there. "It's the back of your head?" he asked.

"Yeah, right . . ." Stoney said, raising his hand. "Here," he added reaching to the back of his head and groaning softly.

"I'll wash up. Be right back." In the restroom, the water was cold but refreshing as Matthew splashed it on his face and then pumped out the antibacterial soap liberally, lathering up to his elbows. With a wad of paper towels, he dried off.

Returning to his patient and trying to get a better view of the back of Stoney's head, Matthew asked, "Can you roll a little more that way?"

"Yeah, I don't want to roll off this table," answered Stoney, sliding to his left and then wriggling to flip over onto his stomach as Matthew held the table steady.

"There's no other furniture down here except folding chairs. This is the best we've got," said Matthew as he pulled gloves from a box in the first aid bag and snapped them in place.

Gently parting Stoney's wavy brown hair to examine the injury, he felt the guy flinch. "You need some stitches to close this gash. It's not deep, but it is pretty wide. Gacoki went easy on you. I'll shave around it and stitch it up. Then, you'll need to rest."

"That was going easy on me?" groused Stoney.

"You can have a couple of Tylenol, but I haven't found any local anesthesia in the first aid bags to numb the area. I'll be as quick as I can," Matthew reassured him.

Stoney grunted. "It's OK, Silkies. Do what you have to do. Rest won't be in the cards for me yet, though," he mumbled into his arms where his head rested.

Neither would rest be in his own for the foreseeable future, Matthew thought, though he wasn't fully aware of the extent of truth in that thought.

32 ~ PHASING OUT

Poised over the back of Stoney's head, Matthew gently tied the ninth and final stitch in a close, neat row. Still holding a synthetic suture material he guessed to be nylon—which wouldn't have been his first choice, but it traveled well—in the forceps, he was about to snip it free when a distant boom made them both jump. If he was honest, he was jumpier than Stoney. Pausing, forceps still in hand, he waited.

When the silence continued, he snipped it free and asked, "Was that a gunshot?"

"Sounded like the RPG Manchester was hauling. Definitely not a hand gun."

"RPG?" Matthew asked, realizing his mind had been divided in multiple directions as he'd tended to Stoney's stitches. If they'd heard the noise clearly from the little chapel, he doubted anybody in the compound to the west had missed it either.

"Rocket-propelled grenade."

"Right, I saw it earlier. What I meant to ask was, 'Manchester took that out there with him?' Isn't that overkill? Wrong expression," Matthew corrected himself. "I mean isn't that heavy artillery for taking out larger equipment? Like tanks?"

"Yeah, he did, and yes, it is. He put it in the Humvee, dragged it out, and hauled it off into the woods along with handguns and a short-barreled rifle stuck through a loop on his thigh. He's got that 'if it's worth doing, it's worth overdoing' mentality right now. He's not taking chances and not planning to take prisoners either."

"Isn't an RPG heavy?"

"It's at least forty pounds when it's loaded," said Stoney, wincing as he lifted himself up on an elbow to squint at Matthew. "You done?"

"I am with the stitching. That was the worst of it. We should cover it, though," he answered as Stoney lay down again, and Matthew retrieved sterile gauze and tape from the bag in the chair beside him. Carefully, he placed the gauze on the wound and taped it in place where he'd shaved Stoney's head. It wasn't a task he normally performed, but he was happy with his work.

"OK, now I'm done," said Matthew, pulling off gloves and tossing them in the trash. "How're you feeling?"

"I've been better," admitted Stoney, propping himself on his side. "But I've been far worse too. It's like my grandpa used to say, 'That'll feel real good when it stops hurting so much.'"

Matthew chuckled at the lack of logic in the colloquialism. "He's right. It will. The Tylenol should help."

"It has. My head aches less," said Stoney, sitting fully upright and groaning with the effort. "A little less," he corrected.

"Here, drink this," Matthew said, handing him a bottle of water. When Stoney began to chug it, Matthew added, "Sip it."

Before Stoney's feet hit the floor, the door swung open, and a blast of fresh but chilly air rushed down the steps along with an assortment of exultant men.

"We're regrouping before phase two," explained Justin. "That didn't go exactly to plan. Obviously," he said, indicating Stoney.

"I am sorry," said Gacoki. "Not to hit you would allow Waruhiu to shoot you. I tried not to hit too hard. I could not let him shoot you."

"Wasaki is dead," said Tumaini. "He was going to shoot Silkies. I fired first."

Matthew turned to correct him but decided it was useless as the others filed in and began checking and reloading weapons.

"Where's Waruhiu?" asked Stoney.

"In the Jeep," said Manchester. "Anything left of him is in whatever is left of it."

"You blew up the Jeep?" asked Matthew. Realizing he wasn't sorrowful that the guy who'd whacked him on the head and left him for dead had been blown up, he decided to process that later.

"I wasn't carrying his huge ass all the way back in here," said Manchester. "Now we regroup. There's no time for chitchat. We need to map out our strategy into the compound and move out."

"Agreed," said Justin, taking charge and moving to the whiteboard. "We load up heavier on ammo. Two vehicles approach, the remaining Jeep pulls up here as we discussed, lights on. That's alpha team. Bravo is behind in the Jeep with Matthew, here. We all bail out, make our way west, and start the climb."

"Wait," said Matthew. "Can we use Gacoki and Tumaini as a distraction and get them inside? Does anybody in the compound know they're compromised?"

"Great question, Doc," said Manchester. "What are you suggesting?"

"That Alpha bails before the Jeep gets this far," he pointed to the spot on the whiteboard where it had been set to stop, a curve short of the final approach to the gates. "Tumaini, you knew which voice was which when Waruhiu was whispering over the communication system. Can you imitate it?"

"I believe so," said Tumaini.

"At least enough to pass for Waruhiu in front of—what did you call them—*mzungu*?" asked Matthew.

"*Wazungu*," corrected Stoney. "Plural, more than one. You're thinking Gacoki and Tumaini return to the compound posing as Wasaki and Waruhiu?"

"Exactly," said Matthew. "They take their Jeep. It's here, right?" he pointed to the spot west monitor and Manchester nodded. "That gets them inside. They are all close to the same size and height, from what I could tell. They were dressed similarly—all in black except the T-shirts. Those can be concealed beneath black jackets. Can you pass for them?" he asked, turning to the two massive Kenyans.

As both nodded in unison, Matthew asked, "Can we wire them?"

"Brilliant, Silkies! We can," said Rex, turning to open and dig through one of the large cases he'd brought in.

Manchester nodded and added, "Useful."

"You trust them now?" asked Matthew.

"Who do you think blew up the Jeep with Waruhiu in it?" Manchester asked.

"Gacoki," said Matthew, realizing both brothers had been responsible for removing their cousins from this realm of existence.

"Can you create a diversion when you get inside? You could heatedly argue about the necessity of killing your cousins, 'Tumaini and Gacoki,' maybe?" asked Matthew.

Both nodded and Tumaini responded, "We can do that. We will get you to your friend. And the other two men?" he asked.

"If we're able," said Teddy. "Extracting Warren Danbury is priority one."

"We'll need Stoney to listen and translate," said Matthew. "Which is good because he shouldn't be scaling rock face right now anyway."

As Stoney began to object, Rex said calmly, "He's right. You're the only one who can understand Kiswahili. Can anyone else inside?"

"No. Not with Waruhiu and Wasaki gone. Only the four of us were left. There are others, younger, being trained. They are not here yet. Not at this facility."

"Perfect," said Rex and began wiring them. "Ticklish?" he asked in surprise as Gacoki squirmed.

"No. Proceed," replied the warrior as his expression grew stern, the look in his eye far away.

"Report on the area inside after you enter, in Swahili, like you're talking to each other," instructed Justin as Rex finished wiring them.

"If you can find where Warren Danbury is being held, or get a better idea, report that. Also report areas where he can't be. And anything else you see that might be helpful."

"Alpha team deploys here," said Justin, turning and pointing at the depiction of the gates into the compound on the whiteboard as he resumed the planning effort. "And bravo team here." He pointed to opposite sides of the cliff they would need to climb.

After a few last checks over weaponry and equipment, Manchester said, "Load up."

Matthew felt the butterflies panicking in his stomach as he added two water bottles to the backpack he'd already restocked with medical supplies. In the pockets of his cargo pants, he carried a stun gun and syringes. The Glock was in the holster strapped under his jacket. He sincerely hoped not to need it.

Climbing into the Humvee he'd driven earlier, Matthew waited while Stoney, Rex, and Teddy stashed supplies and loaded in. Donning the night goggles, he pulled onto the state road, slowly making his way along the tree line. He paused before the path leading to where Wasaki and Waruhiu's Jeep was parked. Waiting until it emerged with Manchester and Teddy in the back, Gacoki driving, and Tumaini riding shotgun, he followed it. The Jeep's headlights showed the road ahead. Matthew followed in the wake of the taillights into the dark night.

Pulling into position, Matthew watched the Jeep navigate the last bend in the narrow road. Before the final approach to the gate, Justin and Manchester slid out and stealthily retrieved their supplies from the back. Rex and Teddy had already vacated the Humvee with their supplies. The four met up and slipped silently into the darkness of the tree cover.

Matthew donned earbuds in time to hear Gacoki identify himself as Wasaki. After a few back-and-forth exchanges over the intercom at the gate, the Jeep entered the compound.

Retrieving the tablets for him and Stoney to watch the satellite images, Matthew settled in. Small handheld devices enabled them to listen to the channels from the mics of the team, including those that were well hidden on the Kenyan brothers.

On the tablet, Matthew scanned to the west where he could see four small heat signatures. Manchester, Rex, Justin, and Teddy were in place to scale the rock wall, two on each side of the compound. The voices of Gacoki and Tumaini, posing as Wasaki and Waruhiu, were debriefing someone about the events of the evening. They calmly explained how they'd located and breached a camp in the woods just down the road, found and executed Tumaini, and blown up the Jeep Gacoki occupied.

There had been, they reported, no other fatalities. The camp was otherwise uninhabited.

"Where were Tumaini's captors?"

"We do not know."

"You didn't ask him?"

"No, I shot him," replied one of them, his voice devoid of emotion.

"And Gacoki? You didn't ask him?"

"There was not time. He saw us coming and fired. We blew up his Jeep," came the remorseless response. Matthew thought that was Gacoki's slightly softer voice, but they sounded so much alike that he wasn't certain. He hoped they sounded enough like the cousins they were impersonating that nobody inside could discern the difference either.

"Now we don't know where they are!" said the voice angrily. "You should have questioned them before you fired! Neither of you think before you kill! You still haven't learned tactics in addition to violence and brute force."

That someone was angry with them wasn't great, thought Matthew, but that the unknown person believed them to be their cousins was excellent.

"I'll report your progress, but Maynard will not be happy that we don't know where the true targets are. That hinders our plans. Go clean up and eat. You smell like skunks. Report back here in thirty. Do not be late."

"Yes, Sir," responded both voices.

"Maynard," whispered Matthew, remembering what Justin had told him earlier. "Arthur Maynard!"

"Who?" Stoney whispered back.

"An advisor to the Secretary of State. Patricia Shrubpeal is investigating him," said Matthew and quickly explained.

The brothers, Matthew thought, must have walked off looking like they were muttering between themselves. Their voices sounded annoyed with the situation, but they were describing the scene as they made their way through the building.

"Nobody in the copse outside," translated Stoney quietly. "Cameras, but no people. There are three security patrols, fully armed. The main entrance to the building faces west. They went through that, and they're headed north inside, toward their quarters, as directed. They've never heard the name just mentioned. Probably Wasaki and Waruhiu had, so they acted as if they knew."

Matthew nodded as Stoney continued to translate the voices in their ears. "Nobody else appears to be in the inside area, but their argument should confirm or refute that. They'll stop in a strategic location to draw attention if anybody else is around. Their quarters should be vacant tonight. It's below grade, part of a larger underground bunker."

Suddenly, the voices of the brothers erupted into an argument, first in Kiswahili and then, when the earlier voice interrupted them demanding to know the nature of the discussion in English, they switched.

"I'll catch you up in a minute," whispered Stoney as he and Matthew listened to the conversation now in English.

"I told him we should have asked questions," said a voice that Matthew thought was Gacoki's. "But Wasaki is trigger happy."

"It was us or them," answered the other voice angrily. "What would you have me do? Let Tumaini shoot us both?"

"No, but we could have paused to question Gacoki."

"We did not know he was alone!" came the angry answer.

"We should have known!"

"Stand down!" said the commanding voice that sounded Midwestern but definitely spoke American English. "Follow orders and do not question them! Shower! Eat! Return in thirty."

"Yes, Sir," said the voices in unison.

Shuffling sounds were all that could be heard through Matthew's ear buds. He pulled one out and whispered, "Do they know where Danbury is being held yet?"

"Not from that exchange. There's no way to ask them, but that's their goal. They'll tell us when they know. Before the American interrupted them and demanded that they respond in English, they were discussing a way to veer off track to sneak into the control room. That's likely where they're going now."

Quieter voices came through the earbud, and Matthew looked at Stoney for translation.

"They heard the guy who stopped them as they walked off radio someone. He was then told to expedite plans and notify the name they didn't know. They didn't say 'Maynard,' which was smart. That would be understood if overheard. They're going to try to determine where Danbury is being held."

A voice came across the communication channel, and Matthew strained to understand what he was hearing from what direction.

"What are you doing here?" demanded a male voice, speaking American English.

"Going to shower, as ordered, Sir," answered one of the Kenyans.

"You're in the wrong corridor! You know you don't belong here. Get back to your barracks immediately!"

"Yes, Sir."

"Wait. Hold the door while you're there!" demanded the voice.

"You! Make yourself useful. Take him," said another voice, this one sounding winded.

"And you go shower," said the first voice.

"Yes, Sir," answered one of the brothers. "Is Wasaki returning to report back at ten thirty?"

"Not your concern. Follow orders."

"What plans are being expedited?" Matthew asked Stoney, while still listening intently to more shuffling noises.

A door slammed as Stoney replied, "They didn't know. Hang on. . . ."

They could hear grunting and loud shuffling noises, and then Gacoki began to speak again over the din, softly this time as if he were mumbling to himself.

"They've taken the body of a white man outside," said Stoney, and Matthew felt every muscle of his body tense. "They enlisted Tumaini's help to carry him out. He's a smaller white man, shot through the head. It isn't Warren Danbury," translated Stoney.

Though it was fleeting, Matthew felt relief wash through him wishing Gacoki had begun with that information. Was killing prisoners the plans that were being expedited? He hoped with every fiber of his being that Danbury was alive there somewhere. Matthew took a deep breath to steady his nerves.

Grunting continued over the earwig, and the two American voices barked orders, presumably to Tumaini who was hauling the body, to hurry up. He must be acting as if the body were heavy and moving slowly stalling for time, Matthew thought. He'd seen the guy haul Stoney, and he knew that wasn't the case. Then, the soft voice came again in Matthew's ear.

"Gacoki can't get in the control room," translated Stoney. "There are too many people around. He's going down to the tunnels to find Danbury."

"Take him to the edge!" ordered one of the voices. "And toss him over," said the other of the American male voices.

"To the edge of the cliff?" asked Tumaini. "I am to throw him over?"

"Yes, you idiot. To the cliff!"

Stoney registered and responded to this information more quickly than Matthew did.

"They're reaching the top of the cliff now. Go!" Stoney ordered as he started the Humvee from the passenger's seat and reached behind him to retrieve an RPG. "GO! Lights on! Ram the gate! GO!!!"

33 ~ FIRE AND FURY

"Bail out and stay down!" Stoney shouted after Matthew had jetted up the hill toward the compound, rammed the fenced gate in the high cement wall with the Humvee, and crashed through it. Three figures in an open span stopped. A guard behind him was yelling and shots rang out.

Matthew's brain was assimilating information and ordering it as quickly as it could to understand all that was happening at once. Without any combat training, it was difficult. Following orders was the easy part. He grabbed his backpack and jumped out beside the Humvee. Ducking, he ran into a small copse of trees he remembered weren't guarded but contained cameras and dropped to the ground as shooting erupted all around him.

Stoney ran through the trees and fired first the RPG at what appeared to be a Jeep, the occupants of which had been firing at them. Switching to some sort of automatic weapon, he sprinted to the edge of the building. Gunfire and explosions seemed to be coming from all directions. Matthew saw a man running toward him from alongside the building and instinct took over. He sprung from the trees tackling the startled man to the ground and jabbing a needle into him.

One of the guards from the gate, who had been pursuing Stoney, saw this and turned, weapon aimed at Matthew. A bullet fired from somewhere to the west caught the guy from behind, and he dropped to the ground. Manchester—who was running toward him along the inside of the fence—had taken him out. Hearing Gacoki, still in his ear, saying in English that he'd found Danbury, Matthew motioned to

Manchester and sprinted along the south wall of the building, heading west toward the main entrance.

Behind him, Manchester pivoted, taking out two more figures that ran firing at them as they turned the corner. In Matthew's ear, Gacoki was explaining to turn left inside the main entrance, look for steps to the right at the far end of the hallway, and descend two flights to the ground floor. Matthew logged all of that as he paused, backed up, and flattened himself against the building while Manchester blew holes in the doors where the handles had been. Turning once more, Manchester fired at two men running from the north side of the building into the melee to their west.

Darting into the building, Matthew turned left, ran down the steps at the end of the hallway, and paused at the bottom of the landing, not knowing which way to go. He had a fifty-fifty chance of being right as he saw first carved hallways and then what looked like underground tunnels, complete with hanging stalagmite, leading off in two directions.

There was no time to be wrong. Manchester yelled something, pointing and running. Matthew turned to see Gacoki motioning to them before disappearing down a passageway. Pulling the ear bud from his ear, Matthew followed them. The noise from above was more than his brain could make sense of and certainly more than he wanted to contemplate at the moment.

Sprinting was difficult along the uneven, rocky ground marginally lit along the way. Matthew did his best, thankful for the hiking boots preventing his ankles from turning. If the blisters were still there, he was unaware of them now. Adrenaline prevented him from feeling pain. The passageway opened into what looked like a room carved from the rock with tunnels running off of it in three directions. Ducking, they followed Gacoki through the passageway to the right. At the end another open space contained the best sight Matthew had seen in days.

Danbury sat on a wooden bench, his hands and feet in chains tethered to bolts set in the rock wall behind him. His head lolled initially. Raising it, Danbury blinked wildly at them. As Manchester removed the gag from his mouth, Danbury looked up and croaked,

"Matthew!"

Matthew's brain registered quickly that there was something wrong with that greeting and turned in time to see the butt of a gun raised above his head in an arm that was quickly descending. He didn't pause to consider why the guy hadn't shot him in that moment. Anger at anybody attempting to hit him over the head again, adrenaline, and muscle memory from Tae Kwando took over.

Dodging, Matthew used the momentum of the man's arm against him, knocking him off balance before he lunged at the man with the full force of his six-foot-three frame. Knocking him to the ground, Matthew landed on top of him. Another quick flick of a syringe pulled adroitly from the side pocket of his cargo pants put the guy out of commission, probably for hours.

Manchester looked up, surprised. "Useful," he said, from where he knelt in front of Danbury assessing the restraints. "I need bolt cutters," he muttered.

"I'm OK," said Danbury, though Matthew had difficulty believing him. He was scruffy with multiple days of beard growth, and dirty, but his face was otherwise unharmed. "You need to get out. Now! Tell Penn," he began but choked on his words.

"Not going without you," Manchester muttered as he set to work.

"We're not," agreed Matthew. "You can tell Penn you love her yourself."

"I will find something," said Gacoki as he slid the hulking unconscious figure from the doorway and dashed out.

"I'm sorry, Conrad," said Danbury, overwrought. "I dragged you into this. It was all a setup."

"I know," said Manchester.

"I led them here. The body like my dad. The shooting at Ogilvy. That wasn't meant to hit anybody. It was planned to do exactly what it did. Scare him into pointing me to you."

"I know," said Manchester.

"How could you know?" asked Danbury.

"You didn't bring them," grunted Manchester, struggling with the chains that held Danbury. "This compound was already here. It has been for a while. They knew where I was. They lured you to me and tried to take us both at once. When that didn't work, they were going to set you up to take the fall for murders, kill you, and then find me and take me out too. Anybody who could point back to them."

"And Doc," said Danbury, obviously distraught. "I'm so sorry. I knew you wanted no part of this."

"Sip slowly," said Matthew, pulling a water bottle from the backpack and holding to Danbury's parched lips.

"Thanks, Doc," he said, wincing in pain as Manchester worked a blade at one of the bolts in the shackles around Danbury's left wrist. Matthew saw the source of the problem.

"Can you start on the other side?" asked Matthew, seeing that Danbury's left shoulder and the three middle fingers of his left hand had been dislocated.

Kneeling beside Danbury as Manchester moved over, Matthew asked, "Are any broken? Or all dislocated?"

"Middle finger is both," said Danbury. "The others are dislocated. I couldn't reach them. Couldn't fix that. My right hand is chained too far away. They made sure of it," he added.

"Can you lay your hand here without moving your shoulder?" Matthew asked, placing the backpack gently on Danbury's thigh. "Good. Hang in there, I don't have a local anesthetic," he said as he began manipulating the fingers back into the joints. The broken middle one was particularly difficult. Matthew tried to ignore Danbury's grimacing face and grunting above him.

"You did great," said Matthew, forgetting for the moment where he was and what was surrounding him as he focused on his patient. "I can splint the finger after we get the shoulder back in place. I'm going to use a modified closed reduction to manipulate your shoulder joint. Ready?" he asked, grasping Danbury's arm.

"As I'll ever be," said Danbury.

Matthew held his wrist in one hand and his upper arm in the other as the chains on the shackles rattled but didn't interfere. Gently, he pulled the arm and rotated it to reposition the dislocated humerus bone back into the shoulder socket. Always stoic, Danbury grunted loudly but said nothing.

"They are for shrubbery but big branches," announced Gacoki, dashing in carrying huge pruning shears. "It was the best I could find. It is quieter outside. I do not know what is happening up there."

"You need to get out now," said Danbury in alarm.

"I've got this," said Manchester, doubling down on the wrist. "Wiggle your hand out."

As Danbury pulled his hand free, Matthew stepped back to allow Gacoki to work on the shackles at his feet. Manchester moved to the other side and began determinedly unscrewing the shackle on Danbury's left wrist.

"You can't shoot them off, can you?" Matthew said, considering the angles of Danbury's body.

"We fire no weapons down here," said Gacoki over his shoulder. "The caves are unstable. We do not want them to collapse. There. One is off. Now for the other."

Danbury stretched his right foot in front of him and his arm above his head. He moved his left foot as far right as it would go on the chain so that Gacoki could duck under Manchester and begin work on it.

"Here, drink," said Matthew, handing Danbury the water bottle now that he could hold it himself. "Is anyone else down here that we need to get out?" asked Matthew.

"They took Otto Edwards out. I don't think he was conscious. I heard a gunshot above. They shot him, I'm sure. He was innocent. Set up to take the fall for his boss. Edwards worked for Arthur Maynard. Advisor to the Secretary of State. Maynard has been on the political scene for years. He's been in all the right ears. But he's involved in this. Up to his eyeballs. In collusion or under the thumb of a security company. One that is contracted to the government. Sounds like it has been for a long time. I didn't catch the name of it."

"How do you know all of this?" asked Matthew.

"I heard them interrogating Edwards," said Danbury, putting the water bottle down beside him, "about what he knew and what he suspected. He'd accidentally intercepted an emailed exchange. One between Maynard and the security company. It made Edwards suspicious. He started poking around and got caught at it. He was forcibly removed from the Harry S Truman building. They took him out of DC, through northern Virginia. He knew he'd been on a plane. But he didn't know where he was. They tortured him. To determine if anyone else knew what he'd learned. He went to somebody with that information. I couldn't hear who."

"Patricia Shrubpeal," Matthew muttered quietly.

"Oh," said Danbury. "That makes sense. The security company was originally Satellife. Remember Penn's computer? When she clicked to learn more about that company. It was a cyber booby trap. Designed to deter anybody poking around. And to identify them. At least by location. Satellife came under scrutiny in 1999. An employee was reported missing. Edwards said it wasn't a person."

"What did he mean it wasn't a person?" asked Matthew.

"The person's name was a code. It defined specific information. Missing meant it had leaked."

"A person wasn't missing, but information was?" asked Matthew, clarifying what he was hearing and trying to make sense of it.

"Right. About an impending strike on a US Embassy. That information was leaked. It must have been what my dad found. It was hushed up. Satellife changed names. Supposedly it changed ownership. But only on paper, according to Edwards. Then it recreated itself and branched into cyber security. Ostensibly to help with the Y2K computer scare."

"You overheard all of that?" asked Matthew, handing Danbury the water bottle again. "Here, drink."

"Edwards confessed it all," said Danbury, taking a sip. "Trying to save himself. Maybe it spared him some torture. It's too late for Edwards. We can't help him. Like my parents all those years ago," said Danbury, his face no longer a mask. The raw pain showed clearly on it. "Whattlesby might still be alive."

"Whattlesby? He's here?" Matthew asked as Danbury nodded. "Where?"

"When you came in," said Danbury. "There were three passages."

"Right," said Matthew, remembering.

"There!" said Gacoki, having managed to cut through the second ankle shackle. "Do you want me to cut this one on the wrist?" he asked.

"Yeah, it's loose enough to get under it now," said Manchester.

"The passageway to the left," said Danbury, "is where Whattlesby was held."

"OK," said Matthew, grabbing his backpack and darting out.

"Doc! Wait!" said Danbury.

"I've got this!" insisted Matthew over his shoulder. He'd made his way back out to the entrance of the three passageways when the lights went out. The darkness was complete, like nothing he'd experienced before. If he were given to swearing, he'd be doing some of that now, as he searched the backpack pockets for the mag light he knew was there. Locating it, he made his way carefully down the passageway to the left. It wasn't as long as the one that Danbury had been down.

It ended abruptly in an alcove where a carved shelf in the rock provided a bed, of sorts, for an emaciated-looking man with dark skin who was sprawled on it. Was he conscious? Breathing? Matthew knelt and took stock. The man didn't stir. His breathing was thready, his pulse weak. That was the bad news. The good news was, in his condition, he wasn't bound by anything other than rope looped through a hook in the wall above that tied his hands together.

Dropping the backpack beside him, Matthew transferred the mag lite to clench it between his teeth, dug through it, and found a knife.

He'd cut the bindings, put the knife back in the backpack, and was trying to determine how to move the man when he heard footsteps behind him. Turning, Matthew found himself in the spotlight of a flashlight and dropped into a fight stance ready to lunge at the intruder.

"Silkies, it's me!" objected Gacoki. "I'll help you."

Gacoki slid in beside him, and together, they pulled the man's arms over their shoulders. Lifting him as they stood, they made their way from the alcove and sideways back down the short passageway. The man was barely alive, Matthew thought, and he weighed very little for one as tall as he obviously was.

Danbury and Manchester were just ahead of them as they entered the open area and darted through the passageway. Retracing their steps through the underground tunnels the way they'd come in, they made their way out.

"Hurry," said Danbury at the bottom of the steps. "When we get up, run. Don't look back. I'll take Whattlesby."

"We've got him," said Matthew, but Manchester pushed him out of the way and took his place as an explosive blast shook the compound.

"Up! Now!" grunted Manchester as Matthew bolted up the two flights of steps with Danbury in the lead. Down the hallway to the main entrance door of the compound they ran. Danbury held a lightweight semiautomatic rifle in front of him, ready to fire, but they encountered nobody. Matthew shoved open what was left of the doors that Manchester had shot up on the way in. He held it for Manchester and Gacoki to turn sideways and pull Whattlesby through with them.

Turning left outside, they dashed across the open terrain toward the wrecked entrance gate of the compound. Matthew ducked behind the Humvee and jumped in. To his great relief, it started. Backing over the gate, he spun it around heading out to the road. The others piled in. A blast tore through the night sky and a fireball erupted behind them as Matthew raced down the narrow road.

"Justin!" screamed Matthew, though the noise was so deafening, nobody could possibly have heard him. Into the cover of the trees he plunged the Humvee and stopped. "Justin," he said again as he stared behind him in dumbfounded disbelief at what had been buildings and a cement fence mere moments before.

"Hey, Doc!" yelled Danbury, from the passenger seat beside him. "They're losing Whattlesby!"

"What?" yelled Matthew. Danbury pointed over his shoulder and down at the figure sprawled between Gacoki and Manchester and sliding into the floor as they struggled to hang on to him.

Matthew jumped out and ran around to the back seats. Pushing Manchester aside, he climbed in. He raised Whattlesby's head, holding it as steady as he could manage.

"Help me slide him into the back!" he yelled. Gacoki took one side and Matthew the other as they slid him backward onto a platform.

"Toss me my backpack!" yelled Matthew as he debated how he could do much to help with limited supplies.

"We need to get out of here!" yelled Manchester as he handed the bag from the front seat.

"We can't leave the others!" yelled Matthew.

"No choice!" yelled Manchester climbing behind the wheel in front. "They're likely already out," he added, tearing out of the tree cover and heading back down the state road to the church. "They probably repelled back down."

Gacoki dropped his head, eyes closed, and Matthew could see his mouth moving. He looked like he was praying, Matthew thought as he bent over Whattlesby. Pulling one of the thin camouflaged thermal blankets from the backpack, Matthew covered his patient and slid down beside him, trying to get the guy's body temperature up as he took his vitals. He was still alive, but his breaths were shallow and his pulse weak.

The Humvee slowed to a stop, and Danbury reached for a weapon as a large dark-skinned man appeared from the trees on the side of the road to block the narrow road and waved his arms frantically.

"Tumaini!" shouted Gacoki, his head popping up and his hands clasped in thankfulness. "Stop! That's my brother!" he yelled at Manchester.

In Gacoki's place, Matthew began praying aloud—knowing that nobody could hear him in a normal tone of voice—for Whattlesby and for Justin's safety. The Humvee stopped long enough for Tumaini to climb in the backseat beside Gacoki.

"We're going to need medical assistance," yelled Matthew from the back platform of the vehicle. "There's only so much I can do with the supplies back at the church. He's severely dehydrated. He needs more than a saline drip."

"I can get that," said Manchester, pulling out a sat phone with one hand while clinging to the wheel with the other. Into the phone, he yelled, "Monkeys munch mangoes! Hey Charity, we need a life flight, stat. Can you get one out if I send you the coordinates?" he said and then paused. "Thanks, Honey."

"Monkeys munch mangoes?" yelled Danbury as Manchester ended the call.

"Code phrase. Means it's me. Or her if she'd called me. It's alphabetic," he said. "Next up is N. If she calls back to verify the location at the church, it'll be something like, 'Nancy nicked Nelson.'"

The platform Matthew was laying on was hard on his body as they bounced along at a speed that shouldn't have been managed, even if everyone had been safely strapped in.

As they pulled in behind the little church where they'd set up earlier, Matthew yelled, "Bring one of the tables out!"

Tumaini and Gacoki jumped out and reappeared with a table while Manchester tapped another handheld device to send the coordinates for their current location outside the church building.

"Slide him out carefully onto the table," said Matthew, directing and holding the man's head.

As soon as he was free of Whattlesby, Matthew dashed the short few steps to the back of the church, in through the back door, and down the steps. The table that Stoney had been on—that felt like days ago, not a mere hour—was still standing. Matthew directed them to put Whattlesby's table, legs folded under, on top of it.

Darting to the restroom, Matthew lathered up to his elbows in the frigid water, rinsed, and dried off with a wad of paper towels. He dug through the large hard-sided case of supplies that Rex, Teddy, and Stoney had brought. Retrieving a saline bag, piping, and a wrapped needle, he snapped on latex gloves.

"Hold this up," he instructed Gacoki, who looked over his shoulder. Matthew tore open an alcohol wipe and quickly cleaned the inside of the elbow of the supine figure. Carefully removing the needle from the packaging, he inserted it into the man's arm, then into the tubing, taping it in place.

"Grab a chair!" he yelled to Tumaini. "And put it up here," he indicated the top corner of the U-shaped table holding the surveillance control panels.

"Now put the drip bag on the chair," said Matthew. "It needs to be higher than Whattlesby." As the brothers stood watching, Matthew adjusted the position of the tubing, then turned to Manchester. "Where's that life flight coming from?"

"The VA hospital," Manchester yelled back. "Charity was there helping out and staying out of sight. It's not far by air," he added. "They're on the way."

"I hope he holds on that long," Matthew muttered under his breath, knowing nobody in the room would be able to hear him.

"Where are the chemical heat packs?" Matthew asked. "Bring me all you can find!" Snapping the packages open, he massaged them to expose them to air and tucked them all around Whattlesby under the thermal blanket. "That's the best I've got for now," he said aloud, checking the man's weak pulse again. "All we can do is wait."

Checking vitals regularly, Matthew was relieved and surprised each time he found a pulse and that the guy was still breathing. Finally, hearing the whir of incoming blades overhead, Matthew turned to see Manchester had gone out some time before, presumably guiding the helicopter in.

34 ~ PULLING IT TOGETHER

The noise grew louder as the door opened. Manchester, Charity, and two young men rushed in carrying a stretcher. Before Matthew had the chance to introduce himself to do the hand off, Charity did it for him. "Dr. Matthew Paine," she said.

"How did you—" Matthew began.

"Hitch a ride on the life flight?" she finished his sentence for him as they worked over Whattlesby preparing to transport him.

"I have friends in low places," she answered, grinning. Then, she introduced the EMS workers as they assessed and moved Whattlesby onto their stretcher for transport. The older of the two guys she introduced as an EMS Paramedic and the younger as an advanced EMT.

"Dr. Paine?" asked the younger of the two guys, chuckling. He looked to be about twelve to Matthew, though he had to be much older to be an EMT.

"Grow up!" said Charity, backhanding him across the chest.

Matthew barked out orders and did the hand off, explaining the brief history he'd had with the patient and the minor treatment he'd managed to provide so far. It wasn't much, he thought, and hoped they could keep the guy alive long enough to get him to a proper hospital with the resources to provide the advanced care he needed.

"Thank you, Charity!" Matthew said as he followed them out and around to the front of the church building, transporting the patient to the waiting helicopter. He was thankful to her for more than just bringing in the life flight. His name coupled with his profession had always drawn attention and comments. As that happened again, he felt a slight bit of normalcy return to his life.

"See you soon, Dr. Paine!" she called as he stepped back, the door closed, and the whirring of the engine grew louder, the blades spinning faster.

Matthew watched the helicopter lift into the dark night. He stood watching until it was a dot on the horizon and then disappeared entirely from his sight. Dropping to his knees in the damp grass and the chilly night air, Matthew began to do what he knew was most important. He began to pray for Whattlesby's safe transport and treatment and in thankfulness that Danbury had been found and would recover. Mostly, in that moment, he prayed for Justin.

This had been one of the hardest days of his life. It was one he'd never want to repeat. His own life had been in danger as well as that of his two closest friends, one of whom still wasn't accounted for. He was beyond exhausted, feeling depressed as he worried about his lifelong friend. Staring up into the dark night sky, he poured his heart out praying for Justin's safety, pleading with God to protect him, wherever he was.

As he rose from the ground—wondering what he'd find if he took the Humvee back down to the destroyed compound, and if it was anything he could bear to see—the clouds above him parted. It was as if the heavens had been pulled aside like curtains at a bright window. A radiant moon and stars lit a pathway across the dark sky. Following it with his eyes, Matthew turned to see movement at the edge of the tree line across the field west of the church building.

Four figures emerged, approaching slowly. Freezing in place, Matthew contemplated ducking and running back into the building to warn the others. Were they hostile refugees from the compound? Poised, indecisively, he noticed the loping gait of one of the figures that was familiarly imprinted on his mind. It was a walk he'd known most of his life. Like Gacoki when he saw his brother, Matthew yelled in exultation and began to run across the field under the now bright night sky.

Though they were genetically and biologically not related, Justin was the closet he'd ever had, or would ever have, to a brother. There was no shame in hugging Justin, his brother in every way that mattered. Nor was there any remorse for the tears that stung his eyes.

"Thank you, God!" he mouthed silently as they locked arms over each other's shoulders. No words were exchanged. None were needed as Matthew fell in step with the group for the final few hundred yards back to the church building. Rex, Teddy, and Stoney trudged alongside them in silence.

Reaching the church door first, Matthew flung it open. The cacophony of greetings, questions, and answers began in earnest with everyone talking at once. It was all a muddle, at first. From the confusion, they agreed the compound must have been rigged with explosives to detonate if it was breached.

After a few phone calls, Justin learned reinforcements were on the way, belatedly organized after Patricia Shrubpeal alerted officials to what she knew of the situation.

"Was Edwards the person who went to Shrubpeal before Justin did?" Matthew asked. "Somebody did. Would his captors have persuaded him to tell them, if he had?"

"I don't know all he told them," said Danbury. "I overheard parts of Edwards' interrogation. They were boasting. That's how I learned what I do know. They got cocky. I wasn't supposed to live to tell anybody anything. I was being set up. To look like I killed them. Both Edwards and Whattlesby. It's why they tortured my left side. The right one needed to be functional. My autopsy would show me capable. And guilty. Of firing the kill shots and then killing myself. Exactly as my father was set up to look like he killed my mother and then himself. 'Like father, like son. And nobody left to say otherwise,' they taunted me."

"Which means that whoever is behind this was probably behind your parents' death, and they were trying to cover it up, for once and for all," said Matthew.

"Likely so," agreed Danbury.

"Different hit men, same killer. At the center, where the lines of investigations, father and son, crossed is the same murderer. Killer convergence," said Matthew so softly he was surprised when Danbury was able to hear him over the roar still in his own ears.

"Exactly," answered Danbury.

"Is it safe to use my cell now?" asked Matthew, pulling it from his side pocket. Shortly after five a.m. in Virginia was already after ten in London, a decent time of morning.

"No," said Manchester. "We got the tail of the dragon and one lair. The dragon is still out there. It has unlimited resources at its disposal."

"Yeah, go ahead," contradicted Justin, who'd been in the corner on his cell phone. "We'll be picked up at zero six hundred."

Rex and Teddy, Matthew realized, had been repacking the cases of tactical equipment and weaponry they'd transported in. Manchester, too, was packing and refusing transport. "I came in on my own. And I'm going out that way."

Justin paused as if to argue, but then shrugged and returned to the corner with his phone.

"Can I borrow a phone?" asked Danbury. "It's early, but Penn won't care. She'll want to know I'm OK."

Matthew tossed him the sat phone he'd been using, and Danbury caught it in his right hand. "When we come back in, we need to splint that finger and put your arm in a sling," said Matthew as they both stepped out into the chilly predawn air.

"OK, Doc," Danbury said agreeably as they parted company, going to opposite sides of the church to make their respective calls.

As Matthew faced east, he was anxious to hear her voice. Turning his phone on, he saw a plethora of missed calls and text messages, all of which he ignored. After he'd tapped to make the call, he heard exactly one ring and then the sound he'd most longed for since he'd been in the Virginia mountains and out of reach.

"Matthew!" Cici choked on his name. "Are you there?"

"I'm here, Cees," he said, soaking in the warmth of her voice and basking in a deep soul-satisfying happiness at hearing it.

"Thank God! I mean, literally, thank God! I was terrified that something horrible had happened to you and I'd be the last to know!"

"Cici," was all he could say choking on the one word that meant everything.

"Are you OK?"

"I will be. It's been rough, but I'm OK," he said.

"Matthew, you don't have to yell. I can hear you just fine," she said.

"Is this better?" he asked, turning the volume up to hear her. "Why would you think you'd be the last to know anything? I called you first thing, as soon as I was able to use my phone."

"I didn't know what to do or what to say! Everyone has been calling me expecting me to know where you were and if you were OK! Your mom called me! Somebody from your office called and said you'd been injured! Your sister called! Penn called me because she hasn't heard from Danbury! Is he OK?"

"He's safe, and he will be OK," he answered the easiest bit of that first. "I'm so sorry that they all bothered you, Cees. Danbury is calling Penn now. I'll call my parents and my office next."

"Matthew," Cici said so quietly that he could barely hear her. "I'm not upset they called me. That's not it at all."

"Well, what is it, Cees?"

"It's that they all recognized and understood what you still don't!"

Matthew tried his best to think what that could be, but he was coming up blank, so he remained silent.

"I should be the person, the one person, who always knows that you're OK, or . . ." Cici choked before she continued, "or if you hadn't been. Don't ever do that to me again!"

As his exhausted mind processed what she was saying, he knew she was right. They were planning to build a life together. It's what they both wanted. If they were honest with themselves and each other, he knew it was what they'd both always wanted.

"I get it, Cees," he said. "You're right. I'm sorry. I am. I mean it. I should have found a way to get word to you."

"Where are you?"

"I'm outside a little church up in the mountains of western Virginia. We'll be picked up in less than an hour."

"We who? Is Danbury still with you?"

"He is. And Justin, and a couple of the guys I met in Miami last year. And Conrad Manchester, Danbury's dad's best friend. And two brothers out of Kenya, Africa."

"What? None of that makes any sense," said Cici.

"It's a long story. I'll tell you when I have time to talk. Now, I'm going to get one of Danbury's fingers splinted and his arm in a sling. Then, I might have to sit on him to keep him from helping pack up to transport out. You know Danbury," he added, trying to make light of the situation to keep her from worrying.

"He's been injured?"

"He has, but he'll heal, physically and emotionally too. We know, without a doubt, his father didn't kill his mother or himself. We might never know exactly who did, but Danbury can clear his father's name and his own from any wrongdoing now."

"Mission accomplished then?" asked Cici.

"I guess you could put it that way. All but one mission."

"What's left?"

"Getting you home, back with me, where you belong."

"I'd love nothing more," she said in the honied voice he knew so well. "When I'm ready to travel again, I won't do it without you." Then, she added, sadly, "The airports here are still closed. At least for commercial flights. I don't know when I'll be able to get home."

"I might have a few favors to call in. I'll see what I can do," said Matthew, not wanting to give either of them false hope but wishing with everything within him that what he'd just said was true.

"I'm scared to hope," she said. "You were right about this pandemic. It's a major big deal. I'm so sorry I didn't listen to you. Of course, in your profession you'd be paying attention to it, and you'd know. I should have come home immediately when you told me to."

Reluctantly, they professed their love for each other, and said their goodbyes. Matthew needed to make other calls and be ready to leave. Who he was being picked up by and where he was being transported to was still unknown. He hoped it'd be home and to his own comfortable bed as soon as possible.

Leaving a voice message with his office, Matthew told them he was safe and would be returning to work as soon as he could get home. He'd update them on when that would be as quickly as he could. The workload had been minuscule, and he was thankful for that timing with his absence.

He called his parents next. It was early morning for them too, so he called their landline, knowing it would be silenced in their bedroom. Anyone who needed to reach them urgently, his mother had reasoned, could call their cell phones. Only important people would have those numbers.

"Dad?" Matthew said loudly into the phone when he heard the familiar baritone answer on the second ring.

"Matthew! Where are you? Are you OK?" he asked, his words coming out in a rush.

"I'm fine, Dad. I'm up in the mountains of Virginia."

"Nobody has known where you were for a couple of days, Son. Even Cici didn't know. Your mom called her to check on you when she had a strong urge to pray for your safety, and she couldn't reach you."

As usual, Matthew thought, his mother was tuned in to a spiritual realm that many people didn't know existed, much less relied on heavily as she did. She worried, he knew, but she prayed more than she worried. "Turn your worries into prayers," she'd told him and his sister when they were growing up.

"I'm not sure exactly when I'll be home, but I hope it'll be soon," said Matthew honestly. "I'm getting picked up in about a half hour to be transported out."

"Transported?" asked Joc Paine. "That sounds official. Transported how? By whom?"

"Somebody Justin knows," Matthew answered, wishing he'd chosen different phrasing and would not be explaining anything further.

"Justin is with you?"

"He is."

"I thought you were with Danbury."

"I am. He's here too."

"Oh," was all that his father said, but the way he said it spoke volumes.

"Dad, I'm fine. Please tell Mom her prayers were answered, and I'll let you know as soon as I'm home."

"OK, Matt. Thanks for calling to let us know. We love you, Son. We'll talk to you soon."

As he dragged himself wearily back into the church basement, most of the equipment had been stowed and packed into the black cases, which stood in rows by the door. On a single remaining table in the middle of the room sat an opened black case.

"You wanted these medical supplies, Silkies?" asked Teddy.

"Yeah, Tylenol all around," Matthew answered. "For Danbury, Stoney, and me, at least. A sling for Danbury's arm and something to splint his middle finger."

Exhausted as they all had to be, they didn't miss the opportunity to good-naturedly rib Danbury about his audacity to flip off the world with his middle finger splinted.

"Yeah, yeah," said Danbury. "What I've always wanted to do."

Rex handed out water bottles, and Matthew doled out Tylenol before he set to work on Danbury. Over his shoulder, he asked as he worked, "Gacoki, Tumaini, you said you were in Peak, North Carolina, locating and following Danbury and me a couple of weeks ago, right?"

"Yes. We were there," answered Gacoki.

"Then we were ordered back here," added Tumaini.

"Were Wasaki and Waruhiu with you?"

"Not with us, no," said Tumaini.

"They were sent there behind us," said Gacoki. "Why? Is it important?"

"It might be," said Matthew, looking up at Danbury. "The drivers of the Ford Aerostar that we saw on Ms. Rosa's video feed. We thought there was either a driver and a passenger, both huge and both dressed in black, or that the driver switched to the passenger side on the way out. Maybe both the driver and passenger were huge and dark skinned. Brothers. Trained assassins, used to following orders and paying attention to detail."

"Not Gacoki and Tumaini?" asked Danbury, looking dubiously at the brothers.

"No, their cousins. Wasaki and Waruhiu," said Matthew. "The other two who brought you to the compound."

"I don't remember much of that," admitted Danbury.

"They were all hired to come over here together to work for a security company. Sound familiar?"

"When was this?" asked Danbury.

"Seven years after the bombing. In 2005," answered Matthew. "But there were others before and after them. Initially, they were all promised money to help their families survive a drought and famine in Samburu, Kenya. Later, they were threatened with harm to their families if they didn't follow orders. It wasn't an idle threat. Wasaki and Waruhiu's families were killed."

"Do you know," began Matthew, turning to the Kenyan brothers, "why your cousins thought the security company you all worked for wasn't responsible for the deaths of their families?"

"No. They shared some things with us, but not that," said Tumaini. "They knew more about operations than we were told. When our families were being threatened, I argued with them about it. Wasaki said they had done nothing wrong, nothing to cause our employers to kill their families. I do not think they had to. I believe it was to make them exactly what they became."

"Assassins who cared nothing about human life?" asked Matthew for clarification.

"That is what we believe, yes," confirmed Gacoki. "I worry now for our families. It is as Mr. Manchester says. The dragon still lives. Whoever is running the security company."

"Maybe, but not for long," said Justin, returning to the conversation. "Arrests are being made as we speak. Our evidence and testimony will be used to hold and prosecute them. And bring further arrests."

"Where are we going tonight? I mean, this morning," Matthew corrected.

"First to a secure hotel," said Justin. "Like a safe house, only bigger. Where you'll be able to clean up and get checked out, medically. All three of you," he indicated Danbury, Matthew, and Stoney. "After you rest, you'll be asked to provide recorded testimony about everything you witnessed."

"We're going to tell all?" asked Matthew. "Everything we did and saw?"

"Exactly as it happened," confirmed Justin.

"OK. All done," said Matthew to Danbury as he finished adjusting the sling. "Keep your arm in that except to shower. Don't use it for anything for the next few days to a week."

"Where is this hotel?" Danbury asked Justin.

"Right outside of DC."

"We're going to Washington?" asked Matthew.

"You are," said Justin.

"Hell no, I am not!" said Manchester, picking up as many of the canvas bags he'd brought in as he could carry. "I'll be right back for those," he indicated others, "and then I'm gone."

"Suit yourself," said Justin. "But there could be a reward and honors coming your way."

"Son, I got everything I need already, and my freedom to boot. I'm not going to Washington. I was done with all of that over twenty years ago, and I haven't changed my mind," said Manchester as he climbed the few stairs up to the landing and kicked the door closed behind him.

The room was sullenly silent until he abruptly returned.

"Warren," he said, patting Danbury on the shoulder before loading up again, "I'll be in touch. I loved your daddy like a brother, and I hate that I didn't get to help you grow up. I can't fix that, but I'd like to get to know you if you'll let me."

"Nancy nicked Nelson?" asked Danbury, grinning at him.

"No. Plain old, 'Hey, Warren this is Conrad,' if they manage to take the head off that dragon. I'll be seeing you, Son," he said as he loaded his hands with the remaining bags and left the church.

They pulled the black paper off the windows, stuffing it into a big trash bag. The remaining tables were stacked against the wall with the others in the ten minutes after Conrad Manchester had loaded one of the Humvees and departed. The peaceful sky of the still-dark early morning was split once more by the sound of whirring blades. Matthew surveyed the room. It looked like they'd never been here at all, he thought as he flipped the breakers off and joined the others outside, locking the door behind him.

Ducking under the whirring blades, he climbed aboard one of the waiting helicopters in the grassy field beside the scenic little church.

EPILOGUE ~ FLASHING BACKWARD AND FORWARD

As Matthew looked out the window at the world below on the dawning of a beautiful May day three weeks after his transport to Washington, his mind drifted beyond the view. Reflecting on the past four weeks and simultaneously on what lay ahead, it all felt surreal. He'd never expected to be grilled by federal agents, or to receive accolades and an honorary civilian voucher, which he was now cashing in.

Excitement rippled through him like an unseen current with thoughts of what he was about to do, what he was so close now to finally doing. All he had wanted was to help a buddy get closure on what had happened to his parents over twenty years ago. What he had helped to accomplish, instead, was exposing a corrupt security company contracted by the government for nearly twenty-five years.

The top brass of the security firm—who remained profitably in place throughout the quarter century—had, like the politicians they worked with, learned the "look over there" trick. It enabled them to direct scrutiny where they wanted it. A sleight of hand, the owners had perfected it over the years.

Their morphing, expanding, taking over other smaller security companies, and changing their name shifted focus from their more nefarious activities. One of those was the transport of Maasai warriors into the US, then training, employing, and selling them to do things corrupt people wanted done but wouldn't dare to do themselves.

"Do you think we'll ever know how Erik Danbury stumbled onto the information about Satellife's activities and the bombing intel twenty-two years ago?" Matthew asked, turning to Justin, who sat across from him. Justin was on the flight to pick up American dignitaries of some description who had not left Europe before the pandemic shut the world down.

"That might always be a mystery," said Justin. "The prevailing theory is based on the evidence provided by the former owner of Iron Clad Security."

"They were bullied out of business by the owners of Satellife?"

"That's about the size of it. The Iron Clad owner archived information for his protection in case Satellife, or whatever it became, ever brought false allegations of wrongdoing against him. Those subpoenaed files revealed some of what had happened." It had, Matthew knew, cracked open the door to the past, but a mere glimpse was visible.

"Was the catalyst for the chain of events a coincidence of location?"

"It might have been. Satellife had a North Carolina politician on their payroll. He was instructed to buy the properties where the Danburys' house was to add a runway to the Raleigh-Durham Airport. If it had been built, that runway would have been used exclusively by governmental contracted security companies."

"Why were they so set on that particular location?"

"It was on the opposite side of the airport from commercial flights. Satellife could have more easily trafficked in the Kenyan Maasai warriors, and whoever and whatever else they chose to."

People would have been easily imported like products, Matthew thought, to be trained to do things he didn't want to contemplate. It made him feel dirty to have been in proximity of all of that.

"One theory is that in fighting to preserve his property, Erik Danbury found the security company behind the property buyout attempts. His findings on that company disturbed him. He took the information first to his police precinct, where he was eventually told to drop it. Then he went to Iron Clad, where he was stonewalled.

Because they were competitors, Iron Clad quietly began to gather concrete information to support that allegation before going forward with it."

"Why did they never do anything about it?" asked Matthew.

"Satellife got to them first and threatened them. Erik Danbury was trying to contact Patricia Shrubpeal with his concern that the US Embassy in Kenya would be bombed, so he had to be removed. She doesn't remember talking to Erik Danbury. Conrad Manchester admitted to being the man she was supposed to meet. He got spooked before she showed up and left."

"It's so sad that Erik Danbury's tenacity in protecting US diplomatic lives was at the expense of his own life and that of his wife. And his reputation. It cost his son dearly too."

"I know clearing Erik Danbury's name came way too late, but I'm glad it finally happened," said Justin.

"For Danbury's peace of mind, me too. The medal awarded posthumously, to add to his father's collection, was a nice touch. Will his father's uniform and other medals and ribbons be returned to him after the investigation is closed?"

"They already have been."

"That's good," said Matthew, thinking of the other thing that reminded him to ask, "Was the body of the man that had Erik Danbury's uniform and medals on it identified?"

"He was. Nothing we've found ties him to any of this. He was just a guy who looked too much like somebody else in the wrong place at the wrong time."

"That's both sad and scary," said Matthew, cringing. Purposefully changing the subject to something positive that had come from all of his involvement, he said, "I'm happy to hear that Whattlesby is recovering"

Whattlesby had finally come out of a coma after over a week in an intensive care unit.

"He admitted that he had been paid off by Satellife twenty-two years ago to look the other way, didn't he?" asked Matthew.

"He did. Contrary to Patricia Shrubpeal's fear that he'd set her up to be killed, Whattlesby insists that he scheduled the meeting with her at the embassy in 1998 to warn her. He was going to come clean about his involvement and report what was happening with Satellife."

"Or so he says," said Matthew. "But there's nobody to dispute that claim. He wasn't there when the bomb detonated, was he?"

"He claims he was late to the meeting, by chance. He swears somebody at Satellife had gotten wind of his change of heart, and that bomb was meant for him. To shut him up. And anybody else he might have already told, probably meaning Patricia Shrubpeal."

"Whattlesby went into hiding immediately afterward?"

"Right. Ogilvy wasn't supposed to have ever heard Whattlesby's name, much less remembered it. Iron Clad's security detail for Whattlesby was part of what drew attention from Satellife and put them in the crosshairs. Nobody could prove that Whattlesby was still alive, and Iron Clad went out of business to protect that information."

Patricia Shrubpeal's words at one of the hearings echoed in Matthew's mind. "I might look old," she'd said, "but I'm not dead yet. It's never too late to do the right thing."

Penn seemed to adopt that philosophy.

"Are you going to the wedding next weekend?" Matthew asked. "Penn said they invited you."

"If I'm in town, I will. She insisted on expediting the wedding, didn't she?"

"She did, and Danbury agreed. They're holding it outdoors at the Lingle Plantation so that COVID distancing rules can be followed."

"Is Danbury still on leave from the police force?"

"He is. Between building a gazebo for the wedding and helping his childhood friend, Jimmy, build an addition on his house, Danbury has been busy. I haven't seen much of him."

"Is he going back to the police force?"

"I think so."

"He's good at his job," said Justin, and then added, "If not, I have some other options for him."

"Any word yet on why he was being targeted from within his own department?"

"Orders to remove him from the cases came from somewhere above the Police Chief. The Chief was as confused about that, and the rumor mill, as Danbury had been. It looks like a staff member in the City Manager's office was blackmailed into falsifying documents, issuing fake orders, and spreading gossip. He disappeared before he could be questioned."

"Huh," said Matthew. "When are Gacoki, Tumaini, and Whattlesby going back to Kenya? They were all pardoned, right?"

"They were. Now that the threat to their families is gone, they'll be transported back to Kenya as soon as Whattlesby has recovered enough to travel."

"That's great," Matthew said. Smiling to himself, he was satisfied with the resolution of a twenty-two-year-old mystery. It gave Danbury closure about what had happened to his parents, allowed his father to remain his hero, and enabled him to move forward with Penn.

Settling into his seat, Matthew contemplated his current mission. He was adopting Shrubpeal's philosophy in undertaking it—the most important one of his life, so far. A change in altitude caused him to peer out the window again. They'd begun their final descent into a remote section of the Heathrow Airport used for governmental and royal transport and for traveling dignitaries.

The landing was smooth, though Matthew hardly noticed. He was having difficulty remaining in his seat as they taxied to a hangar, chocked the wheels, opened the door, and finally lowered the steps of the jet.

The most beautiful woman Matthew had ever seen, her golden hair lit by the sun behind her, emerged from the hangar as workers began loading boxes and luggage into the plane. Floating down the steps that Matthew hardly felt beneath his feet, he took three steps to close the gap between them and pulled her up into his arms, kissing her with his soul.

As he set her back on her feet, her face glowed with the special smile that was just for him. He dropped to one knee. Pulling a gold box from his jacket pocket, he opened it to display the velvet-enfolded emerald-cut diamond ring with side diamonds sparkling in the sunlight.

"Cecilia Lindley Patterson, I love you with all of me. You are the most amazing woman in the world, and I've never loved anyone but you. Will you marry me?"

The radiance of the sun behind her paled in comparison to her face as she beamed at him and said, "Yes, Matthew Landon Paine, a thousand times, yes!"

He slipped the ring on her finger, the box into his pocket, and scooped her up in his arms. Carrying her up the steps, he ushered her onto the waiting plane that would transport them home to their new life together.

*****

Want more Matthew Paine?

Have you read the short story prequel to the series? You can get *Pre Kill* now for free!

https://mpmbooks.cypressrivermedia.com/k3xwi6l5f4

You can start at the beginning of the series with *Dead Spots*, the first book in the Matthew Paine mystery series. Get it from your local bookstore or all major online retailers:

https://mpmbooks.cypressrivermedia.com/bgb7d97qo9

Be in the know!

Join the author group to get all the latest updates on new releases, events, giveaways, and more!

https://cypressrivermedia.com/connect-with-us

Afterword

Boys are trained as Maasai warriors, still, in northern Kenya. The Samburu are regarded as an untamed people group by much of the rest of Kenya. In Nairobi, I overheard the missionaries who work with and live among the Samburu people being told, "You're more Kenyan than I am," when they claimed Samburu as home.

Samburu, the wildly beautiful territory of Kenya above the equator is inhabited by various tribal people groups, many of whom still struggle for survival. Finding and transporting clean drinking water is a daily challenge for many in the towns and remote areas. Life there continues to be difficult as resources are limited. During market days, usually once a week in the small towns, vendors travel in to provide some needed supplies for anyone who has the funds to purchase goods.

What's being done to help, you ask? There are missionaries and relief groups in the area working to improve conditions. Some provide food, water, and other necessities. Others provide schools and trade training. The most successful ones educate local residents, certifying them to move forward by educating upcoming generations.

What can you do to help? I'm glad you asked!

John and Jan Kellogg, of <u>Break the Cycle Global</u> (<u>www.breakthecycleglobal.org</u>) work all over Kenya. From a Montessori school in Mathare—a slum in northern Nairobi that was nearly obliterated after flooding in the spring of 2024—to the Montessori school in Samburu, they train and certify teachers from local communities. Raising up educated leaders truly breaks cycles of poverty. Break the Cycle regularly hosts medical teams who offer help that would otherwise be unavailable. Many conditions or injuries that could be easily treated too often result in permanent handicap or death due to lack of medical resources.

Break the Cycle doesn't stop there. They're spreading the "big gospel" (so called in the tiny fishing village of Usenge in northwestern Kenya on the edge of Lake Victoria) by helping one person at a time—usually people considered to be beyond help that the locals have given up on. "For the one," they tirelessly toil.

Learn more here: www.breakthecycleglobal.org

Feed the Hunger (https://www.feedthehunger.org/) also sends food and relief workers to minister to needs in Kenya. You can sign up on their website to help pack nutritious food to send, globally, where it's needed most. Or, make a donation to help alleviate hunger and prevent starvation. They work with fifty-two partners in twenty-eight other countries, besides Kenya.

Learn more here: https://www.feedthehunger.org/

Have you read the whole series?

Did you enjoy it? If so, I'd greatly appreciate your review of the books!

- On Amazon: https://www.amazon.com/dp/B091ZHDSS1

- On GoodReads:
  https://www.goodreads.com/author/list/21401417.Lee_Clark

- On BookBub: https://www.bookbub.com/profile/lee-clark?list=author_books

- On Barnes & Noble:
  https://www.barnesandnoble.com/s/%22Matthew+Paine+Mysteries%22?

Are you a reviewer on social media?

Please connect and tag me in your review of any of the books!

- On InstaGram: https://www.instagram.com/LeeClarkAuthor

- On Facebook: https://www.facebook.com/LeeClarkAuthor

- On TikTok: https://www.tiktok.com/@LeeClarkAuthor

- On LinkedIn:
  https://www.linkedin.com/company/LeeClarkAuthor

Acknowledgments

My thanks to <u>Mathew Slagle</u>, who provided detailed information about military Marine life, uniforms, ranks, and the lingo that accompanies all of that. <u>Doctor Dick Gilbert</u> supplied guidance for this journey back in time to the early days of COVID by explaining that there were no guidelines to follow in this modernly unprecedented pandemic. He described how he and his office staff responded to continue to help patients. That strategy became Matthew's as his office continued to treat patients, albeit under controlled circumstances.

John and Jan Kellogg were wonderful hosts in exploring various areas of Kenya while introducing the culture and explaining the ongoing needs that they tirelessly work to meet through their ministry, Break the Cycle Global (https://www.breakthecycleglobal.org).

As always, I want to express my most sincere gratitude to Genie Clark, my amazing content editor who takes the first whack at all of my books and keeps me straight—a monumental task!

About the Author

Lee Clark is a coffeeholic and dark chocoholic who resides in North Carolina with spouse, two mostly grown children who are in and out, and a dwindled petting zoo of geriatric dogs and cats.

A North Carolina native, Clark is from Raleigh, with family roots in Virginia. Clark attended Campbell University, obtained a degree in journalism from East Carolina University, and then obtained a master's in technical communication from North Carolina State University.

After working in the software technology industry for over twenty years, creating and building highly technical user information for software developers, Clark decided it was time to pursue a true passion: fiction writing.

Matthew Paine is a fictional character, though inspired by two very important men in the author's life, brother Sean and son Will. Both will see characteristics of themselves in the character and identify with some of Matthew's struggles.